DANGEROUS REFUGE

DANGEROUS REFUGE

Elizabeth Lowell

WM

WILLIAM MORROW

An Imprint of HarperCollins*Publishers*

DANGEROUS REFUGE. Copyright © 2013 by Two of a Kind, Inc. All rights reserved. Printed in the United States of America. No part of this book may be used or reproduced in any manner whatsoever without written permission except in the case of brief quotations embodied in critical articles and reviews. For information address HarperCollins Publishers, 10 East 53rd Street, New York, NY 10022.

HarperCollins books may be purchased for educational, business, or sales promotional use. For information please write: Special Markets Department, HarperCollins Publishers, 10 East 53rd Street, New York, NY 10022.

FIRST EDITION

Library of Congress Cataloging-in-Publication Data has been applied for.

ISBN 978-0-06-213271-0 (hardcover)
ISBN 978-0-06-227192-1 (international edition)

13 14 15 16 17   OV/RRD   10 9 8 7 6 5 4 3 2 1

TO MY READERS, THANK YOU!

ONE

THERE WAS NO doubt about it. He was dead.

Shaye Townsend swallowed hard, breathed carefully through her clenched teeth, and swallowed again. The sick feeling subsided. The grief didn't. Although it wasn't the first time she had seen death, it was the first time she had known the person who died.

Lorne Davis was lying on his back, lean and dark and motionless as the black shoulders of the mountains holding up the western sky. The air had a bite that whispered of summer's end. The first sunlight of day was caressing the highest icy peaks, but there was no warmth yet. The sky was clear, endless.

No need to feel for a pulse, she thought as tears blurred her vision. *No need to cry, either. He died the way he wanted to, boots on, working the land he loved more than anything else.*

The deeply slanted sidelight revealed no sign of a struggle around the body or any flailing pain before the end. Death had come quickly.

It had taken the scavengers a while longer, but they, too, had arrived. If Lorne had been wearing a hat, it had vanished in the restless wind. He wasn't wearing a jacket, either. It must have been warm when he died.

Whenever that had been.

The rising sun showed more than Shaye wanted to see, more than enough for her to guess that Lorne had spent at least a day in the open. Probably more.

I can't even cover his ruined face.

The local deputies would lecture her if she went any closer to the body than she was now. So would her volunteer search-and-rescue unit. Her training had been very clear: If there was no chance of life, the body was to be left undisturbed until the authorities arrived.

He'll never laugh and call me a skinny city blonde again. Never serve me coffee that would etch glass and silently dare me to ask for sugar or cream. Never stand in the dusty yard next to me and watch night flow like a lover up the mountain slopes.

Roosters crowed from the direction of the barn, telling the hens it was time to get out and scratch for a living. Lorne had enjoyed the busy chickens, and Dingo, his half-wild dog, had known they were off-limits for eating or chasing.

Tears streaked Shaye's cheeks as she fumbled in her fleece jacket pocket for her phone. The lining of the pocket felt almost hot against her cool fingers.

Her movement sent a rustling through the nearby sagebrush, where the animals that had scattered at her appearance waited for her to leave. Magpies and crows had come with the increasing light. They settled on the rails of the ancient corral, watching, waiting. Two vultures flapped harshly overhead, fighting gravity for a chance to feed.

It was early for the big birds to be flying. Usually they waited for the sun to heat the air enough to raise thermals. Then the vultures would rise on the warming air and do lazy cartwheels, waiting for something to die.

They must have been here yesterday, knew food was waiting for them today.

She choked off an irrational need to scream at the scavengers. They were what they were—nature's cleanup crew. Nothing personal.

His last words to me were a furious phone message. He died cursing me.

A slow wind blew down from the mountains. It dried the tears on Shaye's cheeks as it dried everything else it touched. The country on the east side of the Sierra Nevada Mountains was arid, unforgiving, and beautiful in a spare, open way.

She punched in three numbers on her cell phone, waited, and then realized there was no cell service where she was. She thought of the backpack of search-and-rescue basics she always kept in her Bronco. The flashlight, first-aid kit, bear spray, and other necessary tools wouldn't help her now, but the SAR beacon could.

I could use the locater, she thought. *It's close and has a radio. I wouldn't have to leave Lorne.*

But the beacon was only to be used in a life-or-death emergency. This was urgent, yet it wasn't an emergency. Death didn't care about a few minutes or a thousand eons.

She muttered something unhappy, waved her arms wildly to drive the waiting scavengers farther back, and retreated toward the weathered barn across the dusty ranch yard. By some quirk of geography, the barn was one of the few places on the ranch that had any cell connection. Lorne had been disgusted when she had discovered it. He had prided himself on needing nothing from civilization—and giving nothing in return.

The only exception to his daily solitude was Dingo, the tawny mutt with erect ears, curled tail, and dainty feet. Lorne had allowed the dog to share first the edges of his life, then his small home. Like Lorne himself, Dingo was aloof with people, independent, but had a reluctant need for companionship.

Both mutt and man had softened toward Shaye in the last months. In Dingo's case it was the treats she brought him. In Lorne's it was the slow understanding that she shared his love for the land in all its enduring, unforgiving grandeur.

A few days. A few days gone and she came back to this.

And all because her boss had never met any paperwork she couldn't trash.

Shaye turned away and walked quickly toward the barn. The dawn wind flexed, ruffling the feathers of the bald-headed black birds sidling closer to Lorne's body. She spun around, shouted, waved her arms, and threw rocks. The birds grudgingly retreated. She thought about pulling out the bear spray and blasting them with concentrated capsicum, but that was anger and revulsion talking. Rocks would work better.

Watching them, she touched the three numbers on her cell phone and waited, automatically turning into the wind so that her hair wouldn't end up in her eyes. Even when she fussed and carefully pinned it up, some of the slippery stuff would always escape to tickle her ears and neck and get in her eyes and mouth.

After hearing Lorne's message, she hadn't taken the time for more than pulling her hair into a clasp at her nape. Now it was flying everywhere.

"Nine-one-one. What is the nature of the emergency?" asked a calm voice.

"A death," Shaye said. Her voice was too hoarse. She cleared her throat and tried again. "I found a body."

TWO

TANNER DAVIS HAD been driving since morning.

The news of Lorne's death had been both surprising and inevitable. He was, after all, eighty-six and counting. The surprise came because it was always that way with death. Young or old, dirt farmer or descendant of great wealth, no one expected to die. Someday, sure, everyone dies. But *today*?

Even after years as a Los Angeles cop—the last twelve of them as a homicide detective—Tanner didn't take death for granted.

He looked into the rearview mirror. Cobalt-blue eyes looked back. Hard eyes. Cop's eyes. He didn't have to see the rest of the package— black hair, dark stubble, angular lines, flat mouth—to know that he wouldn't make a convincing Santa Claus. He'd never looked pretty, and years as an L.A. cop hadn't added any warm-and-fuzzy charm to him.

A road sign told him that Refuge was the home of nine churches and four civic groups. If memory served, there were more than twice as many bars.

The sun was already behind the Sierras and the valley was filled with the radiant not-quite twilight he had loved in his youth. He drove through the center of town, a collection of low brick buildings where merchants served a mostly local clientele. Refuge was close enough to Carson City that people who were on their way to or from the state capital weren't likely to stop. Refuge had never been a destination for anyone but the ranchers who settled the south end of the valley and the merchants, preachers, and pimps who served them.

He turned his Ford—a former police car—up Emery, past single farmhouses where lights were coming on and barns were set in acres of ragged green grass, fenced by barbed wire or wood corrals. From the top of telephone poles, hawks and small falcons watched for a last chance at a warm meal before real darkness came. Without even thinking about it, he knew the birds' names and hunting habits, legacy of summers at Lorne's old house near Glory Springs.

Some of the ranches and farms sported signs on the fences promoting future development, something newer, bigger, better than the way of life that had settled in for more than a hundred-year stay. The smell of wet graze and pastureland flowed through the open window across his face. The water's scent had a subtle mineral tang beneath it. Drinkable, but hard as the rocks it flowed through.

The jagged blue-black line of the Sierra Nevada Mountains loomed large as Emery cut into Ridgeline. For all that he could see, the valley might well have been lost in time. Only the addition of satellite dishes, both large and small, and slightly more modern pickup trucks, disturbed the illusion of having stepped back into the world of his childhood memories.

There were a few more houses than there had been, but nothing like the sprawl of L.A. Most of the newer construction was for people who wanted a ski or gambling getaway but didn't want to pay city prices. The rest was sage and pasture, willows and pines.

If it hadn't been for the slightly drunken telephone/electric power poles strung at the edge of the fence, he would have missed the dirt road leading to the ranch. He had been expecting a Keep Out sign and a cable across the road, enforcing Lorne's privacy, but the cable lay tangled under sagebrush at the edge of the dirt.

By the time the lumpy, rutted road climbed through a notch in the flank of the first ridge of mountains, only the sky was light. The small valley itself was dark. Lorne's house was darker.

Tanner parked the car and threw the door open. Taking a powerful flashlight from the backseat, he switched on the beam and started raking the area with harsh, slanting light. Every small dip and flattened weed leaped out into stark relief.

There was a scattering of different tire and boot tracks in the dry dirt of the front yard, but the tracks were too wind-scrubbed to be of any use for identity. A few yards out, he could see an area where the grass had been tamped down, but the patch wasn't much bigger than Lorne himself would have taken up had he fallen there.

Looks like the EMTs didn't bother trying to resuscitate him.

Nor was there enough trampling to indicate the kind of thorough search a crime scene generated.

Hell, the house hasn't even been secured with yellow tape.

Tanner listened to his own thoughts and laughed roughly. *This isn't a crime scene. This is just where an old rancher had a heart attack. People die all the time and there isn't a crime behind it.*

But it was hard to shake old habits, even if he had been assigned to the morgue lately, trying to match bodies with missing people or felons.

Lorne's old F-150 was still parked near the back of the house. Still the same dirty green color, same Nevada plates that were old enough to show more metal than paint, same internal combustion workhorse waiting for the day to begin. The truck had outlasted Lorne, because the man had taken care of it. No shine or polish, but Tanner knew that everything necessary would be good to go.

He switched off the powerful light and stood quietly, waiting for his eyes to adjust. Other than his own slow breathing, the only thing he heard was a sigh of wind and the distant yodel of a coyote. He knew that there were quail roosting in the bushes near the pump shed, hawks in the big pines across the north pasture, bobcats, bears, and occasional mountain lions prowling the shadows everywhere for the first meal of the night, but the animals were as silent as darkness itself.

The front door wasn't locked. The key hung on a nail just inside the door, where his uncle had kept it. The back door—most often used—hadn't had an external lock, only a bar on the inside.

Tanner pocketed the key, turned on the light, and stepped inside. The place smelled dusty. Familiar. His uncle had been tidy enough, but not much for the finer points of housekeeping. Dusting was done maybe once a month in summer and rarely in winter. The house was like Lorne's truck, ranch, and life. No decoration. Nothing extra. Everything in the one-story house was functional, not fussy. There were old furnishings, but not an antique among them.

Slowly he wandered through the small house. A pair of crusted, hard-used boots resting on a slat bench in the small mudroom near the back door caught his attention. The nail for the truck keys was empty.

Bet they're in a personal-effects box at the local sheriff's office.

Lorne's everyday boots listed sideways, waiting to be worn from the back porch to the barn or pastures, through muck and mud. Tanner didn't know why the boots caught his attention until he remembered what the lawyer had said. Lorne had died fully clothed, apparently headed toward the corral.

If he was doing chores, why was he wearing good boots? Why not the everyday work boots?

A homicide cop's instincts never turned off, even when he didn't need them. File away everything. The little things all point to big things. That was fine when he was trying to figure out the murder of a Jane Doe. Not so helpful when he was supposed to be taking care of personal business.

Tanner turned away and nearly knocked a beaten-up felt Stetson off its hook. Next to it hung a hat that looked new. Creamy white, untouched by dirt, crisp as a fresh dollar bill.

He should have been wearing one hat or the other. He never went out bareheaded.

Puzzled, Tanner really looked around him, rather than sleepwalking through a past he had never asked for. Immediately he saw the dusty red light blinking on Lorne's answering machine.

At least he finally caught up with the twentieth century, if not the twenty-first. Wonder if he had a cell phone, too.

Even as the thought came, he shook his head. There was old school and then there was Lorne.

Tanner crossed the room and grabbed a pencil out of the chipped cup next to the phone. The pencil was gnawed at the eraser end. In his mind he could see his uncle literally chewing out his frustration with whatever conversation he was forced to have by phone. With the eraser stub Tanner pressed the play button on the answering machine.

The system was so outdated that there was no chirpy mechanical voice telling him the date and time of the call. The tape was worn almost through. It hissed and jerked as it worked its way between the spools.

The first message on the phone was from a man.

"Lorne? It's Dr. Warren. Look, about Dingo. He's pretty sick. From the signs, internal bleeding and the like, I'm pretty sure that he got into some rat poison, strychnine most likely. He's touch and go. I'm keeping the dog until he's stable, because I'm not sure I cleaned him out in time. Call me when you can."

Tanner shook his head. It hadn't been a good few days for his uncle or Dingo. He'd have to call the vet tomorrow. Stupid dog letting its nose get it into trouble. Stupid people putting out poison, too.

The next voice on the tape wasn't a man's.

"Are you there, Lorne? It's Shaye. I'm back from the retreat. Pick up the phone, please."

The words stopped, waiting.

Automatically Tanner categorized the voice he had heard—female, young, but not at all childish. A woman. The kind of natural huskiness that made a man think of tangled sheets and bone-deep satisfaction.

The voice came back. Obviously the woman had decided Lorne was screening calls.

"I know why you're so angry, but it was a mistake. Kimberli brought the wrong contract. You know what a disaster she can be. Paperwork is her enemy. Talk to me, let me explain."

There was a plea in her voice. Not the slick oil of a follow-up sales call, but a voice with emotion in it. Tanner had heard enough liars to know when someone was telling the truth.

Unless she was a sociopath. They didn't have human emotions, but the smart ones learned to mimic what they didn't understand. They hid their inhumanity behind manners and pretend emotions, actors on a lifetime stage.

"I had to go out of town on a Conservancy retreat. The kind with no phones. I didn't know what happened until I got back and Kimberli's mes-

sage was waiting for me. And your message. We need to talk. Please, please, give me a chance to explain. I'll bring out the right contract and show you. It was just a stupid mistake."

Urgency and a hurt the caller didn't bother to hide.

Probably real, he decided.

Probably.

It would be something to check on. He scribbled her name and a shorthand description of his own reactions to the message on the yellow tablet Lorne always kept by the phone. The phone itself was too old to have a call log, much less caller ID.

Tanner tapped the pencil on the countertop several times. The local officials obviously were going with a natural death, because any investigator worth the name would have checked the phone to see who had called Lorne lately, and when. But the messages hadn't been touched until Tanner came. Neither had the house.

His glance fell on a stack of mail on the worn linoleum countertop. Postmarks were all within the last week or so. Lots of local advertising aimed at the small rancher—feed sales, pump and irrigation sales and repairs, grocery deals, veterinarians. Only one piece of mail had attracted Lorne's attention. He had ripped it in half and tossed the pieces aside.

Just like the old days. Piss him off and he let you know it.

Tanner stirred the torn, creamy paper with the eraser of the pencil. Whatever it had been, his uncle hadn't even bothered to open it before he tore it apart. Curious, Tanner started to tease out the halves of the letter with the eraser, careful not to contaminate the paper with his fingerprints. Then he realized what he was doing and made a disgusted sound.

This isn't a crime scene and you aren't a homicide detective right now. Get. Over. It.

But he wanted to be. Babysitting stiffs in the morgue and matching them to active cases had almost been enough to drive him away from the job.

Almost.

Yet a deep-down stubborn part of him still believed in leaving the world a better place than he'd found it. Being a cop was the most direct way he knew to do that.

Cursing softly, he assembled the heavy paper. To his eye, the heavy gold embossing on both envelope and letterhead were overkill.

The words invited Lorne and a guest of his choice to be honored by the Conservancy at the Crystal Room of the Tahoe Sky Casino in South Lake Tahoe.

Funny place to throw a local party. But then, the Refuge Grange Hall is as worn out as Lorne's everyday boots.

Maybe that's why he tore up the letter. He hated fancy things.

The invitation looked like it had cost fifty bucks to print. The embossing had the look and feel of real gold. Showy. Not Lorne at all.

Just like he wouldn't have left his hat behind, even if all he was going to do was walk around the yard.

The metallic printing on the invitation glowed and shimmered, bright as nuggets in a streambed.

The gold.

Tanner tossed the pencil back into the cup and walked quickly toward the fireplace in the front room. The chimney and hearth had been built with local cobblestones smoothed by the stream that raced down from the mountains and across the Davis land. Like his father, grandfather, great-grandfather, and all the rest of his ancestors, Lorne hadn't trusted banks. If the family had any extra cash, it went into a homemade safe in the form of gold coins.

Silently he counted stones upward from the left-hand side, starting where hearth met chimney. As he reached for the fifth cobble, he hesitated.

Not. A. Crime. Scene.

He began working the rock free, knowing there was a small hidey-hole behind. When he had turned fourteen, he had been told about it—and the gold coins inside. It was a Davis family coming-of-age rite.

Abruptly the stone came out. Nothing but black dust and darkness filled the opening behind.

Tanner's first thought was robbery followed by murder. He told himself again that it wasn't a crime scene.

Times have been real hard on small ranchers. Lorne probably traded in the gold to keep himself in beans and bread, and pay taxes, and keep the horses in winter hay.

He left the stone on the mantelpiece, a reminder to check the area again later. Then he went through the small house, looking with a cop's eyes. No signs of a search. Nothing out of place. No clothes scattered around. Old wicker basket holding dirty laundry. No notes or doctor's appointment slips or reminders of any kind.

No signs of anything but an old man living alone, keeping up the ranch for a family he hated and a tomorrow he wouldn't see.

When Tanner was satisfied that nothing was out of place, he stripped the double bed and put fresh sheets on from the extras kept in a steamer trunk in the corner of the room. He was too old to sleep in the barn like he had when he was a kid. He started to kick off his shoes, then realized he wasn't fooling anybody, most of all himself.

He couldn't sleep here.

Too many memories. Too many regrets.

Too many questions.

Telling himself he shouldn't even as he punched in the numbers on his cell phone, he waited for it to ring.

Nothing happened.

No cell, idiot.

Then he froze. The sound outside was familiar and wrong. Someone was driving up the dirt road toward the house.

Now what? Isn't being stuck in Refuge again bad enough?

The sound came closer.

His car was still out front, pinging and hot from the drive to the ranch. No way to hide it, or himself. Whoever was coming now was either a close friend of Lorne's who could barge in at any time or someone who had heard about the owner's death and wanted to give the place a quick toss.

He snapped the light off and waited.

There was a crunch of dirt and gravel as the car stopped on the far side of Tanner's car.

"Hello?" called a woman's voice. "Anyone home? Dingo? Here, boy. C'mon, I've got treats for you."

He recognized the voice. No male under eighty was likely to forget that husky sigh of tangled sheets and sex. It was the woman on the answering machine.

Hand on the doorknob, he waited, wondering if she was a thief, a murderer, a neighbor—or all three.

THREE

CALIFORNIA PLATES, SHAYE thought, looking at the Ford Crown Victoria. *Someone didn't just stop by like me to check on Dingo and the animals. We're close to the border here, but not that close.*

She took another step from her Bronco and whistled. Or tried to. Her throat was dry. She didn't like remembering the last time she had been here, the vultures and body that was both Lorne and not Lorne.

No single bark of greeting from Dingo. No lights coming on to welcome her.

Yet there was a car here, its engine still radiating heat into the night. "Hello? Is anyone home?"

She called loud enough to disturb the cows at the close end of the pasture. They rustled and lowed in response. Motionless, she strained to make out a more human sound. All she heard was her pounding heartbeat, blood rushing through her ears like waves on the shore. Fear slid coolly down her spine.

Don't be ridiculous. Whoever is here is probably asleep.

Swallowing hard, she walked up to the door. She didn't want to poke around the barn checking the horses and get shot as an intruder. She rapped hard on the wooden door.

Silently, it opened into darkness.

She made a startled sound. A black shape loomed just beyond the door.

The room light snapped on, backlighting the shape. A man. Taller than she was and then some. Not skinny, not fat. Strong and at ease, yet somehow . . . dangerous.

"You're Shaye," he said.

The sound was barely above a growl.

"Yes," she said. "Who are you?"

"Tanner Davis, Lorne's nephew."

"He never mentioned any relations," she said warily. She wished he would back up into the light so she could see him better. Or back up, period.

"He wasn't a talkative man," Tanner said.

"It must run in the family."

He didn't say anything.

"Look, I'm sorry to bother you," she said. "I just wanted to check on Dingo and the other animals."

"Very neighborly of you."

"You make it sound like an accusation," she said, not bothering to hide her irritation. If he just weren't so damn big. "Since you're here, I won't worry about the livestock. You do know how to take care of the animals, right?"

"Yes."

The man shifted, turning just enough that she could see some of the angles of his face. His eyes were still shadowed. He looked as tired as she felt.

"Ms. Townsend. Or is it Mrs.?"

"Ms."

"I've had a hell of a day getting up here from L.A."

She made a face at the mention of the city. "Los Angeles? I'm sorry."

"I'm not. Beats a one-horse town like Refuge."

"You should meet my mother," she muttered. Then, more clearly, "I happen to love Refuge."

"That's nice." His voice was rough. "Anything else on your mind?"

"I just wanted to help out."

"I'm sure if Lorne was here, he'd appreciate it," Tanner said. "I'm here for as long as it takes to settle his estate. Today sucked and tomorrow doesn't look much better. Go home. You look like you could use the sleep."

"I'm sure you'll be free to go back to your chosen hell real soon," she said before she could think better of it. "Lorne was in the middle of a deal with the Conservancy I work for. We were going to hold the land in trust while he worked it until he—"

"Died," Tanner cut in. "The old buzzard has punched that particular button. Game over."

She gritted her teeth. "I won't bother telling you I'm sorry for your loss. Obviously you didn't lose anything but gas for the trip here."

Though Tanner didn't move, he seemed to get bigger. "Lady, I'm a homicide cop. In a homicide capital. I spend too much time talking to people about how they coulda, woulda, shoulda done something to or for their loved one who recently died. Guess how much good the hand-wringing does?"

Shaye turned her back and headed for her car. Tanner was worse than Lorne had ever been.

But the land was still incredible. Somehow, she had to save it, despite Lorne's looming, abrupt nephew.

She stopped, turned back, and asked, "What are your plans for the ranch?"

"When I decide what business it is of yours, I'll let you know."

"Did you train to be rude or is it a special gift?"

"I deal with corpses and bureaucrats all day. The dead don't care if you push them around and desk jockeys expect it." He raked a hand through his short hair. "Come back some other time when I haven't had back-to-back shifts and an eight-hour drive. Then we can have a discussion like civilized human beings."

She started to say that she doubted that, but he was still talking.

"Dingo is at the vet. They don't know if he'll make it."

"The vet? What happened?"

"Rat poison, likely."

"That doesn't sound like Dingo," she said. "And Lorne didn't keep rat poison around here. He lectured me on it when I brought a box over because the cats weren't keeping up with the mice."

Tanner waited, still blocking the door with his big body. He seemed to expect something from her. She didn't have a clue as to what and she was too tired to play games. Like him, she had been up for the last twenty-four hours.

She turned back toward her car, then remembered. "The mineral lick for the cattle is low."

Silence answered.

"And you don't care about it, either. Gotcha," she said.

Tanner stood without moving as she climbed into the old Bronco and drove off without looking back or waving.

No wonder my captain wants me to go to charm school, Tanner thought, yawning wide enough to put his fist in his mouth. *Too bad. I'm a cop, not a politician. Civilization is always backed by force. The rest is just hot air.*

But coming out of Shaye's mouth, words sound damn good. Bet Lorne loved to have her hanging on his every word.

Were some of those words about gold coins?

Tanner turned and focused on the small black hollow in the fireplace.

The coins were still gone.

And his cop instincts still hummed.

He replaced the stone before he went outside, locking the door behind him. As he got to his car, he pulled out his cell phone. Still no signal. He opened the door, sat behind the wheel, and felt every day of his thirty-six years. Tossing the cell phone onto the passenger seat, he drove until he got a signal. Then he stopped in the middle of the dirt road and called one of the few people he really liked.

The phone rang only once before it was picked up.

"Brothers," the voice said.

In his mind, Tanner could see the other man crammed behind a desk too small for his NBA-size frame.

"Kinda late for you to be at work, isn't it?" Tanner asked.

The chuckle that came back over the line reminded him that there was more to his job than body bags and death. Some people were good. Dave Brothers was one of them.

"Hey, T-Bone. Bureaucracy never sleeps. You too much in the doghouse to make a personal appearance?" Brothers asked.

"Speaks the dude who gets promoted for breathing," Tanner shot back.

"It's my pretty face. It looks so fine behind a desk."

Tanner laughed. Brothers was the only desk jockey he actually liked.

"You're just pissy because I get to go home when it's five o'clock," Brothers said. "Well. Usually. At least I don't have to spend midnights on a nasty crime scene wondering why this mook shot that one. So what do you need that has you calling at this ungodly hour?"

"You saying I only call when I want something?"

"I like a man who knows himself."

"That's because I'm the only one who can stand me."

Brothers laughed richly. "Maybe you'll grow on the new captain."

"I'm trying." Tanner stared at the darkness in the rearview mirror. His childhood was locked up back there, but he didn't live there anymore. "Look, I'll be straight. Thanks to union intervention, I'm on 'paid personal leave for an indefinite time not to exceed twenty days,' which just happens to be the amount of vacation time I have."

"Yeah, I heard about that. Assumed it was window dressing for you pitching a fit about your extended morgue tour."

"Not this time. My uncle died."

"Whoa. That didn't get passed around with the doughnuts. What can I do for you, my man?"

"I need some coins traced—twenty-dollar gold pieces. Specifically, 1932 Saint-Gaudens. I don't know how many there were. I never had the chance to count them. They were in a roll, along with an unknown number of loose Gaudens. Probably less than thirty, total. Since you have more connections than the power grid, I hoped you could tell me if they're as rare as I think they are, or if I'm looking for a needle in a haystack."

"Sounds unusual to me. Liquidating the estate?"

"No. The coins are missing from my uncle's stuff. He could have sold them, but I want to be sure. You know how I am about loose ends."

"Spelled G-a-u-d-e-n-s?" Brothers asked.

"I guess. 1932. I'm certain on the date."

"I'll run pawnshops and coin dealers and let you know."

"Thanks, D."

"You and your loose-ends fetish saved my ass when we were on patrol together. You got a lifetime of favors coming. If I find anything, I'll call or text you."

Brothers hung up before Tanner could thank him again.

He put the phone on the seat beside him and drove toward Refuge. Nothing to do now but find a motel and wait for tomorrow morning, when Lorne's lawyer opened up shop.

Wonder what the tall blonde with the haunted brown eyes is doing now, and who she's doing it with.

He shrugged. Shaye was none of his business.

If that changed, he would care. Until then, she would remain just one more question mark in a world that already had too many unanswered questions.

And deaths.

FOUR

AT PRECISELY NINE o'clock, Tanner parked near the office building where Stan Millerton worked. The Millerton Professional Building stuck up like a modern middle finger between a sagging old Basque restaurant on one side and on the other side a low-rise casino that promised single-deck blackjack for only five dollars. The casino's neon sign flicked on and off, buzzing noisily, but otherwise unnoticeable in the sunlight.

For Refuge, this was prime commercial real estate territory.

Looks like being a lawyer pays a lot better than ranching, but that's hardly news.

A sharply dressed receptionist waited just inside the building, ensuring that visitors had business within. At her back hung a huge landscape showing idyllic fields of cattle grazing near tidy barns and outbuildings in a lush valley ringed by ridges of friendly, snow-topped mountains. It was beautiful and would be forever beautiful and bountiful.

Whoever painted that never tried to wring a living from the unpredictable land, Tanner thought, amused.

As he walked up to the receptionist, she stopped murmuring into the wireless headset she wore.

"Tanner Davis to see Stan Millerton," he said.

"Are you expected?"

"I'm here. He's here. Put us together."

"I see." She blinked. "I'll let him know."

Tanner didn't say any more. Rude came too easily to a homicide cop.

Well, I can pretend that I'm not babysitting the room-temperature class, at least. And that won't last forever, right? Once the captain rotates out, I should be back in the clear.

The anticipation of going back on the beat surprised him. He'd been fighting city hall so long that he'd forgotten how much he enjoyed the actual work.

He glanced at his reflection in the mirrored glass that separated him from the receptionist's area. He looked as bad as the night he had just spent. His sleep had been restless, filled with uneasy dreams and empty darkness. He'd been playing cards and there was something on the table that he didn't want to lose, but every hand came up short.

A dead Lorne was much harder to ignore than a live one. Even when Tanner slept, old memories and new questions poked like sharp, insistent needles under his skin.

The receptionist came back into the lobby. A middle-aged man with short, graying hair, polished loafers, and a crisp suit followed her. His hand shot out with vigor before his receptionist could do more than open her mouth. He looked like the type who dusted off after walking in from the paved parking lot.

"Mr. Davis," Millerton said. "Pleased to meet you in person."

Tanner shook hands automatically. "Sorry I missed you yesterday.

Accident down in the Owens Valley cost me more than two hours."

"No problem," Millerton said. "My condolences on your uncle's death."

Tanner made a noncommittal sound.

"Come back to my office. We have a lot to discuss."

I hope not. I hate paperwork.

Silently Tanner followed the lawyer to his office. Everything from the lush rug beneath his feet to the framed pictures on the wall stated that the lawyer was a big man in a small town.

Tough to imagine Lorne dealing with this guy.

Millerton waved Tanner into a leather chair close to a desk that was big enough to sleep four. "Now, Mr. Davis—"

"Tanner," he cut in. "Every time you call me Mr. Davis, I look around for my dad or my uncle."

"Tanner, of course. Coffee?"

"No thanks. I tanked up at the Corner Café."

Millerton winced. "I'm sorry to hear that. I've never had worse."

Tanner just shrugged and let himself sink into the chair. "Then you've never had precinct coffee."

The lawyer looked startled, then cleared his throat. "Lorne's death was a sudden thing for everyone."

"It always is," Tanner said.

"Uh, yes, of course."

Millerton took the hint that small talk wasn't necessary with this client. He picked a fresh manila folder off a stack on his desk. Inside the folder was a pile of documents. Many of the papers looked old, but the ones on top were new.

As the lawyer stirred through them, Tanner read upside down. Another habit of his past as an investigator. Nothing in particular caught his eye.

"Are you in a suitable state to discuss matters of the will?" Millerton asked, his manner that of a man who kept smelling salts and boxes of tissues for his clients.

Tanner nodded curtly. He'd been around death too much to be intimidated by it.

Millerton nodded. "Yes, of course. As you probably know, you're the only living relative. Normally this would be a cut-and-dried estate to handle."

Silently Tanner waited to hear why things weren't normal.

"Up until a few weeks ago, you were the sole beneficiary," Millerton said.

Tanner's black eyebrows rose. "Huh."

"Lorne made it clear that his holdings would go to blood before they ever went to the state of Nevada. Even so . . . he was discussing an agreement with the Ranch Conservancy just recently."

"Is that like the Sierra Club?"

"Not exactly," Millerton said as he passed the monogrammed papers across the expanse of the desk. It flashed gold, just like the invitation had. "How long has it been since you left Refuge?"

"A long time." He skimmed over the document quickly.

Millerton grunted. It came out judgmental. "A lot has changed since you left. Small family ranches are almost gone because it's just too damn hard to compete in the global market."

"And not many kids want to work twenty-four/seven for low wages, high taxes, and guaranteed uncertainty," Tanner added, scanning quickly.

The desertion of the next generation had been a common theme of Lorne's conversations. It was also true, particularly when there was a small pie divided by a growing number of family members.

"A lot of what used to be family ranches have been snapped up by

San Francisco or Vegas developers and turned into vanity ranches or luxury neighborhoods," Millerton said.

"Gentrification hits Refuge." Tanner thought of all the For Sale and Commercially Zoned signs he had seen along the highway. "Looks like an uphill push."

"It's changed the place some. Enough to make old-timers like your uncle cranky. The Ranch Conservancy is trying to slow down the pace of change. They take possession of a ranch on the contingency that the families keep on ranching or farming and preserve the character of the place."

"And they do this out of the goodness of their hearts?" Tanner's tone was level. "Nice dream."

"And you're not a dreamer?"

"Look, my father left a long time back. There wasn't enough ranch for both him and his brother. My mother couldn't wait to get out. A love of the small-town ranching life doesn't get passed down to kids like eye color or the family name. A hundred years ago there weren't many choices in how to make a living." Tanner shrugged. "Now there are."

"Well, the Conservancy thinks the small-ranch way of life is worth saving. I've helped them negotiate many transfers and trusts. There are plenty of people who think the same way. Even Lorne did, at the end."

At least until a couple days ago, if that torn invitation meant anything.

"Amazing." Tanner meant it. "He wasn't a changeable, much less charitable, sort of man. But good for him. So, when does the Conservancy move in?"

Millerton fussed with the edges of the file. "Uh, that's the problem. Lorne changed his mind a few nights ago. He wanted to change his will, too. Cut the Conservancy out."

"Why?"

Millerton closed the folder. "I don't know. If I had to guess, one of the women over there pissed him off. He was ranting about a 'she' who thought he was 'dumb as a sack of hair.' Last time I saw him was the morning after the regular Tuesday night poker game. And he was none too happy."

"Wouldn't be the first all-nighter he pulled over a poker table," Tanner said, remembering. "High-stakes games?"

"High enough for Refuge. We're not Las Vegas or Monaco."

"Everyone still play in the back of the Stampede Bar?"

Laughing, Millerton shook his head. "Haven't played there since it flooded more than ten years ago. Now we go to the Silver Lode Lodge. There's, oh, I don't know, maybe twenty people who come in and out of the group, usually only ten at any time. I'm not what you'd call a regular. Lorne was. He loved cleaning out men with deeper pockets than his."

"He loved being on top, period," Tanner said.

"You know him better than I expected," the lawyer said wryly. "Anyway, he soured on the Conservancy deal. Said he wanted nothing to do with it. He marched into the poker game and demanded that I change his will back to the original. I told him to go home and sober up. He cussed me out but good and left."

Tanner didn't doubt it.

"When I got here the next morning," the lawyer continued, "he was camped out in his truck in the parking lot, waiting. Still dressed in his poker clothes. He was sober and stubborn as a field of mules, so I agreed to change his will to make you the sole heir again—ranch house, outbuildings, land, stock, water rights, and national forest grazing leases."

"Bet that went down with the Conservancy like a straight shot of gasoline," Tanner said.

Millerton shook his head. "It doesn't help you, either. There will be legal reviews. There's a good chance that Lorne will be ruled intestate, in which case everything will go to the state of Nevada."

"Sounds like I wasted a long drive."

"I really can't say. Legally it's rather a complex question. If Lorne hadn't made any amendments to the old will, then it'd be pretty iron-clad, assuming no outstanding debts or liens or such."

"Is there a document that shows Lorne's intentions to change his will to give the land to the Conservancy?"

"I believe there was a witnessed handshake, sort of a deal to make a deal, which would be finalized at a big party. Then came his verbal, sober instructions to me Wednesday morning, plus a handwritten statement to revert to his original will. I gathered that he was writing his instructions to me when he saw that his dog was sick, so he just tore off the sheet he was writing on and headed to the vet, then waited for me until nine. I have those handwritten instructions, and the new will he requested, but he never came back that afternoon to sign the final document. It's in a legal limbo."

And who benefits most from that? Tanner thought automatically. What he said aloud was, "So he died after he left his instructions with you and before he could sign the final will?"

"Or he changed his mind again before he died. Nobody knows except Lorne. If I were the Conservancy, I'd certainly argue that case."

For a small town, this place is sure crawling with lawyers, Tanner thought. And all he knew about the law began and ended in the criminal codes. "What did the coroner say about time of death?"

"I don't think the death has been certified yet. Sometime yesterday or the night before that, but it's unclear. Only thing I know for certain is that it happened before this could be set out in legal language."

Millerton took a sheet of yellow paper from the folder and handed it to Tanner.

The paper had been torn raggedly at the top. Tanner would have bet good money that the tablet the sheet had come from was on the counter next to the phone at the ranch house. Lorne had written the words so vigorously that the pencil had broken several times, leaving impatient gouges on the paper. This was not the work of a drunk. The language was firm and straight to the point. His uncle had been coldly angry, but well in control of himself.

Like he'd been at his brother's graveside.

Just because your father walked away from his heritage doesn't mean you have to be stupid. Cities will kill you, boy. That was all Lorne had said, and it had been more than enough.

"This letter is pretty clear to me," Tanner said. "And it looks like his handwriting."

"Unsigned, it won't be admissible. Perhaps as an indicator of intent, but it's not a legal document and as such can't automatically replace the witnessed, verbal agreement that Lorne previously had with the Conservancy."

"Interesting," Tanner said. "Neither verbal nor written is definitive, so they're both discarded and the state gets the ranch?"

"The judge will probably rule in a few weeks. Until then . . ."

"Which way is the judge likely to rule?"

"Nothing's sure. Depends which judge is assigned. Some will rubber-stamp this for the citizens' benefit and a couple will let the two parties fight it out. How much money do you want to spend to hold on to the ranch?"

"Doesn't matter. I'll bet that the Conservancy has deeper pockets than an honest L.A. cop."

The lawyer frowned. "Unless you want to simply surrender your claim to the land and the water and lease rights, I'd advise you to stay here and look after your interests as best you can. The personal effects from the house are yours, no question. The truck, too. But without the land, I doubt you want the livestock, much less poor old Dingo."

"Did the dog die?"

"Warren is a good vet. He'll pull him through just in time to be put down at the pound."

Tanner shook his head. "Who do I talk to at the Conservancy?" *Besides the woman I pissed off last night. Nice going, Mr. Charm.*

"I can't advise that you talk to them. Not without someone looking after your interests."

"I'm a big boy. I'll look out for my own rights," Tanner said. "I'm betting the Conservancy is in the phone book."

"There's more of Lorne in you than just his big bones and eye color," the lawyer said ruefully. "Shaye Townsend is the Conservancy's liaison with the ranchers. I understand she works all over the state and even on the California side of things, talking to ranchers about the Conservancy and what it could do for them."

Tanner tried not to wince at the name. "What's she like?"

"She's smart and knows about the problems of small ranchers and modern economics. She's become friends with a lot of old families. Being easy on the eyes doesn't hurt. She's been working with Lorne for some time."

"He could be a tough man to warm up to."

"Hard as flint," Millerton agreed. "Honest, too, maybe to a fault. Not everyone liked Lorne, but they respected him. All the poker boys placed bets as to when he'd kick her pretty ass off his ranch for good. Nobody figured it would be that night, though."

"Maybe they weren't getting all the, uh, benefits Lorne did."

The lawyer shook his head. "It's not a secret that Lorne used to visit the 'ranches' at the far north end of the valley. But that was business, too. Whatever Shaye used on him, it wasn't sex."

"Anything else I should know?"

"The scavengers had been at your uncle's body," Millerton said. "When Shaye found him, it couldn't have been pretty. Deputy August said she didn't come apart, but she was really pale. Right now she's trying to keep it together for Lorne's memorial tonight, the one the Conservancy is giving in his honor."

Tanner thought of all the opportunities he and Lorne had had to reach out to each other in the past. Neither one had. Stiff necks ran in the family.

He also thought about what kind of grit it must have taken for Shaye to come back to the ranch after finding Lorne there, particularly for a woman who wasn't used to tripping over bodies as part of her job.

"Is there any kind of dollar value attached to the ranch?" Tanner asked. "Any other reason for the Conservancy to want it so bad? I mean, it has a nice view, but so do a lot of places here."

"I'd have to evaluate it. There have been offers over the years, especially in the last couple, when real estate looked cheap here compared to Carson City or Reno. That's one of the reasons Lorne hired me, actually. He'd gotten tired of fielding all the queries. He wanted to spend more time actually ranching and not doing the business side of things. He knew he couldn't do everything forever. Frankly it's something of a miracle he worked as long and as hard as he did."

"Any of his poker buddies interested in the land?" Tanner asked.

"If they were, they didn't come to me."

"Anything else I should know?"

"Not at the moment."

Tanner stood up. "I'll be in touch. You have my cell-phone number if you need anything from me."

"Of course," Millerton said, standing quickly. "I'll see you out."

"Not necessary. I have a good memory."

He also had a date with the nearest place that rented suits. Dress clothes were the last thing he'd expected to need in Refuge, Nevada.

FIVE

THIS DRESS IS too small, Shaye told herself.

You just like jeans better.

She could almost hear her mother's accusation echoing down from the past, louder than the party clatter in the Crystal Room of the Tahoe Sky Casino. Her mother was the original girly girl, from a family who could afford all the designer frou-frou anyone could wear.

Shaye had been raised the same. She still wore designer armor, but only for business.

This is business. Quit whining.

The dress still felt too confining and too revealing all at once. The perfect cocktail costume.

So why do men wear cloth head to toe and women wear a minimal, wet-Kleenex look?

She gave a cool glance to a man ten feet away who appeared to be visually counting the stitches in her neckline. When the man, who was easily twice her age, realized he'd been caught staring, he started counting the onions in his empty martini glass.

She swept the large room with a glance, looking for a friendly face. All she saw was more of the designer crowd. The staff of the Ranch Conservancy fit right in. Not for the first time, she was struck by the fact that despite the Conservancy's mission, it spent most of its time catering to the rich with galas like this. Even if the small ranchers had been on the gala's A-list, they would have been be too tired and too broke to attend.

Not to mention the currents of hostility the ranchers felt for the rich outsiders who were changing their life. Locals wanted nothing to do with the fancy Tahoe Sky Casino, much less the ostentatious Crystal Room.

One day, maybe Kimberli will let me throw a barbecue and kids' rodeo for the real people in the valley. In fact, the next time she apologizes to me for her dumb mistake with Lorne, I'll insist on it.

What's done is done, she reminded herself. *Learn from it, pick up the pieces, and move on. Just like you have before.*

Concentrate on all the good Kimberli is doing. She's not IQ smart, but she's a genius at fund-raising.

Trying to look happy and alert rather than sad and weary, Shaye circulated, barely touching the champagne that glowed pale gold in her glass. It was hard not to think about yesterday, and how she had found Lorne. The contrast between then and now was just too stark.

Last night's run-in with Lorne's nephew had been almost as bad. *Just who the hell does he think he is, treating me like an intruder. I'm a better friend to Lorne than Tanner Davis was. Or anyone else in this room, for that matter.*

Giant capital letters silkscreened on a banner suspended from the ceiling spelled out LORNE DAVIS. Jewelry flashed among the attendees, and clothing gleamed with wealth.

Lorne would have taken one look and walked out.

Shaye certainly wanted to. But unless she planned on returning to San Francisco and being her parents' trophy daughter, she had to make a go of the Conservancy job. None of the city jobs she had tried had worked out. Neither had her personal life. The men on the party circuit were too much like her ex—users and losers.

She glanced at her watch. Too soon. She simply couldn't leave until the hastily knocked-together "memorial" speech in Lorne's honor was over.

"Smile, darling. It's a party, not a funeral."

Shaye bit back a sigh. If there was one thing that grated on her, it was her boss in full happy-happy mode. Reminded her way too much of her mother.

"Kimberli, you look wonderful as always," Shaye said, proving that childhood lessons in social manners and maneuvers hadn't been a waste of time after all.

The older woman brushed the words aside. She knew she looked good. It was what she did best. That and vacuuming money from checking accounts for the Conservancy. She was dedicated to her job the way some people were dedicated to religion. The hours she routinely worked should have been illegal. Not to mention after-hours visits to families and properties to keep the relationship going.

Shaye wondered if Kimberli knew about Lorne's rude nephew, but didn't bring it up. Shaye was in no hurry to have her boss sweetly and passive-aggressively chew her out when the situation was Kimberli's fault in the first place.

God, I should never have let her anywhere near the closing of that deal. My bad. Her bad.

A mess.

"Lovely to see you in something other than old jeans," Kimberli continued. "Now smile and look like you're having fun. I don't want this night to be a downer just because Lorne Davis isn't here."

"You make it sound like he was called away on a short trip," Shaye said, then wished she hadn't.

"Our cause is bigger than any one person."

"Of course." Shaye smiled her social smile, the one that didn't touch her eyes. "It looks like everyone is having a great time."

"I did what I could," Kimberli said absently, checking out the bunting and cheerful, fresh flowers.

Framed in mascara and touched by glitter, Kimberli's pale blue eyes searched the room endlessly, ready to pounce if anyone wasn't having a good time. Again, Shaye was reminded of her mother. Shaye knew how necessary—and relentless—raising money was, but she didn't enjoy the process.

"If only Lorne—" Kimberli stopped abruptly. Her smile got even brighter. "I do hope that Harold Hill gets back in time to be here. He's such a dear. So handsome, too." She gave the man hanging on to her arm like a purse an air kiss. "Not that you aren't, Peter. You're gorgeous and you know it."

Shaye glanced at Kimberli's escort and live-in lover. Peter Mann was half Kimberli's age and fond of marijuana, which did nothing for his already mediocre IQ. He was apparently content to be a boy toy. Without complaint he stayed by her side through the tangled wilderness of cosmetic surgery and all-night parties. He had the tan skin, streaked blond hair, and toned body of a tennis, ski, or surf pro willing to give lessons on the side. Quite good-looking, if you liked the sort.

Kimberli did.

Shaye didn't. She'd had a handsome athlete for a husband. It hadn't worked out well. But then again, nothing after that had seemed to work, either. Men figured Shaye was supposed to be arm candy or a mommy.

Maybe Kimberli has the right idea. Screw them and lose them.

Kimberli had invested a lot of time, money, and energy in being forever twenty-one. At fifty, it was hard to do, but her boss pulled it off beautifully. That wasn't what grated on Shaye. What made her teeth clench was the Marilyn Monroe act that went along with it. Kimberli wasn't as breathless and stupid as she sounded.

Unless it involved paperwork.

But Kimberli was brilliant at fund-raising, which was all that mattered to the big bosses in the Conservancy. Paper pushers could be picked up at minimum wage.

"Peter, don't you be staring at our pretty little rancher liaison," Kimberli teased. "Shaye won't be able to think straight for blushing."

"Peter has the most beautiful woman in the room on his arm and he knows it," Shaye said matter-of-factly. It was the truth.

At the reminder, Peter shifted his focus from Shaye's body to Kimberli. "I sure do, you sweet thing."

Thanks to hard schooling by her parents, Shaye's thoughts didn't show on her face.

Kimberli rolled her eyes. "Please don't ruin the image by talking, Peter. Especially if Hill comes."

"Did he actually say he would be here?" Shaye asked. "I thought he was out beating the sagebrush for votes."

"He promised," Kimberli said, ruffling her fingers through Peter's well-styled hair. "Took time out from the campaign and everything."

"He's never not campaigning," Shaye said. "I'll bet he shakes hands in his sleep."

"Of course. You won't get elected to govern Nevada unless you eat, sleep, and breathe the job. He should be able to coax some campaign money out of the party tonight."

"Which you pointed out to him," Shaye said.

"Of course. He's very qualified for the job." As Kimberli spoke, she searched the room like the practiced hostess she was.

Qualified? Shaye thought. *He'd float away if his staff hadn't carefully nailed his Bruno Maglis to the ground.*

Other than being telegenic, charismatic, and descended from old money, Hill didn't have much to offer. He had made an art out of leading from the rearview mirror. His opinions were shaped by focus groups. He was always camera-ready, outwardly friendly, and socially polished.

"We could use a governor helping the Conservancy," Shaye said neutrally.

"Then in Washington, D.C. Of course, that would be a few years from now," Kimberli said, still scanning the crowd.

Shaye made a doubtful sound.

"You can't rain on my dreams, sweet Shaye," her boss said. "I have Teflon umbrellas to spare. I carry sunshine in my pockets. Have some."

"You don't have any room for pockets," Shaye said, looking at the fiery, fitted dress Kimberli wore.

"Then you don't want to know where I keep that sunshine." Kimberli hugged Shaye. "Smile like you mean it. Please. I've worked so hard to . . ."

Make up for one mistake, Shaye silently finished for her boss. Then she shook herself mentally. *It's not like I've never made mistakes. Big ones. Supporting a man-child until he broke into the major leagues being at the top of that list.*

L.A. can have Marcus. At least I won't be paying for his training anymore.

Shaye put more wattage in her smile.

Kimberli looked relieved. "Much better. This is a celebration of a fine and generous man's life." She pointed out the display at the head of the room, where a black-and-white picture of a cleaned-up, much younger Lorne Davis stood between two outrageous fountains of ruby and gold petals.

"Lorne's land passes to the Conservancy and becomes part of living history. Everyone's happy," Kimberli said. "In fact, I . . . I feel a tear coming on. There it is."

Peter passed her a clean white handkerchief before her mascara could run into a raccoon mask. She dabbed at the corner of a black-rimmed eye.

"You're horrible," Shaye said, laughing in spite of herself. This was the Kimberli who made the wide-eyed act bearable, the Kimberli who acknowledged that she was fake and damned good at it.

Her boss smiled her first real smile of the evening.

"I might be a bitch, but I'm our bitch," she said, winking at Shaye. "And as our bitch, I say that we go work this crowd and remind them that giving generously to the Conservancy is exactly what Lorne would have wanted."

Really? But Shaye held her tongue. She didn't want her boss to have to pull sunshine from a handy body cavity in order to dazzle all the sadness away.

There was a stir in the crowd. Sheriff Conrad's trademark white Stetson appeared in the doorway above the throng. Conrad was what Lorne would have called a long drink of water. Tall, lean, almost as telegenic as would-be governor Hill. But unlike Hill, Conrad had a high, almost girly voice, and no charisma worth mentioning—which limited his political future to appearing in stern photographs in local papers. The position of sheriff of Refuge County was about as far as he would get with voters.

Like most of the people at the gala, Conrad was here to do business and get his picture in the news and on local TV screens.

"Go find Jonathan Campbell," Kimberli said. "He can afford more than his recent donation. Or maybe Ace. Ace likes you. And on him, bald looks sexy. Stop drooping around. Make people feel welcome."

Before Shaye could point out that people like casino owner Wilson "Ace" Desmond hardly lacked company, Kimberli was gone.

The sorrow Shaye had felt since yesterday wasn't helped by all the chattering voices and fancy dresses. Her eyes kept burning and her throat felt squeezed dry. Blinking against tears that wouldn't come and wouldn't go away, she dutifully scanned the room for a male or female who was alone and didn't like it—and she prayed she wouldn't find anyone. She felt too raw to make nice with people who had money to spare for the Conservancy.

Her glance caught on a man in a dark suit that was too tight across his shoulders and too loose everywhere else. He stood with confidence, not at all intimidated by people who were accustomed to handmade clothes and a house for every day of the week.

He was doing the same thing she was, searching the room. Probably part of someone's security detail.

Wonder what he hopes to find, she thought. *He's good-looking in a hard sort of way. Dark and rangy, solid, not overly muscled like a gym rat. Not a perfectly dressed escort like Peter. Come to think of it, the guy looks familiar. Maybe I should do what Kimberli said and—*

The stranger was staring at her. She suddenly had an eerie feeling she was watching a much younger Lorne. Same long bones, stark jaw, and—

Oh God, it's him. Lorne's nephew. What the hell is he doing here?

Despite his lack of fine clothing, as he walked toward Shaye, people gave way to him like a covey of quail avoiding a hawk.

SIX

THE SOUND OF silverware tapping a crystal glass vibrated through the PA and the room itself, leaving a quivering kind of silence in its wake.

Automatically Shaye turned toward the head table, where Kimberli burned like a carmine flame beneath a spotlight. The tousled, flaxen fall of her hair gleamed in silent testimony to the best shade of blond ever made in a chemistry lab.

She lowered her glass and the knife she'd used to make the crystal ring. "Good evening. For those who don't know me, I'm Kimberli Stevens of the Nevada branch of the National Ranch Conservancy. I won't keep you long, just enough for a few words of appreciation. First, I want to thank Wilson 'Ace' Desmond for providing the ballroom and such lovely catering."

A spotlight picked out Ace as she spoke. His head gleamed as he smiled and nodded to the scattered applause. "What good is having a casino if you can't throw a party for your friends and an excellent cause?" he asked clearly.

"Just one casino?" called someone from the back of the room.

"I hear you out there, Campbell," Ace said, laughing. "Don't worry, when it comes time to build another one, Campbell Construction is first on my list."

The crowd laughed and clapped. Casinos were good for business, and this was a gathering of businessmen.

"Thank you, Ace," Kimberli said, recapturing attention with a beautiful smile and just enough of a bow to emphasize her cleavage. "Your generosity is legend."

More scattered laughter.

Kimberli's smile faded and she drew a deep breath. "This is a bittersweet night. We should have been standing here with our dear friend Lorne Davis, in honor of his gift of more than a thousand glorious acres of ranch land to the Conservancy."

A low murmuring passed through the crowd. Smiles and small conversations faded.

"Just last month, Lorne verbally agreed to have his will amended. Tonight he would have formalized the eventual transfer of his ranch to the Conservancy by signing a contract. Instead . . ." She trailed off and touched just beneath her right eye as if to stop a tear. Then she straightened and said, "Instead, we raise a glass in his memory. To Lorne Davis, taken away from us too soon." She lifted her champagne glass.

Tanner was still half a room from his destination—the slender honey blonde in the simple, heart-stopping dress—and was doing his best to ignore the speaker's breathy words. He knew he'd seen the honey blonde before, but was having a tough time remembering where.

Last night? Was she the one I was so abrupt with?

He'd been blocking most of the light last night and cross-eyed tired, but still . . .

I was just mad that her voice made me hot. Actually, I was just mad, period.

God, he really didn't want to be in Refuge, Nevada. Not last night, not now. Not ever.

And here he was.

"Lorne was a vibrant gentleman," continued the Hollywood blonde in the siren dress.

What? Tanner thought, not believing his ears. The uncle that Tanner remembered shared very little with the Lorne Davis being celebrated at this party. Either his uncle's grip on reality had slipped, or these party people hadn't known the living man.

"He loved the land above all else."

Well, she got that right, Tanner thought. *The old bastard loved dirt more than he loved kin.*

Mentally he dismissed the speaker as one of those L.A. or Vegas females he couldn't stand—showstoppers at thirty feet, and too thin and anxious up close. He'd take the real blonde he was heading for. Hopefully tonight.

He heard his own thought echoed in the elevation of his pulse.

Dude, you're crazy. You all but kicked Shaye's lovely ass off the ranch.

My bad. Temporary insanity.

And this isn't? his rational self shot back.

He dropped the mental argument. He couldn't remember the last time his pulse had kicked this hard outside of sex. Shaye had wide dark eyes, sunny hair piled loosely on her head, and a smile that kept wanting to slip into sadness.

Her simple dress made his mouth dry.

The cloth wasn't spray-painted on and it wasn't loose. It was a dark silk shadow flowing over a body made for a man's hands. Her shoulders and neck were exposed, showing fine bones and sleek skin. Nothing was cut too low or too high, nothing demanded attention.

Unbelievable. Last night she was dark circles, working clothes, and temper.

And I was an idiot.

Good thing I have something she wants. It's the only way I'm going to get within spitting distance of her.

With a cop's eye, Tanner measured the man who had beaten him to Shaye. Ace Desmond had a shaved head and a dark blue suit tailored for his solid body—money, power, and plenty of intelligence to use both to his advantage. Gold flashed at Ace's white cuff as he put his hand on her mostly bare shoulder.

She flinched, then caught herself and smiled.

Dutiful and polite, not spontaneous and happy-to-see-you, Tanner thought, more satisfied than he should be. *She might be taken, but not by him. She reacts like a woman who isn't into kissing everyone.*

Ace chucked Shaye lightly under the chin, brushed a kiss to her cheek, and allowed himself to be drawn back into the crowd by someone who probably had something to sell him.

Tanner made himself look away from the woman who had caught him off balance. Twice.

I should be checking out the rest of the crowd. Somebody here might have actually known Lorne. Played poker with him, anyway.

Yet for all that Lorne's name was hanging from a ceiling banner, none of the conversations Tanner had overheard had told him any more about his uncle than he already knew.

Maybe that was why Tanner kept looking back at the natural blonde in the unnatural setting. She was real. The rest of the people were onstage.

He walked close enough to see that her eyes were clear brown, probably deep amber in daylight and dark crystal in artificial light. Her tight smiles didn't hide the aura of sadness that clung to her. She didn't wear enough makeup to conceal the dusting of freckles across her high cheekbones. Her mouth was wide, full, and not painted on. Either she had nibbled off her lip dye or wore only a pale gloss. She brought her glass up to her lips with her left hand, but didn't actually drink.

So much that he'd missed last night in his anger at being summoned back to a place he wanted to forget. And couldn't.

No rings. No trophy jewelry. What is a single woman like her doing in this plastic party set?

There were several ways to answer that question, but only one of them appealed to Tanner. He moved closer to her, close enough to smell her light perfume.

"I think you're the only person here who is genuinely sad at Lorne's death," Tanner said. "And I owe you an apology."

Shaye took a quick half breath and turned fully toward the man she had watched across the room. He was standing within easy reach now, as close as he had been last night.

But tonight he didn't look and act like a grizzly bear.

"A lot of people are sad," she said carefully. "I'm just not as good as they are at hiding it. Don't tell me you came here to mourn. I won't believe you, even if you do have his eyes."

"My dad turned red every time he heard that," Tanner said. "I'm sorry I was such a dick last night."

"Really?" she said, surprised.

"Let's start over," he said, holding out his hand. "My name is Tanner Davis."

"Shaye Townsend," she said automatically, shaking his hand.

Her touch was cool, polite. Hesitant. Like her eyes.

He wanted to replace hesitation with heat.

Should have been polite last night, stupid.

"I wasn't expecting visitors last night," he said, holding her hand. "Hell, I wasn't expecting to be in the state."

"I'm sorry. Your uncle's death must have been a shock."

"Yes," he said, meaning it for the first time. "For you, too."

He squeezed her fingers gently.

She realized she was still holding on to his hand. She tried to let go, only to find her fingers tangled with his.

"I don't think anyone gets used to death," he said. Then he thought about what he'd said the first time they met. "Or should."

And that was another truth he hadn't thought about in years.

She looked at his eyes again and realized they weren't exactly like Lorne's. They were both darker and more clear. And they were too old to belong to a man whose hair was black instead of silver.

Belatedly she realized she was staring.

And still holding his hand.

No, he was holding hers. Before she could pull back, he gently let her fingers slide free. It felt like a caress. The dark blue eyes she had first thought of as bleak were anything but. He looked at her mouth like a man with some thorough tasting in mind.

"Do you have a rude, identical twin?" she asked. Then she heard her own words and blushed. "Sorry, I must have an evil twin, too."

He smiled, then laughed. "We're quite a pair. Or is it a quartet?"

"Just make sure there are no sharp objects around and we'll do fine."

"Truce?" he asked, taking her hand again.

"Ah, sure. I guess." She shook her head. "Ignore my inner teenager. Truce."

"Did you know Lorne well?" he asked.

I shouldn't have come here tonight, she thought. *I'm not ready for this. I'm not ready to look at Lorne's ghost. A really sexy ghost.*

"Yes. No." She shook her head again.

Wrong place, wrong time.

"Why?" he asked.

She stared. "Are you a mind reader?"

His smile was as slow as it was hot. "Only when you think out loud."

She felt the flush that spread from her breasts to her cheeks. "Did I? I'm not usually so . . . scattered."

"Good thing I'm here."

"Why?"

"Putting pieces together is part of my job description."

Even if it's just matching John Does with a missing persons report.

But that wasn't something he wanted to talk about with Shaye Townsend. He wanted to know what she liked, what she hated . . . and just how she wanted to be touched by a lover.

Too bad she isn't giving off free-to-a-good-home vibes.

A round of applause went up. In a flash of red, Kimberli stepped out of the spotlight. Part of Tanner's mind caught her final words, something about honoring Lorne's intentions and giving to his dream of preserving small ranchers.

So much for the eulogy, Tanner thought. *Back to business—for the Conservancy and for me.*

"I'll bet you're the only real mourner here," he said. "Lorne wouldn't have pissed on these people if they were on fire."

She turned a laugh into a cough. "Kimberli understands how to turn glitter into money. For the Conservancy, that means galas, which are underwritten by corporate sponsors. All but a handful of the people here tonight paid at least a hundred bucks a head to come."

"So the showgirl act in the red dress is shilling for a good cause."

"My boss truly enjoys parties."

"You don't?"

Shaye shrugged, but the shadows under her eyes and the tightness in her mouth said a lot.

"Well, it's true, isn't it?" he pressed, wondering how deep her temper was buried beneath the polite exterior.

"There's true and then there's polite. When I'm in a place like this, I do polite. When I'm on the valley floor, with the livestock and the flies, I do truth."

Tanner's smile was slow and hot. "No wonder you got assigned to my uncle. He didn't have any use for lies, polite or otherwise. That's why I'm having a hard time believing he was anybody's guest of honor."

"He was just himself," she said simply. "He didn't have a fancy suit and he wouldn't have rented one for tonight." She looked pointedly at the dark, almost-tuxedo Tanner was wearing. "Why did you bother?"

"Maybe I like champagne and short dresses."

A smile came and went swiftly from her lips. "I can believe half of that. Is that why you never visited your uncle? No short dresses?"

"He and my dad had a real fence-lifter of an argument. No dresses involved, short or otherwise. Lorne could be a real bastard, in case you didn't know it. My family left Refuge. End of argument."

"Your dad never made peace?" she asked.

"You ever try to make peace with Lorne Davis?"

She rubbed her hands over her arms as though chilled. "No. I didn't have the chance."

It was just the opening Tanner had been waiting for.

But before he had the chance to ask a question, he felt a hand on his arm. Perfume slid around him like a jungle night, alive with primitive possibilities.

"Shaye, you simply must introduce me to this handsome stranger," Kimberli said breathlessly. She looked up at him with wide blue eyes. "I know we haven't met before, because I'd remember a man like you."

Normally Shaye was amused when her boss turned up the heat on a male, but this time it wasn't funny. Kimberli could ruin everything. Despite the rocky meeting last night, Shaye didn't think the ranch was lost, but it was far from a done deal. She could tell that Tanner was about as thrilled by Kimberli as Lorne had been.

Kimberli wouldn't see that as a problem so much as an opportunity.

Shaye's voice was just a bit clipped when she spoke. "Kimberli Stevens, Tanner Davis. Tanner, Kimberli. She's your hostess."

"Davis?" Kimberli asked. "What an odd coincidence."

"Lorne was his uncle," Shaye said quickly.

Kimberli blinked as though unable to comprehend. "Uncle? You're his nephew?"

"Pleased to meet you, Ms. Stevens," Tanner said, hoping she would vanish as quickly as she had appeared.

"Well, I certainly wish someone had told me sooner," Kimberli said breathlessly, pouring wattage into her smile. "We have so very much to talk about and so many people to meet!"

Kimberli couldn't be deflected short of a very public battle. Tanner considered just that, then decided he might as well meet the local movers, shakers, and players. Some of them might be helpful when he started asking questions about Lorne.

For the next half hour Tanner was paraded in front of wealthy businessmen and their trophy wives. The former greeted him like an old friend. The latter sized him up for sex before Kimberli saved him by throwing him to a fresh pack of wolves.

Through all of it he hung on to Shaye's hand, ignoring the fact that Kimberli's brassy hair and cleavage were always in his face.

Shaye allowed herself to be pulled along, telling herself that the movement of Tanner's thumb back and forth across her palm wasn't a caress.

But it was. And she liked it way too much.

"There's the judge who will be overseeing the probate of Lorne's will," Kimberli said into Tanner's ear.

And she knows this before my lawyer does? Tanner asked silently. *Let the good times roll.*

"Judge, I'm so pleased to introduce Tanner Davis, Lorne's nephew. Isn't he just the spitting image of Lorne?"

The judge was a steel-haired, hawkish man who looked like he'd just eaten a serving of frozen nails. He nodded curtly, whether to the introduction or to Tanner's supposed resemblance to Lorne.

Tanner nodded. "Judge."

Shaye said, "Mrs. Hudson, you look like you've been to a spa rather than riding herd on your grandsons while your daughter and son-in-law are celebrating their twentieth anniversary in Hawaii. How do you manage it?"

As if surprised at being noticed, the white-haired woman standing in the judge's shadow smiled. "They're good boys. Lively, but good."

The judge rolled his eyes. "Hellions will be lucky not to stand before my bench in a few years."

But he smiled at Shaye.

"Judge Hudson will be taking care of things, since Lorne died intestate," Kimberli said.

Tanner decided the good times were over. Sooner or later, everyone would know. Sooner saved time.

"My uncle didn't die intestate," he said easily. "He left a handwritten document with his lawyer stating that he was severing all connections with the Conservancy. As I'm my uncle's executor and beneficiary, it looks like we'll be seeing a lot of each other, Judge."

The other man nodded and held out his hand.

While the two men did the polite, pleased-to-meet-you dance, Kimberli looked like she'd found half of a mouse in her champagne glass.

"But he said in front of witnesses that he was leaving his land to the Conservancy," she protested finally, watching Tanner with wide, confused eyes. "You'll honor that, of course."

It wasn't a question.

"Lorne's written and dated instructions specifically and categorically revoke any preceding business with the Conservancy," Tanner said. "He left the ranch to family. To me. You'll honor that, of course."

"But—I—we—" Kimberli said.

"A pleasure, Judge, Mrs. Hudson," Tanner said, nodding to the couple before turning back to Kimberli and sliding another secret caress along Shaye's palm. "It has been a long, unexpected two days for me and the next few aren't going to be any easier. You'll understand if I leave early."

"But—but," Kimberli said, "we need to talk about the ranch."

"That's why Shaye is coming with me. We're going to discuss Lorne, land, and the Conservancy. I'm sure she'll present your case well to me."

With that, he led Shaye toward the exit.

She knew she should have at least put up a minor objection, but she was too relieved for the excuse to get out of the party.

"Call me with progress reports," Kimberli said.

"Of course," Shaye said over her shoulder.

She wondered which twin she was leaving the party with. If it was the rude one, she'd lose him in the parking lot.

SEVEN

LESS THAN AN hour later, Shaye was relaxed with the nice twin that had saved her from the party. "It's a good thing Kimberli needs to stay on your sunny side."

Tanner made a sound that could have been agreement.

Hard to tell, since he had a mouthful of burger. She took a delightfully sinful french fry from the container she held on her knees and wondered if he had the same fizzy feeling in his blood as she did.

Maybe it was just escaping from a gala. Maybe it was Tanner, her unlikely knight in rented armor, rescuing her from a dragon in a red dress and making her wonder how it would feel to be thoroughly kissed by a man like him.

Stupid teenage thoughts. But I can't stop thinking them.

Tanner's eyes reflected the moonlight coming through the windshield.

She shook her head. "You look like a wolf with a lamb chop. And

Kimberli . . ." Shaye's laughter bubbled up in the darkened car. "Oh, to have a picture of her face when you whisked me out of there. She's too used to having men hanging on her every word."

"More like her cleavage," he said, licking ketchup off the side of his thumb.

Shaye tried not to agree, but it was impossible.

Like being here, now, with Tanner. Impossible.

Smiling, she savored another fry while he wolfed the rest of his burger and reached for another.

"Good thing I wasn't hungry," she said.

"I offered to share." In fact, he'd like to share a lot more than a hamburger with her. She was surprisingly easy company, unafraid of either silence or conversation.

"When I went to the gala, the last thing I expected was to be eating dinner overlooking Lake Tahoe with the mythical tall, dark stranger sitting next to me," she said. "Especially since he could have scared off a dragon by looking at it last night."

"I said I was sorry," he answered without complaint. "I'm different, not strange. And this is a greasy take-out snack. But I'll give you the lake."

"Really? I've always wanted a place on the water."

He smiled and wondered if she'd bolt if he gave her the kiss he'd been thinking about since he first saw her at the party and wished he hadn't been such an ass the night before. "I can see how you got around Lorne."

"I didn't 'get around him,'" she said instantly.

"Relax. It was a compliment not a poke. You have an easy way about you, that's all."

She sighed. "Sorry. It's been a rough few days."

"The lawyer told me about the scavengers and Lorne's body."

Tanner licked up another stray drop of ketchup. "Must have been a shock for you."

She just stared at him.

"Look, when you're a cop, you get used to poking at the grim and grimy details of life and having it not kill your appetite," Tanner said. "Or you starve."

She opened her mouth, closed it, swallowed, tried again. "That explains the bedside manner. Do you . . . like the work?"

"It's complicated. And you swiped my fries."

"I was just holding them for you," she said, chewing one, wide-eyed and innocent.

"Prove it. Feed some to me."

She met his eyes. The dare and the male heat made her feel like she was sixteen again. She picked up a fry and held it in his direction. He took her hand and nipped the greasy bit of potato from her fingers.

"You left some ketchup on me," he said in a deep voice.

For an instant she thought about cleaning his lips with her tongue. Then common sense kicked in. Flirtation was one thing, expected in a social setting. What was in his eyes was another thing entirely.

Without a word she handed him a napkin and the rest of the fries. He ate some more as if nothing had happened.

And licked his fingers.

Is it crazy to find a man's tongue sexy? she asked herself as she watched him.

Then she forced herself to look at the moonlight instead of the man.

Stupid inner teenager. You've just gone too long without. And maybe you want some of tall-dark-and-handsome, but are you ready for an old-fashioned fling?

Why not? God knows marriage didn't work.

For a while there was silence broken by munching sounds as

Tanner finished off the food. Through half-closed eyes, Shaye watched the night and the black water turning silver in the moonlight. Slowly her pulse went down to normal.

Finally she let out a silent sigh, feeling herself uncurl in the quiet. For all his hard edges and male hunger, Tanner was an easy man to be with—when he wasn't biting into her like a burger. He didn't require constant conversation, admiration, and attention. Like her, he was at home in his own skin. Not smug or arrogant. Just not anxious for approval.

"Don't judge the Conservancy by Kimberli's public persona," Shaye said finally. "Both of them do good work, necessary work."

"So does a cop or a garbage collector."

"And nobody dresses up to thank either one of you."

He smiled slightly. "I knew there was a reason I became a cop. But you wear that little black dress like it was designed for you. Ditto for the glitter party."

"My mother is like Kimberli, only more subtle. Either way, up-front scarlet or modestly pastel, I was raised to make the cocktail and charity circuit."

Tanner chewed on that, then shook his head. "You must have driven your mother nuts."

"My older sister made up for it. She never met a party or a volunteer committee she couldn't take by sheer breeding and polite persistence."

He noted that there was no resentment in Shaye's voice, simply acceptance of the reality that she and her sister were different, and her mother and her sister were alike.

"You take after your father?"

"Nope. His mother. She did her own thing before it became the thing everyone had to do. So who do you take after, besides Lorne?"

Tanner accepted the change of subject, for the moment. Then he would switch it back to Shaye the first moment he could. He should be asking questions, not relaxing or wondering if the rest of her tasted as heady as the smell of her next to him.

"I've got Lorne's eyes," Tanner agreed, his voice deep.

"Noted. And his no-BS manner," she said, sneaking a fry from his stash. "His height, and a few inches more. More muscles. Same steel core. Stubborn, too, I'd guess. And we've established that you have his temper."

"Steal any more fries and you'll find out all over again."

She swallowed and licked her fingertips and wished she had the nerve to sample the bit of ketchup on his lower lip. "Terrifying thought."

He watched her looking at his mouth.

She reached for another french fry.

"You were warned," he said.

Slowly he put one big hand around her nape and eased her forward until their lips almost touched. Then he stopped, his muscles tightening against his thoughts.

"That was a little wishful thinking on my part," he said finally against her lips.

She didn't complete the kiss, but she didn't pull away, either. She gave him a look that was level, curious, and warm. "Well, let's say you're a lot closer to it than when we first met."

Tanner breathed out and hoped he didn't look as disappointed as he was. "Close, but not there?"

"The thing about twins? There are two of them. Yes and No. My Yes twin can be dumb as a rock."

"So No is in charge right now." Tanner pulled back a bit but didn't remove his hand from her nape. "Bad luck with Yes?"

She let herself enjoy the caress of his hand against her neck. "I made a bad choice with a marriage."

"Burned, huh?"

"Yeah. Knowing you have bad taste in men really makes it easy to say no." She shifted herself against his hand, savoring the masculine texture and heat. "This is the first time I've regretted it." Her breath brushed the back of his hand as she spoke. "But not enough to give in to temptation."

"At least I tempt you."

She sat back and blew out a long breath. "Tanner, you're a living, breathing temptation to anything female with a pulse."

He gave a crack of laughter. "You're the first woman who's noticed."

She doubted that, but she knew better than to argue it. She had a suspicion that verbal fencing with him would lead to more temptation than she wanted to handle. A quick mind appealed to her more than a hard male body.

Tanner had both.

"Did you really think Lorne would change his mind if you talked to him?" Tanner asked.

"You're giving me conversational whiplash. Wait—" She blew out a breath. "You're right, time to change the subject. When I returned from a fund-raising retreat, there were two messages on my phone. The first was from Kimberli, who said she'd made a mistake with the contract she took out to Lorne, along with the letter of intent he was supposed to sign to firm things up before the party."

"Must have been a bad mistake."

She closed her eyes for a moment. "The boilerplate contract allows the Conservancy to modify land usage according to the overall conservation plans for the entire Intermountain West. Lorne wanted a guarantee that the land wouldn't be traded for any reason under any circumstances. It's hardly an unusual response. We agreed to make the change. He agreed to sign."

Tanner waited. The weariness in her made him want to pull her into his arms, but that wouldn't answer any questions except the hot, male-female kind. Death was a cold business.

"Kimberli was late, as usual, for the appointment. She grabbed the wrong contract from Legal and didn't have time to check it."

"So Lorne found a mistake."

"He accused the Conservancy of everything but stealing children for the sex trade and kicked Kimberli off the ranch. She left a message on my phone that I was supposed to go to Lorne and talk reason into his thick head."

Tanner raised black eyebrows. "She has a lot of faith in you."

"She knew Lorne was more than a job to me."

"You said there were two messages."

"The second one was from Lorne. He was . . . very angry. Wanted me never to set foot on his land again. He wouldn't answer my return calls. I tried to sleep. Finally I gave up and headed for his ranch. I knew he got up before dawn."

Tanner listened to Shaye's words with the skill and intensity of a man who made his living sifting lies from truth. Nothing in her body language or tone rang any alarm bells.

"Did he ever complain about pain or shortness of breath or being stiff in his left side?" Tanner asked.

"No. Other than a knee that bothered him on cold, damp mornings, I never heard him say a word about pain. I never saw him hesitate to pick up a bale of hay or a bucket of water, either."

"He got the sore knee when he was bucked off a horse that was meaner than he was," Tanner said, remembering his uncle's blistering language as he was slammed into the corral fence. "He got back on, rode the horse into the ground, and sold him the next day."

"Sounds like Lorne." She hesitated. "He died quickly. He didn't thrash around or try to crawl back to the house. Just lay faceup to the sky."

"You found him on his back?"

Shaye nodded.

Tanner's fingers tapped once on his thigh. "Odd."

"Why?"

"Unless the person is already lying on his back, most quick, natural deaths fall facedown." He rolled up the paper trash and stuffed it into the fast-food bag. "Had he argued with anyone else lately?"

"Other than Kimberli, not that I know of. I warned her not to be late with the contract because it was poker night and—"

"Wait. If he was signing a contract, why the letter of intent?"

"Lorne doesn't—didn't—trust anyone. Before he signed the letter of intent, he wanted to review and initial every clause of the contract. He was going to officially sign the contract tonight, at the gala, and wanted to be certain he was signing the same contract that he had approved."

Tanner nodded. "Sounds like him."

"Anyway," she said, "Tuesday night was his poker game and he hated being late. With Kimberli, late is a religion. I wanted her to wait until I got back from the retreat so I could handle the whole thing, but she wanted to nail down every detail as soon as possible."

"Go on."

She looked at Tanner and saw nothing but the moonlight drawing dark planes and angles from his face. "My guess is Kimberli was late as usual, and just grabbed the contract from Legal without reading it over herself."

"Is that what she said?"

Shaye shrugged. "It's what she does—rush from one thing to another, leaving a scatter of papers. She's goal-oriented rather than detail-oriented. The details are left to the rest of the staff."

Tanner's long fingers did a single, rippling tattoo against his thigh. "When you usually saw Lorne, was he wearing work boots and an old Stetson?"

"Unless he was in town. Then he wore the boots I found him in. And he was in town clothes, too." She frowned, remembering. At the time all she had cared about was the scavengers. "All these questions aren't giving me a good feeling."

"Hey, I'm a cop," he said absently, watching moonlight glide over Shaye's smooth skin. "We do a lot of questions. Second nature."

"Try the sheriff. He knows more than I do."

"I will, and I doubt it."

Moonlight and silence and a slight breeze ruffling the water.

"One more question," he said finally. "Are you seeing anyone?"

Shaye blinked. "What?"

"Serious dating, live-in lover, that sort of thing. Seeing someone."

"If I was, I wouldn't be here. Are you stepping out on someone?"

"No." He tossed the bag of trash into the backseat. "I'll take you back to your car and follow you home to make sure you get there."

"Why would you—"

"It's a cop thing," he said. "We're the last of the real gentlemen." He turned the car key and flipped on the headlights. The engine made a snarky sound, balked, then started. "I'll pick you up tomorrow morning at nine. Earlier, if you're the dawn type."

"I'll meet you at nine, but I can get myself home just fine."

Even though my gas gauge isn't trustworthy.

"I'm sure you can. I'm also sure not going to leave a woman alone in a vehicle as old as the wreck you drive."

She started to argue, then shrugged. "You're not coming inside with me."

He nodded.

"Why will you pick me up at nine?" she asked.

"We're having breakfast and you're working hard to talk me into giving the ranch to the Conservancy, remember?"

"Hey, a girl has to eat, right?" she said neutrally.

"We need to talk about your enthusiasm."

She looked sideways at him, focusing on his mouth, imagining the smooth, resilient heat of his lips and the sensual textures of tongue and teeth.

"Tomorrow," she said.

And she wondered where that low, sexy voice had come from. Obviously Tanner had a bad influence on her.

Or a good one.

Maybe.

She had all night to decide.

EIGHT

S HAYE STILL HADN'T decided whether Tanner was good or bad for her when the doorbell to her condo chimed happily. She put down the brush she had been running through her hair and looked at her sturdy, all-weather watch. Twenty minutes before nine.

The peephole assured her that it was Tanner rather than a salesman. She opened the door to her second-floor condo.

"You're early," she said.

In the daylight, his eyes were a deep, deep blue. He was looking at her from head to toe and back again.

As far as Shaye was concerned, there was no reason for the utterly male appraisal. She was wearing faded jeans, a plain khaki-colored sweater, and shoes that could take sidewalks or trails. No makeup, hair pulled back. Nothing fancy. Certainly nothing worth a second look.

He met her eyes. "Dressing down today?"

"Cocktail dress for breakfast means the 'Walk of Shame.' It's like wearing an I-did-it sign."

He laughed and looked at her lips. "I'm hungry."

Oh my God, she thought as her pulse kicked. "I'm feeling like Little Red meeting the wolf."

"If you get me fed, I'll be no more dangerous than a border collie pup."

"In that case, I won't take time for makeup."

"You don't need any."

"And you need glasses. Come in while I get my jacket. The wind off Lake Tahoe can have a bite to it even in late summer."

As Shaye disappeared into a bedroom, Tanner walked in and shut the door. A few glances around the condo told him that she was well organized without being militant about it, liked bold colors more than pastels, and preferred comfort over style. That was more personal information than the Google results he'd read about a white female, thirty-three, five foot eight inches tall, one thirty-two, blond and brown, divorced, reclaimed her family name, no tickets, no warrants, no arrests, no children, no unpaid bills.

Which was more than could be said for her ex, a handsome low-level Major League ballplayer named Marc Nugent who liked wild parties and wilder women. Good thing he had a Dodgers paycheck to cover that.

From the envelope Tanner could see on the entryway table, they were still actively corresponding.

Is that why she isn't seeing anyone? Still too involved with the ex?

Or did she get burned but good?

The thing about growing up was that there were so many potholes in the road. Some of them were deep enough to swallow you whole.

"I thought you were hungry," Shaye said, waving a hand in front of his face.

"I am. Who's Marc Nugent?"

Shaye looked at the envelope. "You mean you haven't heard of the famous deep bench player for the Dodgers? My ex. He has a high opinion of himself."

"You could kill scorpions with that tone."

"If only. What about you? Any ex-wives?"

He smiled slightly, liking her directness. He had never been drawn to coy women. "I stopped collecting at one. I got married too young, before I knew how hard a cop's life is on a relationship. Way before I'd grown up enough to make it work anyway."

"Still paying alimony and child support?" she asked sympathetically, picking up her purse. "I was. Alimony, not child support. The court finally decided that my ex could get along without an allowance from me. He wrote me a nasty gram about it."

Okay. She's not really corresponding with the ex.

"No kids or alimony for me," Tanner said. "My ex remarried the day our divorce was final."

"It's better that way. No children to grind up between adult realities." Her voice was matter-of-fact. "Takes a while to stop feeling stupid, though."

He put his fingers beneath her chin, tilted her head up. "It stops?"

She half smiled and half frowned as she gently stepped away. "Anything else from the deep past that we need to exorcise before breakfast?"

"Not on my side."

"Then let's eat."

"I'll drive, you navigate. Deal?"

Automatically she hesitated. Then she reminded herself that nothing in her Google-stalk of him before she went to sleep last night had raised any flags.

"Deal," she said.

Tanner followed Shaye's directions to a nearby breakfast place. On

Sunday morning, the hungry clients should have been lined up out the door, but no one was waiting for a table.

"You sure this is a good place?" he asked before he turned off the car.

"Yes."

"Couldn't tell it by the parking lot."

"Wait until it snows, or until high summer. Place is buried in people then. It's only quiet in the shoulder seasons."

The coffee shop was done in extreme skiing decor. The front-door handles were miniature skis. Signed posters of Olympic ski luminaries lined the walls. Brightly clad ski daredevils shot off cliffs to fly down to snow far below.

Tanner spotted a booth in the back and persuaded the hostess that she wanted to seat them there, rather than at a table with a view of the parking lot.

"She saves this booth for regulars," Shaye said, sliding in on one side.

"You aren't?" he asked.

He took the same side of the booth, following her in. He sat down too close to her at first, smelling her shower soap. He made himself ease away, give her room.

"I usually eat at home," she said, "but I haven't had a chance to go grocery shopping since I went to the retreat." Her husky voice said she was feeling the heat of his body close to hers.

"You like to cook?" he asked.

"When I have time."

"Me, too. Maybe breakfast tomorrow. We can shop for stuff later."

She didn't know which assumption to deal with first—her place, breakfast, his presence, shopping together—so she said, "Kimberli will be expecting me at the Monday staff meeting."

"Not after I tell her that the Conservancy's best chance of ever seeing Lorne's property again is letting you soften me up. That will take time. She'll understand. For her, sex is a sales tool."

"Do you think she'll buy it?"

"I'm not selling," he said with a hard flash of teeth, "I'm telling."

She blinked. "And the evil twin returns."

His smile changed, softer now, hotter. Tempting.

Without realizing it, she licked her lips.

He openly watched her response. He didn't try to tell himself that he wanted to stay close to Shaye only as a way to find out more about Lorne's last months, the Conservancy, and Lorne's death. Tanner had given up that kind of self-deception about the time he came off shift early and found his wife energetically shagging her yoga instructor. He'd known something had been off-key with his wife lately, but he had told himself that he was being too much of a cop.

Too suspicious.

That was the last time he ignored his inner voice—the one that had sat up and howled when he first saw Shaye in that little black dress. One look at her and he had decided to work his way into her life using whatever means was at hand.

At least part of him had decided. The other part of him was laughing its ass off. *L.A. meets Refuge? Really? You'll be lucky to stay here long enough to tie up all Lorne's loose ends without going stir-crazy.*

A waitress came with coffee and menus.

Gratefully Tanner took the coffee and gave her his order without looking at the colorful print and cute ski-slope names for eggs, omelets, breakfast meats, potatoes, and granola with a side of yogurt.

"Scrambled eggs and hamburger," he said. Eggs Benedict cop-style.

Shaye's order followed on the heels of his.

"No waffles and whipped cream?" he asked when the waitress left.

"Sugar and fluff don't last until lunch. Eggs do."

He grinned. "Good. Waffles are a pain in the butt to make."

"All you do is open the box and pop them in the toaster," she said with a sideways look.

"Not if I'm cooking. I start from scratch. I don't pour eggs from a carton or thaw cut-up fruit from the freezer, either. I get enough of that eating out."

She smiled. "All right. You can make breakfast for me tomorrow. I hope your hotel isn't too much of a drive."

"It isn't."

Breakfast came quickly. It was hot, fresh, and plentiful. He didn't bother to make small talk while he neatly demolished his platter of protein.

She concentrated on her food, too. She hadn't been particularly hungry since she had found Lorne, but this morning her normal appetite wanted to make up for lost time. When she was down to chasing a few stray hash browns across her empty plate, she looked toward him. He was watching her with an intensity that took her breath away.

And he was smiling a hungry kind of smile.

"What?" she asked. "Is there egg on my chin?"

"No. I'm just glad you aren't a carrot-shavings-and-lettuce kind of eater. After last night, I wondered."

"I've been off my game since I found Lorne."

"You good now?"

"Better. But still . . ." She shrugged. "Like roots on a trail. Memories keep tripping me."

"Yeah." He took her hand and pulled it onto his thigh. "Do you mind talking about it?"

"I thought you were going to the sheriff."

"Reports can only tell you so much, especially when everyone is taking what they see at face value."

"What do you mean?"

He watched the hostess walking toward them. Trailing behind her were four people he vaguely remembered from the gala. She seated the group in the booth just in front of Tanner and Shaye.

"You feel like doing the meet-and-greet with anyone from the party last night?" he asked quietly.

"Not particularly. It's my day off. I haven't had many of those lately."

He caught the server's eye, got the bill, and gave the woman enough cash to cover everything before Shaye could unzip her wallet.

"I'll be back with your change, sir."

"It's yours."

The waitress brightened. "Thank you."

She turned around and hurried back down the aisle as if afraid he would change his mind.

"I go Dutch," Shaye said.

"I'll keep a tab for you."

He pulled Shaye out of the booth and headed for the back door. After he tucked her into the passenger side of his car, he got in behind the wheel and turned the key. The engine wasn't happy about it, but finally coughed to rough life.

Needs more than a tune-up, he thought.

Working overnight made normal chores a pain.

Maybe that's why our shiny new captain smiled when he changed my hours.

"Would it bother you too much to go to Lorne's ranch?" he asked.

"It won't bother me. I was going to check on the animals before I saw your car. I didn't want to leave Lorne's body, and then the cops . . ."

"Yeah, we're heartless bastards until the forms are filled out."

"They were just doing their job."

"I know that, too. Doesn't make it any easier on civilians."

"No, it doesn't."

She leaned back against the seat and watched dark green trees whip by on either side of the windshield. The two-lane road twisted, rose, then dropped down until the solid wall of evergreen needles gave way to stands of aspen and tongues of grass and sagebrush among the pines. Granite boulders polished by long-ago glaciers gleamed in the sun.

Tanner turned onto a dirt Forest Service road that led to an aging asphalt road. Within minutes the road crossed above Lorne's ranch. A few hundred yards later they were bouncing along the ruts leading to the ranch house.

"You're going to scrape bottom," she said. "We should have brought my Bronco. The gas gauge has a split personality, but I could have bought fuel in Tahoe."

"Long as it doesn't rain, we'll be fine. This is a former LAPD squad car. The suspension is a lot better than the car looks."

And I hope the engine is better than it sounds.

"But if the weather goes sideways, there's always the ranch truck," he said.

She murmured a word that could have been Lorne's name.

Tanner drove into the sunlight flooding around the ranch house. Shaye's glance intently probed shadows and sunlight alike.

"Looking for something in particular?" he asked.

"I keep waiting for Dingo to come out and investigate."

"He's still at the vet, and I'm wondering how he got into that poison."

That, plus the missing gold, is just too damned convenient for this homicide cop to swallow without choking.

One or two—or even three—mismatched details he could accept. Life was that way. Messy. Death was the same.

"So am I," she said. "Dingo stayed away from roads and other people. He was as shy as a coyote."

"I called the vet before I picked you up. Dingo won't be chasing rabbits for a while, but he's getting better. We can see him later."

"I'd like to. He must hate being penned up."

Tanner parked on the shady side of the ranch house, several hundred feet away from the area where Lorne had died.

Shaye unfastened the seat-belt harness, which had dialed itself up to choke. She had closed the car door behind herself when he reached her side of the sedan. He took her hand and gave it a squeeze that lasted just long enough to remind both of them how much they liked it.

"Dessert with breakfast," he said, smiling at her.

"Never saw that on any menu."

"You've been going to the wrong restaurants."

He liked seeing the humor in her eyes and on her pink, naked lips so much that he wished he didn't have to grill her like a murder suspect. But he knew he was going to just the same.

Some questions just had to be answered.

NINE

*E*VERYTHING IS GOING *well.*

 Lorne Davis's death will be certified as natural.

 The nephew is an unexpected problem, but not insurmountable. Tanner Davis has no attachment to the ranch, so even if he ends up with it—unlikely—he'll sell it to the highest bidder.

 If that doesn't work out, or if the inconvenient cop gets in the way somehow, there will be a really convenient, and fatal, accident in his near future. Nobody will care, especially the brass in L.A.

 Nobody will miss Rua, either.

 Really, killing him will be a public service. The sooner the better.

TEN

TANNER LED SHAYE close to the flattened patch of grass and brittle weeds where his uncle had died.

"Was Dingo a carrion hound?" he asked.

She flinched and tried not to think of Lorne's body and vultures sliding out of the air. "Not that I know of. He was more a hot-rabbit-and-fresh-kill kind of canine."

Tanner smiled faintly.

She watched him study the area where Lorne had died. His eyes were intent, narrowed, looking for or seeing things that others wouldn't see.

"It's different, now," she said.

"How?"

"Full sunlight," she said simply.

He switched his attention to her. "Was Lorne wearing a jacket when you found him?"

She remembered the scene all too clearly. "No. And the first deputy didn't ask about that."

Tanner grunted. He wasn't surprised. The deputy probably was doing back-to-back shifts just to cover his part of the county. There was never enough money to pay for full coverage, especially in rural areas. An old man dying alone on his ranch wasn't going to raise enough interest to get much more than a body bag and an obituary in the local weekly.

"The second deputy, Nate August, started to question me about Lorne's clothes, but another call came in and he had to leave."

She stared at the beaten grass and reminded herself that Lorne had died quickly, no time to be alone in fear and pain.

"Are you okay?" Tanner asked gently.

"Yes. No. Not really." She pulled off her ponytail holder and rubbed where some hair had been caught the wrong way. "I know his death was quick. That helps."

"I don't want to make it harder on you, but . . ." He shrugged. "It sounds like nobody in the sheriff's department is paying attention to this one."

"Everyone is spread thin in the county, and they concentrate on the towns."

"They're working the odds. More people, more chances of needing a cop. What makes you say that Lorne died quickly?"

"I'm a volunteer with the local search-and-rescue group," she said. "They taught us to read and follow disturbances in the land—tracks, broken brush, or trampled grass, anything that was out of place."

"You could see the ground that well? I thought you found him before sunrise."

Her eyes narrowed, but she was looking at the past, not at him. He waited, letting her reexamine the picture in her mind of the moment she had first seen his uncle's corpse. Something, or things, had led her to believe he died a quick, painless death. Tanner needed to know how she had arrived at her conclusions.

"It was the gloaming time," she said.

"What?"

"Those clean, beautiful moments before the sun clears the mountains across Carson Valley, when the stars are mostly gone and light seems to bloom from an invisible source. There aren't many details, just darkness at your feet and the day coming up with the sun. You get the same feeling at twilight, after the sun has set and light drains away, leaving the stars behind."

He watched her, listening to her describe the beauty of the times when night and day passed each other. "Are you a dawn person?"

"I won't get up to see one, but if there's another reason to be out, I like that hushed, waiting-for-something feeling."

"Lorne's message must have really upset you," Tanner said quietly, understanding what she hadn't said—she really hadn't slept well after hearing his uncle's anger.

She nodded and closed her eyes. It made no difference. She still saw Lorne's body condensing from the shroud of night, the marks of scavengers getting clearer and clearer on his corpse with the rising sun.

She opened her eyes. It was too easy to remember how he had looked lying slackly on his back, his ruined face lifted to the merciless sky and his thin silver hair lifting in the occasional wind.

"What are you seeing?" Tanner asked in a low, undemanding voice.

"Lorne. The marks of scavengers. Vultures sliding out of the brightening sky to get their share of the free protein."

He waited, hating that he had to put her through this. And knowing that the only other choice was to walk away and pretend that everything was as neat as the first deputy's report, all gaps filled in, certainty crisp in every line, no dangling ends or unanswered questions.

"This kind of ground doesn't hold footprints well," she said, "unless the person stays in place for a long time or paces back and forth or drags himself around. I didn't see that kind of disturbance in the vegetation until they lifted Lorne's body. Everything beneath him was crushed. His boot heels . . ." She waved her hand. "You can still see the marks. His arms were out from his sides."

"Sounds like he fell hard."

So hard his heels bounced.

"Like a puppet without strings." She cleared her throat. "Sorry, I—"

"Don't apologize. I asked for what you saw. You're telling me." He took her hand and rubbed his thumb across her fingertips.

"Do you console every grieving civilian?" she asked softly.

"No."

His thumb stroked her palm.

She let out a breath. "He wasn't wearing a hat. I guess it blew away in the wind."

Tanner waited, caressing her, saying nothing, silently encouraging her to remember each painful detail.

"I'm not sure I ever saw him without his hat," she said.

"He only went bareheaded in bed or in the shower."

She almost smiled. "He wasn't wearing one of his work shirts or his work pants. It was his go-to-town clothes. And . . ." She frowned, remembering. "The little pouch of chewing tobacco had spilled out over his shirt."

"The one he kept in his left shirt pocket?"

She nodded. "I could tell he had died well before the scavengers came, because they didn't draw blood. There were . . ." She drew a deep, careful breath. "Marks, gouges, but no bleeding. No rigor mortis. No bruises on his hands, no grass or dirt under his nails that I could see from ten feet away. Except for the scavengers, I didn't see any sign of facial injury. Nothing to make me think he'd struggled or fought or anything like that."

"Like I said, you see better than an overworked deputy. Sheriff wrote it off as a heart attack before he ever looked at the body. If he looked at all."

Shaye watched Tanner with shadowed, beautiful eyes. "You don't think that's what happened?"

"A heart attack is always possible, but in this case it leaves a lot of dangling ends."

"Such as?"

Tanner started naming the facts that he was having trouble swallowing. "Lorne's home, but he's in his town clothes. Shortly before Lorne died, Dingo ate poison. Dingo's a hunter, not a scavenger, and Lorne didn't put out poison. Lorne's dogs—the ones that lasted more than a year, anyway—hunted in the national forest in the daytime, not out of garbage cans at night. Lorne was trying to change his will. If he had lived, the Conservancy would have been cut out."

"We've had a lot of people refuse us," Shaye said. "They're all alive and a lot of them had more land than Lorne."

Tanner nodded. "That's what I figured. Which leaves the missing gold. Did he say anything about being close to bankruptcy?"

"No. He complained about the price of feed and taxes and what a lousy amount of money he got from the cattle when he shipped to the feedlots, but so does every other rancher I know. He was looking at new trucks, and had just bought a new dress hat and the boots I found him in, so he couldn't have been that broke."

Then, as if it had just registered. "Gold? What gold? He had a silver belt buckle or two, but I never saw him wearing gold."

Tanner watched the sky with the measuring eyes of someone who had grown up where weather mattered. The morning was sunny with puffy clouds, but almost cool. Autumn was settling in, leaching the heat from the ground. Once the sun went behind the mountains in the late afternoon, the furnace went off and things got chilly real fast.

Clouds slid over the sun like gray fingers, threatening rain. But the clouds were being pushed by a hard wind that chased and scattered them before they could get together and cry.

Shaye waited, seeing cloud-shadow and sunlight change Tanner's face. He looked like a man chewing on something he couldn't swallow and wouldn't spit out.

"Sorry, that was my mistake bringing it up," he said. "So you found him out here?" he asked quickly. "On his back, wearing his new town boots?"

She wanted to pursue the question of the gold, but doubted that he would tell her much more than he had.

All he has is questions to ask, not answers to give.

It irritated the hell out of her. Then she took a better grip on her roller-coaster emotions and said, "Yes."

"Wonder why," he said to himself. "He and my dad were raised alike. Dad didn't change. I'm having a hard time believing Lorne did."

"What do you mean?"

"On the ranch you had your work boots, then you had the boots you wore into town, and for really special occasions you had a pair of fancy boots. Your work boots didn't leave the ranch, and you weren't on the ranch without being in them unless you were heading into town or coming back from town."

Shaye didn't know what to say. Obviously the boot thing meant more to Tanner than it did to her.

He sat on his heels and ran his fingers through the dirt, testing the dryness of the soil.

"If you found Lorne here, he wasn't coming back from his truck or heading toward it," Tanner said, "yet he was wearing his town boots. With a town shirt. What about his pants?"

She looked at the ground, seeing the past and not wanting to see it at all. "They weren't work pants. Maybe he was just out admiring his land."

"He respected the land, but I never saw him stand around and admire it. Did you?"

Wind gusted down the mountain, swirling her hair. Automatically she tucked it back behind her ears. "No. When he was outside, he was always doing something. Mending fences, cleaning the irrigation ditches, checking the cattle, cussing the deer and rabbits that kept raiding his garden, despite Dingo's teeth. Even when we were talking, his hands were busy oiling a bridle or wielding a hoe or . . . something."

"Yes, that's how I remember him." Tanner stood and brushed his hands off. "No footprints around the body?"

"I didn't look for any." Absently she pushed windblown hair back from her face again. "Even ten feet away, it was clear that Lorne was dead. If I can't give aid, I'm supposed to leave everything untouched for the deputies. I called 911 and chased scavengers until a patrol car showed up."

And I cried, but I'm the only one who cares about that.

"If it was important, wouldn't the first deputy have seen it?" she added.

"Not if he wasn't looking for it," Tanner said.

She shook her head. "I should have looked. I'm sorry."

He heard the emotion in her voice and touched her chin. "Why would you? You're not a cop. And maybe there was nothing to see."

"You don't sound convinced."

He changed the subject. "Lorne's lawyer said that there had been offers on the ranch. Was that something he talked about with you?"

"He laughed about it. Said the idiots thought they could eat the view."

"If you could, you'd be fat," he said wryly, waving a hand at the surroundings.

Behind the ranch house, the Sierra Nevada thrust granite spires up into the sky, creating a vast barrier to anything that didn't have wings. In the winter, winds routinely reached more than one hundred miles an hour on the upper ridgelines, lifting snow like white fire from black rocks. The mountains were a wilderness of tall trees and rushing white streams, hidden valleys and stands of aspens that burned molten gold in the fall.

Below the ranch to the east, Refuge spread out, far enough away to be interesting rather than intrusive. Around the town, sunlight glittered off the groundwater and irrigation channels that were wet even in the driest season. A hundred shades of green fields and marshes shimmered in the sun, surrounding farmhouses and town alike.

Glory Springs and Lorne's narrow ranch valley lay between the mountains and the main valley floor where Refuge was, part of both but at the same time distinct, aloof. Like Lorne.

"The ranch is one of the most beautiful places I've ever seen," Shaye said quietly. "I wish . . ."

Tanner waited, but she didn't finish. "What do you wish?"

"That Lorne was alive and the land was safe with the Conservancy." She turned and faced him. "What are you going to do with the ranch?"

ELEVEN

A T FIRST SHAYE thought that Tanner would ignore her question as he had the one about the gold. Then he shook his head.

"I don't know," he said simply.

"You weren't in touch with Lorne, you haven't been here since you were a kid, yet you dropped everything and drove here when he died. Because of the ranch?"

"No."

"Then why?"

He shrugged. "I wondered myself. I think I was . . . looking for something."

"What?"

"If I knew, I would have found it by now." He hissed out a long breath and put his hands on his hips. His mouth settled into a flat line. "Whatever, I'm here now, and I keep tripping over questions. As for the ranch, when I'm sure I understand why you found Lorne lying on his back for a vulture buffet, then we can talk about the land and the Conservancy."

Because I'm sure I don't want much to do with the land anymore. Right?

He made an impatient sound. The ranch reminded him of too many things that never had had answers and never would—his father, his uncle, himself.

If she picked up his uneasy thoughts, she hid it well. Or it didn't bother her.

And why should it? You're nothing much to her, and while she's a damned intriguing woman, she isn't into casual sex—and that's all I can offer her. She loves life in a place that drove me crazy.

Or was it the teeth-grinding tension of growing up as a buffer between my uncle and my father that made me eager to get out?

Tanner had never thought about that possibility and he didn't have time or patience for it now. The past was over. The questions about Lorne's death were here and now.

The wind flexed across Tanner and Shaye, bringing with it the smell of evergreens and stone. Like the day, the wind was balanced between sunshine and chill.

"What if we don't find out all the answers?" she asked.

"We will. It's just a matter of knocking on enough doors."

Or kicking them in.

"Let me see your badge," she asked.

"Why?"

"Because you come in with the wind, and you're going to blow out just as quick. I'll still be in the here and now, though. I have to live with all this."

With an odd curl of his mouth that was too hard to be called a smile, he pulled a leather wallet from his jacket pocket. A quick, practiced motion of his wrist opened the wallet, revealing a bronze shield and ID card. They gleamed in the light.

"Detective Tanner Davis. LAPD Homicide," he said in a voice that had an edge like the wind. "Western B, representing the great Olympic district. When I'm not in the cooler shuffling papers and stiffs."

A situation that is going to change when I get back to L.A. I'm a good cop. I should get back to being one.

Curious, Shaye took the badge and examined it. The metal item was a lot heavier than she thought it would be. She wondered if he noticed its weight. "And you believe that Lorne didn't die of a heart attack?"

"I believe that it's certainly possible. Does that mean a crime was committed? I won't know until I find out more."

He retrieved his wallet, flipped it shut, and stowed it with the automatic motions of someone who has done it countless times.

"If you really think something was . . . off . . . about Lorne's death, you should talk to the sheriff."

"I couldn't get past the door with what I have now. The last thing a sheriff wants before an election is an important, unsolved case."

"You think the sheriff is corrupt?" she asked, startled.

"No. I think he's as much politician as cop. Unless I can come up with a lot more than a few loose ends, the politician will mourn at Lorne's funeral and the cop won't look anywhere he isn't forced to. I'm hoping the gold will be a lever."

"What gold?" she asked bluntly.

"Pirate treasure," he said with a straight face.

She considered smacking him like a little brother. But he wasn't her brother and he certainly wasn't little.

"Would that be treasure he dug up while shoveling bull manure?" she asked sweetly.

Tanner smiled. "C'mon. I'll show you."

After the sweeping views outside, the interior of the old house seemed small. It hadn't been empty long enough to have an abandoned feel, but it was beginning to need a good airing.

Shaye kept expecting Lorne to come out from the back bedroom and ask what the hell they were doing in his house.

"I recognize Lorne," she said, gesturing to the framed photo on the fireplace mantel. "When I asked him who the other man was, he ignored me. Is it your father?"

Tanner didn't even look up from the chimney stone he was poking around. "The one on the right is my dad."

"You don't look like him."

"Nope. I'm meaner."

"Tougher," she corrected. "Like Lorne."

"Don't kid yourself. We both got a full helping of mean."

She wanted to argue that Marc Nugent had taught her all about mean. Tanner wasn't. Tough? Sure. But not striking out at every target just because it was there and he was frustrated. Like Marc had.

Tanner was different. It showed in simple ways . . . like the gentleness of his hand against her cheek even though he knew sex wasn't on offer.

I could get used to that kind of man, strong enough to be gentle.

And that was something she shouldn't be thinking.

"Did they argue a lot?" she asked.

"Lorne and my dad?"

"Yes."

Tanner stopped worrying the stone and leaned against the cold chimney, watching Shaye, remembering just how good she had felt with only a brief touch, wanting to taste her long and deep.

"Two men," he said, "one ranch, one boss. Lorne. Dad was much younger. In Lorne's eyes, he always would be. Lots of friction. But that's all from an adult perspective. As a kid, I just accepted that they fought through me. I enjoyed the ranch, horses, cattle—hell, even shoveling manure. I worked hard bucking hay and fixing fences, and my uncle taught me how to shoot, ride, drive, drink, and judge livestock. Dad worked in Reno. I loved him, but I didn't see much of him until we moved to L.A."

She thought of what Tanner must have been like, an energetic kid with the whole world to discover. "What about your siblings?"

"By the time I was old enough to care about the ranch, my two sisters were through with their horse phase and chasing boys. They're both married and have kids. One lives in D.C. and one in Atlanta. How about you?"

"Older sister, married, no kids, doing the San Francisco social thing with my mother. Brother overseas, divorced, no kids. My parents have been doing laps about having grandchildren for almost as long as I can remember."

"Sounds like family. Never satisfied."

"Not in my experience. And you've ducked the gold question long enough."

His mouth lifted at both corners. "I'm easy. I'll trade info for a kiss."

For a moment both of them looked equally surprised.

Her breath backed up in her throat. She cleared it. "Speaking of gold," she said firmly.

He laughed and gave up teasing her.

Later, he had some serious teasing and tasting in mind. He could tell that she wanted him, but she was resisting. He respected that.

And he planned on getting around it real soon.

Shaye watched Tanner and let out a silent sigh when he turned his attention back to the fireplace. The look in his eyes had made her feel like the sexiest woman alive.

Hunted, too.

Wonder when I'll let him catch me.

If, she thought quickly. *If.*

The sound of stone grating over stone startled her. She walked close enough to look over his crouching body. His hands looked lean and capable as he pulled out one of the river cobbles on the side of the fireplace.

There was nothing but darkness where the stone had been.

"It looks empty to me," she said.

He straightened carefully. She was close now, close enough for him to smell the clean scent of her hair. No perfume this morning. Just warm, soft female.

"The coins were kept in here," he said huskily. "I saw them several times after I turned fourteen. Knowing about the hidey-hole was a Davis rite of passage for the men."

"The gold was Lorne's fortune?" she asked, turning from the black hole to Tanner's vivid blue eyes.

Falling into them.

Yanking herself back.

"No," he said, watching her lips. "They were Max's continuing 'screw you' to the government and the crazy idea that he owed it money from land that generations of family had fought and died to hold against Indians, drought, envy, and politicians."

"Max? A Davis ancestor?"

"The original hard-ass," Tanner agreed. "Lorne learned it best, but my dad was no amateur. The gold was my family's form of Social Security and Medicare. Originally it was nuggets and dust panned up the mountain or traded for steers. Then Max decided to celebrate a good cattle sale by converting everything into a gold coin that had caught his eye at the poker table. He'd never seen one like it before."

"Was it really a Spanish doubloon? Pirate gold?"

Tanner leaned in closer, close enough to feel her startled breath, smell her warmth, all but taste her sweetness. "The coins were 1932 Saint-Gaudens," he said in a deep voice. "They were a family relic. Each generation added some. Loans from the hoard were always repaid. It was our independence, our freedom, our solid gold 'screw you' to civilization."

"Maybe Lorne cashed in the gold when he decided to give the ranch to the Conservancy."

"Possible."

"But you don't believe it." She frowned. "Do you think the gold was stolen during a robbery and then Lorne was somehow killed?"

The cry of a hawk fell out of the sky like a silver talon.

She started and saw that the wind had opened the front door. Automatically she headed toward it.

"Leave it," Tanner said. "Place could use some fresh air. As for the gold, in L.A. people get killed every day for a lot less than that."

Wonder when Brothers will get back to me.

When he has something, mook, Tanner said to his impatient half.

Shaye opened her mouth, but said nothing. The thought of him seeing hard ways to die on a regular basis closed her throat. She stared at him, eyes dark and wide.

"I'll bet murder happens in Carson Valley, and even Refuge," he said. "After all, humans live there."

She swallowed. "I know. It's just that . . ." She shook her head. "Seeing that much death must wear you down."

Saying nothing, he put the stone back into place, pressing it tight, like he wanted the secret to stay hidden even now that it was out.

She got the silent message. He wasn't going to talk about his work.

"The gold," she said, "explains why Lorne said that he wasn't hard up for tax money, so if the Conservancy was waiting for him to get that desperate, they'd wait a long time."

"When was that?" Tanner asked, turning to face her.

"A few months ago, about the time I finally got him to sit down and really listen to what the Conservancy was trying to do for the small ranchers in the valley."

"Huh. You actually got to the old buzzard."

Shaye winced and remembered vultures condensing out of the dawn. "Not my favorite word right now."

"You prefer 'bastard'?"

She ignored the choice. "I finally convinced Lorne that we weren't trying to evict him or sell his land to developers or turn it over to the mustangs."

"Mustangs?" Tanner asked, lifting his black eyebrows.

"Oh, don't act like that around Kimberli. She'll bend your ear for hours and have you writing a check just to get her to go away. Mustangs are her special cause."

"Why? Mustangs might have had good bloodlines once," he said, "but that was hundreds of years ago, when they came to the New World with conquistadors on their back. Those horses went feral as soon as they could get away. When settlers came, the feral animals were crowded off into the scrublands and inbred down to something small and tough enough to survive on sagebrush. Like burros."

"You sound like Lorne. But to a lot of people, mustangs are romantic. People have become attached to them."

"City people, yeah. Ranchers? Not so much. They compete with cattle and game for food."

"So do city people," Shaye said blandly. "Kimberli is city down to her expensive pedicure. She adores mustangs."

"She ever been close to one?"

"The license plate on her car, does that count?"

He gave up the mustang discussion. "So you convinced Lorne to put the land in trust with the Conservancy? And he'd still work it for as long as he could?" There was an unspoken *not real long* in his words.

"Lorne, and six other local families who agreed to put their ranches in trust with the Conservancy. They're still able to live and work on the land they love and the Conservancy makes sure the land stays as it is, rather than being abandoned or turned into shopping malls. And that's only ranches in and around Carson Valley. The Conservancy is all over the Intermountain West."

Tanner's fingers did the tattoo thing on his leg again.

"Come on. Let's go talk to your Sheriff Conrad," he finally said.

"He's not mine."

"Okay." Tanner held out his hand. "Take a ride with me. You can sit in the car while I talk to the sheriff. Afterward I'll buy you lunch."

"Um, the sheriff is Kimberli's kind of person."

"Yeah, I got that last night."

"I'm sure he's good at his job," Shaye said.

"I'm not."

TWELVE

I'M COMING INSIDE with you," Shaye said as Tanner parked in Refuge. "Sheriff Conrad will probably be polite to me."

"It's worth a try." But he smiled to take the edge from his voice.

Come on, Brothers. Call. I'm going to the sheriff with a double helping of nothing much.

The county office was small and brightly lit, papered in the kinds of public service posters that made civilians feel that things were completely under control, with all bad guys numbered, known, and destined for justice. There was a door off to one side, leading to a small office. Tanner assumed that if the sheriff was in, he was behind the closed door.

The secretary's desk had a nameplate—*Ms. Jones*—and a man frowning over the phone system like a spaniel confronting a page of quadratic equations. The tag over his right pocket said he was Deputy Feldt. His attitude said he wasn't interested in visitors.

"That's the first deputy on scene at Lorne's death," Shaye said in a voice too low to be overheard.

"The one who didn't ask about Lorne's clothes?" Tanner asked quietly.

"Yes."

That, plus the deputy's attitude right now, told Tanner all he needed to know. He walked up and loomed over the desk like the Sierras over the valley, threatening to slide down at any moment.

At first Shaye thought he had growled. Then she realized he was only clearing his throat.

"Yeah?" the deputy said without interest.

"I'm Tanner Davis. I want to talk to the sheriff about my uncle's death."

Without looking up, the deputy punched a button. He frowned when nothing happened. "Sorry for your loss," he said, eyes on the phone.

"So am I," Tanner said in his cop voice. "Is the sheriff in?"

No wonder Tanner expected the sheriff to be rude to him, Shaye thought. *Cops have it down to an art form.*

"Listen, Mr. whoever-the-hell—"

A newspaper rattled loudly.

Tanner glanced to the rear corner of the room. Separated only by a waist-high wooden divider and a gate made of the finest wood laminate that the taxpayers would foot the bill for, another deputy sat with his boots propped up on a tiny desk. He didn't look up, simply rustled his newspaper again, sharply, making the sound of dry weeds harried by the wind.

Deputy Feldt straightened like he had been smacked. "Sorry, I hate this damn phone. What's the name of the deceased?" His gaze shifted to the phone.

"Lorne Davis."

"Oh, of course. Same last name and all."

The deputy in back glanced up from his paper.

Shaye nodded, recognizing him. When Deputy Nathan August wasn't being an investigator, he often moonlighted as security for Conservancy galas. He had been the second official on scene, but had been called away before he could take pictures with his cell phone.

"Oh, *that* Davis," Deputy Feldt said. He looked as earnest as the spaniel breed he resembled. "I was sorry to hear about that. Lorne was a real . . . uh, real."

"Uh-huh," Tanner said. "Has there been a ruling on the cause of death?"

"We, ah . . . gimme a moment." He glanced back toward the other deputy. No response. "I think the sheriff was just looking at the results for that, not sure . . ."

"I'll need to see them," Tanner said in a tone that was just short of a demand.

From the back of the room Deputy August said, "Not until the sheriff signs off on the report."

"Hello, Deputy August," Shaye said, trying to add some politeness to the conversation.

"Nice to see you, Ms. Townsend." He looked from the newspaper to Shaye. A long look of male appreciation. "You left the party early last night."

"Um, it had been a long day," she said, surprised he'd noticed.

Tanner wasn't. He made a sound that could have been a growl. The deputy was giving her a visual pat-down.

August looked away from Shaye to Tanner. "My sympathies for your loss." His gaze went over Tanner, sizing him up like a cop.

Tanner returned the favor.

The other deputy hurried back to the closed door of the office and disappeared. The light came on. A few moments later he returned to the front, carrying a folder.

"I'm sorry you were the one to find him," August said, switching his focus back to Shaye. "That was a grim bit of business."

She stood up straighter, shaking off the chill of memories. "It was . . . difficult."

Without appearing to, Tanner watched her closely. If she realized that August was interested in her as a woman, she didn't show it.

"Okay," Feldt said, clearing his throat and paraphrasing from the paper he held in his hand. "'It is the judgment of this expert that the deceased, one Lorne Maximilian Davis, residing at'—hell, you know where he lived—'is hereby ruled to have died from natural causes, likely stemming from cardiac arrest due to the age of the individual.'"

"Bullshit," Tanner said flatly.

Shaye gave him a sideways look.

"Ex-cuse me?" August said, coming to his feet.

"Can't be the first time you ever heard the word," Tanner said, his voice flat.

"What Tanner is saying," Shaye said in a calm voice, "is that there are some new facts he'd like to add to the investigation."

"Not what I said," Tanner muttered in a low growl, but only she heard him.

"Yeah, I figured that out all by myself," August said. "He must be some kind of city expert come to teach us rural folks how it's done."

Feldt looked very unhappy.

"It doesn't take an expert, city or otherwise, to notice my uncle wasn't wearing a hat," Tanner said. "You know any rancher in the valley who doesn't put his hat on before his boots?"

August said, "Feldt, what's the time of death there?"

"Hard to tell. Body wasn't exactly in prime shape, what with the scavengers and all."

Shaye's mouth thinned at the reminder.

"What does the report say?" August asked bluntly.

"Uh, best they could decide, it was probably Wednesday, give or take." Feldt looked at August. "If it was night, he maybe wouldn't need his hat."

"Then he'd need a jacket," Tanner said. "He wasn't wearing one."

Feldt looked intently at the report, a man hoping to find a jacket. There wasn't one.

"Then there's the question of his boots," Tanner said.

"He was wearing boots," Feldt said, tapping the report. "We got 'em all wrapped up waiting for someone to claim them."

"His regular work boots were on the bench inside the house," Tanner said.

"The ones on his feet were shiny," Shaye added.

August lifted his hat, ran his fingers through his thick hair, and resettled the hat. "I thought about that, even brought it up to the sheriff more than once. But it didn't have much weight." He shrugged. "Not enough to order an investigation, for sure. From where we are, you can't even see circumstantial."

Point made, Tanner thought. *August tried to do cop work and was shut down by the sheriff.*

"So you're sure it was an accidental death?" Shaye asked.

There was a flash through the front window, sun glancing off an approaching car. August looked over Tanner's shoulder to the front door behind him. His suntanned hand closed around the newspaper once again.

The front door opened, rattled in its frame by someone in a hurry.

"Morning, Sheriff," August said.

The cop in Tanner knew that August had deliberately ignored Shaye's question. What Tanner didn't know was why. Unless it was Conrad's presence. Turning slightly, he got a good look at the sheriff.

Without the stage lighting of the Conservancy gala, Sheriff Conrad had the command presence of dryer lint. His long, slight frame was drawn. Dissatisfaction with life radiated from him like heat ripples off asphalt.

Two cell phones hung on the sheriff's belt. Instead of making him look important, they made him look ridiculous, especially as one of them was a cheap piece of crap any kid could purchase by the handful at a convenience store.

Since Conrad had settled for being sheriff of the rural county of Refuge, Nevada, Tanner doubted that the man could afford much more than a free dog to worship him. Tanner also had no doubt that he was looking at a man who was like his new captain back in L.A.—huge ambition but no real talent to back it up.

Must be real good at ass-kissing, Tanner thought in disgust. *When it comes to promotions, that beats good work almost every time.*

If Sheriff Conrad recognized Tanner, he didn't show it. He nodded curtly to Shaye before he stalked through the open area to his office and closed the door. Hard.

"Never saw a man wearing a Do Not Disturb sign that big," Tanner said into the silence.

"You'd think somebody would be happy he's the bookies' favorite in the next election," August said.

The corner of Tanner's mouth kicked up. Under other circumstances, he probably would have liked August. But right now the deputy stood between Tanner and the answers he wanted.

He leaned over and said very softly to Shaye, "Am I the only one who looks at the sheriff and sees a kid playing dress-up?"

She tried not to laugh, and settled for not being loud about it.

"FELDT!" The window-rattling yell came from behind the closed door. "Where in the sainted name of Jesus H. Christ is that final inquest? It's supposed to be on my desk!"

"I've got it right here, Sheriff. All ready for your signature."

The door opened and Conrad stalked toward them.

Tanner knew that Conrad was trying to project someone-is-going-to-die, but he just didn't have the right stuff.

Probably why Conrad hired Feldt. Somebody he could intimidate.

"Damn it! That was supposed to be put to bed already!" He stood so close to Feldt that the edge of his hat brushed the deputy's eyebrows.

That's got to tickle, Tanner thought in disgust. He'd known too many fear-biters like Conrad. Give them a little power and they were hell on the half shell.

In Refuge, the sheriff had more than a little power.

"Uh, sorry, sir," Feldt said. "I was just—"

Tanner interrupted. "That has to rank as the fastest inquiry ever spit out by a county bureaucracy."

"Who the hell are you?" The older man's voice had an unfortunate tendency to squeak under pressure.

"Sheriff, you'll be pleased to meet Tanner Davis, nephew to the deceased in question," August said, deadpan. "He has some questions and observations to share with you."

Conrad looked at Tanner like he was boot scrapings. Then the name seemed to register. "Kin to Lorne Davis?"

Tanner nodded impassively. "Sheriff."

Conrad's mouth tried for sympathetic and settled for harried. "Look, I'm sorry for your loss. But what we have here is a natural death. Nothing more. Nothing less."

"What about the gold?"

Shaye made a startled sound. She hadn't expected Tanner to mention anything about gold.

August watched the sheriff like a man interested in what he would say next.

"What gold?" Conrad asked before turning to the deputies and asking the same question, only louder because it was much more important right now. "WHAT GOLD?"

"I—I—I—" stuttered Feldt.

"Never heard of it," August said calmly.

"No damn good, either one of you!" He exhaled a curse and turned to Tanner. "What gold?"

Since the sheriff had dropped his voice, Tanner answered. "At least one roll of pre-Depression gold twenties."

"What?" Conrad's voice was rising again.

"He kept them in a family hiding place in the house. A place you could only find with a wrecking crew. The house wasn't wrecked. Wasn't even messy, so nobody conducted a search before or after Lorne died."

"Son," Conrad said. "You've been away too long to know how hard times have been. Lorne probably spent any gold he had long ago. Doesn't change the fact that he died a natural death at eighty-plus years."

"He wasn't wearing a jacket or—" Shaye began.

"Hello, Ms. Townsend," the sheriff interrupted. "Looks like the Conservancy has bagged another ranch. Which tells me Lorne was flat out of cash or he'd never have given the land to you." He glanced at Tanner. "You got a problem with your uncle's death, take it up with the Conservancy. The sheriff's office has real crimes to fight."

August's creosote-dry voice filled the silence growing between Tanner and the sheriff. "The hyoid bone was intact, no strangulation. Toxicology came back clean, no poison. No gunshot wounds, cut marks, or major trauma. His body was good until the coyotes and vultures got to him."

Without looking away from Tanner, the sheriff nodded curtly. "There you have it," he said. "Your uncle died on his own ranch with his boots on. There are worse ways to go."

"Yeah, and I've seen most of them," Tanner said. "I've also learned that face value often isn't worth a handful of cold spit." He turned and walked toward the front door.

Shaye watched August watching Tanner. When the deputy's attention switched to her, she turned and followed Tanner out.

"Thanks for your time," she called over her shoulder.

"Don't mention it," August said.

She was certain that underneath his deadpan exterior the deputy was laughing his ass off.

"It could have been worse," she said as they approached Tanner's car.

He gave her a look of disbelief and opened the passenger-side door. As she sat down, he asked, "How?"

"The sheriff could have arrested you for contempt. Didn't your mother tell you that a smile goes farther than a snarl?"

"Not in a place where people want to ignore you. And Sheriff Conrad wouldn't know a snarl if he saw the teeth." Tanner slid in behind the wheel and slammed the door. "He's a leaky balloon trying to float a badge. August is probably a good cop when he's allowed, but the sheriff keeps a real short leash on everything except himself."

"August knows more than he's saying," she said.

"He figured out real quick that I'm a cop."

"That's a no-brainer. One look at you out of a semi-tux and anyone would know you're not a citizen."

"I think I'm insulted."

"Tanner, surely you look in the mirror when you shave."

"Every day. So what?"

"You don't look like the guy next door," she said.

"I'll leave that to August."

"News flash. August is a hard case."

"August wouldn't mind patting you down real good," Turner said, starting the car.

She turned her head so fast her hair swung out. "What?"

"Trust me. A guy knows." He glanced at her and smiled. "You should see the look on your face."

Shaye told herself she wouldn't blush. For once, she didn't.

"I get August," Tanner said as he backed out of the parking spot and turned into traffic. "What I don't get is the sheriff. You mind checking at the vet's before I buy you lunch?"

"I'd like to see how Dingo is, too. Is that who you're going to piss off next? The vet?"

"I'm expecting a call," Tanner said. "If it doesn't come, we'll start talking to the men who played cards with Lorne. Do you know who the regulars are?"

"Berne Mason would. He manages the Silver Lode Lodge, where they played on Tuesday nights."

"Do you know Mason well enough to get in to see him on short notice?"

"The Conservancy makes it a point to use the lodge for meetings with ranchers. It's a favorite with the locals. I often handle the arrangements."

"Good," Tanner said. "Call him and find out if you can get in to see him early this afternoon. With a guest."

"Why?"

"To talk about Lorne and poker buddies. As a favor, if nothing else will work. You're the Conservancy and the Conservancy brings money into the lodge. And you're a sexy woman."

She made an inelegant sound and reached into her purse. "I'll see what I can do."

While she talked to various lodge employees, the town sputtered out along the road, becoming boarded-up tourist stores, Mexican restaurants, fields of Black Angus, and ranches all the way up to the mountains on both sides of the valley. Horses posed as if at shows, muscles defined beneath tight skins that gleamed in the pouring light. Hawks and falcons patrolled the grasslands.

"We're on," she said. "Two o'clock."

"Good work. Thanks."

Damn it, Brothers. Call me. I could chase Lorne's poker pals all over Nevada and not be any closer to the truth.

It's called a homicide investigation, Tanner reminded his impatient half. *Suck it up. Impatience is a rookie mistake.*

"If it helps," Shaye said after a few miles, "the sheriff sold Mercedes-Benzes until just a few years ago. I guess he got the political itch before that. I heard he ran for supervisor, right around the time that Harold Hill was vacating the spot."

"Wonder how much the post cost him?"

"Hill?"

"Yeah."

"We go cheap in Refuge," she said coolly. "But we like the appearance of law and order. You know, breaking up rustling rings and making sure the hangings go on time."

Tanner gave her a sideways glance. "Not what I meant. Whatever the sheriff did in his past life, he doesn't take the stress of this one real well."

"How could he? The population of the county is small. The sheriff knows every missing person or robbery or domestic violence or car wreck or whatever else that comes across his desk. He can't drive the street without seeing problems he should fix."

"I hear if you can't take the heat you should stay out of the kitchen," Tanner said. "Yet the sheriff walked in today with the oven on high and frying pans blazing. Something is bugging him. And something is riding August. Notice how he took Conrad's side the second he walked in the room?"

"And let me guess—you argue with your bosses all the time?"

"Hey, I give them Fridays and holidays off."

Smiling, she shook her head. "I don't think that August is any happier with how things are going than you are. Only he doesn't have the luxury of coming right out and saying it to the sheriff's face."

Tanner didn't argue. He'd told the truth to power and now he was opening drawers in the morgue. He didn't blame August for being politic.

He just didn't like the way the deputy had looked at Shaye.

Since when have you been territorial about a woman? You weren't mad at your wife or her yoga instructor—you were mad at yourself for being stupid.

No answer came to Tanner but the memory of first hearing Shaye's voice and thinking of tangled sheets and sex.

THIRTEEN

THE VET HAD silver hair and beard, and blue eyes behind wire reading glasses that he peered over half the time. Tanner was surprised to find the vet's face unlined.

Dr. Warren smiled like he could read the other man's mind. "I went gray when I was thirty," he said. "Good for business. Been getting early-bird specials since I was forty."

Smiling, Tanner shook the vet's hand. "Sorry to put you to the trouble of a private consult."

"I was one of the few people in the valley who actually liked Lorne," the vet said. "Cantankerous old coot, but he took care of his animals and paid his bills. Left a gold coin with me to pay for Dingo, because he didn't have any other cash."

Shaye went still.

"Did he do that often?" Tanner asked easily.

"A couple times," the other man said. "I'd hold the coin until he got the cash. He always paid."

"What kind of coin?"

The vet shrugged. "Looked like the same one every damn time. I'm not a coin collector. It's in my safe. You can have it when Dingo is released or you can use it to pay for the dog and I'll give you the change."

Tanner nodded. He could insist on seeing the coin, but there was no reason to irritate the vet. "When did Lorne bring Dingo in?"

"Early Wednesday morning, and I do mean early. Rousted me out of bed. Good thing, too. The dog nearly died."

"How's Dingo now?" Shaye asked.

"As good as can be expected. Like I said, Lorne didn't ignore his animals. He caught on real quick that Dingo was deadly sick. But the dog still suffered some seizures and hyperthermia. That's elevated body temperature, really high. Nearly lost him." His eyes glanced down at the rest of the chart. "He's stable now, still on fluids and light sedation to keep him comfortable. He should pull through, but it will be a long time before he eats steak again."

"Steak?" Tanner asked.

"Yeah. Found some red meat in Dingo's gut that he hadn't puked out yet. Too weak. Lorne said he didn't remember having any steak lately, and Dingo wasn't a counter thief anyway."

"My uncle wasn't the kind of man who fed steak to his dogs."

The vet nodded. "Lorne was cussing fit to scorch paint, trying to figure out what kind of damn fool son of a bitch, pardon my language, would leave varmint bait where his dog could get it."

"Was it carrion?" Shaye asked.

"No. Meat was fresh beneath the stomach acids."

"Maybe Dingo went onto a neighboring property," she said.

And maybe someone wanted Dingo out of the way, Tanner thought. But he kept it to himself.

"Could be, but Dingo didn't wander around roads or other ranches,"

Warren said. "Dogs that do end up as bobcat or coyote bait, or get run over. I patch those dogs up or put them down too often. And I yell at the stupid owners, for all the good it does. Dingo was seven. Only time I ever saw him was for his shots. Except for the time when he took on a porcupine when he was young and stupid."

"Did the toxicity levels look like an accidental dose?" Tanner asked.

Dr. Warren looked at him curiously. "And here I was explaining hyperthermia to you. What line of work are you in?"

"Public safety."

"Dingo weighs about twenty-two kilos, just shy of fifty pounds. He ingested maybe twelve or thirteen milligrams of the active ingredient. I've seen dogs die with less and I've seen dogs take a lot more and still be ticking."

Tanner looked interested.

Dr. Warren took the hint and kept talking. "From the severity of the symptoms, I'd say that Dingo got a pretty good dose. Maybe it was some idiot trying to get rid of coyotes and getting ranch dogs instead. Whatever, Dingo paid the price."

Tanner nodded. "Accident?"

"He's the only dog anyone has brought in during the last few weeks with poisoning, but not everyone brings a sick animal to the vet. And sometimes people put out poison without thinking about what happens to the squirrels or varmints after they die, or thinking that something you like having around might eat the poisoned carcass. People . . ." Dr. Warren shrugged. "Never could figure them out. That's why I like animals. They can't lie to me."

Shaye still looked worried. "But Dingo's going to be okay, isn't he?"

Dr. Warren put a hand on her shoulder. "You can come back and see him if you want, but he'll be sleeping. We're keeping him that way so he won't pull out the IV line."

"Thanks, I'd like to see him."

"Been a rough week for you, hasn't it?"

She smiled wanly. "Yes."

Tanner and Shaye followed the vet to another area of the office. Quietly they looked inside the animal hospital's version of a critical care unit. Dingo lay on the towel-lined floor of one of the kennels. An IV line led into the cage. He was breathing shallowly, legs twitching like he was chasing dream rabbits.

"Huh," Tanner said softly. "Looks like that mutt out of the *Mad Max* movies, only tawny instead of black."

"That was a Queensland Heeler in the movies," Warren said. "Dingo is, ah, well, Dingo. Probably Aussie and Queensland mix mostly, with some bigger dog in his ancestry. I hear Lorne found him hiding under the porch some years back."

"He looks skinny," Shaye said, her voice worried.

"We had to intubate him and hit him with a light dose of ammonium chloride to clear the last of the poison. That's hard on a system."

"Beats dying," Tanner said.

"So we assume. We'll give Dingo a lot of rest and keep him under observation here for a couple days. Then . . ." The vet shrugged and looked at Tanner. "You're paying the bills. You tell me what you want to do."

He blew out a breath. "My apartment has a no-pet rule."

"My condo doesn't," Shaye said instantly.

Dr. Warren looked at her. "Dingo isn't a condo dog, but maybe he can learn."

"Surely some rancher needs a good dog," Tanner said.

"I'll check around, but I wouldn't count on it."

"I'll take him," she said. "I couldn't leave him to be put down because his owner died. It's not the dog's fault."

"Be sure to leave your contact information up front with Betty, then, Ms. Townsend. We'll be in touch."

Tanner held his tongue until they were alone in the car again. "I doubt if Dingo will take to being shut up."

"He can come to work with me most of the time. I'm out on ranches more than I'm in meetings." Her voice was like the set of her mouth. Stubborn.

"Dr. Warren knows a lot of ranchers."

"So do I. None of them are looking for dogs."

"If Dingo is on his feet before I go back to L.A., I'll take him back to the ranch he knows. We don't have to decide things right now."

Before I go back to L.A.

Shaye knew Tanner was going to leave, but hearing it said so casually put her on edge. "You do what you have to do. I'll do the same."

He opened his mouth, then closed it. She was right, so why did he feel like arguing?

"I'm doing the best I can," he said after a few minutes.

"So am I."

Neither of them said much over sandwiches at a place in South Tahoe. After lunch, Shaye settled back in the car and tried not to see Lorne every time she closed her eyes.

And not to think about Tanner leaving.

I'm crazy, she said to herself. *The dog, Tanner . . . Crazy. At least the dog needs a home.*

The part that made her doubt her sanity was her growing belief that Tanner did, too.

FOURTEEN

S HAYE DIDN'T SHAKE off her edginess until Tanner turned onto
the curving driveway up to Silver Lode Lodge. Instead of watching
his hard-cut profile and gentle hands, she forced herself to look at the
expanse of irrigated green grass and blue spruce.

"People were taking bets on whether the spruce or the grass would
die first," she said, breaking the long silence. "They can live here, but
they belong at different elevations."

"Who won?" Tanner asked. It beat thinking about Lorne's death
and Shaye's tender smile. Or thinking about Dingo alone at the vet's,
and of himself alone in L.A.

"Nobody. The trees don't grow much and don't quite die. The grass
has been redone piecemeal after every winter. Lot of arguments over
whether that constitutes 'death,' but no winners."

The lodge itself was old, made of logs and local rocks, a three-
dimensional definition of rustic. There was nothing backcountry about

the service, though. A valet appeared instantly and took Tanner's wheezing car without a single disparaging look.

"I don't remember it like this," he said as the valet drove the car away and parked it out of sight.

"What's different?" she asked as they walked up to the lodge entrance.

"Everything from grass to trees to whole logs gleaming in the sun."

"Nothing has changed in the time I've been here," she said, "except chunks of grass."

"It was well established back when I remember it." His mouth curled up at one corner. "Only then it was called the Lucky Uncle. I still remember the look on my dad's face when I asked him what went on in there."

"Your dad didn't like gambling?"

"He didn't care one way or the other. It was the women in the back rooms that made him squirm to explain."

Tanner opened the wide lodge door.

Shaye looked at him, surprised and a little horrified. "This was a . . ."

A pair of kids about ten years old thundered past them.

"Brothel," Tanner finished when the kids lined up across the lobby in front of an elevator. "Wonder if the folks who stay here now complain that their rooms are a touch on the small side."

"I hope it was remodeled," she said, looking at the place from a different angle now. "Thoroughly."

"I imagine it was. Most cribs aren't any bigger than they have to be to get the job done."

"I'll take your word for it."

He looked amused. "Homicide detectives have a broad education. On the job, only, for me. Forget what you see in movies—real-life prostitutes are about as sexy as a public toilet."

"New topic, please."

He laughed and put his arm around her, pulling her against him. "You're good to be with."

When she met the intense blue of his eyes, she let the last of her irritation slide away. He would leave and she would stay. Until then, she would enjoy.

"But I'm not illegal," she said.

"Too bad. You'd look great in handcuffs . . . and nothing else."

She felt the flush climbing her cheeks and punched him lightly. "Stop."

"It's the truth, the whole truth, and nothing but the truth, so help me God."

She gave up and laughed. And tried not to wonder how he would look in her bed. Handcuffs optional.

Tanner smiled at her like he knew what she was thinking.

Shaye said the first thing that came to her mind. "Wonder where they got the marble."

He glanced around at the decor without real interest. There was a lot of light, sandy-colored wood and fine pink travertine shot through with veins of white and carmine.

"Reminds me of blood spatter," he said without thinking.

"Lovely. You see a lot of interior decor in your line of work?" she asked.

"Crime cuts across all classes."

"Cheery thought."

He shrugged. "Fact of life."

The fresh flower arrangements dotted around the room gave a softer edge to the efficiency of the layout. The only way a person could tell that this was Nevada rather than California was the come-hither gleam of slot machines set off in an alcove. A man stood unobtrusively nearby, making sure that kids didn't sneak in and lose their allowance.

The concierge could have been a showgirl with a really fine boob job. She watched with a professional smile and rather predatory eyes as Tanner walked up.

"May I help you?" she asked, looking only at him.

"We're here to see Mr. Mason," Shaye said.

"Who should I say is asking for him?" the concierge asked, watching Tanner like he was the Second Coming.

Shaye almost rolled her eyes. "Shaye Townsend and guest," she said coolly.

And no, you can't have his telephone number. While he's here, he's mine.

The thought startled her. She had never felt this territorial about a man before, including the one she had married.

The concierge smoothed her long, dark hair away from her perfect face and scanned the computer. "You're early, but I'll tell him. He's in a meeting. Please wait here."

"No problem." Shaye's voice was of the scorpion-killing variety.

The concierge turned, opened a door behind her that led to a wing of offices, and walked quickly. Her stilettos clicked like cat claws across the hardwood floor.

"Are you still angry about the dog?" Tanner asked, eyeing Shaye warily.

"The showgirl can keep her hungry eyes to herself."

He looked at her. "That's what put razor blades in your tone?"

"I'm also peeved about wanting a man who has one foot out the door. I'll get over it."

His eyes widened. Then he caught her face between his hands. "You're honest."

"Rare in your line of work?" Shaye shot back.

"Rare anywhere, anytime." He touched her lower lip with his thumb. "I'll be as honest as you are. When Lorne and my dad had their shouting match and my family left town, Refuge died for me. Lorne gave me a backhanded kind of 'forgiveness' when he came to my dad's funeral and told me not to be as stupid as my dad had been. Let's just say I didn't fall into his arms with joy."

"So now you hate Lorne and everything about Refuge?"

"No. I made my life somewhere else, that's all. Yesterday I found out that Lorne hadn't written me off entirely. Then all the questions about his death started digging at me."

"And when you answer all your questions here, you'll go back to your life there. I get it. Until then, let the good times roll, right?"

Before Tanner could decide how to answer that and the tangle his life had become—here and in L.A.—the concierge returned, stiletto heels announcing her presence.

Just as well, he thought. *I'm no damn good with people. Corpses? I'm the best thing that ever happened to them. Living, breathing, warm women? Not so much.*

A man was following the concierge.

"This time," Shaye said to Tanner in a low voice, "try not to be a quarrelsome son of a bitch."

"I'll take my cue from him, just like I did from the deputies," he said in an equally soft tone. Hard, too.

"Am I interrupting?" Mason asked, dismissing the concierge with a motion.

"Not at all," Shaye said. "Thank you for making time for us."

"It's good to see you, always," Mason said. "Especially when it isn't strictly Conservancy business. You're a breath of fresh air."

Smiling politely, Shaye stepped away before he could kiss her cheek. She had never been into the social kissing game. Or any other kind of casual kissing.

"Berne Mason, Tanner Davis, Lorne's nephew," she said.

"I thought you were going to say grandson," Mason said.

"You wouldn't be the first," Tanner answered, holding out his hand.

Without seeming to, Tanner cataloged details about the other man. Mason's salt-and-pepper hair was swept back from a tanned face. He didn't have the tan of a workingman, the kind with pale creases from squinting at the sun and a white stripe across the forehead from wearing a hat in the sun. It wasn't a tennis tan, or a skiing tan. It looked like Mason spent most of his time indoors with side trips to a tanning oven for the color. His clothes were tailor-made. He looked fit and didn't walk like a man whose feet hurt.

The watch on his wrist would have cost Tanner a year's rent.

Bet he started out as a pit boss, Tanner thought. *He has eyes like a cop—and some crook thrown in to keep things lively.*

"Terrible tragedy," Mason said. "We'll miss Lorne around the poker table, though I'm sure there are some players who will be relieved." He leaned in confidentially. "Lorne could read about half of them like a road map. He was one of the few men I've played poker with that didn't have any 'tells.' Never knew what he had until he laid down his cards."

"You'd know more about that than I would," Tanner said. "I haven't seen him since I was a kid. That's why Shaye brought me here. Said you knew him as well as anybody. I feel like I missed a lot of his life."

"Lorne was one of a kind. Come on back to my office. I'm expecting some Norwegian investors soon. Very punctual people, so I don't want to keep them waiting. But until then, I'm all yours."

"I appreciate it," Tanner said. "Very kind of you."

As Mason led the way across the lobby, Tanner took Shaye's elbow like a good city gentleman.

"Would the aliens who took the old Tanner please keep him?" she muttered.

He gave her a smile that was all teeth.

They walked past an early crowd of hotel guests coming in from the pool, heading up to their rooms to dress for dinner, dancing, and some low-key, laid-back gambling.

Tanner walked with a pleasant smile and eyes that never stopped looking around. Card rooms opened up on either side of a wide aisle. The main casino was nearby, judging from the hustle and hum that came through a wide archway. In the casino, there would be hidden catwalks and cameras patrolling for cheats. The card rooms were low-ceilinged, quiet, under camera surveillance, and mostly empty. A few players threw in their cards or raked in modest piles of chips.

"So Lorne was a regular here?" Tanner asked.

"Yes," Mason said. "Lucky room number seven is where we meet. The group he played cards with is taking the next session off in his honor."

"Sounds like you take poker seriously," Tanner said. "If I could have their names, I'd like to talk to them, thank them personally."

"I'll have my concierge send them to Shaye's e-mail, if that will be all right?"

She nodded. "Thank you. The Conservancy is doing everything we can to help Lorne's nephew enjoy Refuge."

"Do you play poker?" Mason asked Tanner.

"Not seriously."

Mason laughed. "Weather, cows, land, and cards. We take them all serious around here."

"High stakes?" Tanner asked.

"No, but bragging rights on winning are real important." He winked at Shaye. "Drives the wives crazy."

She smiled politely.

"No bad feelings among losers?" Tanner asked, watching Mason while not seeming to.

"It wasn't that kind of poker," Mason said. "Lorne and the boys come here to shoot the bull and have a few drinks. Man-cave time, my wife used to call it. Guess I spent too much time that way. She left me years ago."

"Good reason to stay single," Shaye said neutrally. "Never can tell who will turn into a poker nut."

"Must have been an unusual group of men, never to lose their temper," Tanner said.

"If someone got too tight in the collar, I'd make sure they took a break from cards for a week or two, tell them to spend time with their wives or mistresses or kids. Whatever. Didn't have to do that more than a few times."

"Lorne ever step over the friendly line?" Tanner asked.

"Not once. He could be an abrupt, abrasive man, but it wasn't personal. Just his way. The men he played cards with were used to it. A lot of them were as hard-shouldered as he was."

Mason opened his office door, looked in, and motioned Shaye and Tanner to go first. The room was small for the desk parked in its middle, but not crowded. The desktop was a cross section from a single, huge pine log. The concentric growth rings looked like amber water rippling out to the still-intact bark.

"How did you get this inside?" Shaye said with wonder.

"That's right, you've never seen my office before," Mason said. "When we did the renovations, I basically had the room built around my desk."

"And changed the name of the lodge," Tanner added.

"Oh, you know the history of this place?"

"Despite my mother's best efforts, Lorne told me about the 'cathouse up the hill' before I was ten."

Mason laughed. "That's Lorne. He never appreciated much beyond the basics. Too bad. There are many profitable uses for land. Cows often aren't one of them, but men keep raising them anyway. Good thing, too. Steak is a beautiful thing."

"Sure is. I remember Lorne always used to eat a big, rare slab of it on Saturday, chicken on Sunday. Tuesday was poker, which meant he ate out."

"He never changed that routine, so far as I know."

"Anything else change in Lorne's life? How did he seem at the last game?" Tanner asked.

Mason frowned at his desktop. "I got in late, but Lorne was later. We had several tables of players that night, with some left over to hold down the bar. Don't think he took cards, though. Went straight to the bar and started jawing at his lawyer."

"Was that usual?" Shaye asked.

"No. Stan Millerton only plays now and again. I assumed that Lorne had been drinking," Mason said with a shrug. "It happens."

"Did Lorne drink a lot?" Tanner asked.

"A fair amount, especially if his knee was hurting or he was pissed off about something, which usually amounted to the same thing."

"So he was angry," Tanner said.

Mason waved them into chairs near his desk. "Hard to tell with Lorne. Even when he wasn't playing cards, he kept things close to the vest. Could have been as simple as he was late and the tables were full and he didn't like waiting, so he bent his attorney's ear instead."

"You hear what Lorne was saying?" Tanner asked casually.

"I wasn't part of the conversation," Mason said. His phone buzzed. "Excuse me." He listened, tapped a clean fingernail on the wooden desktop, and hung up. "The Norwegians are early. Sorry, but I really must cut this short. Can you find your way out or should I call the concierge?"

"We're good," Tanner said, coming to his feet. "Don't want to keep people from their business. Thank you for seeing us."

"Call if I can help you," Mason invited, shaking hands. "Lorne was a good man. Shaye, always a pleasure to see you. You should drop in more often."

"Thanks for talking to us," she said. "I know how busy you are."

"For you, anytime."

With that, Mason hurried from the room, straightening his coat and tie as he went.

Shaye looked at Tanner in silent question.

He shrugged. Nothing about Mason had tickled his cop meter. At least, nothing to do with Lorne's death. Mason wasn't nearly as civilized as he looked. But you could say that about a lot of men.

Tanner and Shaye headed for the exit. They had just dodged another herd of kids in the lobby when his cell phone pinged, indicating a text had arrived. He took out the phone, saw it was from Brothers, and felt a rush of adrenaline.

FIFTEEN

TANNER SHUT THE car door behind Shaye and started reading the text while he walked around the vehicle and slid in behind the wheel. Several names and addresses, ranging from Tahoe to Reno and Carson City.

The phone vibrated before he could call Brothers and ask *What the hell?*

"Hey, D. What do you have?" Tanner said into the phone.

"Reputable coin dealers took me about three seconds," Brothers said. "Best they could do was along the lines of if I find any coins like that, give them a call. The shady ones took a lot longer, because there's a lot more of them. They don't talk to cops unless you have a twist on them, so I've been trolling the sites where dealers talk to dealers and don't know I'm a cop."

Tanner waited, trying not to remember what Shaye had said about *wanting a man who has one foot out the door.* He should be concentrating on Lorne's death, not a sexy woman.

Shaye wasn't an easy-answer kind of woman.

And the sweet curves of her body were making him hard.

"I hit on some recent dealer-to-dealer sales or trades of Saint-Gaudens," Brothers continued.

"Is that unusual? To have hits like that on something specific?"

"I was curious about that myself. That's another reason I took so long. I dug down for months of cached site histories. Only found a few requests for that particular coin, not any trades or sales."

"Good work, D."

"Bet your ass. Best part? The sales or trades they did talk about were all within fifty miles of Carson City. And all since last Wednesday."

"Bingo," Tanner said softly, coldly.

Shaye looked at him. She had seen the same predatory focus in Dingo when he caught the scent of a rabbit.

"Plug the addresses I gave you into the nav computer," Brothers said.

"On it. Did you give them to me in any special order?"

"First two are actual I-have-the-coin hits. Rest are just dropping hints and/or trolling for price info. And don't talk about badges unless you have to," Brothers added. "You're a long way from L.A."

"D, I graduated higher in my academy class than you did," Tanner said.

"Then why do you keep calling me?" Brothers retorted.

"You're better at computers."

"So I'm told."

"I owe you," Tanner said.

"Not in this lifetime. Stay out of trouble, T-Bone."

"Hey, no worries. I have it on good authority that the aliens took me and left a polite pussy in my place."

Brothers was still laughing when he hung up.

"Are we talking to the sheriff again?" Shaye asked.

"I thought we'd take in some of the local Tahoe color." As he spoke, he began feeding numbers into the nav computer with the speed of someone who had done it a lot.

"Shopping? Spas? Casinos? Boating? Hiking?" she asked.

"Pawnshops."

She blinked. "Pawnshops. Really?"

"Really." He gave her a wolfish grin. "Those aliens you mentioned taught me how to show a girl a good time. No butt probes required."

"That's a relief." Then, "You have a lead on Lorne's coins, don't you?"

"That's what we're going to check out. You're my sweetie, and you have your heart set on a Saint-Gaudens for your engagement ring."

"I do?" she asked, startled.

"It's a classy coin and you're a classy sweetie," he said blandly. He wondered if he should be insulted that the idea of being engaged to him made her do a double take.

"So we find the coins and go back to the sheriff?" she asked.

No engagement ring required.

"Conrad has made up his mind that everything is kosher in Refuge. Who am I to harsh his mellow?"

"But—"

"Fasten your seat belt," Tanner said, starting the car. "Wouldn't want my classy sweetie to hurt her pert little nose on the nasty hard windshield."

"I've changed my mind about the aliens. I want the other Tanner back."

He gave her a crooked smile. "No problem. They're getting tired of him, too."

The closest place on Tanner's hit list was a rented corner in a pawnshop masquerading as a secondhand store on the California side of Lake Tahoe.

"Looks like a locals-only joint," he said as he parked the car in front.

"Why do you say that?" Shaye asked.

"The window displays. This is where full-time residents go who get hard up and hope to cash out their fad collections—Pokémon cards or Justin Bieber records and signed sweatbands—and catch up on their rent or car payments. Or a woman whose boyfriend screwed around hocks the engagement ring and buys some new outfits. Small-time community stuff. The owner will have receipts for most of it and a lame explanation or a faulty memory for the rest."

The shop was small, no cleaner than it had to be, and smelled of the cigarettes someone had smoked in the back office. The squeaking front door brought out a woman who was just like the shop. She watched while they worked their way to the corner where odds and ends of mostly costume jewelry were for sale. A locked case held the items with supposedly real gold set with possibly real stones. Some coin and arrowhead collections were in the same case.

"CanIhelpya," she said.

"Hope so," he said, glancing up from the coins with a smile. "My sweetie wants a gold coin. What do you have?"

"You're looking at it."

"Nothing in the safe?" he asked easily. "She really wants it."

"Not just any old coin, babe," Shaye said, smiling like a sweetie. "A 1932 Saint-Gaudens. My daddy taught me to be real particular. Family tradition, you know."

Tanner reached into his pocket and came out with a twenty. "If you'd look for that coin in your safe," he said to the woman, "I'll pay you for your time. If you find the coin, we can talk about price."

The woman held the twenty up to the overhead light before she pocketed the bill and vanished into the back office again. She returned with a gold coin in a transparent plastic box.

Tanner took the box. A tag stuck on the bottom had a recent date in black ink.

"Gimme," Shaye said. She turned the box until it caught the light well enough that she read both sides. "That's a 1932, all right. Looks good."

The woman took back the box and named a price that made Tanner's eyebrows rise.

"Hell, sweetie," he said to Shaye, "I'd be better off buying a diamond." He turned to the woman. "Is this a consignment item?"

"Nope. Bought it outright."

"Did the woman who brought it in leave her name?" he asked.

"Man."

"Did the man leave his name?" Tanner asked patiently.

"Nope. Took my cash, cussed me for not paying more, and left."

"Huh. Usually old men don't cuss at women."

"Who said he was old?"

"What did he look like?" Tanner asked.

"A useless steak-head like my second ex. That was thirty-six years ago. You gonna buy that coin?"

Tanner knew the end of question-and-answer time had arrived. He thought about showing his badge—the shop was on the California side of the line—but decided he would wait until she was the best lead he had. Whoever had stolen the coins hadn't done much business here. It was probably the first place the thief came across.

Or the one he lived closest to.

"I have to go think about it," Tanner said.

And to find a better twist than sweetie's engagement ring. Or D could put in a word to the local business-license people. The old lady's memory might improve if her license was threatened.

"You sure he didn't leave a name?" Shaye asked the woman. "Maybe he wants to get engaged."

The woman laughed, coughed, and shook her head. "Near as I can remember, he swore he was John Smith."

Tanner swore, period.

"Hey, I'm Jane Doe," Shaye said. "Match made in heaven, right?"

The woman looked at Tanner. "Got yourself a live one. Hope you can keep it up."

Shaye snickered.

Tanner took his sweetie's arm and headed out the door. Maybe the next place would be run by someone with a better memory, or more vulnerability to a badge.

"Are we any closer to circumstantial?" Shaye asked as he started up the car.

"Not nearly enough to budge the sheriff," he said. "Lorne didn't sell the coin to her, but the timing is right. Someone marked the day of the week it was received on the box. Ink was new and tag was clean, so it probably was recently applied."

"Nothing else in the place was fresh."

"Better than a lot I've seen."

"Oh, I'm so looking forward to the next pawnshop," she said.

"Sweetie would be more enthusiastic."

"Sweetie has the brains of a baked potato."

Tanner's grin was a flash of white against the beard shadow that was already showing. "You did real well back there."

"The joys of being raised by a society maven. I can act with the best of them."

"Good thing," he said. "In L.A. I could threaten to jerk her license if her memory didn't improve real quick. Maybe I could even pull a name and address or license plate off the purchase slip."

"She didn't look like she was long on paperwork."

He didn't disagree. He lowered his window, grateful for the fresh air after the close, dusty shop. Though Lake Tahoe was more than a quarter mile away, it smelled like they were parked right on it. Breathing deeply, he pressed a button on the navigation system and punched in the second address.

"Aces Up," Shaye read on the screen. "That's in Carson City. It's the first casino owned by Wilson Desmond. You met him at the party-turned-memorial—he's one of the chosen bald. Everyone calls him Ace."

"Chosen bald?"

"Shaves his head rather than give in to male-pattern baldness or a ridiculous comb-over," she explained. "Quite a few city men in their early forties take that route."

Tanner smiled slightly. "Tahoe Sky wasn't a locals kind of place. Too high end."

"Aces Up attracts high-end local, with the dedicated gamblers from Reno and Tahoe coming down for a change of scene," Shaye said. "Ace told Kimberli the place is kind of a dress rehearsal for his dream casino. He wants to turn Carson Valley into a gambling and resort destination."

"So Ace and your boss are close?"

Shaye shrugged. "She's a fund-raiser. He's a man with funds. Besides, Kimberli already has a boy toy."

Tanner remembered the *GQ*-handsome Peter and asked, "How many casinos does Ace have?"

She shrugged. "Not enough. He and his backers own three and are looking to build one as big as the biggest in Reno and as fancy as any Las Vegas palace."

"Maybe whoever stole the coins likes to gamble locally, and Ace ended up with the pot," Tanner said. "Whatever, let's have a chat with Ace's pawnshop manager. You know Ace, right?"

"Not as well as Kimberli wants me to."

"Sex as a sales tool?" Tanner asked, trying not to snarl.

"Not quite that bad."

I hope.

Tanner started the car. It made some really unhappy sounds, spewed blue smoke, and died. He muttered under his breath and tried again. The car had a lot of miles on it—hard city time for the most part—but he'd hoped it would hang on for at least another six months.

Not looking good, he thought.

The starter ground, the car farted mightily, and the engine caught. It kept running, ragged but game.

"Some machines don't like altitude," Shaye said. "Like you don't like small towns."

Tanner didn't know why the truth irritated him, but it did. "The real problem is LAPD cut back on maintenance in ways you can't make up for later."

"What do you mean?"

"If something breaks, there's always emergency money to fix it, but upkeep? Not so much. Same with the roads, sewers, water pipes, and everything else the city controls. Bad maintenance wears things out faster."

"But you bought the car anyway."

"The price was right."

"That's what Ace said about the casino in Carson," Shaye said. "Word is, he bought it for a tenth of a cent on the dollar—or won it in an all-night poker game."

"Why don't you make an appointment with him and he can tell me all about it?"

"I won't bother Ace if I can help it. His assistant can do what we need."

"Pawnbrokers don't like to talk to assistants. It will be faster to go straight to Ace."

"These are my connections, not yours," she pointed out.

"Good thing we've got a lot of time."

But he didn't argue the point. He knew that investigations involved turning over a lot of rocks in hope of finding the right worm. Besides, he hadn't enjoyed sharing a ride with anyone since Brothers got promoted to a desk.

Brothers never turned me on.

Shaye worked him like a light switch.

SIXTEEN

TANNER DROVE INTO the Aces Up parking lot and turned off his car's unhappy engine. "Looks more like Monaco than Glitter Gulch," he said of the building. "Fresh paint, artsy sign, no burned-out bulbs or flickering neon, and a clean parking lot."

"Like I said, a dress rehearsal. Locals gamble here, but only the high rollers get upstairs. No shorts or sandals allowed on the upper casino floor. You want to play slots next to people wearing flip-flops, surfer pants, and Hawaiian shirts? You can do that at ground level, but you won't make it past the bouncers guarding the mezzanine entrances."

"No wonder Lorne and his poker pals drove to the Silver Lode."

"The old ranchers might have anniversary dinners at Aces Up— the restaurant is almost painfully classy and has really fine food—but the old ranchers don't really care much for Ace himself."

"He's not their kind of people?" Tanner asked.

"They don't trust manicures and Italian loafers."

"Yeah, I can't imagine Lorne getting all fancied up in a tie and suit just to enjoy a drink and a card game."

"From what Kimberli says, you might get away without a tie upstairs, but only if you've been gambling for more than twelve hours and have lost a bundle already."

He looked at Shaye. She was the least produced, turned-out, or self-conscious woman he'd ever met—and the sexiest. He liked knowing that if he went to bed with her, he wouldn't wake up to raccoon eyes and a face that needed an hour with a makeup artist.

"So Kimberli likes Ace's casino and you don't," he said.

"Nothing personal. Gambling just doesn't light up my blood. And the casinos . . ." She shook her head. "Forget quiet desperation. They're noisy desperation. So I don't spend any more time than I have to in them."

He laughed. "Smart lady."

"Ace is smart, too. Underneath that glossy surface is one very shrewd businessman. The local gambling competition is strictly small town and downscale. He bought Aces Up cheap, renovated, and proved that he could attract a high-end crowd to the valley floor."

"Yeah. From what I've seen, his local competition has to lure people through the doors with soft slots and easy tables, low-dollar single-deck and guaranteed ninety-seven percent payouts. Three percent of the day's take in penny and nickel slots isn't much."

She listened and realized all over again that Tanner was more than a hard body and a compelling face. He had a brain and wasn't afraid of using it.

And he was good company.

"That's why the Conservancy spends a lot of time charming Ace," she said. "He has enough money to keep Kimberli's mustangs in hay for the rest of the century, and land to let them run."

"Yet Ace will make time to talk to you if you ask," Tanner said.

Her expression said she wasn't thrilled. But she was game. "C'mon. Let's get it over with." Then she heard her own words and sighed. "That didn't come out right."

"Ace isn't your kind of guy?"

"About the only thing we have in common is the Conservancy. Makes conversation pretty limited."

Tanner's smile was a flash of hard teeth. "We'll see what we can do to expand his horizons."

"I'm hoping we won't have to go to him at all. If we do, please remember that Ace may make Conservancy donations for his image, but his money spends just like a true believer's. Whether he means to or not, he's done a lot of good."

"Don't worry. I won't bite or piss on the rug."

She just shook her head and bit her lip against a smile.

No sooner did they walk in the front entrance than a thin, nervous young man with startling natural red hair approached them. The suit he wore was ill fitting and his string tie was lopsided and frayed at one end.

"Shaye Townsend?" he asked.

"And guest," Tanner said.

"Oh, uh, yeah. Ace told me to give you any help you needed. I'll take you upstairs."

"Thank you," she said. "I was wondering how we would get past the clothes police."

He almost laughed, then cleared his throat. "I promised the pit boss we wouldn't stop for a game. Follow me."

An employee elevator was waiting for them. Their guide used a key card, then fidgeted for the short ride up. The instant the door opened, he set off at a brisk pace down a hallway that paralleled the second-floor casino, looking neither right nor left. The wall dividing them from the casino was made of a smoky kind of glass that allowed anyone in the hall to watch the action without being seen.

Tanner had seen one-way glass windows in interrogation rooms, but never an entire wall. Well-dressed people were drinking from crystal glasses and pushing chips on the line for bets. Some of the players were still wearing clothes from last night's parties, though no one seemed obviously drunk. The feel of money was everywhere, but there was no cash in sight.

"Hell of a place for a pawnshop," Tanner said quietly to Shaye.

"Vertical integration. You can experience an entire resort getaway—food, drink, shops, exercise room—and never leave your hotel. It doesn't look like it from the outside, but Aces Up covers a city block."

"So if you come up short for a bet, you can hock a watch or a ring or your lady's jewelry without actually leaving the casino."

Shaye nodded.

The red-haired guide used his key card on the door at the end of the hall. It opened onto a mezzanine of shops and restaurants. One of the shops offered jewelry and other portable, expensive items. Though it was richly laid out and discreetly lit, it was difficult to hide the fact that Brilliant Moments was a pawnshop.

Tanner took it all in with the eyes of the cop he was. The front was run like a jewelry store with a big side order of collectibles. People who got lucky in the casino could come to the shop and buy diamonds, guitars, solid gold watches, coins, or the collector's case of *Star Wars* figures that had haunted their dreams as a kid. Unlucky people sold their personal Brilliant Moments for pennies on the dollar.

Vertical integration with a vengeance.

He wondered which back room was used to disappoint losers who found out that the $6,000 watch they had bought retail was worth maybe $600 cash right now in their sweaty hands. When all the shine was rubbed away, gambling was about losing money, not winning it.

"The dude who manages the collectibles section is back here," their guide said. "Name is Fred."

Tanner and Shaye dutifully followed their guide through a locked gate. The two salesclerks up front looked at the redhead before they went back to waiting for the next person, someone who might be a buyer instead of a guest.

Fred was moon-faced, dressed to gamble on the second floor, and didn't glance up when the redheaded admin guy showed his two charges into the room and left, shutting the door behind him. Fred was giving a quick and thorough examination to a teardrop-shaped guitar lying on the counter in front of him. Next to the guitar, a laptop computer waited to research online databases.

Tanner suspected that the computer was backup only. People like Fred knew the difference between retail dollars and pawn dollars without resorting to machines.

"Best I can offer for this Vox is five bills," Fred said. His voice sounded like Chicago, bourbon, and cigar smoke. His attitude was take it or leave it.

The tall, gaunt man with shaggy hair, worn jeans, and moccasins picked up the guitar and walked out a back door without saying a word.

"My turn," Shaye said softly.

Tanner didn't object. Fred wouldn't be any more interested in Tanner's L.A. badge than the guitar player had been in giving away his Vox.

Fred looked at Shaye like a man who was tired of questions. "Why did Ace's boy bring you here?"

"I heard you had some 1932 Saint-Gaudens twenty-dollar gold coins."

"Where did you hear that?"

Tanner moved like a man impatient to be somewhere else, and fully capable of kicking the ass of anyone who got in his way.

Interest flickered in Fred's pale eyes. Then he gave Shaye his full attention. "And are you buying or inquiring?"

"Depends on what you have," she said.

Silently Tanner cheered the society maven who had taught Shaye how to make someone feel like gum on a sidewalk without even curling her lip.

"Unusual pieces," Fred said. "Sure you don't want a coin specialist?"

"We're here, aren't we?" Tanner said to himself. His voice was pitched like he expected privacy, but it was just loud enough for Fred to overhear. "C'mon, sweetie, I told you this would be a waste of time."

"Hush, sugar pie," she said. "I want those coins. Preferably uncirculated. I was told Brilliant Moments had them."

"When I think you can afford them," Fred said indifferently, "you can see any Saint-Gaudens I have. If I had them. Which I didn't say I did."

As Fred spoke, he started cleaning his nails with a letter opener he kept at hand.

"I assure you, I am quite capable of buying whatever you have for sale," she said.

"Then it's too bad I don't have any Saint-Gaudens, isn't it?"

She turned to Tanner. "Your turn."

"We're not buying. We're tracing," he said. "Word is, you have what we're looking for."

"You have any ID?" the man asked without looking up.

Tanner dropped his badge onto the counter.

"Long way from home," Fred said after a glance. "And we're not in California, so I wonder why I'm talking to you without a warrant."

"Because you don't want to piss off your boss," Tanner said. "I don't care how much you paid for the Saint-Gaudens. I just want to know who sold them to you."

"If I have them."

Tanner spun the laptop computer toward himself, clicked up to the menu that would give him the search sites for the last week, and struck gold.

"You're researching Saint-Gaudens for the hell of it? Starting Thursday?" he asked sardonically. "Lame, mook, really lame."

Fred stopped working on his nails for a heartbeat, then continued. "I research a lot of things."

"Uh-huh. Looks like you spent some time on dealers' forums where they brag about how cheap they buy and how dear they sell coins. Your handle is Auric1953. Now, you want to do another lap around this track and make me call Ace?"

Fred sighed like someone who had a junk poker hand that wouldn't float him long enough to get him to the other side of the river. "Yeah, I've got some Saint-Gaudens. And yeah, they're fresh."

"Your turn," Tanner said to Shaye.

She smiled. "Thank you." She looked back to Fred, who had given up cleaning his nails. "How did you hear about the coins?"

"Same way you did. Off the casino floor."

"When? This post on the forum was made on Thursday."

"Couple hours before I hit the forum," Fred said, disgust in his voice. "I just had to shove some of their snotty noses in it."

"And you got five of them for two thousand cash?" Shaye asked. "How much do they usually sell for?"

"Depends on the buyer."

"According to the reaction on the forum," Tanner said, looking away from the computer, "you made one screaming hell of a buy."

"The guys who come here want cash and they want it now. We

make good buys after we make sure the goods aren't on anyone's hot sheet. Ace would fire my ass in a heartbeat if he thought anything different."

Shaye looked at Tanner.

"You have to take a copy of the driver's license, right?" Blue eyes bored into Fred.

"Of course. Like I said, we're legit all the way."

"Then you won't mind showing us the copy and the data from that transaction," Tanner said, gesturing to the cameras he was sure were hidden in the ceiling.

"We delete every forty-eight hours. Storage doesn't come free. And no copy of the driver's license until Mr. Desmond personally tells me different."

Tanner looked at Shaye.

"You're right," she said. "We should have started with Ace."

SEVENTEEN

ACE STRODE INTO Brilliant Moments, his shaved head in shining contrast to the dark silk shirt and wine-purple double-breasted suit he wore. Beneath the sheen of skin on his skull lay the outline of male-pattern baldness.

"Shaye," he said, his smile wide and welcoming. "If you'd told me you were stopping by, especially with an out-of-town guest, I'd have arranged a full tour."

He half embraced her and put out his hand to Tanner at the same time. Ace was thick through the body, but it wasn't fat. He was built like a wrestler. Though he was stronger than a lot of men, he didn't try to prove it with a crushing handshake.

"Ace Desmond," he said easily.

"Tanner Davis, Mr. Desmond. Pleased to meet you."

"Davis—now I remember. You were at the Conservancy gala. You're Lorne's son, grandson?"

"Nephew," Tanner said.

"I truly regret your loss," Ace said. "Lorne was an icon to the valley ranchers. When he died, an era ended. If there's anything I can do for you, please let me know."

"Well, I really hate to bother you with this—Shaye told me how busy you are—but we're trying to track down some coins that might have been stolen from Lorne's house before he died," Tanner said.

Surprise flickered across Ace's face. "I hadn't heard about that. What brings you to Brilliant Moments rather than the sheriff's office?"

Fred shifted his feet behind the counter, looking like he wanted to curl up into his own belly button and disappear. He'd called Shaye's bluff about Ace and found himself holding a losing hand in a game whose stakes were bigger than he'd thought.

"We got reports that some similar coins have shown up recently in a couple of shops around the area, including this one," Shaye said. "There's no point in bothering the sheriff when all we want to do is verify that the coins were sold to Brilliant Moments, and who sold them."

"Of course," Ace said. "If there's a thief in the valley, I don't want him anywhere near my guests." He looked at Fred. "Have you any information about the coins?"

"Yes, sir."

"I commend your discretion, but this is a special case. Please give them what they need. Now."

"Yes, sir."

Ace turned back to Shaye as Fred hurried off. "I'd give you some chips and tell you to enjoy the casino, but Kimberli tells me you don't care for gambling. How about an early dinner on me in the restaurant?" He winked. "I hear good things about the food."

"That's very gracious," she said, "but we're hardly up to the dress code."

Ace waved it off. "That's what private rooms are for."

She quietly salivated at the thought. Her half sandwich at lunch was barely a memory. The food at the casino restaurant was justly famous. Despite her uneasiness at trading on the Conservancy's connections, she looked at Tanner.

He was watching Fred with predatory intensity.

The pawnshop manager hurried toward them holding two enlarged copies of a driver's license. He gave the first to his boss and the second to Tanner.

Tanner's glance swept down the page, taking in information.

A hard-looking guy named Antonio Rua stared back from the driver's license. Dark hair and eyes, five foot ten inches, thirty-five last February. He had a buzz cut, a scarred left eyebrow, and a stony jaw suggesting plenty of testosterone.

"Don't recognize him," Ace said, handing back the paper to Fred.

Neither did Tanner, but he had dealt with a lot of Rua's type. Gifted physically, but not gifted enough, so they ended up finding dumb ways to make money, or got shot, or both. Along the way, there were usually some misdemeanor arrests. Maybe a felony or two.

Tanner folded the paper and tucked it into his pocket. "Thank you for your help and your offer of the best dinner in the valley," he said. "But frankly, Mr. Desmond, I'm not feeling up to doing justice to your chef."

"Call me Ace. And I understand. Mourning and a full stomach don't do well together." He turned to Shaye. "A rain check, then. I insist."

She smiled. "Rain check it is."

"Just so long as you cash it sometime," Ace said as he hugged her gently. He turned to Tanner. "Again, I'm sorry for your loss. It was the valley's loss, too. And if there's a thief selling hot goods on my property, I'll find him and let the sheriff know. I have a lot more eyes than you do," he added, casually indicating the cameras concealed behind smoky domes and in ceiling lights.

Like all gaming establishments, on the premises of Aces Up the only places where you weren't observed were the public restrooms and the hotel rooms themselves. Everything else was photographed and stored.

"Fred, send a copy of that license to Security," Ace said. "If that man shows up again, I want to know." He frowned. "He looked local, like maybe there's some Basque blood in him."

"There are Basques all over the valley," Shaye said. "Ranching is in them as much as it's in any westerner."

Ace nodded and turned to Fred. "Keep those coins in the safe until I tell you otherwise."

Fred didn't look happy about losing all that profit, but he said, "Yes, sir."

With a barely noticeable sideways glance, Ace checked his watch.

Quickly Shaye said, "Thank you again. Please don't let us keep you. I'll bet you were called out of a meeting."

"Remind me never to play poker with you," Ace said wryly. "Mr. Davis—"

"Tanner."

Ace nodded. "A pleasure, Tanner. I'll look forward to seeing you and Shaye in the restaurant very soon."

The redhead passed his boss in the doorway to Brilliant Moments. Tanner wondered if Ace had his admin assistant wired for sound.

Neither Tanner nor Shaye said much on the way back through the casino and out the front door. The sun was well behind the peaks of the Sierras now, and even the warmth from the ground wasn't taking much edge off the chill.

As soon as his butt hit the driver's seat, she said, "Tell me we're going to eat dinner somewhere. My treat. My stomach is gnawing on itself."

He grinned. "Sorry. I just wasn't in the mood to be the owner's special guest."

"Neither was I, really. Doesn't mean I'm not hungry."

"Is Wrigley's still open?"

"Wrigley's?"

"Fried chicken and biscuits. Decent salads. They're soaking tomorrow's chicken in buttermilk today. Rumor was they used it in the biscuits, too, which made them taste extra special. It was about the only place in town we went to on anything like a regular basis."

"Must have closed. I've never heard of the place, and I've eaten about everywhere there is between here and Tahoe."

"Damn." Tanner sighed over the lost biscuits. "Antonio Rua—the guy who sold the coins—lives in Meyers. Or that's what the driver's license said. California license."

"There are some good barbecue joints on the way to Luther Pass, back through Refuge."

"You know your way around, don't you?"

"Why do you sound surprised?" she asked.

"Because I never saw girls like you when I lived here."

"Probably because you left before you were interested in girls."

He shook his head. "I grew up fast," he said. *And then started up a chain of serial disappointments.*

But he didn't want to spoil anyone's appetite by talking about his rock-stupid past.

"Barbecue it is," he said. "Right after I make a call."

She listened while he called Brothers and relayed Antonio Rua's stats and license number, and Brothers promised to drag the name through some files and get back.

The car started—smoky, noisy, rough—but it started.

"Maybe we should take my Bronco," she said.

"It's in Tahoe. We aren't. If you're worried, I can swap this for Lorne's truck."

She muttered something about frying pans and fires.

He ignored her, driving quickly to the place she had recommended.

After they placed their orders, she fidgeted at the table, waiting for food. Tanner leaned back like he was in his favorite chair and had nothing on his mind but his hair.

"How can you be so calm?" Shaye demanded in a low voice.

"Other than you, I haven't found anything to get excited about."

"But we aren't getting any answers."

"Honey, I've barely started asking questions. I'm just feeling around for rattlesnakes in the dark."

She frowned. "I don't like the sound of that."

"Then don't come with me on a rattlesnake hunt. I'll take you back to your condo after we eat, then I'll go talk to Rua."

"That's a lot of time wasted for you. From here, Tahoe is on the far side of Meyers."

He smiled. "I've got a lot of time."

But inside he wasn't smiling. The more he thought about Antonio Rua, the more Tanner didn't want her anywhere near the man.

"What are you thinking?" she asked.

"That I'm going to talk to Rua alone."

"No," she said instantly.

"I thought you were bored."

"Impatient, not bored. I feel like something's gnawing at me. And you spend as much time looking in the side and back mirrors as you do watching the road. What are you expecting?"

"Just hoping to see that our questions pissed somebody off or worried them enough to follow me around. It would make my life easier. I'd lay a trap for the tail, spring it, and find out who set him on me."

Shaye looked startled. "Does that work?"

"With amateurs."

"How about today?"

"Nothing so far."

Before she could say anything else, the server came and dropped off plates of pork ribs. Tanner had intended to eat on the way to Meyers, but Shaye had ordered ribs for herself, all but licking her lips. Since he wanted to lick her lips for her, he tripled the order and joined her.

He really was going to have to do something about those lips of hers. They couldn't be nearly as wild and hot as they looked.

With quick white teeth, Tanner cleaned meat off a savory bone, wishing Shaye was on the menu. On the other hand, watching her fearlessly dive into the food was a sensual revelation. He had discovered that a woman who was afraid to get messy at the table often carried that attitude into bed. He supposed the haughty, touch-me-not routine worked for some men, but he wasn't one of them and never would be.

Hungry in too many ways to count, he concentrated on the only appetite he could appease at the moment. Barbecued ribs and various vegetable sides vanished with impressive speed. Though he had twice the food Shaye did, he finished at the same time.

"Like a starving wolf," she muttered as he put the last clean rib bone on his plate.

"Like a man who is used to being called out during dinner. And breakfast. And lunch."

"Ah." She tilted her head to the side and looked at him. "You missed a spot."

"Of food?" He glanced at his plate. "Where?"

"There's still a little patch on your chin that isn't covered in sauce. Makes me want to dab some on and finish the job."

He looked up and gave her a slow smile. "Dab away."

She gave him a sideways look, then deliberately touched him with a saucy fingertip. With a speed that was almost startling, he took her hand and began thoroughly cleaning each fingertip. She shivered as he kissed her little finger and slowly released her hand.

"All done," he said, watching her with vivid blue eyes.

"I've got another hand." She heard herself and laughed, shaking her head. "You're bad for my impulse control."

"Good," he said huskily. "You're hell on mine. Fair warning, if I clean your other fingers, I won't stop there."

There was an electric silence, then she sighed and tore open a package containing a damp wipe.

"You sure?" Tanner asked.

"I'll lick fingers in public, but that's as far as I'll go. Here." She handed him the damp napkin. "Wipe your face. I don't trust myself to do it for you. And that's a first."

"Not wiping faces?"

"Not trusting myself."

He smiled slowly. "God, you're beautiful."

She gave him a look of disbelief and wiped off her own face with a second damp napkin before she went to work on the hand he hadn't licked. "Since sex isn't on the table—"

"—here," Tanner said. "I've got a table at the ranch that—"

"—let's go find out where Rua got his gold coins," she said firmly.

"I'm taking you home before I talk to the mook with the California driver's license."

"I said I was impatient, not bored."

"Up until now, this has been civilized ride-along stuff, talking to mostly civilized folks who aren't likely to try to crack my skull. All we know about Rua is that he might have killed Lorne and damn sure had five of his coins to sell. I'm going alone."

Her chin came up. "Would anyone give you a warrant—for anything, much less murder—on the basis of what we know right now about the 'mook' and the coins?"

"That's not the point."

"Really? It sure looks like the only point that matters. You can't see circumstantial from where we are and you know it. And FYI, sweetie. Overbearing men are high on my never-again list."

"It's not overbearing to want to keep you safe," Tanner said reasonably. The fact that his fists were curled under the table was his secret.

"Okay," she agreed.

His hands relaxed. "Good. I'll take you home and—"

"I want to keep you safe, too," she cut in, looking reasonable. "So neither of us goes."

"I'm a cop."

"Which means I'll be safe, right?"

He bit off the response he wanted to make. He had known one thing about Shaye from the beginning—treat her with respect or take a hike.

"Let's compromise," he said. "You wait in the car with the doors locked while I chat up Rua."

"If the guy knows anything about what happened to Lorne," she said, "I want to be there to hear it. Damn it, *I found Lorne*. Let me do something to make me feel less like I hurt him and never had a chance to make it right."

Tanner pushed away from the table and shook their tray of dinner debris into a nearby trash can. The bones rattled on the way down. He was still hearing the unhappy clatter when he got back to the table.

It's my own damn fault, he thought. *I wanted to know her better—a lot better—and figured I was pretty much on a wild-goose chase and that would be as good as any excuse to keep her with me.*

Now the chase doesn't look so wild, and the quarry sure as hell isn't goose.

It's time to start thinking like a cop and less like a hound dog.

"Fine," Tanner said to Shaye. "The compromise is that I don't dump you at your condo. In return, you stay in the car and play JAFO."

"Is that like charades?"

"Just Another Observer," he said. "Eyes open, mouth shut, out of the way."

She filled in the missing word and knew he wasn't going to change his mind. "Okay."

For a moment he looked surprised. "I'm not kidding."

"Neither am I."

EIGHTEEN

TANNER'S PHONE VIBRATED as he was paying—over Shaye's protests—for dinner.

"Licking fingers makes it a date," he said, answering the phone. "Not you, D. I'd sooner lick asphalt. What do you have?"

"In your e-mail."

"That was fast. Thanks—" Tanner snapped his phone closed after realizing he was talking to himself.

When he and Shaye were in the car, he picked up his phone and punched buttons until he got his e-mail. As he read, he summarized for Shaye.

"Rua's last known address is Meyers. Lives alone. Minor rap sheet. Several drunk-and-disorderly, twice for assault and battery—bar fights—dismissed for lack of testimony. No drugs. No B and E. No stolen goods. No listed place of work, but since he's never been on probation, there's no reason we'd have it."

"That's a 'minor' rap sheet?" Shaye asked.

"To me? Small beer. To the average citizen? Not someone you want your daughter or friend hooking up with. Certainly not anyone I want you getting within a country mile of."

"Then park more than a country mile away from Rua's house."

He didn't know whether to laugh or swear, so he turned on the engine, waited for it to die or fly, and was relieved when it chose life. Ever since engines had gone electronic, he'd left their care and feeding to professionals.

"What's Meyers like?" Tanner asked.

"Quiet. A lot of forest. Small. Mostly a relatively affordable town for the folks who work in Tahoe. Meyers gets some of the tourist money coming and going to the city, but not much. Its primary claims to fame are the largely ignored California State ag enforcement station and the marine inspection station, where people hauling boats to Tahoe get vetted for invasive plants or animals stuck to hulls."

"Gotcha. D and D and small-time drugs, occasional spousal battery."

"D and—oh," she said. "Crimes. Is that how you see a place?"

"I'm a cop. I look under rocks."

"Right. Ever look at the flowers, too?"

"I must. I'm riding with one."

Shaye smiled and tried not to think about Tanner's tongue neatly licking her fingers clean. It was impossible. The longer she was with him, the more she saw that her first impression of him had been misleading. He was tough, yes, but he wasn't a bully and a whiner like her ex. And she wasn't the insecure, anxious-to-be-loved young woman that she had been.

Time to cut myself some slack. I've paid for Marc again and again. Thank God the Dodgers are paying his rent now.

Forget him. He was a loser.

And who says you have to marry Tanner because you'd like to peel off his clothes and find out just how hard he is? This is the twenty-first century. Marriage isn't required for good sex. It sure didn't help with Marc.

Tanner and Shaye turned off Highway 50 for the half mile between it and Antonio Rua's last known address. Wind tousled the pines in the moonlight, making them look like a shaggy herd of animals flowing by on either side. She felt like she was speeding through giant wild things out of a children's book. It was primitive. Eerie.

"You really shouldn't be here." Tanner's first words in many miles broke the silence.

"Already decided." Her voice was clipped, angry without knowing why.

"Not what I meant. You're smart, fine-looking, city bred, able to live and work anywhere. Why are you stuck way out in ranch land and wilderness? Why a place like Refuge, where most of the men think women's rights means being a slut?"

"You mean, why live like a country bumpkin?" Shaye asked acidly, thinking of the running argument she had with her family. "Lemme just spit out my chaw, scratch my crotch, and tell you to—"

"Go to hell," he cut in. "Whew. Stepped on a land mine there, and I don't mean a cow pie. Sorry, didn't know you were so sensitive about—"

"I'm not sensitive," she said across him. "I'm just damn tired of everyone second-guessing my choices."

"By everyone I assume you mean family?"

She shot him a look. "Been checking into my background?"

"Nope, just a good guess. Nobody pushes old buttons like family."

She took a deep breath and let it out slowly. "Sorry. You're right. Old buttons lovingly polished by my parents and sister. Like you and Lorne, I suppose."

"Don't know about the loving part, but the polishing? Oh yeah. As for the rest, I still get surprised that a woman like you chooses to work with ranchers who are as hard as the land."

"Is that why you never came back?" she asked. "Too hard a life?"

"I wanted to make a difference in the world, make it better, so I became a cop." He laughed without much humor. "Yeah, I was real damn young. I got older telling the grieving widows that their husband of too many years got whacked because he was in the wrong bed screwing the wrong woman, and said woman earned her keep on her back and her knees, and the widow should make an appointment with her doctor for the kind of tests you don't talk about with your friends."

Shaye looked at Tanner. In the reflected lights of the dash, his face was stark and his eyes like cut crystal. He should have frightened her.

He fascinated her.

"Then I got a lot older telling frantic parents that their son or daughter died because some sick son of a bitch got off on little kids," he continued. "And by the way, the sicko just happened to be the kid's uncle or the husband's best friend or the nice neighbor down the street."

Silently she put her hand on Tanner's thigh. It seemed like such a small comfort to offer a man who had known too much of the underside of life. A man who was more interested in helping out than being famous.

His hand settled over hers, squeezed, then returned to the wheel.

"So my youthful shine got scuffed off on concrete, and I finally got the memo that people weren't going to change no matter how many killers I put in jail or how many hours I worked."

She waited, but he didn't say any more.

"Why didn't you quit?" she asked.

He shrugged. "I'm good at what I do. Now I'm back in Refuge with a flower in my front seat, hoping like hell I don't bruise her petals along the way to finding out why my uncle died in the wrong clothes with tobacco spread over his shirt."

"I don't have petals."

"You do to me," Tanner said. "And I have all the finesse of asphalt. Don't let me hurt you."

"I won't," she said, and hoped it was true.

She could all too easily be haunted by Tanner when he left. Especially if he was her lover.

He lifted a hand, brushed the back of his fingers over her cheek. "Petals," he murmured, then returned his attention to the road.

Her heart turned over. She wanted to crawl inside his skin. And stay there.

Just as a few, widely scattered lights appeared, the nav computer pinged. He glanced at it, turned off onto a narrow road that needed new gravel, bumped into the weeds near a clump of mailboxes, and killed the lights.

The darkness was another kind of intimacy drawing Shaye to Tanner. She wanted to brush her fingers down his cheek. He wouldn't feel like petals. He was warm, slightly rough, with surprisingly soft lips.

In too fast, too hot, too deep, she told herself, and wanted to believe it.

She breathed out in a rush and forced herself to look anywhere but at him. Houses out here were lonely, built away from the main roads by people who preferred their privacy and the company of the trees. The moon hung silver over the forest, neither full nor crescent, giving a flat metallic light to the gravel road. Beyond the pale line of the lane ahead, the trees ate moonlight, leaving only shadows.

"See that light just off to the right?" Tanner asked.

She blinked and stared through the windshield. Several hundred feet away, at the end of a dirt driveway off to the right, she glimpsed the pale yellow of porch light winking through the wind-stirred trees.

"A cottage?" she asked.

"The last one on the road. Nothing after it except forest and ridge-lines. No other lights on anywhere, even though there are five mailboxes at the turnoff."

"A lot of the places here are owned by people who rent them out to skiers or summer tourists," Shaye said. "Summer's over and skiing is a few good snowstorms in the future."

"Stay here out of the wind. I'll check the mailbox." He opened the car door.

"Your overhead light is out," she said, noticing it for the first time.

"I don't need it to drive."

The door closed softly behind him.

She watched him walk back toward the highway, a shadow moving among shadows. She glanced back at the gravel road leading to the cottage. The light had vanished. Either it was on a motion sensor that had been set off by wind-tossed branches, or someone had shut the light off.

Her skin rippled and tried to raise a nonexistent ruff. For all her ease in the wilds, this place was different. It was civilization, yet it . . . wasn't. The pale gravel lane went past deserted homes to a dead end at the isolated house of a man with a "minor" rap sheet, a man who had sold coins that someone stole from a man who was recently dead or soon to be so.

It wasn't a comforting thought.

How can Tanner do this all the time? Is this what my parents feel when they think of me on lonely ranches or out looking for hikers who were supposed to check in yesterday? Is that why they're always on me to move back to the city?

What was normal to her wasn't normal to her parents.

What was normal to Tanner wasn't normal to her.

You insisted on coming along. Don't wuss out just because it's a dark, windy night. You've camped alone in bear country. Suck it up.

A small light flashed briefly as Tanner read the mailboxes. Darkness returned while he walked back to the car.

He got back in with a minimum of noise. "Rua's box is crammed with junk mail, local newspaper throwaways, and what looks like bills. Either he's been gone several days or he doesn't check his mail real often."

"We'll find out."

He tapped his right index finger on the steering wheel. "I will. You're going to slide over and get ready to drive if somebody who isn't me approaches the car." He glanced at her, his eyes like slices of midnight. "Don't give me any grief. This is borderline stupid as it is. I'm going in at night with no real backup—and don't say you're backup because you aren't armed."

"I can shoot a pistol, a rifle, and a shotgun."

"Not if you aren't carrying one."

"And you are?" she shot back.

"I'm a—"

"—cop," she finished. "So where's your gun?"

"Closer than yours."

She wanted to be angry, she wanted to laugh, and most of all she wanted to hold Tanner's arms and tell him not to let go.

I'm all over the emotional map and it's nowhere close to my period, she thought. *Suck. It. Up.*

He makes me laugh instead of looming over and intimidating me. Or trying to. God, how did I marry my ex? I was more desperate than I knew.

She watched Tanner reach under the front seat, then straighten and clip something to the back of his belt. A big handgun.

"If Rua is home, what will you do?" she asked.

"Tell him I want to buy some 1932 Saint-Gaudens."

"Right," she said through her teeth. "I'll wait here like a good little girl."

"Thank you." He ran his fingers over her cheek in a brief caress. "Don't worry, honey. If it's me or the other guy, I have no problems with it being him."

"But if there's no trouble, you'll come and get me, right? I don't like being a helpless little flower."

"I'll come get you and teach you the finer points of B and E."

She smiled crookedly, touched a lean, warm cheek whose stubble had passed five o'clock hours ago, and smiled. "I'll look forward to it."

"If you see a car turning onto the road, duck out of sight."

"Yes."

"Sure hope I hear that word again soon, under better circumstances."

Before she could answer, he was gone, devoured by shadows and at home among them.

Tanner stayed in the deepest pools of night he could find and looked for any sign that Rua was home. The weak porch light he'd seen as they turned onto the road was nowhere in sight. There was no garage or visible vehicle.

A hard gust of wind bent the trees. The dim light at the front of the porch came on.

Motion sensor, he thought.

Not unusual for a rural house, but not real helpful on a windy night. At least the wind would cover the inevitable small sounds his boots made on the gravel.

Of course, the same would be true of anyone sneaking up on him.

The light was either set on a very short cycle or had a short, period. It went dark again. From inside the house came a bluish glow that had been too faint to be seen from the road. It flickered, too, but not from a faulty contact.

TV is on.

Not good.

Tanner began circling the house, listening, hearing nothing but the wind and an occasional sound from the TV.

No dog, thank God.

A motorcycle with worn, all-terrain tires was parked under a lean-to in back.

That would take him up a ranch road, no problem.

He touched the engine. Cold as the wind. In the moonlight, scattered empty beer cans and caffeinated energy drinks gleamed like jewels. He had to be careful not to kick one every other step.

He continued working his way slowly, carefully around the small house, keeping to each bit of cover nature offered. When he had made most of the circuit, he hunkered down in the shadow of a thick pine and watched the house.

Still nothing happening, nothing moving but the wind.

Tanner eased up onto the worn porch as quietly as he could. He could hear the TV but not what was playing. No refrigerator door slammed. No toilet flushed. No lights were on anywhere else in the house. He debated for a few seconds whether to knock or call out. Rua might have done some petty crime, but there was no sign in his rap sheet that he dealt drugs from the house, or was the kind of habitual offender who would shoot or rabbit at the first knock on the door.

Still, Tanner waited. Something about this just wasn't right. A primitive part of his brain, the part left over from times when animals hunted men for food, screamed at him that he was being watched by a predator. It was the sort of message he would be a fool to ignore. It had saved Brothers's life when they were on patrol as rookies. Saved his own, too.

He listened to the fitful murmur of the television, louder during the ads, muttering during the program. It sounded like sports of some kind, cheering and booing and crowd noise. It wasn't the full-throated roar of a football or hockey stadium. Maybe a boxing match.

Quietly, he eased up to the side of the porch for a better look into the house—and to avoid setting off the motion sensor, which was an unpredictable light at a time he needed darkness. Blending into the shadows, he waited for some sign of life other than the electronic variety.

He would wait until he lost that nagging feeling of something being off. He had been on enough stakeouts to know that impatience could be a deadly mistake.

Tanner wanted the other guy to make it.

NINETEEN

*F*OURTEEN MINUTES. NO. *Fifteen and a half.*
Sixteen.

Shaye looked away from her glowing watch face. She told herself she should keep waiting, but her hand kept closing around the door handle. She kept thinking about all the ugly things that could be happening to Tanner.

Two or three minutes to walk up there, she thought for the tenth time. *At most a few minutes to find out if Rua is home. Maybe five minutes to get him talking. Then two minutes to walk back.*

Unless something went wrong.

Like Lorne, lying faceup.

She told herself again to wait, everything was fine, she was letting her imagination run away with her mind. She even tried to believe it.

Seventeen minutes.

Twenty minutes.

Shaye opened the car door and got out as quietly as she could. She told herself she was just going to check and make sure everything was all right. If it wasn't, she would call the local 911 and do whatever she could until people with badges arrived.

Trees shivered and rushed around her, wind making sounds like distant conversations and whispered warnings. Pale-barked aspen gleamed like bone in the moonlight.

Nothing moved but the wind and her.

The wind was a lot more confident than she was. Every noise she made sounded like a cannon shot to her.

Damn it, Tanner. Where are you?

Wind died into the kind of silence that quivered with dark possibilities. Moonlight on the granite peaks gleamed like remembered snow. A look over her shoulder assured her that no one was coming up behind her on the gravel lane.

Carefully, she circled the house as quietly as she could, but didn't see one of the beer cans in time to avoid kicking it. The racket it made sounded huge in the empty night.

Nobody called out.

Nobody came to a door or window to check out the noise.

Part of Shaye's mind yammered at her to go back and wait in the car like Tanner had told her to. The other part of her, the part that had vowed never to let her desires come in second to a man's again, kept her going. She was an adult who could make her own decisions.

Warily she eyed the front of the house again.

Nothing moved.

Okay. If Rua is there, I just need to make a phone call because my cell ran out of juice and my car quit. If I look nervous, so what? What woman wouldn't when she's stranded on a dark road and has to approach a strange house to ask for help?

At least I have on shoes I can run in.

Not bothering to be quiet, she climbed the steps and went to the front door. It was slightly ajar. Nothing moved in the narrow strip of light coming through the doorway but the restless flicker of the TV.

Now would be a good time to call the cops, she thought.

Without it meaning to, her shoulder brushed against the door. It opened wider in silent invitation. It didn't creak like she half expected it to, just waited silently for her to make up her mind.

A sudden rush of wind startled her and pushed the door farther open. The motion sensor light at one corner of the porch came on with an irritated buzz and died seconds later with a crackle.

The room beyond the doorway looked so ordinary she felt like a fool for being jumpy. The biting smell of stale beer flowed out as the wind retreated. There was an underlay of gym odor in the air, probably explained by the crumpled workout clothes and stray socks scattered at one end of the room. The television was happily chattering to no one.

Maybe the owner had gotten bored with the ads and gone back to the kitchen for another beer. The erratic lights and shadows cast by the television were distracting—imitations of life in an empty room.

She thought about calling out, but her mouth was too dry. So she tiptoed inside the room. No matter how hard she listened, there was no sound but her breathing, her rapid heartbeat, and the television selling vitamins to dirty socks. Weights, some empty food containers, and the big LCD screen rested on a cinder-block shelf.

The TV lights shifted from vitamins to sweating, beefy men. Across the bottom of the screen a scrolling line displayed the logo of MMA and the dates of future matches. One of the men had a shaved head and wore eye-watering colors on his shorts and shoes. Feints and tentative poking exploded into brutal clutches. If there were any rules, or anyone to enforce them, it wasn't reflected on the screen.

Off to one side of the TV, the worn set of dumbbells and cracked vinyl bench reflected the light from the television in sickly shades of blue.

When Shaye stepped all the way inside, she saw another source of light, almost as blue and restless as the TV, yet different. The light moved slowly, almost hypnotically, but there was no sound coming from it.

Tanner, where the hell are you?

She crept closer to the second source of light, somewhere in a room off a bare hallway. The television covered any of the small sounds she made.

The room that was the source of the flickering light was at the end of the hall. Two other doors gaped open, advertising a bathroom and another darkened room. The hall itself was barren, its pine floor scratched and scuffed. The empty room before the end of the hall looked like the floor was the same.

She was walking toward the odd blue light at the end of the hall when she decided to check out the room that had no light at all. She would feel better knowing that there was nothing at her back but the yammering TV.

Tentatively she entered the unlit room.

If Tanner isn't here, I'm going back to the car.

What good does that do? He could be hurt, needing help, and there I'll be shivering in the car like a kid afraid of the dark.

The thought of Tanner needing her, and her too much of a coward to help, pushed Shaye's reluctant feet forward. She went in a few steps, feeling her way. The black shine of a window across the room was her only light. Despite her care, she kicked something on the floor. The sound it made seemed like an avalanche echoing in the silence.

She froze, waiting for her heart to settle, and felt carefully in front of her. The back of her wrist brushed over a wastebasket. She let out a long breath and gathered up her nerves. When her heartbeat finally slowed, she could hear more than the hard bang of her pulse.

That was the only reason she noticed the small sounds coming from somewhere behind her. Footsteps.

In the hall.

Coming toward her.

Shaye's heart hammered inside her chest and tried to jump up her throat and strangle her. Even as she was berating herself for being *stupid stupid stupid,* she knew that the only exit left to her was the window across the room. She started toward it, tripped over the wastebasket, and barely managed to stay upright.

The window was just ahead. Beyond it, the safety of the forest was only twenty feet away.

Screw stealth.

She lunged for the window.

At the same instant that she registered a whisper of movement behind her, a hand clamped over her mouth and a man's muscular strength banded her arms against her waist. She was yanked back against him with dizzying speed.

And she was helpless as a child.

TWENTY

S WEETIE, YOU DON'T obey orders worth a damn." The words were softly spoken and colder than the wind.

Tanner. Thank God.

As his hand lifted from her mouth, anger replaced fear in a rush of heat. She spun to face him.

"My name isn't sweetie and you were gone more than twenty minutes," she managed to whisper, though her heart felt like it was running a marathon behind her ribs. "Did you have to scare me?"

"You're lucky I didn't coldcock you. What the hell do you think you're doing?"

"My car quit and my cell phone is out of juice," she shot back in a low tone.

He made a strangled sound and shook his head. "Unbelievable."

"Am I the only one having a hard time yelling in whispers?"

Tanner didn't know whether to laugh or bang his forehead against hers. "Go back to the car."

"You scared the hell out of me," she said between breaths. Her mouth tasted like a hangover laced with bile.

"Good. Go back to the car," he said again.

"Is anyone else here? Why is the TV on? Why are we whispering?"

"Not quite. I don't know. It beats yelling until I figure out what's going on. Then I'm going to be so loud you'll get a headache."

"Wouldn't it help to turn on the lights?" Shaye asked, ignoring the threat.

"Doubt it. Go back to the car."

"If no one's here—"

"I don't have time for this," he said curtly. "Just stay out of the way and don't touch anything you can leave fingerprints on."

Wanting to argue some more, quivering from too much adrenaline, Shaye followed Tanner down the hallway and into the room at the end.

The source of the eerie blue light was a big aquarium. The water was faintly cloudy. Fish that looked like bloated Japanese drawings hung in the water and gulped at her with goggle eyes. A trickle of moisture hung on the outside of the tank, transparent beads trailing down, glowing like a cat's eyes in the odd light.

"Over here," Tanner said. "I found him like this."

Shaye's emergency training overcame her nerves. "Is he alive? Does he need help?"

"No."

She glanced past Tanner's feet. Rua—if that was who it was—was a heavyset man, more muscle than fat, arms thick in the black T-shirt emblazoned with the logo FIGHT FOR YOUR LIFE.

At least, that was what Shaye thought it had said when it was intact. Some of the lettering had been ruined.

"Bullet holes?" she asked, not quite believing.

"Yeah. He lost his last fight but good."

She swallowed. "Is it Rua?"

"The driver's license showed a buzz cut, but the rest looks pretty much the same. I'm assuming it's Rua until I find out otherwise."

Rua's shaved head looked gray blue in the aquarium light. His eyes were open, still shiny with moisture.

Carefully she bent down and touched the dead man's neck. The skin was resilient, slightly cool to her touch, but nothing close to cold. "He hasn't been dead long," she said.

Tanner watched her with new respect. She'd been so frightened her cheeks were bone pale, but her hand didn't shake as she checked a corpse for life.

I shouldn't be surprised. She ran scavengers off Lorne's body, waited for the deputy, and gave a coherent report.

She's too damn brave for my peace of mind—sneaking into the house, hoping to find me, and not knowing what shape I was in or who else might be here.

Tanner couldn't help thinking how badly it could have gone if the killer had still been in the house. It made him want to yell at Shaye.

Later, he promised himself. *When we're a long way from here.*

That was the most important thing—not being found at a murder scene he had no intention of reporting.

"I didn't hear anything," she said.

"Neither did I. It must have happened about half an hour before we got here. He's still warm, considering the temperature of the room. And the floor underneath his right hand is still damp."

"Someone other than you was mad at Rua," she said.

"I'm not even mad at him," Tanner said, low and hard. "I just wanted some answers."

"And then maybe you'd get mad?"

"Depends on the answers."

Rua's eyes stared up, seeing something a lot more distant than the ceiling.

"Let's go," Tanner said. "I'd like to search him and the house. Coins likely are here somewhere. No landline, so a cell phone might tell us who he's been talking to. But we've been here too long as it is."

"Did you call the police? Don't we have to wait for them?"

"If I was working this case, I'm the first guy I'd lock up, no matter what I said."

"But you didn't do anything."

Tanner smiled grimly. "B and E followed by a corpse? Yeah, sure. Nothing at all. Like Lorne."

"But if we don't tell the police, isn't that a crime?"

"Only if we were here. Did you touch anything?"

Shaye felt like reality had shifted and she was stumbling around trying to stay on her feet. "I . . . not with my fingertips."

"How about the front door?"

"The wind opened it for me. I didn't see anything I wanted to touch except that window, and you yanked me back before I reached it."

Mentally Tanner retraced his route, and the one Shaye had taken. He knew he hadn't touched anything. He'd have to hope she hadn't. There wasn't time to wipe down every possible surface.

Not that he was real worried about it. The lab techs—if they were called in at all—were usually six to eight weeks behind in their work. Unless there was something important about the death, it would be written off as a drug deal gone south, a B and E and an unlucky home-owner, or a falling-out among marginal thugs. A red case, with no one to snitch on the murderer.

It would take a chain of similar deaths before anyone official would be interested enough to demand a full, expensive effort to find the murderer.

But Tanner didn't want to be caught because some D.A. wanted a reelection cause.

"Are you sure about the fingerprints? If they're around, and someone cares enough to spend a lot of taxpayer money, your prints will be found."

"Which is why we should stay here until the cops come," she said.

The innocence of a civilian who has never been on the wrong side of the law, he thought wryly.

"Look," he said. "You and I have no alibi except each other. I'm from out of town. My uncle might have been killed by Rua. It wouldn't take a rocket scientist to find out I had Rua's address."

"But—"

Tanner kept talking. "The first thing the cops here will do is check with Sheriff Conrad. He won't be interested in a complex story that leaves me innocent. He'll be much more interested in a simple story that has me locked up. And in the meantime, whoever actually did this is still running around."

She sighed. "Maybe Rua had bad friends. Maybe he was selling drugs."

"Place smells like sweat, not drugs. His death is connected to Lorne's gold, and maybe to Lorne himself. Wishing it was different will get us in trouble. Move it, honey. I don't want to meet any neighbors."

"You're sure about this?" Shaye asked as he led her away from the aquarium's glow.

"I'm sure that we won't get any answers on the inside of a jail cell."

She looked at the fish tank. The water drops outside the tank still glowed, but there weren't as many. "What about the water on the outside of the fish tank? It's drying up, so it's not a leak. Something splashed."

"Yeah, I saw that," Tanner said. "The bottom was disturbed, too. But I don't have time for a fast search, much less a thorough one."

Shaye looked over her shoulder as he hustled her from the room. The fish were staring up at their own watery ceiling, as motionless and silent as the corpse a few feet away.

TWENTY-ONE

FINALLY.

The watcher had almost given up on Tanner and Shaye leaving.

Guess they decided not to call the cops.

In some ways, that was too bad. It might have made things easier, because everyone's favorite suspect would have been Tanner. In other ways, it was just as well. Everything was back on track. Better than back. There was nothing to tie Rua's murder into anything else.

Two down, none to go.

Unless Tanner becomes a problem. He sure connected the dots fast.

Be a shame if Shaye gets in the way, but shit happens.

I'll worry about that later. Right now my pistol has an appointment with the deepest part of the lake.

TWENTY-TWO

TANNER'S CAR WENT downhill toward the valley, gravity assisting the balky engine. Shaye barely noticed. The adrenaline jag was wearing off, leaving her feeling tired and edgy at the same time.

"You doing okay?" Tanner asked after a long silence.

"I don't know."

"Tell me if I can do anything," was all he said.

You could hold me.

But she kept that thought to herself. He couldn't hug her like a child and drive. She turned away from the side window where night rushed past her and looked at Tanner. His expression was neutral, his hands calm as he coaxed and guided the unhappy car through the twists and turns of the mountain road.

The strength in him should have frightened rather than soothed her. He was one of the people who knew all about bullets and flesh. Yet his undemanding presence eased her in ways she couldn't describe.

"I know that people kill people all the time," she said finally. "At least, I know up here." She tapped her forehead. "But knowing it right here"—she put her fist against her stomach—"is a whole lot different."

"It changes you," he said. "You get used to it, but you never look at people the same way again."

"I'm not sure I like it," Shaye said after a few miles. "And I know that liking has nothing to do with it."

"I'm sorry. I shouldn't have let you come along tonight."

"You warned me. I don't blame you. I don't even blame myself. I'm just . . ."

"Adjusting?"

She sighed. "I sure hope so. I'd hate to feel like this forever."

"Like what?"

"Edgy. Adrift. Like I want to scream but don't know why. Waiting for something else to blow up in my face. Not knowing how or when to duck, but certain I'll have to without warning."

Tanner knew what she meant. He had felt that way. So had every other intelligent person confronted by unexpected, violent death.

The road straightened out, allowing him to take one hand off the wheel. He touched her cheek, soft yet taut, cool yet with life beating just beneath. She was as pale as granite in the moonlight.

"There's a small blanket in the backseat," he said. "Or I could turn up the heat."

At his words, she realized she was cold. She reached into the backseat, fumbled, and connected with something as soft as a sigh. Pulling the blanket into the front seat, she wrapped it around herself and rubbed her cheek against it.

"Nice," she murmured.

"I have touchy skin," he said. "I like soft things. I think I became a detective because I hate starched uniforms."

She made a sound that was suspiciously close to a giggle.

"I took a lot of crap for it from the other cops," he said. "I just smiled and agreed I'm a pussy who likes to snuggle up with something that feels good on my skin."

Definitely a giggle.

He glanced over. She was relaxing a little, looking less like she might bolt or throw up.

"Good thing I live in the modern age," he continued. "Wool underwear would have made me miserable. China would have been an okay place to live, as long as I was one of the elite who wore silk underwear."

She laughed much too hard at his words, took a shaky breath, and then another, and another, until her breathing evened out.

He touched her cheek again. "You're doing a lot better than most rookies with their first murder."

And she had seen two in only a few days.

But he wasn't going to talk about that. She had had enough for tonight.

Tanner didn't even offer to take Shaye back to her condo. He knew she didn't want to be alone tonight any more than he did. He might have seen a lot more violence than she had, but it still bruised him. He had just learned to live without it showing on the outside.

Bare granite was bleached white by the moon that was now high in the sky. The valley below looked pale where the pastures were dry, dark where they were irrigated, and became hammered silver wherever there was surface water. Random lights lay like colorful embers scattered unevenly across the land.

"It looks the same," Shaye said to herself.

Tanner heard, and understood.

"The land lives in a different time than we do," he said.

And that was one of the things he had left behind without knowing it. And missed it the same way. For him, somehow the enduring land balanced the uncertainty of human life.

She leaned against the seat and sighed. "I don't like to think of Rua lying in that room staring at nothing."

"He doesn't care."

"Do you?"

"I can't afford to care about him beyond the fact that if Lorne was murdered, then Rua is the link," Tanner said evenly. "Now that link is broken. I don't have any direct way to find out how the hell Rua knew about Lorne's coins and if he killed Lorne for them or for another reason entirely."

She made a small sound. "What other reason?"

"Someone got fed up with Lorne's abrasive ways and wanted him dead. Someone heard about the coins and wanted them and Lorne was in the way. Someone wanted the land to go to the Conservancy and killed Lorne to speed the process. Someone wanted his land and killed him before he could give it to the Conservancy. Someone lost too much on Tuesday nights and—"

"You're giving me a headache," she interrupted.

"Only fair. I have one big enough to share."

"But then who really killed him?"

"Lorne or Rua?" he asked.

"Now I have your headache. Do you think the same person killed both of them?"

"Possible."

"But not probable?"

"Given Rua's history, I could draw up a long and interesting list of people who might have had reason to kill him," Tanner said. "I'm having a hard time believing any of them also would have a reason to kill my uncle."

He turned off onto the dirt road leading to Lorne's house.

"So we're stuck unless more coins turn up and we find out who sold them this time?" Shaye asked.

"Or we find a suspect that connects Rua to Lorne."

"That's a stretch. Lorne wouldn't have let someone like Rua on the ranch, and someone like Rua wouldn't have known who Lorne was."

"Exactly. You'd make a good detective."

She stared at Tanner. "Why? All I can think of are reasons why their deaths *aren't* logically connected."

"Except by the coins."

"Maybe whoever killed Rua knew about the coins and wanted the ones he hadn't traded and didn't want to pay for them."

"Robbery has led to more than one murder," Tanner agreed.

"You aren't helping my headache."

"Nothing will help your headache but a soak in the hot springs at the ranch."

"I don't have a bathing suit."

"The hot springs don't care." He glanced at her, saw she was nibbling on her sexy lip, and said, "You can go in naked, or in your underwear with me, or in your underwear without me, or—"

"No more choices!"

"Okay." He touched her cheek for an instant before he returned to driving the rough road. "We'll figure it out. Death has a way of really clarifying what's important."

When she realized he was right, she let out a long sigh.

They were silent as he drove up and parked behind the small house next to Lorne's truck. They got out at the same time and looked at the dark windows.

"I feel like an intruder," she said as they headed toward the front door.

"I wish I did."

"Why?"

The door opened easily to Tanner's key.

"It's too damn familiar," he said, "like I never left, like I can just pick up where Lorne left off and never miss a beat."

"And that's bad."

There was no question in her voice, just a sadness that surprised both of them.

"It's not real," Tanner said. "I have a life in L.A." *Even if I don't want to go back and kiss the captain's ass until he giggles. Two years and I'll have twenty in.* "I was happy on this ranch, but it was a kid's happiness. That kid is as dead as Lorne."

He walked by memory through the darkness until he had gone all the way to the back door, a test he wasn't sure if he had passed or failed.

He found the light switch. The overheads in the kitchen and mudroom flickered on slowly, pinging in the quiet. The blue-green light made the room seem even smaller, casting odd shadows and creating pools of darkness. At least one of the bulbs needed replacing. It had been out last night, too. He just hadn't really noticed.

She followed him into the small mudroom on the back of the kitchen, walking past Lorne's beaten up work boots and battered Stetson, trying to shake off the feeling of being an intruder.

"I'll get some towels for the hot springs," Tanner said. "If you want coffee—"

"I'll make some," she said. "I've watched Lorne do it, so I know to only add half the coffee he does. Unless you like it his way?"

"I learned to drink it that way. I'd just as soon keep the enamel on my teeth, though."

She smiled. "So would I."

She walked to the stove, lifted the pan Lorne had always used to boil water, and filled it at the sink. While she made coffee Tanner found towels in the old trunk that served as a linen cupboard. The towels, like the bedsheets, were worn but serviceable.

The condoms were where they had always been, at the bottom of the trunk. The box was unopened. The expiration date on the package said the contents were a long way from being past their shelf life. His uncle might have stopped going to the whorehouses at the northern end of the big valley, but apparently he hadn't stopped buying condoms at the town drugstore.

Whether his uncle had been motivated by pride or pragmatism, Tanner was grateful. He opened the box and stuffed some of the contents in his hip pocket. When he had rushed out of L.A., he hadn't expected to find in Refuge a woman who made him feel teenage hungry just by looking at her. If she was willing—big if—he damn sure wanted to be able. The condom in his wallet had been there too long to be trusted.

He picked up the towels and headed into the kitchen.

"Water's almost boiling. It will take a few minutes to drip through," she said.

"We'll have some when we get back."

After stacking the towels on the small kitchen table, he went to the counter. He opened the top drawer. It jammed halfway out.

I'll have to find some paraffin to put on the wood, Tanner thought. *Everything about this place needs work. I should go to the hardware store, and while I'm at it, I should get some lumber and fix that old mudroom, maybe build another room and—*

Abruptly he realized where his thoughts were going. He was actually looking forward to swinging a hammer and tightening screws, fixing drawers, and replacing window casements and the sagging corner on the front porch.

Are you crazy? You're not a kid anymore. Stop thinking like one.

He wrenched the drawer open with the kind of casual strength Lorne had lost to age. Part of the contents flew out and scattered on the floor. Swearing under his breath, Tanner bent to pick everything up. Among the screws and rubber bands lay a pocketknife. Its handle was black plastic made up like wood with tarnished metal hubs on either end. He knew without opening it that the blade was black and dull.

The knife had once been his. It was a child's toy, not a real tool.

That child grew up, he told himself.

He pocketed the knife with automatic motions, realized what he'd done, and tossed the knife back in the junk drawer.

"Something wrong?" Shaye asked.

"I'm an idiot. Nothing new."

He picked up the rest of the odds and ends on the floor. There was a matchbook and a couple of bullet casings, a chewed-up comb, and a photograph so faded that you could barely see the woman in it. When he turned it over, he saw the words *From Millie xoxoxo* written in ballpoint ink, blue as the summer sky. He dumped everything back in the drawer and searched until he found the spare set of truck keys. They were on a chain with a black-and-white compass floating in its still-clear globe.

"Is that the treasure drawer?" Shaye asked.

"Lorne called it the junk drawer." He put the keys in his pocket. "Guess everybody has one, right?"

"Several, in my case," she admitted. "I call it my desk."

He smiled despite his double-edged memories. The rechargeable flashlight waited in its bracket near the kitchen counter. He wished he could plug himself into a wall socket and get new energy. He felt cold and drained and at war with himself over the childish lure of the ranch.

And he wanted Shaye until he had to remind himself to breathe.

He knew he shouldn't touch her. She was off balance, bruised by violence, too soft for a cop who had seen too much. He felt too full, like his skin was going to split and open into something new, something utterly unexpected. Part of him was frightened. A bigger part of him couldn't wait.

He closed his eyes and fought for control.

When he opened them again, she was watching him, knowledge in her eyes. She saw everything in him, all the cold and unease and consuming need. He didn't like being that transparent and couldn't do a damn thing about it.

And she was afraid of him.

Smart woman. Way too smart for a dumb piece of meat like me.

He slammed the drawer, catching some of his skin in it along the way, burning a jagged star of pain up and down his forearm. He grabbed a hand towel off its wall hook and headed for the sink.

"Tanner?"

"The water is boiling," he said, turning on the faucet. "Make the coffee and I'll drive you to the hot springs."

"What about you?"

He shoved his hand under the cold water. "You're better off without me."

"When I believe that, I'll tell you myself."

He didn't look up. "It was written all over your face. You're afraid of me."

She poured the water into the drip pot before she went to stand beside him. Close.

"I'm afraid of myself," she said, taking the cloth from him and holding it under the faucet.

He looked into the dark brown warmth of her eyes and saw only truth.

"Why?" he asked.

"You make me want."

"What do you want?" he asked in a low voice.

"Everything." She wrung out the cloth and turned off the faucet. A thin line of blood welled along the webbing between his thumb and forefinger. "Wiggle your thumb."

He did.

"You'll be sore, but you didn't do any real damage," she said. "No stitches required."

When he didn't say anything, she glanced up. The light framed him against the darkened window, and in its reflection she could see him watching her. His eyes were rimmed with pain and weariness, echoes of too many emotions in too little time.

She felt the same way. Without thinking, she brushed her mouth against his chin. "C'mon. A soak will do us both good. You give directions and I'll drive."

"I can—"

"So can I," she interrupted. "Keys."

He searched her eyes, then smiled slightly.

"Left pocket," he said, holding up his towel-wrapped left hand. Daring her.

She hadn't had a brother for nothing. She shoved her hand in Tanner's pocket and felt for the keys. She found more—a lot more.

"That's not the keys to the truck," he pointed out.

"Feels more like a gearshift," she agreed. "Ah, here we are."

He made a half-throttled sound that could have been a laugh or a growl. She had had an emotionally bruising few days, but she wasn't physically afraid of him. He didn't understand it—most people flinched if they got even a taste of the cold, cutting edges of his life as a homicide cop.

But Shaye didn't.

TWENTY-THREE

TANNER GRABBED THE flashlight from its charging cradle and followed Shaye outside. The night was still, silence defined by the distant sigh of water finding its way down the rugged mountainside. He waited for her to ask for light. When she simply paused for a few moments to let her eyes adjust to darkness, he smiled and felt something uncurl inside him. Like him, she was at home in the night.

"I can't check fences very well in the dark," she said, "but I can make sure the horses have food and water."

"Everything should be fine until morning. I fed the horses before I picked you up for breakfast, then turned them out into the east pasture. The fences and cattle were where they should be, all water troughs were full, mineral lick has been replaced, and the old salt licks are only about half gone."

What he didn't say was how much he had enjoyed the simple physical chores, the clean air, and the increasing light of morning flooding the quiet land.

It's a dream, he told himself roughly. *Like Shaye.*

"Where to?" she asked as she swung easily up into Lorne's truck.

"Take the track along the west pasture. You know the one?"

"Yes." She started the truck, waited for the engine to even out, and shifted into first. As they bumped along the road, she said, "We should talk to Deputy August."

"Hard to do that without implicating ourselves," Tanner said.

In the pale gleam of the dashboard, the full line of her lower lip made him think about licking, biting, sucking.

"But . . ."

"Yeah," he said, forcing himself to look away. "I'll go in tomorrow and tell him what we found at Brilliant Moments."

"But not at Rua's house."

"I'll tell August I'm going to see Rua, and ask for any info he might have. Then I can drive up, find Rua, and call it in like a good citizen."

Without meaning to, Tanner found himself studying the curves and shadows of Shaye's mouth again.

"Where will I be?" she asked.

"Sleeping in. You've had a hard few days."

"Not that hard. If you leave me here, I won't be here when you get back and I won't be taking any of your calls. I'm in this to the end or I'm gone."

He started to argue, then decided it wasn't worth the energy. He'd rather taste her. "Don't snarl when I wake you up early."

"I won't."

"And we agree on our story before we get there. I got lucky with an online check of coins—"

"Do you have a computer with you?" she asked.

Despite the ache and hunger prowling through him, he smiled. "Like I said, you'd make a good investigator. I don't have a computer, but I know people who do. So I got two addresses. The first was a dead end. The second was Brilliant Moments, where we got Rua's ID."

She nodded, downshifted, crept around a pile of rocks, and shifted into third again.

The pale flesh of her hands caught his eye. Her fingers looked delicate. Edible. He remembered how it had felt to suck one into his mouth. Then he wondered if she would let him suck anywhere else, somewhere hotter, wetter.

Wanting her was bad enough. Sensing that she wanted him but wasn't sure was making him nuts.

With a mental curse, he kept on talking. "We were hungry," *no shit,* "and we went to a rib place you knew. Then we decided to soak in the hot springs rather than try to track down Rua in the dark. We slept, we ate breakfast, and we went to see Deputy August. Short and simple. No embellishments. Turn right just before those big pines."

Shaye turned. The ranch track became nothing but a ghost trail. She downshifted again and stayed in second.

"You know what August's going to think," Tanner added. "About you and me."

She watched the brush that seemed to leap out of the darkness. Sage scraped against the sides of the truck.

"He'll think whatever he wants to," she said.

God, I hope he's right, Tanner thought.

"Good thing this truck has high clearance," she said, slowing and downshifting into first as the truck crawled up and over a stone shelf that covered half the track.

"We could have walked, but you look tired and I know I am."

Needing to take his attention off her, he unwrapped his hand and examined it by flashlight, casually bracing himself as the truck bumped around.

"How is your hand?" she asked, not wanting to take her eyes off the miserable excuse for a road.

"I'll live."

"That's a relief. Yikes, those boulders—"

"Stop at the wide spot," he said, bracing himself on the dashboard as he slid toward her. "There's a path to the first pool."

"Good," she said, relieved, "because there sure isn't any more road."

She shut off the engine and turned off the lights.

He got out immediately because he didn't trust himself not to grab her. The bench seat of the truck had looked more inviting every instant. He took the chill air into his lungs and hoped it would settle to his crotch.

No such luck.

Overhead, the partial moon had outlasted the clouds. The stars looked close, sharp enough to cut. He had so many memories of them overhead as he curled up in his sleeping bag in the hayloft and dreamed of being a grown man.

Now he was.

His childhood memories were as bright as the stars, and as sharp-edged. He listened to the night and heard nothing unfamiliar, nothing threatening. He clicked on the flashlight and swept the ground ahead. The path to the pool was more overgrown than he remembered, but the boulders and pines hadn't changed any.

Shaye surprised him by pulling a thumb-size penlight from her jacket pocket and falling into line behind him.

"You didn't use that at Rua's," Tanner said, resettling the towels under his left arm.

"I was afraid to."

"Smart." He thought about adding that it would have been a lot smarter to stay put in the car as he had told her, but let it go. The scare she'd gotten was more than enough to make the point.

They walked in an easy silence until they reached the first pool.

"This one is only about ninety degrees," he said. "We jerry-rigged some plank seats for the next pool. It's about a hundred and two. The one above that is hot enough to cook trout and smells like the mineral stew it is."

"Lead me to the second one," she said quickly.

The idea of soaking was delicious.

The idea of having him next to her was hotter than the third pool.

She squashed the thought. She was too tired and too off balance to be thinking about sex, much less to follow through on it.

The second pool steamed gently in the moonlight, surrounded by rocks and tall pines.

Tanner left the towels on a boulder by the edge of the pool. Then he sat on another waterside rock and began pulling off his shoes and socks. With quick efficiency he stripped off his jacket and shirt, folded them, pulled the gun and holster from the small of his back, and stacked everything neatly on the ground.

"I've never gone in the springs wearing more than my skin," he said, standing and reaching for his belt. "It's one of the best things about being here."

She wasn't surprised, but she was intrigued. "Clothes or no clothes, no promises about anything else."

A deep laugh floated up as he peeled down his pants and underwear in a smooth motion. "Gotcha. No touching without an invitation. It goes both ways, you know."

"Damn," she said without thinking.

Thinking was the last thing on her mind. The shine of moonlight on his bare, muscular chest, the intriguing dark swirls of hair, the clean, strong line of his legs, and his obvious hunger for her made her breath back up in her throat. She had thought her ex-husband was beautifully made, but next to Tanner her ex was . . . insignificant.

"Both ways," she said, watching Tanner disappear into the pool a few inches at a time. Then, "You sure?"

"You already have your invitation," he said, sinking in up to his waist, then ribs, then his chest.

"I do?"

His head turned toward her. "Anytime. Anywhere."

"I see," she managed.

"Yeah, I'll bet you did."

She tried not to laugh, or at least not to let him hear it. But she was sure he could see her blush. Hastily she bent to undo her hiking shoes. Like him, she folded and stowed everything within reach. By the time she was down to her underwear, she was feeling the biting edge of chill in the air. Hurriedly she peeled everything off and walked to the pool.

"There's kind of a gravel path into the water," Tanner said. "Go about a foot to your left. Feel it?"

"Smooth but not slippery?"

"That's it."

The playful breeze raised gooseflesh on her skin. The hot pool was a gleaming lure promising warmth. It wasn't her first time in one of the many natural hot springs in the area, so she knew to walk carefully on the uneven bottom of the pool until she was almost hip-deep. Then she sank into the water and did a half float, half walk over the rocky bottom. The contrast between cold air and heated water made her take a ragged breath.

The pool became deep enough to swim in.

"You said something about benches?" she asked.

Tanner barely heard her. He was still seeing her careful, graceful entry into the pool. Her body was slender, lithe, and so female in its dips and curves that he was having a hard time breathing.

A hard time, period.

"Benches?" she reminded him.

"Come closer. You're in the deep end." His voice was too husky, but he didn't care. She'd already had an eyeful of just how much he wanted her.

"How deep?"

"Over your head."

"What about yours?" she asked.

"Depends on how well I keep my footing." He held out his hand to her.

She took it, letting him float her to the underwater bench.

"Splinters?"

"Nope. Lorne and Dad sanded it in the barn workshop. What they couldn't smooth out, the water has. Careful, though. It's wedged between two big boulders and they're rough on the skin."

"I'm surprised the plank hasn't washed away in a spring melt."

"The springs aren't a runoff channel," Tanner said, "so floods aren't a problem. Hot water bubbles to the surface, makes a chain of three pools, and drains back into the earth again. Probably seeps into the stream somewhere, but we've never found where."

Shaye settled lightly onto the plank, found a place to brace one foot so that she wouldn't float off—if she concentrated—and sighed. The silence was like a texture of the night, as endless and deep as the starry sky. Heat seeped into her, unraveling her. She closed her eyes and simply let herself be, until she was a part of the hot spring and the forest and the night.

Tanner watched her eyes close and her body relax. When she started to float away like moonlight on water, he gently captured her with his arm around her waist. She opened her eyes, smiled, and curled into him, wrapping her arms and legs around him, letting him anchor both of them. Then she sighed and let herself relax utterly.

He held her in return, ignoring the insistent ache of his erection. The peace she brought him was new, staggering. He didn't want to disturb it. For long, long minutes they sat in the pool, wrapped in hot water and each other.

An owl called softly. The sound was slow, rhythmic, the heartbeat of the forest given voice.

Finally, reluctantly, Tanner stirred against Shaye. "Time to go back. Too much more of this heat and we won't be able to crawl, much less walk."

She nodded. "I know. But this is . . . incredible. I didn't know how cold I'd become."

"Me, too."

She tightened her arms and snuggled closer. His erection lay taut between them. A heat that owed nothing to the pool bloomed through her. She had thought the pool had totally relaxed him, drawing out all the tension in his body.

She had been wrong.

"That doesn't feel cold to me," she said, rubbing against him.

She felt the involuntary leap of his flesh as it hardened even more. Deliberately, gently, she bit the muscular curve of his shoulder.

"You sure?" Tanner asked almost roughly, knowing how spent she had been.

"Yes."

"Hold that thought."

Without moving anything but one arm, Tanner fished a condom from his nearby jeans.

"Let me," she whispered.

He opened the packet and handed her the contents. When she fitted it to him with great care and attention, he thought he would come right there.

"Shaye," he said with a strangled sound.

"Right here."

She raised her head for his kiss, tangling her tongue languidly with his, then more deeply, urgently. When their mouths separated, their rapid breaths mingled with the twists of steam rising from the pool. Her tightly drawn nipples rubbed against him each time she drew in air.

"I wanted to go slow," he said. "I wanted to spread you out on a bed and taste you until you were screaming and clawing."

A shudder rippled through her. "I've never . . . God, Tanner. I want to do the same to you."

"Next time," he promised.

He lifted her and sucked on first one nipple, then the other, until she was twisting against him and making small sounds. His hand slid between her spread thighs and probed, testing and caressing, sliding deep into her clinging sheath, until her sounds became both pleas and demands.

She felt the broad, smooth head of his penis replace his fingers and tightened her hold on his shoulders until her nails dug in.

Tanner hissed between his clenched teeth. "Take me at your own pace, Shaye. I'm all yours."

Her eyes half opened, dark slices of night and desire. She eased down on him, retreated, returned a little deeper, retreated until it was more than the hot springs that made him sweat.

"You're a tease," he said hoarsely.

"You're bigger than I expected," she said, licking her lips. "I'm really enjoying it."

"Enjoy more of it."

She laughed and sank down slowly until he was locked in her so deeply she could feel his heartbeat inside her.

"Your turn," she breathed against his lips. "I'm all yours."

"I can feel that. You. Me. Us."

His voice became a low groan and then he began to move, measuring both of them again and again with increasing speed. His tension became hers until she was riding him as hard as he was riding her. She started to say his name, then lost her voice as everything flew apart in pulses of ecstasy that were neither hers nor his, but theirs.

TWENTY-FOUR

S HAYE AWOKE, FEELING both disoriented and safe. She was on her side in a bed, one bare leg over an equally bare male leg, her cheek on a man's smooth, muscular shoulder, and her arm around his lean and naked waist. Gradually she realized Tanner was as wrapped around her as she was around him. She sighed and enjoyed the simple intimacy, wondering when the last time was that she'd awakened to such peace. Or been so thoroughly satisfied by a man.

Then she realized that she never had.

Before she could get nervous about it, strong, tapering fingers gently counted down each vertebra in her spine, stroked her bottom, then slowly counted up her spine to her nape, caressing, and going back down, lingering at the curve of her hips.

"A woman could get used to waking up like this," she said, nuzzling closer, breathing in the scent of clean man.

"So could a man," he said. "How do you feel?"

"Fine, why?"

"It was a tight fit. Did I hurt you?"

He felt the blush that spread from her breasts to her face.

"Any sounds I made had nothing to do with pain," she muttered against his chest.

"You sure?"

"Trust me. I would know." She bit him on his shoulder with enough pressure to make her point.

He smiled and his fingers continued their journey down her spine, but this time they lingered in the shadow crease below her tailbone. His other hand slowly caressed the soft breast that was plumped up against his chest. The feel of her nipple drawing tight was lightning in his blood.

The telephone in the kitchen rang.

"Ignore it," he said. "I'm going to."

He shifted and brought her mouth to his. While the phone rang and rang, they enjoyed the kind of utterly lazy, exploring kiss that they'd been too impatient to have the night before. His biceps flexed and his body tightened. Without breaking the kiss, he pulled her up over him like the sweetest kind of blanket.

The phone in the kitchen stopped ringing.

The cell phone in his discarded jeans started clamoring.

"Who has both numbers?" Shaye asked against his mouth.

"No one."

"You wish."

"Yeah. I wish."

With one hand he groped on the floor next to the bed. Finally he fished the still-yammering phone from a pocket. The incoming call was local, but that was all he could tell. He answered the damn thing.

"What?" Tanner snarled.

"Hell of a way to answer the phone. This is—"

"Deputy August," Tanner said.

Shaye stiffened and began to slide off him. He held her in place with casual strength.

"How was Meyers last night?" the deputy asked easily.

"Who is Meyers?"

"Not who. Where. The town."

"It's barely after seven," Tanner said. "Is there a point to waking me up or do you just harass citizens at random?"

"I'm having breakfast at the Western Café at eight. You can join me there or you can see me at nine at the office. You'd rather eat breakfast. If Shaye happens to be handy," he added sardonically, "bring her. It will save time."

August hung up.

Tanner stared at the phone, thinking like a homicide cop—hard, fast, and mean.

"What is it?"

"Deputy August wants company for breakfast at the Western Café at eight or I can talk to him at the sheriff's office at nine. He recommends breakfast. He said it would save time if I brought you."

She blinked. "Really."

"Yeah, that's what I thought. Remember what we did yesterday?"

"Computer search, grubby pawnshop, fancy pawnshop, Rua's name, ate at the rib joint, came back here, soaked in hot springs, and crashed. Plan on talking to Rua today, after we find out what August might know."

Tanner's grin was as hard as his eyes. "Short and simple. If August tries to make it complex, you don't remember. Got it?"

"Sweetie, I was so lost in your midnight-sapphire eyes I didn't remember my middle name."

He laughed so hard she nearly fell off his chest.

"I can't wait to see August's face when you hand him that one," he said.

As Tanner and Shaye drove down the east face of the Sierras, slanting sunlight filled Refuge valley.

"Beautiful," he said, as if seeing it for the first time.

The fields gleamed bright green and every pond and irrigation ditch looked like liquid diamonds. Beyond the settlements and pastures, the sagebrush and mountains fell away in shades of silvery gray and navy blue. Clouds cast an ever-changing patchwork of dark, silky shadows.

"If we had time, I'd pull over and just enjoy the view," he added. *And you. Last night was barely an appetizer.* "But if we had that kind of time, we'd be back in bed and I'd be so deep inside you we'd both scream."

"I thought you liked the way I tickled your fancy."

"That wasn't a tickle, honey, it was a full-on, full-length squeeze. And I can't wait to do it again."

Shaye felt heat liquefy her. "Change the subject or I'll have to go back and change my underwear."

"Don't say things like that when I'm driving."

"Pot, kettle."

"If you stick out that sweet tongue at me, I'll take it as an invitation to get naked right now."

She looked at her watch and said reluctantly, "We're late as it is."

"What else is August going to do but wait for us?"

"Start on his pork chops or chicken-fried steak."

"I'd rather start on you. And finish." His breath hissed out in a curse and he did the smart thing—changed the subject. "Is the food where we're eating any good?"

"Don't know about the chops, but the chicken-fried steak with country gravy is awesome. None of this frozen, pre-breaded hamburger garbage. They make their own from scratch, including pounding flour and seasonings into the round steak until it's tender."

Tanner's mouth watered. He realized that he was hungrier than he'd been in a long time. "Steak it is."

The café wasn't big, and looked even smaller with its dark wood paneling and cast-iron light fixtures shaped like wagon wheels. Photos of several generations of western actors hung everywhere in sight. Many were signed. Despite the photos and movie posters, there was no attempt at glitz. Like the West itself, the café was what it was.

The early-morning rush had already come and gone, and the breakfast-at-leisure folks weren't quite ready to venture out yet. All of the patrons looked like they worked and lived locally.

A waitress—and they were waitresses here, not servers—led them to August's table, which was next to the back door so that he could make a fast exit without disturbing the other patrons. John Wayne stared down at the booth, young and radiating the quality that had made him a star.

August radiated the mood of a man with a rock in his boot.

Having delivered her two charges, the first waitress went back to chat with the patrons at the counter. They were old enough to be her father or grandfather, and she obviously enjoyed their company, smiling and swapping jokes.

Tanner and Shaye took the same side of the booth.

"Here y'are, Deputy," a different waitress said as she slid a steaming plate of pork chops and eggs in front of August. "Gravy on the side just like you like it."

"Thank you, Darla," he said.

"Can I get you two anything?" the waitress asked.

Tanner summed up the woman as automatically as he had summed up the café and its patrons. She was around thirty-five, pretty in a lean sort of way, like many of her generation who were raised on ranches.

"Two coffees and two orders of chicken-fried steak," Shaye said.

"Sure you don't want to split an order? They're big."

"No problem," Shaye said. "If he can't eat all of his, I'll help him."

Tanner snickered.

August shook his head.

Smiling, the waitress poured two more cups of coffee and left.

"I shouldn't be seen taking my breakfast with you two," he said, reaching for his knife and fork. "Well, at least one of you."

"And I have strong feelings about you," Tanner said. "Yet here we are."

"Yeah." August sawed off a chunk of pork, dipped it in the gravy, chewed with obvious pleasure, and swallowed. "Sheriff won't be here anytime soon."

"And the staff will alert you if he comes into the parking lot," Tanner said.

"You don't miss much, do you?"

"Only my mama's cooking."

August looked at Shaye. "Never figured you for the type to hook up so quick with a clown."

"Aw, how sweet of you to notice," she said. "Is that why you wanted to see us this morning? Or did you want all the juicy deets about how we spent the night?"

Under the table, Tanner's hand clamped on her thigh. Hard.

"Get to the point, August," he said.

The deputy smiled faintly. "Your lady sure has a mouth on her."

"And he loves every bit of it," she assured the deputy.

Tanner's hand tightened on her leg as he said, "You wanted to talk, August. Talk."

TWENTY-FIVE

THE DEPUTY SLICED off a neat strip of chop and ladled gravy over it. "Was there frost up in Meyers last night?"

"What is this fixation with Meyers?" Tanner asked.

August chewed, swallowed. "They always get frost before we do. I just wanted to know if we're due."

"Try one of the online weather sites," Tanner suggested.

"How much did Tony Rua tell you?" August asked, watching him over the rim of his coffee mug.

Shaye didn't need Tanner's fingers squeezing her thigh to know to keep her smart mouth shut.

"I've never talked to Antonio Rua in my life," Tanner said easily.

"But you know who he is."

"Yeah. He's the mook who sold some gold coins to Brilliant Moments."

"If you thought he stole from Lorne, you should have told me," August said flatly.

"Unless and until I prove it, talking is a waste of your time and mine. The sheriff just flat doesn't want to know."

Shaye sipped coffee and hoped her face didn't show how glad she was not to be the one the deputy was grilling for breakfast.

"Is that why you went to see Rua last night?" August asked.

"Who said I did?" Tanner asked.

The waitress returned with impressive speed, carrying two platters. Tanner would bet the fast service was a tribute to the deputy's presence, especially because patrons who had been seated earlier still were looking hopefully toward the kitchen. August must eat here often and tip well.

Shaye took one look at the food and decided she would be too busy eating to talk. She grabbed a knife and fork and focused on breakfast.

Tanner was already cutting and chewing with the same easy, impressive speed he had showed at the rib place.

August smiled a faint, hard-edged smile. "Saved by the breakfast bell."

Tanner ignored him.

So did Shaye.

The deputy began eating his breakfast with the same neat speed that Tanner had. Shaye decided it must come with the badge. Both men finished at about the same moment, leaving her to eat in peace.

"I'm here on my own time," August said, wiping his mouth with his napkin. "The sheriff doesn't care about much more than the shine on his badge and his boots. Usually I try to do the same."

"Wish I'd learned to be that smart," Tanner said.

"Yeah, I'll bet you do. Your new captain sounds like a real prick."

Startled, Shaye looked at Tanner.

"Nobody likes to gossip more than cops," he said to August. "Are you here to talk shop with me?"

"I'm here because somebody put three bullets into Tony Rua last night."

Shaye's head snapped up from breakfast.

Tanner was relieved she was staring at the deputy, not him.

"Damn, that's going to make it hard to talk to him," Tanner said, shaking his head.

"Real hard. He's in the morgue."

"Huh." Tanner settled back and waited.

Shaye chewed and swallowed and chewed and swallowed. Her appetite had taken a hit, but she needed fuel. She and Tanner had spent more time discovering each other than sleeping.

She couldn't wait to discover more. She hadn't had any idea of what she'd been missing in the sex department.

"That all you have to say?" August asked mildly.

Tanner sipped coffee. And never took his eyes off Nathan August.

The deputy glanced around, saw that no one was close enough to overhear, and began talking in a low voice. "Most of the time I can go along and get along with the sheriff, because there's no real crime worth mentioning. We roust drunks, make life hard on drug dealers and petty thieves, keep the sidewalks clean, and keep the citizens happy."

Tanner nodded, watching the other man.

"But murder pisses me off," August said. "Your uncle and Rua and the gold coins just keep sticking in my throat."

"I hear you," Tanner said, and meant it. "Who found Rua? And where? Was it a bar fight?"

"It was a cold call to the Tahoe cops. Rua was murdered in his home in Meyers. Were the coins he sold your uncle's?"

"They were the same type as the ones that were gone from the family hidey-hole. That's all I know for sure."

"If you're telling the truth, whoever called was probably the murderer," August said.

"Yeah. Try convincing your boss," Tanner said.

"I'm not dumb enough to take on hell with a cup of water. I need at least a garden hose." August finished his coffee and set it very carefully on the table, like a man who wanted to slam it down instead. "Look. I always figured Lorne might have been murdered. I just couldn't figure out how, much less why."

"It wasn't for the gold," Tanner said. "Nobody knew about the hidey-hole except family."

August grunted. "You're not helping me. I was hoping that Rua was good for Lorne's murder and gold was the motive. Now I've got squat. And you should be grateful the sheriff isn't interested. If someone—like the local press or power structure—leans on him, sure as shit he'll make a connection between you and Rua and mistake a simple solution for a real solution."

"What do you mean?" Shaye asked, pushing her plate away.

"Your new buddy," August said to her, "had reason to be looking for stolen coins. Ace—remember him?"

"Yes," she said impatiently. "We spoke to him yesterday."

"Figured. Ace keeps the sheriff in the loop when it comes to bad actors circulating in town. Rua's face turned up on the fax this morning as a possible receiver of stolen goods, or possibly the thief himself. If and when the sheriff is forced to connect the dots, he'll do some damn fool thing like arrest your new friend on suspicion of murder and hold you as a material witness, or worse. You two went to see Rua last night, didn't you?"

"Sounds like I should call my lawyer," Tanner said before she could speak.

"If I thought you did Rua, I'd have you cuffed and in the tank. But I'm not connecting any dots for the sheriff. As long as things stay uncomplicated, my boss won't be interested in you for anything other than being a pain in the ass."

"Your boss and my boss would love each other."

"Oh, we know all about KISS, even out here in the sticks," August said drily. "Just like I know you didn't mean to knock my brother's teeth loose when you laid him out after football practice."

"What?" Tanner asked, wondering if he had heard right. His football career in high school had been short, mostly due to his having moved soon into it. But there was that one fight . . .

August put a hand up. "Don't strain yourself. My mama was married to a different man back then and she took her own name back. You'd have known my brother as William Stewart."

"You've done some homework."

August smiled slightly. "Willie had it coming. Hell, I wanted to shake your hand after the game. My mama told him, 'Now you've gotten your bell rung, maybe you'll learn you aren't so tough and shape up.' I looked you up in the yearbook after you stopped by yesterday. Thought it might've been you, but now I'm sure."

The waitress came with more coffee, putting a hole in the conversation. When she moved back down the aisle, August started talking again.

"I'm also sure that if I'd had family killed, I'd want to know why," he said to Tanner. "You say it wasn't the gold. Was anything else missing? Did the place look like it had been searched?"

Tanner shook his head. "Not so far as I can tell. Lorne didn't have much to take."

"Shame that guy who was selling the coins can't talk. Wonder what he'd have to say."

"He'd probably have lawyered up and shut up," Shaye said, swallowing the last bite of her breakfast. "Or he'd have kicked a hole in the door and run. I did a fast Google-stalk after my shower this morning. Rua was one of those UFC fighters. Or he wanted to be. The best he did was undercard status, whatever that means."

"Second string," Tanner said. "As for the coins, I found one in a pathetic pawnshop on the California side of Tahoe. You might get something useful if you squeeze the old lady who runs it, but I doubt it. We already have Rua. And I have feelers out."

August said, "California isn't my jurisdiction. But Rua's fight background explains the Ground and Pound."

"What's that?" she asked.

"A hangout for the aspiring fighters."

"That wasn't on Google," Shaye said. "He won nine fights and lost ten. And there was a line about being a regular on the small-casino fight circuit."

"Hard way to make a living," August said. "You don't get paid much for getting the hell beat out of you for a small crowd of drunken gamblers."

"This is a Mongolian goat-roping," Tanner said in disgust. "A lot of people might want to get even with a small-time tough guy."

"Smile," August said. "That's the good news. The bad news is that once California's El Dorado County Sheriff runs out of suspects, he's going to ask for help from Refuge County."

"Given how close Meyers is to the state border," Tanner said, "I'm surprised they haven't been talking to you already."

"Oh, they have. But their sheriff is like ours—a problem won't become a *problem* until the easy explanations are all burned up. I've got friends up there who told me about Rua's murder, but it won't be too long before someone who cares takes a good look at this, and you two. Ace sends his casino alerts to Meyers cops, because it's a downscale place for those folks who tend to play and prey on the Nevada side."

"If that happens, it would help to have a friend in Nevada with a badge," Tanner said.

"I'll do what I can. In the meantime, you might want to check out that gym in person. It's off Highway 395. Stubby Jasper runs the place, ex-fighter. Might be a good source. Just a suggestion."

"Thanks, I'll—"

"We'll," Shaye cut in.

Tanner started to argue, knew he would lose, and shut up. The idea of leaving her by herself bothered him on too many levels. Lorne had been alone. Rua had been alone.

And then they were dead.

August's smile was as big as a breakfast platter. "Let me know if anything useful turns up, Ms. Townsend. You've got a twist on the L.A. cop that I don't want to have."

Tanner ignored them, took money out of his wallet, and tucked it under the edge of his coffee mug.

"You keep paying for my food and you'll go broke," Shaye said. "I'm not a dainty eater."

"I'll take it out of your silky hide. Every last calorie. Excuse us, Deputy, we have a gym to visit."

With a faint smile, August said, "My money is on the lady." Then the smile faded and he said in a low voice, "While you're out kicking over beehives, be damned careful. Shaye, you might want to swallow your modern-woman routine and stay home. Safer that way."

She started to give him the cutting edge of her tongue.

"No," the deputy said. "Two people are dead. All it takes is a bullet to make it three. Think about it."

"I already have," Tanner said.

"I wasn't talking to you." August gave her a level gaze. "Stay alive. Stay home."

"Did Rua live alone?" Shaye asked.

"Yes."

"Sounds like staying home alone can be deadly."

August looked at Tanner, but there was no help there.

"Damn it," the deputy said under his breath. Then, to Tanner, "She gets hurt and I'll skin you out like a coyote."

"If she gets hurt, it means I'm already dead."

TWENTY-SIX

THE GROUND & POUND gym sulked in the corner of a mostly abandoned strip mall, notable only for its swath of dirty white stucco and black glass windows. A ragged assortment of pickup trucks beaten into varying colors of submission by dirt and sun were parked out front. Lorne's truck looked right at home.

A glossy white Lexus LS stood out like a coonhound in a cat show. The license plate read STUBBY.

"Looks like the boss is in," Shaye said.

"You could wait in the truck," Tanner said.

"I thought we'd settled this. Twice."

"The deputy is right. This isn't a game."

"And we begin one more lap around the track," she said. "Even if you didn't need me for my local connections, I'm safer with you than I am driving lonesome back roads and talking to ranchers, which is what Kimberli will have me doing the instant I'm not with you. Whoever the killer is, he or she prefers victims one at a time."

Tanner wanted to argue, but Shaye was right.

"From now on," he said, "if I tell you to jump, hide, or shut up, promise me you'll do it."

It was her turn to want to argue and discover herself holding the losing hand. "As long as we're together, fine."

That was less than he had asked for and more than he had expected. She was smart and independent, and had guts. Taking orders like a recruit wasn't her specialty.

"Unless the guys inside that gym go all gooey and helpful at the sight of a pretty woman," he said, "I'll do the talking."

She nodded.

"August would like there to be something between you and him," Tanner said.

She blinked at the sudden change of subject. "There isn't. Not like you mean."

"Good. I don't make a habit of jumping into bed with any female I meet, and after the way we fit together, I'm damn well sure you don't sleep around."

She ignored her blush and said, "So?"

"You're an independent woman, I get that. But all the same, I want whatever we have to be exclusive."

"You're bossy. I'm independent." She unfastened her seat belt. "But the fringe benefits are spectacular. So, yes, whatever we have for as long as it lasts, exclusive."

That hadn't come out the way Tanner had meant, but it would have to do for now. "Okay. I'm not very good with words . . ." He pulled her across the bench seat and kissed her until her hands went to his shirt buttons. "But I sure do know what I like. You."

"If you 'like' me any more right now, we're going to be arrested for lewd acts in public."

"Mmm, lewd acts," he said, savoring the words like a fine wine. "Does that mean getting naked, hands on, and mouths, and—"

The truck's passenger door opened and closed, hard, on his speculations. Smiling, he got out and followed her inside.

Beyond the front door, Ground & Pound was loud and sweaty, with an open floor plan broken up by support beams and movable wall panels for private instruction. The center of the big room was dominated by an octagonal ring that was nearly thirty feet across. Eight chain-link fences, taller than an NBA player, surrounded the octagon. The junctions were padded in battered plasticized canvas.

It looked like child-safety equipment made for monsters.

As pairs of men grappled with each other, the sound of grunts and meat slamming into meat thickened the air. A lot of the fighters had shaved heads. All of them were naked but for trunks and boots, which resembled the fancy padded Reeboks that had been in style when Tanner had gone to high school. They looked more silly than impressive.

Nobody smiled or joked. The Ground & Pound wasn't for laughs. It was a grim, sweaty path to fame and riches. Or so the occupants hoped. Everyone was looking for a golden ticket out of dead-end physical jobs. All the men were solid muscle, burning so fiercely for their shot at the big time that they gave off more heat than the air-conditioning could handle.

"Holy Toledo, as my grandmother used to say." Shaye spoke so that only Tanner could hear. "Some of these guys are riding a wave of desperation that's going to break and send them facedown into despair."

"Good enough to hope, not nearly good enough to achieve," Tanner agreed. He had seen plenty of gyms like this in L.A.

"No wonder they're so serious. They're trying to put off failure every time they breathe."

"Steak-heads. And Rua was one of them."

The man behind the counter looked like he'd been shaved out of granite that was the color of brown skin. His mouth was a thin curve of unhappiness and his black hair was cut down to a skullcap. He didn't smile when he saw them.

Shaye took one look and knew Tanner would do better with the man than she would. Women weren't as strong as men, and the meat behind the counter was only interested in strength.

"Tag, you're it," she said in a low voice.

Tanner wasn't surprised.

"Looking for something?" the man asked. His tone said he didn't care.

Tanner put his hands on the counter before him and leaned into the man's face. "A dude called Stubby."

"Mr. Stubbs doesn't see walk-ins."

"I'm not here for training. Got that covered." He smiled his cop smile, cold and uninterested.

"He's not here."

"You just said he didn't see walk-ins, which is like saying he's here but you don't want to help us. Too bad. Stubby wants to see us."

Shaye put a hand over her mouth and coughed rather than laughing out loud.

The man's skull turned purple underneath the short pelt of hair. "What do you want?"

"Antonio Rua. He trains here."

"Tony hasn't been around in days," the man said sourly. "Lazy bastard."

"Then Stubby must have a hole in his schedule. We'll help him fill it up."

The man scowled, but was smart enough to know that Tanner wasn't the least bit intimidated. He just had the kind of patience that wasn't going anywhere until he got what he wanted, and a confidence that said he didn't have to prove himself to anyone.

"Wait here. The fighters don't like to be bothered."

"Yeah, I could feel the love all the way from the parking lot," Tanner said.

She coughed again.

"You need some water, honey?" Tanner asked. "I'm sure the receptionist could find some."

She shook her head and tried to squash her laughter. It shouldn't have been so funny, but watching Tanner casually face down the gym's tough guy amused her. Tanner didn't bluster or posture or yell, he simply, calmly knew he would win if it came to a throw-down.

So did the "receptionist." He turned on his heel and stomped off into the center of the sweat and noise.

"It's a good thing I've already decided that I like you," she said with a voice that loosened his knees. "You can be a donkey, but you're very hard to pin the tail on."

"Rent real estate in your opponent's head, take them off their game." He shrugged. "Same reason ass-poking and crotch-gouging are used in these fights. It's not the pain, it's the shame."

"I didn't know you fought."

He shook his head slightly as he glanced around the ersatz dojo. "Not like this. The people I take on are fighting for their lives. These guys are tough in the sense that they can absorb pain. The ones who make the big time can give and take a whole lot of hurt and be smart at the same time. It's a real scarce combination."

"That's what I keep telling these dumb sacks of meat," a man said as he walked up. "The ones who get it move on to the next rung of the fight card, and the next, until they find someone smarter or tougher than they are."

"Mr. Stubbs?" Shaye guessed.

Stubbs didn't live up to his name. He was nearly as tall as Tanner and probably had twenty pounds on him. He was too old to be active in the fight game, but still in shape. His T-shirt had ripped-out sleeves because they didn't fit around his biceps. His chest looked like a well-cut sculpture. His thighs bulged beneath his faded jeans.

"Yeah, I'm Stubbs." He looked at Tanner. "Is there a problem?"

"We're trying to learn a bit more about a guy, Antonio Rua. People call him Tonio or Tony. He trains here."

"Name's familiar," Stubbs said.

"No surprise. He's enough of a regular that your receptionist missed him after only a few days."

The boss gave the counter steak-head an unhappy look before concentrating on the unwanted guests. "Let's talk in my office, Mr.—"

"Detective Tanner Davis."

Stubbs didn't ask for a badge.

Tanner didn't offer one.

Shaye felt invisible, so figured no one would notice if she followed along quietly behind them.

As they wound through the gym, Stubbs pointed out the brightest prospects, pretty much ignoring the guys who'd never be more than glorified practice dummies. Tanner was more interested in Stubbs's information about Rua than hearing about the rest of the clients, but he nodded in the right places.

She ghosted behind, treading water in a testosterone sea. The place was cleaner than she had expected, with the sharp scents of bleach-based disinfectants, male musk, and a hint of copper, which she realized must be fresh blood. More than one of the men she passed had a face like a fright mask.

"Occupational hazard," Stubbs said, following her glance. "Even the best bleed here."

"How good was Rua?" Shaye asked.

"At this gym he was close to the top. Little on the short side, but he made up for lack of reach by being able to eat pain like some guys down six-packs. Not that I encourage anyone training here to drink."

"But he hasn't been here for a while?" Tanner asked.

There was a meaty smack and a clang of chain link as a fighter was thrown against the barrier.

"Hey!" Stubbs yelled. "You save that for Saturdays!"

Shaye winced. The man had a voice like a jet engine.

"Some of these guys have a lot to prove," Stubbs said, shaking his head. "They get overexcited."

"Take shortcuts?" Tanner asked in a voice far more lazy than his eyes.

Without looking away from the fighter peeling himself off the chain link, Stubbs shook his head. When he was satisfied that there was no meaningful damage to the fence or the fighter, he gave his attention to his guests again.

"No. I run a clean shop here. No drugs. No juice. No payoffs." He counted off the infractions on his meaty fingers. "I find otherwise, I kick 'em to the curb." The fingers became a fist.

"You could be putting human growth hormone in the watercooler and pumping steroids in the air—I don't care," Tanner said. "We just want to know about Rua."

Stubbs measured the other man, then nodded and led them to his office, which was set off from the gym by a waist-high wall of concrete blocks. A few filing cabinets, a phone, a copier, an old computer, a small desk, and some stacked metal folding chairs occupied most of the space. Stubbs sat behind the desk, where he could still see out over the gym.

Tanner grabbed two folding chairs and pulled them up to the side of the desk. As he and Shaye sat down, Stubbs started talking.

"Rua might have gone places. He was one of the best of the lot here and had caught some Reno gigs. And he looked real good cleaned up. That's an important part of the game, too—not looking like a mutt on cable TV. About a week ago, he cleared out his locker and quit the gym."

"Why?" Tanner asked.

Stubbs shrugged and spoke with genuine regret. "He outgrew me. He came in, told me he had the deal, and left."

"That happen often?"

"It's the dream of every fighter out there. The good ones move on. The rest hang on."

"What is 'the deal'?" Shaye asked quietly.

For a moment Stubbs studied something out in the big ring, then he nodded and turned back to the conversation. "We're all nothing until the day we get the deal that makes us something."

"And Rua got the deal," Tanner said.

Stubbs nodded. "He sure thought so. He was talking about breaking out of the casino circuit and getting second bill on big matches." He flicked his hand at the gym beyond. "Most of those guys won't even make undercard material. They might lie to themselves, but they can't lie to me."

"Was Rua really that good? Or did someone die and leave him a pile of money?" Tanner asked.

Stubbs gave a rusty laugh. "At this level, money doesn't win fights. Determination, muscle, and guts do. Undercard status and a good manager—and a sponsor—are the next step up. That's where Rua is going. He likes fighting a lot better than his day gig supervising a bunch of Mexicans on construction sites."

"Did you manage Rua?" Tanner asked, wondering if Stubbs cared enough to shoot the man who got away.

"I did what I could, but I have a couple hundred guys in and out of the gym every month."

"Did he mention a new manager or sponsor?" Tanner asked.

"I got the feeling he was going to Reno. A new job."

"Did he say where he was going to train?"

Stubbs barked out a laugh. "That would be like telling your girl-friend that you have a piece on the side and like the piece better than her and you're moving out."

Shaye could only nod. Stubbs had just described how her marriage had ended.

"What kind of a job did Rua get?" Tanner asked.

"Security detail for some politician's personal appearances. Holden or Mills or someone—I don't really keep up unless I have to play nice with the licensing agencies. If you run a bar or a gym, being a sweet-heart doesn't get the job done."

"Do you mean Hill?" Shaye asked.

"Yeah." Stubbs snapped his thick fingers. "That was the name. Isn't he running for county board or something?"

"Governor, actually," she said.

Stubbs grunted. "No wonder Rua looked so happy." He gave Tanner a long look. "You have a badge and a lot of questions about Rua. He in trouble?"

"Not anymore. He's dead."

Stubbs shook his head sadly. "Head injury?"

"Bullets," Tanner said.

"Well, shit."

Shaye thought that pretty much summed it up.

TWENTY-SEVEN

T ANNER DROVE TOWARD Carson City while Shaye talked on
her cell phone, working her way through underlings until she got
one who admitted to having access to Harold Hill, the gubernatorial
hopeful. The man who, according to Kimberli and the odds makers in
Las Vegas, was very likely to get the office of his dreams.

Make that the stepping-stone on the way to his dreams, Shaye
thought.

The idea of a pretty face and empty head in the Oval Office made
her wonder how often it had happened in the past. It was an open secret
that Hill had his eye on the presidency and plenty of moneyed backers
who were just waiting for him to get seasoned in the governor's office
until the next national election.

Thinking about Hill and his hoped-for future made her shake her
head, but it was better than the deputy's words echoing in head.

Stay alive. Stay home.

She could have done without August's reminder of the two corpses she'd recently seen. Or how much she wanted to live to enjoy one very alive man.

"Yes, I'm still here," she said into the phone. "Really, you don't have to bother Mr. Hill. I just need to know who handles the staffing on his security detail."

"I'm sorry. Nothing about Mr. Hill's security arrangements is available to the public," the aide said. "However, Mr. Hill has five minutes between engagements late this morning, if you would like to talk to him personally. He has a keen appreciation of all the good work the Conservancy has done for the state of Nevada."

She resigned herself to waiting around for a little face time with Harold Hill. "Should my guest and I sign in at the front desk?"

"Yes, please. You'll receive badges and an escort there. Now, if you'll excuse me, I have several calls waiting."

"Thanks for your help." She was talking to herself.

"Any luck?" Tanner asked. "Sounds like Mr. Hill was very busy shaking hands, or shaking down donors."

"Same difference," she said, putting her phone back in her jacket pocket. "No one will talk about security, so we have to ask the man himself."

"I'd have been surprised if the future governor's security staff was any other way. Frankly, I'm impressed you had the juice to get us in at all. I was going to ask a friend to do some not-quite-legal hacking."

"Would this be the same one who discovered the coins for you?"

"That was legal." He glanced in the rearview and side mirrors. No takers yet. "Thanks for getting through to Hill."

"The National Ranch Conservancy backs candidates who share its views," she said. "One of them is Harold Hill."

"Interesting. How does it feel to work for a kingmaker?"

"Kimberli is too busy putting on mascara and attracting donations to have much time left for making kings. But from what she's said, Hill is one of the Conservancy's favorite politicians, which makes him a big deal for her."

"Can't fire a gun in the desert without hitting an interest group," Tanner said wryly. "When do we see Hill?"

"Before noon, if we're lucky. But we have to be there on *your* best behavior and wait until he has a free moment between meetings."

"Does that mean no waiting-room sex?"

She gave him a sideways look and bit back a smile. "None. But thinking about it should help pass the time."

"Thinking about it will make me wish I had a hat to put on my lap."

She was still smiling when they hit the security at the main door and showed ID. An underling led them to one of the several private offices reserved for people who had appointments to see Hill. The chairs were okay, the coffee was drinkable, and the selection of magazines numbing. The muted TV in one corner didn't offer relief.

It was almost one o'clock before Hill was available. Shaye had plenty of time to remind Tanner to smile and be pleasant, rather than acting like he was grilling a suspect with white lights and a black attitude.

Mr. Hill strode in with the vigor that was his trademark almost as much as his charismatic smile. He was the best of the past and the promise of a bright future rolled into a sharp gray suit with silver buttons on his cuffs and jacket front. When he looked at someone, they were the only person in his world.

I was too tired to appreciate him at the "memorial," Tanner realized. He's good. I'll bet he can change course to pick up every political breeze and explain any change of direction with a handshake and a smile.

He makes the mayor of L.A. look like a three-legged dog in a greyhound race.

"Shaye, I'm so glad you dropped by," Hill said. He signaled informality by unbuttoning his suit coat and giving her a warm handshake. "I was just going to ask the Conservancy for advice on building up a policy with regard to keeping ranchers in the valley."

"I'm sure Kimberli will be happy to help in any way she can," Shaye said. "This is Tanner Davis, nephew of Lorne Davis. You probably met at the Conservancy gala, but you meet so many thousands of people, I figure it doesn't hurt to introduce both of you again."

"Mr. Davis," Hill said. As he turned toward Tanner, his suit coat opened enough to show two cell phones. One was dark, flashy, and expensive. One was a muddy shade of blue and cheap.

Tanner thought of the sheriff and wondered if the men used the cheap phone when out getting votes from the common man.

"My condolences on your uncle," Hill said. "He was a good, respected man."

"Thank you," Tanner said politely.

An aide tapped on the open door. Hill looked over.

"A moment, Rowan," he said. "Surely it can wait while I talk to my friends?"

"Yes, sir," the young woman said as she shut the door.

"Sorry," Hill said to them. "My staff is told to keep me on time. I have a meeting with one of the president's economists. We're going to put our heads together and find an environmentally sound solution for the high unemployment rate that is dogging our state. That's what's important—jobs and the environment."

Tanner nodded, and knew that if Hill had been talking to another interest group, he would insert their cause in the place of the environment. Not sleazy, just political savvy. Everyone wanted to feel important.

Hill and my captain would trip over their own shoes trying to kiss ass first, last, and best, Tanner thought. *Wish I could learn the knack.*

Or even want to.

"Jobs are important," Tanner said. "Hard to live without them."

"A man of intelligence," Hill approved. "I have many plans for the state, and Refuge in particular, but I need to ensure that the government only promotes and doesn't interfere too heavily."

The aide knocked again, lightly, and didn't open the door.

"Blast," Hill muttered. "I'm sorry, Shaye, Mr. Davis, but my aide said that you needed some information about security?"

"Are you familiar with a man called Antonio 'Tony' Rua?" Shaye asked.

Hill looked blank. "Forgive me, I meet so many people. Rua . . . Rua." He shook his head.

"He was recently hired in connection with your security," she said.

"Oh. That explains it. Rhonda handles security staffing. Has there been a problem?"

"Nothing major," Shaye said. "Could you clear it for us to talk to Rhonda?"

Hill frowned. "This is rather odd."

"Rua was murdered last night in Meyers," Tanner said calmly. "The Conservancy would hate to see some eager reporter slime your campaign by connecting the two of you. There would be nothing to it, of course, but headlines are headlines."

Shaye couldn't believe what she had just heard. This was Tanner's idea of being *nice*?

"What my associate means," she said, smiling, "is that we're trying to find out the relationship between you and a member of your security detail. Unfortunately there is evidence to suggest a connection between him and a recent crime."

Hill smiled. "I have to say, I'd been having a terrible day before this. But this . . ." He struggled not to laugh. "This is rich. Where are your little cameras—you're recording this, right?"

"Um, no cameras," she said, trying to think of a tactful way to tell Hill there was no joke, either.

"Where are you from, Mr. Davis?" Hill asked with a snicker.

"Los Angeles."

"Gotta love that California sense of humor. Not everyone appreciates it, but I enjoy a joke, even at my own expense."

"Does Rhonda have a sense of humor?" Tanner asked easily. "Or do you do the final security-staff hiring yourself?"

Hill laughed again. "That's like asking me if I hire the gardeners. I do love the innocence of a citizen when it comes to the complexities of politics. I encourage my staff to hire locally when the skill set and talent allow. After that, it's up to individual department heads." He gave Tanner a smile. "If you're looking for a job, I'll put you in touch with Rhonda. You certainly look fit enough for security work. I'll have to warn her about your sense of humor, though."

Tanner smiled back. "I'd like that. Working for someone with a sense of humor would be a happy change. But that still leaves you with a murdered man on your security staff who is under suspicion of receiving stolen goods."

Hill frowned at the unwelcome reminder.

Tanner wasn't surprised. He had a knack for irritating important people.

"I'm sure there's no real problem," Shaye said, touching Hill's arm. "Rhonda will sort it out, if you give her permission."

After a moment of uneasiness, Hill's face settled into its usual smile. "Yes, Rhonda. No problem." He turned his head to the side and called out, "Rowan!"

The aide popped open the door like she'd been praying for the summons. "Yes, sir."

"Take my guests to see Rhonda."

"Of course, sir. The representative from—"

"In a few moments," Hill interrupted her. "I'm expecting a call on my private line. I'll let you know when I'm available. Shaye, I'm sorry this was so brief. Again, Mr. Davis, my condolences."

"Please come with me," the aide said. "Ms. Spears just returned from lunch."

Shaye envied her. Breakfast was a savory memory.

And Tanner looked good enough to eat.

Again.

TWENTY-EIGHT

RHONDA SPEARS WAS aptly named. She looked like she could cut steel with her fingernails.

"What is this nonsense about my staff and murder?" she asked.

That told Tanner the security staff had Hill's private offices wired for sound and probably cameras as well. Good idea, as long as you deleted the data daily, if not more often.

"One of your recent hires was murdered in Meyers last night," Tanner said. "He is connected to another murder as well. Antonio Rua isn't the kind of man you want connected with the future governor. What made you hire him?"

"You're talking about Tony Rua?" Rhonda asked.

Tanner nodded.

She opened up some kind of PDA, entered a few words, and read the file. "No wants, no warrants, no arrests, no jail time, no outstanding bills worth mentioning, excellent ratings in unarmed combat, good rating with a pistol, licensed to carry, tested negative for drugs." She looked up. "I don't see the problem."

"Is Mr. Hill expanding his security staff?" Shaye asked before Tanner could point out the obvious—murder was a problem.

"Not at this time. If the odds in Hill's favor go up several more points, we'll hire."

"But you hired Rua recently. Was there an unexpected opening on your staff?" Shaye asked.

"We get recommendations and requests from backers," the other woman said, shrugging. "If possible, we accommodate them."

"Who recommended or requested Rua be hired?" Tanner asked.

Rhonda hesitated, her manner plainly saying that if Hill hadn't cleared it, she wouldn't be giving out the information. After a moment she scanned through the file until she found the notation she was looking for.

"Jonathan Campbell," she said. Her attitude said she was out of patience.

Tanner would like to have used the Rhonda-Hill connection to get in to see Campbell, who was no doubt as busy as every other mover and shaker they'd cornered today. But he knew when he'd worn out his welcome.

Shaye had known before they ever got to Rhonda.

"Thank you for your time," Shaye said. "I'm sure Mr. Hill's lead in the race will have you out hiring more staff in no time. The Conservancy very much appreciates his support."

The subtle reminder that Shaye represented one of Mr. Hill's significant supporters put a smile on Rhonda's face. "You're welcome. Mr. Hill has great personal and professional admiration for the Conservancy."

Silently, Tanner and Shaye walked back through the building, discreetly watched by a member of security.

The instant they were alone in the truck, she said coolly, "May I remind you that I have to work in this valley when you're gone? The more wells you poison, the harder it will be for me to live."

He started the truck and drove onto the highway, thinking carefully about his answer. She was mad enough to skin him out and clean toilets with his hide.

And he wasn't as eager to get back to L.A. as he should have been. The night with Shaye had only sharpened his need, not sated it.

"Maybe a place with such easily poisoned wells isn't a healthy area to live," he said carefully.

"Why do you think I left San Francisco?" she shot back. "I have to make it work with the Conservancy or I sign up for food stamps. Got it?"

"Yeah. That's why I was the one to ask the really unhappy questions. I can take the heat."

"There doesn't have to be any heat to take! We're civilized people working with civilized people."

He gave her a sideways look. "Hate to be the bearer of bad news—again—but murder is damned uncivilized."

"Surely you can ask questions without angering people."

"Look. We could have made nice and kissed ass until Hill rushed off to another important meeting and we were left standing there with tired lips and no place to go but out to lunch. Hill needed a good reason to open his staff files for us. I gave him one."

Her head hit the back of the seat. "You're saying there's no polite way to ask questions people don't want to answer. And no answers means somebody literally gets away with murder."

He gave her a wary look. "Right now we have what amounts to a handful of beads. They're intriguing, but without a way to string them together, they'll slide through our fingers and get lost in the cracks of everyday life."

"You're assuming that Rua was a tool, and the gold was purely incidental to Lorne's death, not the reason for it," she said.

"So far, that's the most logical way to assemble the beads."

"What on earth is logical about Hill being directly connected to Rua's murder, and therefore, logically we hope, to Lorne's murder?"

"I don't know," he said impatiently, glancing in the mirrors repeatedly. No one had taken the bait. "That's why I'm asking questions, touching pressure points. Sooner or later, the killer will start getting jumpy. Jumpy people make mistakes."

She began to understand just why August had wanted her to stay home. Waving a red flag at a killer bull was a good way to get hurt.

Tanner didn't let the silence bother him. Much. Instead, he started looking for a place to eat lunch. Maybe her outlook would improve if she got some food in her. People with turbo-metabolisms didn't do well without fuel. He knew because he was one of them. He had learned that Shaye was another. Watching her destroy breakfast had been a revelation.

He'd discovered that he liked feeding her. Primitive, but there it was. Under some circumstances, he was a real primitive sort of guy.

Silence settled into the cab of the truck. The lack of conversation was neither easy nor uneasy, it simply was.

Shaye looked out the passenger window, trying to decide whether she should scream or laugh or swear, and if so, in what order. Or run and hide.

No.

Lorne deserves better than that.

And so do I. If I have to spend the rest of my life seeing his ruined face, at the very least I want to know why.

Trying not to think about how she had found Lorne, she focused on watching Carson City's fine old state buildings and casinos slide by, reminding her of a mingling of moneyed gentlemen and brassy tarts. In the side mirror, a smudge of smoke caught her eye. She watched the smoke grow quickly into a column.

Somewhere between Tahoe and Reno a fire was burning. Judging by the rate the column was spreading, it was wind-driven and out of control. It had been a bad fire season already. Now it would be worse.

A nagging sound pulsed in the cab of the truck. The noise was somewhere between that of an early-morning alarm and the grate of sheet metal dragged on a gravel road.

"What the hell?" Tanner asked.

"Crap," she said. "That's my ring tone for Kimberli. Hope she isn't going to yell at me because Hill yelled at her."

"You can always sic me on her."

Shaye ignored him and answered her phone. "Hi, Kimberli. What's up?"

"Are you with Lorne's luscious nephew?"

"I'm working to uphold the Conservancy's interest in the Davis ranch, if that's what you mean."

Kimberli laughed. "Well, that's no reason not to enjoy the man. I could just grab him and lick him all over."

I already did, and went back for seconds. He returned the favor until I screamed. But that's not something I want to talk to my boss about.

"Is Tanner feeling more charitable toward the Conservancy?" Kimberli asked.

"Hard to tell, but I'm working on it."

"Do you have any idea how quickly you can win him over?"

"Not at this time."

"I'll check back later," Kimberli said. "Ace may have a line on another rancher who's tired of fighting taxes and bureaucrats. The land is out in the middle of nowhere and would make a great mustang preserve. Apparently the rancher is a crusty old cocker, just like Lorne was."

Shaye filled the gaps in Kimberli's conversation and said, "Tag, I'm it?"

"You do so well with those backcountry sorts. If you have any breakthroughs on your end, call me soonest."

"Of course."

Tanner gave Shaye a sideways look as she ended the call. "What did Queen Botox want?"

You. Naked.

"A progress report and a hint of another project for me," Shaye said.

"I'm your full-time project."

"Kimberli is big on multitasking."

"Good idea," he said.

"It is?"

"Yeah. We'll grab some sandwiches and figure out how to get an appointment with Jonathan Campbell. Multitasking."

"I'll make an appointment the usual way," she said. "I'll call."

"He's another friend of the Conservancy?"

"He owns one of the biggest development companies in Nevada. He works off any bad karma with regular, hefty donations to the Conservancy. Business has been in the toilet lately, but he's still an important contributor."

"The Conservancy is starting to sound like the confessional," Tanner said.

"A guilty conscience is an expensive thing."

TWENTY-NINE

W E'RE LUCKY CAMPBELL lives close to Carson City," Shaye said to Tanner. "His main office is in south Reno, but he lives here."

"Wouldn't you?" Tanner asked.

"In a heartbeat."

The Sierra Nevadas thrust into the sky, forming a glorious backdrop to a handful of low buildings. Long-limbed horses with clean lines and lustrous coats grazed in pastures with white fences. A hot spring steamed invitingly within a luxurious man-made pool. The buildings themselves were done in a semiranch style with stone and wood and desert-colored stucco.

"The one on the left," she said. "See the small parking area?"

"Yeah."

He drove toward the building, which was a lot bigger than it looked, because the mountains dwarfed everything in their shadow. Two golf carts with sunshades were parked in the lot, along with several modest sedans. There was space for at least twenty more cars.

"I wish the Conservancy headquarters had a parking lot like this," she said.

"Paved?"

"Big enough for more than two cars at a time. It's so bad that we all leave a second set of keys on the keyboard so nobody gets trapped in the lot. Some days it's like solving a puzzle to get out."

Tanner's mouth curled up at the corner. "Any car ever get 'borrowed'?"

"I wish. The only one worth stealing is Kimberli's Lexus."

"Rhinestone wheels?"

Shaye snickered and shook her head. "Not yet." She looked around at the lush, beautifully tended landscape. "I'll bet Campbell writes off all but the main house as a business retreat. There's as much of a resort vibe here as anything else."

"Is that what the Conservancy does?" Tanner asked as he parked the truck.

"We're not-for-profit. We just borrow beautiful places for our retreats."

"And the owner writes off a chunk of overhead as a donation," he said, turning off the engine.

"That's the way the tax system works."

"Works the same in L.A., if you get far enough up the bureaucratic food chain."

Shaye balled up the remains of their lunch and stuffed everything into the carryout sack. "I'm glad we didn't have to go to Reno. I'm not dressed for city business." She yawned. "And I'm hoping for a nap. Something kept me up most of the night."

"That's because someone kept *me* up most of the night." His long arms reached out, wrapped around, and pulled her into a hug. "Too bad Campbell was able to see us so quickly. I was looking forward to fooling around in the truck after lunch."

She gave him a sidelong glance from dark eyes. "You're too big for the cab."

"Ever take yoga?"

"No."

"Neither have I, but I'm told they can do it in a glove box."

Laughing, she kissed him and then got out of the truck before she kissed him again. Harder, deeper, hotter.

He caught up with her at the front door, which looked like it could lead into the lobby of a small resort hotel. The receptionist was in an alcove to the left, entranced by his computer screen. From his expression and quick, repetitive hand movements, he was playing some kind of game.

Shaye waited to be noticed. She was still waiting when Tanner cleared his throat. Loudly.

The receptionist started. His eyes went wide as he realized he had company. Hastily he shut down the game.

"You made good time," he said hurriedly. "I—uh—" He looked down at his phone. "Unc—uh—Mr. Campbell is still on that conference call." He stood up, displaying the gawky limbs and social unease that were as much a hallmark of geek as his neon shoes and matching shirt. "I'll—uh—I'll take you to the conference room."

"Thanks," Shaye said, smiling.

The receptionist blushed, making him look too young to drive.

Tanner watched the kid as he took them to his leader. The geek didn't walk so much as shamble, like he could only be bothered to move three-quarters of his body at a time. He could probably type faster than most people could think. On the computer, he was invincible. In reality, he was chained to a boring job.

Get used to it, kid. People invented games because reality sucks.

They walked down a long hallway broken by occasional doorways on either side. Several doors were half open, showing glimpses of what looked like a video room, then a room with displays and models of various Campbell projects, and a room with a large pool table and racks of cues on the wall.

"My unc—uh—Mr. Campbell's office is at the end of that hall," their guide said. "The conference room is over here." He opened the door to a medium-size room with a wall of glass facing the mountains and a circular table with upholstered leather chairs around it. "Can I get you some soda—uh—coffee or water?" When there were no takers, he said, "He'll be here as soon as he's off the phone."

Tanner waited until the kid was halfway back to his video game before saying to Shaye in a low voice, "I saw something I want a closer look at."

"What?"

"A restroom. If Campbell comes, go ahead and make nice without me. I'll be back to do the wet work."

She winced. "From what Kimberli has said, Campbell hates all conference rooms. Prefers to do things in his office."

"Down that hall." Tanner pointed with his thumb as the kid had. "Got it. I'll make it quick."

Instead of sitting, Shaye wandered the conference room, looking at the photos on the walls. A few were of buildings with striking architecture. Most were of industrial parks, subdivisions, modest apartments, condos, and malls.

Jonathan Campbell entered the conference room with a broad smile on his equally broad face. His frame was as burly as that of the construction worker he had once been. Though his hands were smooth and manicured now, they still showed signs of too much sun and the random scars of rough labor. He had a belly and an empire, and had enjoyed building both.

"Shaye. How's my favorite preservationist?"

"I haven't talked to Kimberli lately," Shaye said. "As for me, it has been a long few days."

"Such a loss to the community. But Lorne Davis had a good life."

"Yes," she said in a husky voice.

Wish I could say the same about his death.

"Freddy told me you weren't alone."

"Tanner ducked into the restroom. He should be right back. If you want to talk to us in your office down the hall, I'll bring him there when he comes back."

"Good. I hate conference rooms. A man can never get comfortable."

When Campbell left, she went back to studying before-and-after pictures on the wall. Intellectually she knew that people needed places to live and work, raise and educate families, and that not everyone was made for the concentrated life of cities. Even so, emotionally, too many of Campbell's constructions were an insult to the landscape.

Don't be a snob. Not everybody can afford to buy even those low-cost houses. Just because I'd rather look at sagebrush than industrial parks and suburbia doesn't make me right.

Sure does make me want to work harder for the Conservancy, though.

Tanner ducked his head in the door. "Campbell still in his office?"

"He's waiting for us there."

"He can wait another minute or two. Come with me."

"I don't need a restroom," she said.

"You will after you see this." He looked quickly up and down the hallway. Nobody in sight. "Come on. We don't have much time."

Curious, she followed him, listening to his low-voiced explanation.

"I wanted to explore inside one of these rooms, but I didn't want to make the kid nervous," Tanner said.

"Which room?"

"This one." He pulled her through a half-open door.

She looked around. "I didn't know you had a thing for model buildings."

"I really liked that one," he said, pointing.

She looked at the far end of the room, where there was a long table holding a three-dimensional relief map of mountains, a narrow valley, and a stream winding through. Low, clean-lined buildings clustered around a landscape featuring bike paths or trails, model trees, and what looked like both a hot-spring pool and the more standard Olympic kind. Farther upslope, the stream had been diverted into a series of randomly sized pools and cascades, which could be for fishing or even kayaking. The steep mountain slopes showed miniature ski runs and surprisingly tasteful chalets.

"So Campbell built a resort," she said. "So what?"

"Look again. It hasn't been built yet. Imagine yourself about here," he said, pointing to the map, "and pretend you're looking up at the line of taller mountains."

Silence filled the room, followed by a low sound, the kind made by someone taking a body blow. "That's Lorne's valley!"

"Keep it down," Tanner said swiftly. "Campbell's office shares a wall with this room."

She gritted her teeth and said in a low voice, "This should get the sheriff's attention."

"The fact that Nevada's premier developer would like to get his hands on Lorne's land? Hardly a news flash."

"But this . . . this is evidence. Motive!" For all that she was whispering, it was obvious she was mad enough to wreck the model with her fists.

"It's another bright, shiny bead, not the string we need to hold all the beads together."

"But—"

"Think," he said urgently. "There are too many ways the sheriff could explain this away, the most obvious being that wanting something isn't the same as murdering to get it, plus there's still no way to prove Lorne was murdered in the first place. "

She opened her mouth, closed it, opened it again. "Are you saying this doesn't *mean* anything?"

"I'm saying even a lawyer provided free by the county could scatter our beads to hell without breaking a sweat. Campbell's lawyers wouldn't be free. They'd blow us out of the universe."

She knew Tanner was right. She just was too furious to accept it quickly, much less graciously.

"Put on your party face," he said.

"This is my party face."

"I've seen you do a lot better."

She glared at him.

"Look, if you can't keep it together," he said, "I'll pretend to be interested in selling the ranch if the court gives it to me."

Her eyes widened like she'd been slapped. "Are you?"

"I don't know," he said impatiently. "But if you have to yell at someone, yell at me."

There was a tight silence.

"I'll keep it together," she said. "We need to know how close Campbell is to Rua. Someone wound that thug up and aimed him toward Lorne."

Tanner didn't point out that they didn't know that for certain and they sure couldn't prove it. He didn't want to set her off. She was a passionate woman in more than sex.

"Okay," she said, even though it wasn't. "Let's get it done."

THIRTY

FEELING LIKE A rebellious teenager, Shaye followed Tanner out of the room—and nearly tripped over the geek in the neon shirt and shoes.

"I was just coming to tell you that Unc—uh—Mr. Campbell has another appointment real soon."

"Thanks," Tanner said. "I saw the models and couldn't resist."

"Really?" The kid's voice said he'd never looked at the models once, much less twice. "I'll take you to his office."

"We know where it is."

"It's my job."

Tanner took Shaye's arm. She was stiff, like someone who was keeping vicious control of each breath. He hoped she wouldn't explode before he got her back to the truck.

They stood in the office doorway behind the kid. Campbell had his back turned to them, gesturing as he looked out the window that made up the back wall. Tanner couldn't decide if the posture was defensive or aggressive. It sure wasn't relaxed. He held a cell phone to his ear, listening, not talking. The gold in his wedding band looked liquid against his weathered hand. The diamonds set in the band gleamed like frost.

Shaye counted nubs in the Berber rug under her feet and forced herself into her party persona. The hated lessons learned at her mother's nylon-clad knee finally snapped into place like the armor they were.

Tanner kept looking at what he could see of the cell phone in Campbell's hand, trying to figure out why he cared. Then he realized that there was a landline on the desk, and an expensive cell phone lying right next to it. Plus a BlackBerry on Campbell's belt.

Why does he need another phone? And a cheap piece of junk at that. I can understand why an elected official like the sheriff has a cheap phone, and why someone running for office might want an anonymous cell phone, but Campbell? Is it some kind of Nevada fetish?

I feel like I'm in south L.A., where drug dealers use throwaway cell phones like other people use toilet paper.

The kid knocked on the open door.

Campbell's stance tightened. "Later. My guests just arrived." He ended the call, tossed the phone into the center drawer of his desk, and closed it with an angry motion. But he was smiling when he looked up. "Thanks, Freddy. I'll take it from here."

The kid vanished.

"The guy on the phone has been stringing me along for a couple months now, never coming through. You know how it is," Campbell said to Shaye. "Some deals have to be nursed like babies." He narrowed his glance on Tanner. "Have we met? Something about you is familiar."

"Tanner Davis," he said, holding his hand across the desk with a toothy grin. "Real happy to meet you, Mr. Campbell."

"Lorne Davis is—was—his uncle," Shaye said, and watched closely.

"Oh, right, the Conservancy benefit," Campbell said, smiling and shaking hands. "I only played poker with Lorne a few times, but I liked him."

"He was a hard son of a bitch," Tanner said. "But he was family."

"Family. What're you gonna do?" Campbell asked, shaking his head. "Got some hardheads in mine. Still, you miss them when they go. Sit down and tell me how I can help you."

Tanner looked at Shaye, saw she was in control, and nodded slightly. She was already talking, using the polite, social voice that made him want to strip her naked and go down on her until she forgot to be civilized and screamed with pleasure.

"Thank you for making room in your busy schedule," she said. "I know you're pressed for time, so we'll make this as short as possible. We had a few questions about a man you recommended to Mr. Hill's security detail. Antonio Rua, called either Tonio or Tony."

Campbell sat back in his leather office chair and let the name roll around in his head. "Sounds vaguely familiar, but I can hardly keep track of every man I've hired."

"Rua was a supervisor, so you might've talked with him directly."

There was a moment of puzzlement before Campbell leaned forward and snapped his fingers. "Got him. Yeah, sure I remember Rua. He kind of drifted in and out of construction, but when he paid attention he was good. He kept the men on the site in line, and not everyone can do that. Cleaned up real nice, too. Was comfortable talking to suits when we took potential investors to sites."

"So you remember recommending Rua to Mr. Hill's security manager?"

"Yeah, I guess. I mean, if Harold said so, I must have. Over time

I've recommended a number of guys to help handle crowds for him. I already require random drug testing and I screen pretty heavily, so if they work for me, they'll pass Harold's sniff test without a lot of wasted time."

"Did Rua?" Shaye asked, her face aching from keeping the social mask in place. The vision of Lorne's ravaged body and Campbell's cheerful model of Lorne's transformed valley kept pinging around in her head.

"If Rua worked for Harold," Campbell said, "he passed the tests."

"I checked with Mr. Hill and Rua was indeed hired on," she said. "I don't think he has started work yet."

Silently Tanner gave her points for not mentioning Rua's death by lead poisoning.

"So is Rua in some kind of trouble with the Conservancy? Building condominiums on sacred land or the like?" The corners of Campbell's eyes crinkled as he grinned.

Her training held and she smiled her social smile. "We were hoping to talk to him."

"Cell phones work on construction sites. Did you get his number from Hill?"

"The last number we had for him is disconnected," she said.

Tanner decided she'd make a very good partner. *Don't lie, but don't tell any truths you don't have to.*

"He probably just got a prepaid cell phone on payday and used it as his number until it ran out," Campbell said, shrugging. "A lot of people in the valley are living real close to the bone."

"I see that in my line of work, too," Tanner said gravely.

"Oh?" Campbell asked. "And what would that be?"

"Social work over in L.A. County. Lotta people living pretty tight there. I mean, I do what I can, but I'm only one man, y'know?"

"I surely do."

Tanner looked around the office, which was three times as big as the conference room. "Just glad to see someone around here is making money and jobs. Surprised you don't have more building sites close by. They all in Reno?"

The phone on the landline buzzed once.

Campbell ignored it. "So far, all my sites are near Reno. Land enough to do big things with is hard to come by here in the valley. What little the government or the tribes don't own is locked up in old landholdings."

And will stay that way, Shaye thought savagely, *as long as I do my job.*

"But that doesn't mean you don't have big dreams for the place, right?" Tanner asked with a knowing smile.

"Who doesn't want a better life for themselves and their community?"

"We all do," Shaye said with a smile as empty as a desert sky. "It's just that everyone doesn't agree on what that better life is. For some, it's the family ranch and open land and maybe a touch of the wilderness at the edges."

Campbell shook his head sadly. "I hear you, but if we're going to bring jobs back to the valley, something has to change. You've been here less than, what, two years?"

She nodded and her cheeks felt numb from smiling.

"Well, there was a time when every business pad on 395 between here and Carson was a beehive of jobs and building. New businesses— family businesses, most of them—starting everywhere you looked. Now, hell," Campbell said in disgust, "now you could fire a shotgun down those same streets and not hit anything but For Sale signs."

"There is still a place for family ranches," she said through gritted teeth.

"Sure, but not every place." Campbell leaned back and sighed. "Like you, I have a dream for one or two of those ranches. Unlike you, my dreams will bring money into the valley."

"Like that ski resort in your model room?" Tanner asked. "That would bring in a lot of jobs."

Campbell grinned. "That's my baby. I've been working on it for five, six years now."

"What made you think you would ever own the land for it?" Shaye asked, forcing another smile.

The BlackBerry signaled an incoming message. Campbell ignored that one, too.

"I've got several long-term projects like that," he said. "The modeling and all is expensive, but if the land ever comes on the market, I'm ready to go before my competitors have a chance to blink and look around for an architect."

"Designing a casino, hotel, cottages, recreational area, ski run and chalets, trails and all the trimmings—pretty expensive for an if-come project," Tanner said.

"I've got the backers to compete with Tahoe," the other man said. "It'll probably take a decade or more to gather the land, but imagine if it happens—jobs for thousands, a new market for local goods, a new destination for people from all over the world. Why should all that tax base stay in Tahoe? It's overbuilt and overpriced for what you get. We can do better than that."

"What if someone didn't want to sell? Wouldn't that derail your dream train?" she said neutrally.

"You gotta use your mind as well as your heart," he said to her. "Remember *Kelso v. New London*? Supreme Court says the state has an overriding interest in the case of private landowners who stand in the way of beneficial local or state developments. Eminent-domain laws would apply. But that shouldn't be necessary. People here know we are desperate for jobs."

"What if they didn't care?" she asked, her voice still polite, interested. Controlled. "As you said, everyone has different dreams."

From inside the desk came the strident noise of a cheap cell phone.

"That's why we have laws, cops, politicians, and courts. Sure, it would be a hassle to use *Kelso,* but if the politicians are with you, it'll get done. Me? I'd rather work with the Conservancy to make sure not just one dream comes true. There's room in Nevada for everyone to get a piece of the pie. We just need the right people at the political helm to make sure things happen."

The cell phone rattled again.

"Sorry," Campbell said. "Gotta take this call. Great talking to you, Shaye, Mr. Davis."

Apparently Freddy was aware of the incoming calls, too. He appeared in the doorway as Campbell opened his desk drawer.

Tanner knew he wasn't going to be able to eavesdrop.

So did Shaye.

Without a word, they followed the neon shirt and sneakers out of the building.

She had never been so grateful for an interruption in her life. Her social armor was fraying, her skin too tight, her jaw and shoulders aching. She pulled herself up into the truck and counted the seconds until Tanner pulled out of the parking lot.

"It's safe now," he said. "Let it out."

"I can't. I'm afraid I'll never be able to shove it back in again."

THIRTY-ONE

THE THROWAWAY CELL phone vanished into an anonymous Dumpster behind a restaurant and bar.

Enough of this.

Nevada is full of empty spaces and unmarked graves. Nobody will notice another one.

Or two.

Three.

Whatever it takes.

THIRTY-TWO

T ANNER PICKED THE first motel close to Refuge that advertised more than clean rooms and weekly rates. He knew that Shaye was going to crash sooner rather than later. Dealing with death was like being in a race—at first your adrenal glands run a marathon a minute. More training, more races, and less adrenaline each time, until finally the mind rather than adrenal glands ruled the body.

She was new to the murder business. She needed a safe place to let down. The ranch had too many memories and her condo in Tahoe was too far away.

He parked and turned off the engine.

"What are we doing here?" she asked.

"Taking a time-out where nobody can find us."

He realized how spent she was when she simply nodded her head.

It took him about five minutes to get a second-floor room—the cop in him knew how dangerous first floors were. He told the clerk their luggage had been lost on a Reno flight and checked in as Mr. and Mrs. T. L. Davis. Those were his initials, verified by his driver's license and credit card, so the clerk didn't think there was anything odd about a couple checking in without luggage.

After all, this was Nevada, where prostitution was licensed and taxed.

"Come on, honey," Tanner said, guiding her up the outside staircase to their room. "You need some downtime."

She wanted to argue, but didn't. There was no point. She knew she was on the breaking edge of her control. Too much had happened, too quickly, too horribly, for her to absorb. And then there was Tanner . . . a wild wind sweeping away her certainties, leaving her nowhere stable to stand but in his arms.

And those arms would only be around until Lorne's estate was settled.

"Maybe my parents were right," she said as Tanner stripped off the bedspread on one of the queen beds. "Maybe I'm not cut out for rural life."

"Death goes everywhere. Statistically, you're safer out in the boonies."

He began undressing her as efficiently as he had the bed. Shoes, socks, jacket, and outer shirt hit the floor.

Though his touch was caring rather than hungry, she felt a rush of heat melt through the ice in her bones.

"But—" she began as he nudged her backward until the mattress hit her knees and she sat suddenly.

"That's it, honey. Into bed." He bent and whisked off her jeans. "I'll wake you in an hour or so. We can talk then."

"An hour," she repeated. "No talking."

"There you go."

She lay back under the gentle push of his hands—then hooked her arm around his neck and pulled him off balance, into her arms. For a moment he lay full length on her. Then, reluctantly, he made a grab for common sense.

"I meant you should rest," he said, bracing himself on one arm above her.

"You're hard."

"Honey, around you, that's like saying my heart is beating."

"I'm sorry I've been so——"

"You've been incredible," he said, putting his fingers over her mouth, stilling her words. "You saw the model, wanted to take out Campbell's throat with your teeth, but you hung tough, questioned him like a pro, and never so much as hinted at Rua's death. You can be my partner anytime."

Her dark brown eyes examined him intently, then accepted that he was telling her the truth.

"I almost lost it," she admitted against his fingers. "That damn model was the cherry on top of the crap pile of the last few days. You, on the other hand, are the cake." She lifted just enough to kiss him. "But I just discovered that I'm greedy. I want the whipped cream, too."

He didn't know whether to laugh or groan.

Then her tongue slipped hotly between his fingers. Twice. Three times.

"Shaye . . ." It was all he could force out his suddenly tight throat.

"Take off your jeans."

He removed his fingers from her mouth and kissed her until she was writhing and rubbing against him, wanting more. Demanding it. He stripped off her underwear so that he could do what he'd wanted to do before the deputy's call had interrupted them this morning.

Tanner's teeth raked gently, hungrily, down her throat. He kissed her collarbone, the hollow of her neck, the pulse in her throat, trying to tell her how beautiful she was to him.

Her fingers pulled out his shirt and tested every texture of his back, biting into his resilient heat, both impatient and appreciative.

"More," she said.

Her husky demand went through him like lightning. He laughed deep in his chest and bit her carefully. Her back arched, reminding him that he hadn't touched her breasts. Her nipples were already hard. He sucked one into his mouth for a long, thorough loving.

"Jeans," she groaned. "Now." Her hands tugged at his waistband, then pulled his fly open.

His breath hissed in. "You should sleep."

"I will. After. I need you so much I'm aching. Help me, Tanner."

He kicked off his shoes and socks and helped her peel off his clothes. Moments later they were a hot, moving tangle of mouths and searching hands. She kneaded down his back with her hands, short fingernails digging in. Then she slid into the crease until she found his balls drawn hard and tight. She loved the feel of him, the hunger and the heat.

"One day I'm going to make it slow," he groaned, arching at another lightning strike of need.

"Not today. Not now."

"Not now," he agreed.

He sucked her lower lip between his teeth and bit down just enough to get her attention. Then he released her with a slow promise that had her hips lifting urgently against him. His hands moved down her back and over her butt until his fingers slid down the seam between her cheeks to the hidden flesh below. The feel of her seething and wet and eager against his fingers made him light-headed.

"Damn, you're a miracle," he said, easing her over until she covered him. "Never felt a woman half as hot."

"I don't want to hear about your other women."

"What women? Bring me home, Shaye."

She shifted until she could take him hard and solid and so deep they felt like one being. With urgent, hungry motions they rode each other until they were both breathing too hard, too fast, and the only possible end was a sensory explosion that left them spent and at peace.

The sound of Shaye's phone dragged her out of sleep.

"Ignore it," Tanner said.

The rumble of his chest beneath her cheek made her smile. She rubbed against the sensuous texture of hair and flesh while she fished blindly around for her jacket, which had landed within reach of the bed. Her fingers found the phone.

"It's Ace," she said.

Tanner made a snoring sound.

Snickering, she took the call. "Hi, Mr. Desmond."

"Ace," he corrected. "I found something that may help you. Or rather, Tanner. McCurdy's 8 lets women in because it has to, but no one will talk to them."

"What's McCurdy's 8?"

"A Reno gym where Rua signed up recently."

"Hang on. I'm putting you on the speaker."

Muffling a yawn, Shaye put the phone on speaker and said, "Can you hear okay?"

"Just fine," Ace said. "I've been really bugged by Rua and those gold coins. Have you gotten any further on that?"

"No," Tanner said. "My source hasn't sent any more leads."

"Hell," Ace muttered. "I told Personnel to go through Rua's file and give me any contact numbers he had. He only listed two. One was his cell phone, which I assume was found at the scene . . . ?"

"I haven't heard one way or the other," Tanner said. "The death of some mook in Meyers isn't exactly a fire burning under the El Dorado County sheriff's ass."

Ace said something muffled to somebody on his end. Then, "Sorry. I've told Security to go through the tapes we saved and see if Rua appears on any of them. We might pick up a friend of his with him or something. I'll tell my people to forward anything they find to Shaye's number."

"Thank you," she said.

"You mentioned two numbers for Rua?" Tanner asked.

"The second one is a mixed-martial-arts training gym I was telling Shaye about," Ace said.

"McCurdy's 8?" she asked. "A gym that will let women in but then ignores them?"

"That's the one. I put it through the cross-match site online and came up with a place north of Reno." A paper rustled as Ace read off the address. "I'd go there myself, but I'd planned a fishing overnight in the mountains, and if I don't get away today, I won't get away at all."

Shaye stifled another yawn—or tried to. "Sorry."

"You sound as tired as I am," Ace said. "Want to go fishing?"

Tanner glared at the phone. "She's going to take a nap while I check out McCurdy's 8. Thanks for the tip, and I hope you catch a mess of fish."

He hung up before she could stop him.

"That was rude," she said.

"It's a gift," he agreed as he slid out of bed and started pulling on clothes.

Her head hit the pillow with a muffled thump as she buried a yawn in it. "How do you keep going?"

"Practice. I don't blow through all my adrenaline at once. Close your eyes, beautiful, or I'll be tempted to demonstrate just what you do for my stamina."

She opened one eye. "Rain check?"

"For you, always." He bent and gave her a gentle kiss before he pulled the blankets up to her chin. "I'll put out the Do Not Disturb sign, but don't turn off your phone. I'll be calling you."

"Shouldn't we call August?" she mumbled against the pillow.

"And tell him Campbell has a model-building habit? I'd be lucky if he didn't cuss me out as an amateur. Go to sleep while I check out the woman haters."

"I could—"

"Sleep," he interrupted. "I'll call if anything comes up."

She mumbled something, then gave in to sleep.

He turned and quietly left the room before he could demonstrate just what had come up. Again.

After the gym, he promised himself.

THIRTY-THREE

I T TOOK TANNER about two seconds to realize that McCurdy's 8 was everything the Ground & Pound wanted to be. Stubby's place had been held together with duct tape, sweat, and desperation. McCurdy's 8 was all about professional fighters who had already proved themselves in the octagon under hot lights with screaming and jeering fans surrounding them.

McCurdy's 8 was where men oiled themselves in their own sweat, ready to fight or die for the crowd. It was ancient Rome minus the lions and lead plumbing. Posters of meaty champions hung on the walls in oversize images of blood and triumph, adrenaline smiles holding off the pain that would come as surely as dawn.

The biggest poster was of Nick McCurdy, grinning through bruises and blood, holding up a championship belt buckle almost as big as his chest.

Beyond the reception area, men hit padded steel bars and heavy bags, grunting with effort, sounds that filled the place with a peculiar, primitive rhythm. Part of Tanner understood the sheer physical joy of going one-on-one with a worthy opponent. The rest of him wondered if the fighters had ever tried sex instead.

He didn't bother trying to talk to McCurdy himself. He just badged the mountain of meat on the other side of the reception desk. The name tag read *Bulldog*.

It should have been *Gorilla*.

"Got a few questions about a fighter called Antonio Rua, goes by either Tonio or Tony," Tanner said, putting his badge back in his pocket.

"Don't know him."

"He's a new member."

"Gotta check with the super," Bulldog said.

Tanner nodded, relieved that Bulldog was a man with nothing to prove. Even if Tanner fought dirty—and really, why fight any other way?—Bulldog wouldn't be much fun.

While he waited he looked around, noting the cameras that recorded everything that happened in the gym—including the reception area. The thumps and grunts from the various octagons in the big room were the only sounds. No trash talk, no cursing, just the kind of determination and ability to eat pain that were a vital part of the training.

This is a waste of time, he thought. *Shaye said Lorne's body wasn't torn up by anything but scavengers. You beat a man to death and it leaves real marks.*

But the gym wasn't the first wild-goose chase Tanner had ever been on while investigating a case. It wouldn't be the last. Investigations where murderers didn't leave witnesses, or brag about themselves in bars or on the street, were time-consuming bitches to solve. If they were solved at all. He didn't like that, but he knew it just the same.

All he hoped was that Shaye wouldn't have to live with that kind of knowledge.

Bulldog returned. "Super says we always cooperate with cops. What do you need?"

"Information about Rua."

"Why?"

"He's dead."

"Ah, man. Super really hates when the fighters take it out of the ring."

"Bullets, not fists."

Bulldog shook his head. "Coward."

Tanner shrugged.

The other communed with his computer, pulled up Rua's file, and spun the machine toward Tanner.

There was nothing on the screen that helped.

"Rua have any friends here?" Tanner asked. "Anyone who touted the place to him?"

"McCurdy's 8 doesn't need touting," Bulldog said, unwrapping a piece of sugarless gum and stuffing it into his massive jaws. "Anyone who don't know about us don't know shit about fighting."

"He hang with anyone in particular?"

"I never saw him come in or leave with any of our fighters."

Tanner tried another direction. "Does this place take anyone who walks in the door?"

"Nope. Waste of time. Super watches a wannabe fight, then decides."

"So Rua made the cut?"

"Barely. What got him in is he had this really fast, tricky heart punch that rocked fighters twice his size. The Super thought it might win him a few matches."

"What's a heart punch?"

Bulldog chomped his gum a few times. "You hit a guy hard enough on his heart and it can take him down. I saw a heart punch kill a guy once."

Tanner kept his face neutral. "Must have left a hell of a bruise."

"Dead dudes don't bruise. Plenty of other bruises from the fight, but not from the one that killed him."

"Huh. I thought that sort of thing was bullshit."

"Saw it. Never forgot it. It's not just strength, its speed and timing. Super can give you a medical explanation, but it's like a concussion on your heart instead of your brain."

Tanner spent some more time asking questions about Rua's training schedule, sparring partners, anything and everything that might bury the heart-blow discussion in Bulldog's mind. Then he thanked him and headed out.

As soon as he got in the truck, he called August.

"I know this won't raise the sheriff's eyebrows," Tanner said, "but Rua had a fighting trick known as the heart shot."

"Keep talking."

"It's a fast, single blow to the heart that can take down a trained fighter—even kill him. The result looks like a heart attack and doesn't leave a mark."

"Bullshit."

"Think about it. Bruises form because blood is pumping, under pressure, and leaks out of injured veins or arteries. No heartbeat to cause pressure, no bruises. *Bam.* Lights out forever."

Silence, then a long-drawn-out curse followed by, "Well, ain't that a kick in the butt. You sure about this?"

"I'm sure that it wouldn't require much to take out a man Lorne's age. It was the lack of body marks that was bothering everyone. This is an explanation."

"With Rua dead, it's blowing smoke. Sheriff won't inhale. He's at some national peace officers' meeting over in California, learning how to be even better at his job. But if the reports of the fire that are coming in get any worse, he may come back."

"He could try pulling his head out of his ass," Tanner said. "Once his ears stopped ringing, he might be able to connect Lorne to Rua and figure out why Rua was whacked and who did it. Anything new on that, by the way?"

"Haven't heard a word. Could be everyone's at the same conference, learning all kinds of new things about how to make jail more like a nice resort."

"Makes me want to rush out and get arrested," Tanner said. "Oh, wait. Nobody's around to do that job. They're all at the conference."

"You might have a future here after all."

"Thanks, but I have one just like it waiting in L.A."

August laughed. "Damn, but I could like you. Look, I'll do what I can, but it's not a hell of a lot. If you come up with any link between Lorne, Rua, and a third person, then I can ignore the sheriff and get some investigating done. Until then, my hands are tied. I'm under direct orders to 'quit chasing my ass and get busy on community relations.' Solving a murder in El Dorado County and starting rumors about a senior citizen's perfectly natural death in Refuge County isn't any part of my job description."

Tanner hung up and called Shaye.

She answered on the first ring.

"Did I wake you up?" he asked.

"No. I've just been sitting here, watching the shadows lengthen across the first floor's heating and air-conditioning units. What did you find out at the gym?"

"Ever heard of a heart shot?"

"As in bullets?" she asked.

"Fists."

"Missed that memo."

"I thought it was a myth, but the dude at McCurdy's 8 said it's real. A single blow delivered just right sends a shock wave to the heart. Most of the time it just knocks the fight right out of an opponent. Once in a while it's lethal. Looks like a heart attack. Doesn't leave a mark."

"Did Rua know how to do it?" she asked immediately.

"It was a specialty of his. The only thing that got him in the door of McCurdy's 8, where the guys make the Ground and Pound look like preschool for pussies."

"I'll call Deputy August."

"I already did. No joy. Sheriff flat-out told August that his job is to let sleeping dogs lie and concentrate on community relations."

"You're kidding."

"I wish."

There was silence while Shaye watched shadows lengthen. "Now what, Detective?"

"I'll be back in an hour, maybe hour and a half, depending on traffic. Reno isn't L.A., but lots of cars are hitting the freeway, heading for happy hour or home."

"We're not getting any closer to who told Rua to murder Lorne, are we?"

"*Investigation* is another word for *patience,*" Tanner said.

"Is it true about the first forty-eight hours after a murder?"

He didn't have to ask what she meant. It was a brutal fact of life that every investigator faced—solve a murder in the first forty-eight hours after death or the chances were high that it would never be solved.

"Do you want to let it go?" he asked.

"No," she said instantly. "Do you?"

"No."

What he didn't say was that she was the one holding him in the valley. She was right about the trail getting colder at an exponential rate. But part of him was coming alive even faster.

"Shaye?"

"Yes?"

"You don't have any deeply buried yen to live in L.A., do you?"

"I . . . oh, Tanner, I wish I did," she said in a husky voice. "But when I first saw Refuge it was like coming home. My ex taught me that burying what I want in order to give him what he wanted was a losing combination. And I was the one on the losing end. What about you? Do you have a deeply buried yen to live here?"

"All I know is I don't want to lose you. Don't leave until I get there. It will be a while. Have to gas up. Be there, honey."

"I will."

"I'll hurry."

She heard the sound of an open line. She stared at the phone, her heart beating too fast.

I don't want to lose you.

And she didn't want to lose him.

For all the good it would do either of them. Sometimes being an adult sucked.

THIRTY-FOUR

S HAYE TOSSED THE phone onto the bed, got dressed, and went to the tiny balcony that had a slice of a view of the parking lot. The angle of the sunlight transformed the asphalt into a charcoal landscape, ripples of cracks and rivers of tar like veins throughout. The lot had been patched together a hundred times over the years, but never would be whole.

I used to think I was like that, never able to be whole again.

But I don't anymore. When did that happen?

Maybe loving Tanner would be a kind of freedom I've never known, never even dreamed of. Free of the past that ripped me apart. Free to take a chance on the future.

Believing, finally, in a future, instead of simply gutting my way through every problem alone, every day, every week and month and year until I'm as old and dead as Lorne.

She knew she could keep living alone and doing a good job of it. She had done it for years.

Her phone rang.

Shaye hurried back to the bed to pick up her phone and answer.

"Tanner?" she asked quickly.

"It's Kimberli. Where's tall, dark, and sexy?"

Shaye frowned. Despite the teasing words, Kimberli's voice was flat, thin, stretched by an anxiety she'd never heard from her boss. And she wasn't using her own phone, or the ring would have been different.

"What's wrong?" Shaye asked.

"What isn't?" Kimberli said shakily. "Somehow the Conservancy is the bad guy because Lorne had a senior moment and pulled out before he signed the letter of intent."

"That doesn't make sense."

"When do emotions make sense?" Kimberli retorted. Her voice was rough, like she had been screaming or crying. "I was told that growing old meant outliving your enemies and dancing on their graves. Now I feel like someone is dancing on mine. Lorne changing his mind screwed us. Ranchers are saying that the Conservancy tried to pull a fast one and get him to sign a contract that gave us everything and him nothing."

Shaye knew she should tell her boss, *It's not your fault, everyone makes mistakes,* but she wasn't feeling charitable right now. If she had made the kind of mistake Kimberli had, she'd have been fired, and rightly so.

"Who are the ranchers?" Shaye asked. "Are they mine? I can talk to them and—"

"The head of the National Ranch Conservancy called and reamed me over Lorne," Kimberli said as if Shaye hadn't spoken. "He said the Conservancy can't take that kind of scandal. Something would have to be done. I'm afraid that 'something' is firing me."

Shaye waited while Kimberli fought to control her voice. After long, long moments she succeeded.

"You know what the real hell of it is?" Kimberli asked, then rushed on without waiting for an answer. "My guess is that Lorne never was going to sign the ranch over, but thought he could have a little fun and keep a pretty woman at his beck and call for months and months."

For a moment Shaye was too shocked to speak. "I know you and Lorne didn't like each other, but we all managed to be civil and keep our ultimate goal in mind—saving Lorne's ranch for future generations."

"Yes, yes, that's just good business," Kimberli said in her raw voice. "But now the Lester family up north is one lawyer's appointment away from withdrawing their offer and the Gunthers on the east side of the valley are talking to realtors about putting their land on the market. We've been blindsided. The Conservancy is reeling and looking around for people to blame and they're dumping the load on me. But I've poured *everything* into the Conservancy. No one will hire me and my great-uncle's inheritance can barely keep me, much less Peter. I'm too old to start over. I'm ruined!" she wailed. "I have nowhere . . ."

Shaye gave up trying to interrupt Kimberli's monologue. There was no point. Though the presentation was over-the-top, what she said was the simple truth. If the Conservancy fired her, Kimberli was finished. All the attention, all the galas, all the businesses and politicians courting her for the Conservancy's approval . . . it was all gone.

When Shaye realized that her job right now was to listen, she went to the bed and settled in for as long as it would take Kimberli to run down. With her boss, it could be quite a while.

Shaye looked out the window. Somewhere in the Sierras above and north of Carson City the fire was still burning, smoke rising thick and black from the far side of the closest mountain ridge. The color of the smoke announced the arrival of a fire trying to get big enough to generate its own furious winds. She hoped it was burning in an unpopulated area, but those were getting harder and harder to find.

Someone tried to beep through twice, but she didn't feel right about putting her distraught boss on hold. Then the line went dead. She checked her own cell battery. Plenty of juice. Apparently Kimberli had talked her borrowed cell phone's battery into the ground.

She listened to Tanner's call-me message and was just getting ready to hit the callback button when someone slid an electronic key into the lock on the only door into the motel room.

Crap. Tanner must have forgotten to put out the Do Not Disturb sign.

"Maid service," said a muffled voice.

"I don't want—"

She had an instant to realize that she hadn't put the chain or dead bolt back on after Tanner left. Then the door opened and Ace stepped into the room, with Kimberli right behind him.

Part of Shaye's mind noted that Ace wore hiking boots, jeans, a warm shirt, a waterproof jacket, and a floppy fishing hat that all but concealed his face. He was friendly, smiling as warmly as he ever did, but there was something about him that was off.

He's wearing surgical gloves.

THIRTY-FIVE

A CE? WHAT ARE you doing here?" Shaye asked.

"Remember the acreage Kimberli told you about, the ranch beyond the far side of the valley where mustangs are? She insisted I show it to you today, before my fishing trip."

"I thought if we could get a new ranch in the bag, then the Conservancy would be happy with me again," Kimberli said hurriedly.

Shaye felt like she'd been dropped into an alternate universe. "Wait. Wait. How did you know where I was?"

"If you have the right connections and enough time, cell phones can be traced just like landlines," Ace said. "Tracking via IP address while triangulating off cell towers is quite easy. As for getting in the motel, I own it, along with five others. Did you enjoy your stay?"

She stared at him. "What would you have done if I didn't stay in one of your motels?"

"Sent Kimberli knocking on doors. Your location coordinates were rather precise." He smiled. "Sorry to rush you, but I really want to get this over with and go fishing."

The certainty that something was very wrong made cold sweat slick Shaye's spine. Above her racing heartbeat she heard Tanner's voice.

Be there, honey.

Her phone cut into her clenched hand.

"I can't go," she said. "I have something else to—"

"Give me the phone."

Ace's voice was as pleasant as always, but now it made goose bumps rise on her arms. She got up, then stumbled, using the motion as cover for punching the callback button.

Tanner picked up immediately.

"A—" was all she got out before a measured punch knocked her back onto the bed, paralyzing her breathing and sending her cell phone flying.

Ace picked up the phone, turned it off, and pulled out the SIM card. He flushed the card down the bathroom toilet, then bundled the phone in a mess of toilet paper and threw it into the bathroom wastebasket.

All the while Shaye fought to draw wheezing, strangled breaths.

Kimberli watched everything like it was a television show and she was thinking about changing the channel. But really, it was too much trouble to press the button.

"Get up," Ace said. "You're not hurt."

Easy for you to say, you bastard, Shaye thought.

"Sorry about that," he said. "I should have spotted the phone sooner. I don't like to be physical. I thought I'd left those days behind long ago." He shrugged. "One adjusts as life requires."

By shooting Rua? Sounds plenty physical to me.

But she kept the words to herself. She was in enough trouble with a calm Ace. Prodding him would be really stupid.

That left Kimberli.

"Kimberli," Shaye said, breathing unevenly around the ache in her solar plexus, "what's going on?"

Her boss looked like she had dressed for a party and then decided not to go after all. Her makeup was overdone, her silk shirt glittered with rhinestone swirls, but her jeans were faded, her tennis shoes were a scuffed metallic silver, and her eyes were glassy with adrenaline or something less legal.

"I told you," Kimberli said. "I need that new ranch, so get it together and we'll make a quick trip of it."

"The switched contract wasn't a mistake," Shaye said, breathing unevenly, still not getting of the bed. "You *meant* to trick Lorne."

Kimberli shrugged. "We needed the ranch more than he did. Besides, there weren't any mustangs on it, so no big deal."

"We? You and Ace?"

"Well, sure. You don't think Peter is smart enough to help me, do you? Besides, he was just arm candy so people didn't notice that Ace and I were getting busy as often as we could."

"We can talk over old times while Kimberli drives," Ace said. "There's a trout or five with my name on it waiting for me up in the mountains."

"I'm not going anywhere with you," Shaye said.

"You have a choice," he said. "Come with me or die here."

Kimberli rolled her eyes. "Do we really need the drama, Ace?"

"You won't kill me here," Shaye said without looking away from him. "The people in the motel's front office would remember you."

"They never saw me. I have a master electronic key to all my establishments. So much easier that way," he said pleasantly. "Are you coming or staying?"

From his tone of voice, he could have been asking if she liked sugar with her coffee. The alternate-universe feeling was making her doubt her own sanity. He was so calm, so polite, as he waited for her answer.

It didn't take but a heartbeat for her to decide that given a choice between dead now or dead later, she'd take later.

"Looks like I have a ranch to see," she said through her teeth.

Kimberli let out her breath in a rush. "Oh, good. I told you, Ace. She is a very bright girl. She doesn't want to be on the losing side. And there's no need to talk so rough."

"You were right," he said. "I think there will be a soft, lucrative place for her in our new business. She has a way with the old-timers."

I think that aliens have taken me to Area 51. Or is it 52?

Shaye couldn't remember because it was taking all her strength not to scream or do something equally stupid.

"Grab her jacket," he told Kimberli. "It will be chilly where we're going." He looked at Shaye. "If you scream or give me any trouble, you'll break your neck in a fall down the stairs and we'll be gone before you hit the bottom."

Kimberli made a sound of distaste.

Shaye remembered the restrained force of Ace's blow. He had known exactly what he was doing and how to do it.

Unlike Kimberli, Shaye knew Ace wasn't just talking rough. He *was* rough.

"How long have you been into mixed martial arts?" she asked.

"You go first," he said, ignoring her question. "I'll be right behind you. Shut the door on your way out, Kimberli, and don't forget to put out the sign for maid service."

Shaye had already decided to scream if she saw anyone out in the parking area, but the only life out there was a weed pushing for survival through a narrow crack in the blacktop.

Go for it, weed. Life is worth fighting for.

"That's my Bronco," Shaye said, noticing the faded orange vehicle for the first time.

"Kimberli's Lexus wouldn't be much good where we're going." He handed keys over to Kimberli. "You're driving."

"How did you—oh, the keyboard," Shaye said.

"I made copies of everyone's keys as soon as they started work," Kimberli said cheerfully as she opened her clever little purse that could double as a very small backpack. "My next office will have a real parking lot where more than two cars won't cause a jam."

"Sweet," Shaye said, and wondered just how far the gas in her tank would get them.

"Parking lot," Ace said.

Although she walked as slowly as she dared, and stumbled twice— only to feel Ace's hand yank her back upright with surprising strength— no one else appeared in any of the empty doorways surrounding the parking lot.

Kimberli's car was parked on the opposite side of the lot from the Bronco.

"Go to the front passenger side of your car," Ace said to Shaye. "Get in and put your seat belt on. Be careful not to move afterward. Not one bit. Life is precious and very, very fragile, and I'm told I have wicked fast hands."

"Ace," Kimberli said in exasperation.

Shaye didn't argue or ask him to repeat his instructions. She just kept looking for a way out of the mess she was in—a way that didn't involve dying.

Nothing offered itself.

Reluctantly she got in, stumbling a bit over the search-and-rescue backpack she always kept in the passenger footwell in case she was called.

The emergency locater, she thought with a surge of hope. *I've got to turn it on.*

Somehow.

"What's the problem?" Ace asked sharply.

"I'm a little shaky," she said. "I just tripped over some junk in the footwell."

Before she fumbled the seat belt into place, Ace was in the back cargo space on his knees with his left hand under her chin. It was horribly easy for her to visualize how quickly he could break her neck. Because the old Ford Bronco had been built for desert sun, the tinted glass in back made him virtually invisible from the outside.

Kimberli got in behind the wheel and started the Ford. She stalled coming out of first gear, started, stalled again.

"You said you can drive a shift car," Ace growled.

"I can," Kimberli said. "I'm just rusty."

"Nervous, too," Shaye said. "Kidnapping won't look good on your résumé."

"Shut up," he said. "Kimberli has enough problems without you sniping at her."

For an instant outrage struggled with fear for control of Shaye's tongue. Fear won. She shut up.

Kimberli started the Bronco again and lurched toward the exit.

Shaye felt an instant of hope when a car pulled into the parking lot, but Ace's fingers tightened on her chin in silent warning as he crouched down behind her. She would be dead before she could make any move to catch the other driver's attention.

"Ease off," she said through her teeth. "The way Kimberli is driving, you could break my neck by accident."

"I assure you, it wouldn't be an accident." His fingers tightened.

Shaye held herself like a store mannequin, as relieved as her boss was when Kimberli finally got the hang of the Bronco's balky clutch. Obviously Ace had driven the vehicle from her condo in Tahoe to the Carson motel.

She hoped his knees would go numb on the hard metal floor of the cargo area.

"You're too tall, Shaye, dear," Ace said, as if they were at a dinner party or a movie theater, completely casual and loose. "Lean forward a touch so that I can get a clearer view of the road."

She bent down perhaps more than he might've expected, resting her forearms on her knees and glancing at the fuel gauge. It said three-quarters full.

It lied.

"See how pleasant things can be?" he asked. "You're a lot more comfortable than I am. Kimberli, be sure to obey the speed limit."

Shaye glanced down at the SAR backpack and wondered how she could get to it before Ace killed her.

THIRTY-SIX

TANNER HIT REDIAL four times, got nothing four times, and pulled out of the gas station fast enough to make the tires bark. He drove Lorne's truck like it was a wide-stance sports car until a red light stopped him just before he got on the freeway. He thought about blowing through it, but there was too much cross-traffic. As he waited, he punched in the number of the sheriff's office, hit the speaker, and put the cell phone on the seat.

By the time he got August, the light was green and Tanner was breaking every speed law he could get away with.

"Glad you called," the deputy said. "The sheriff has been crawling up my ass about Lorne and Shaye and how he doesn't need that kind of grief right now. What the hell is going on?"

"Shaye's in trouble. She called me, tried to say something, and then made a sound like someone kicked the breath right out of her. The phone went dead a second or two later. I called four times and got nowhere. Then—"

He broke off, laid on the horn, and shot through a slot between two cars. One driver gave him the middle-finger salute. The second slammed on the horn and brakes at the same time.

"Where the hell are you and what are you doing?" August demanded.

"Just getting on the freeway north of Reno. All the traffic is like me, southbound. It will take me an hour to reach the place I left Shaye— Mountain View Motel, room twenty-three. Ask for a welfare check. Then call and—son of a *bitch*!"

A red Caddy and a station wagon held together with duct tape and rust were blocking both lanes ahead. Tanner got in the Caddy's business and flashed his high beams while leaning on the horn. The Caddy guy hit his own horn and flipped Tanner off, but sped up just enough for him to squeeze through.

"Good thing there was a five-car pileup with injuries northbound about twenty minutes ago," August said blandly. "Otherwise you'd have cops all over you like flies on fresh shit. As it is, southbound ahead of you will slow because all the yahoos just have to have a look at the pretty flashing lights and hope to see some poor citizen's fresh blood. Now tell me which hornet's nest the two of you kicked over."

"Welfare check. Room twenty-three."

"I can multitask," August said. "The closest patrol unit will take about twenty, thirty minutes. We've got a wildfire in the mountains."

"Whoever is with Shaye has already killed two people."

She could already be dead.

But Tanner refused to believe that. "Get someone's ass down there now!"

"Can you prove that?" August asked hopefully.

"No time."

"The sheriff told me to stay put and shuffle papers," August said, sounding angry and disgusted. "And he made it damn clear that every-thing to do with Lorne, Shaye, or the Conservancy goes through him first."

Tanner made a sound too savage to be human. "Call the motel. Find out if anyone signed in or out after Mr. and Mrs. Davis in room twenty-three. And if the sheriff asks, you're trying to find me, not her."

"I'll call you back."

"Thanks."

Without giving August his callback number, Tanner disconnected. He knew that calls to the sheriff's station were automatically logged by time and number as they occurred.

He wove in and out of increasing traffic. August had been right. Although the pileup was across the freeway, every idiot just had to slow down and goggle at someone else's bad luck. Using horn and brakes, he got through the slowdown and went across the rest of Reno at eighty. Apparently there were a few cops not busy with the accident or the fire, because he just missed getting nailed by an officer with a radar gun on the overpass. The three chase cars working with the cop on the overpass were already busy writing tickets.

Then he was out of Reno and on the miserable stretch of 395 that wound through tiny ranches, junkyards, and tourist shops. One car in front of him, someone made a bad left turn, heading across the busy highway for an antiques store. Tanner saw what was coming and aimed for the side of the road where there was just enough room to squeeze by between a stalled driver and a cottonwood tree.

There was a rending, metallic sound as he slid by the tree. The wheel bucked hard, then settled. He shot out of the narrow gap minus the mirror on the passenger side and a few coats of paint.

Behind him, traffic slowed to walking pace.

No harm, no foul.

The mirror hadn't come completely free. It hung down and banged on the door like someone trying to get in. Tanner ignored it and the unhappy rattle of a fender. He watched the oncoming traffic ahead of him, searching passing cars for any hint of Shaye.

It was a long shot, but when that was all you had, you didn't sneer at it.

His phone rang. He laid off the horn long enough to take the call. It was August, and he was on a private phone.

"Nobody checked in or out after you," the deputy said. "The sign outside the room requested maid service, so the kid at the front desk went in. Nobody there. No possessions left behind. He figures the guest took off in the old orange Bronco he saw on his way into the parking lot. Two blondes in the front seat. Couldn't see if anyone was in the back, but a lot of those old Broncos don't have a backseat. The blonde drove like it was her first time with a shift car."

"Shaye owns an old orange Bronco, but she knows how to drive a shift. The other blonde could be Kimberli. Put out a bulletin on the Bronco."

"I'd have to go through the sheriff."

"Why?" shot back Tanner. "I borrowed Shaye's car and it was stolen from the motel parking lot. Nothing to do with nothing important, so why bother him? Get her license number and—"

"On it already," August said. "But doing you favors is going to get me fired."

"Working for Sheriff Conrad, *breathing* could get you fired."

A rusty chuckle came out of the speakerphone. "I'll keep you posted, but unless I get something solid, I don't think the sheriff is all that interested in helping you out. He's got other dogs in this hunt. Hill, Campbell, and Mason have called him today. Whatever they said didn't make him happy."

"Huh. They call him often?"

"Sure. Helped him get elected. Paid for it, actually, along with Desmond and some other casino owners. Conservancy even kicked in."

"And I'm betting someone in that group is good for murder one."

Silence, followed by a hissing curse. "Davis, you are a great big helping of shit, you know that? I've put out the BOLO on Shaye's orange Bronco. Now I'll start looking for work. Don't call except on my private cell, which should be in your call log now."

August disconnected.

Tanner drove like he was in second place on the last lap of the Indy 500.

THIRTY-SEVEN

S HAYE SAT MOTIONLESS. The unnatural position made her stiff, but since her feet were busy trying to push apart the Velcro closing of her backpack, she didn't complain. What really irritated her was that her shoes were made for trails, not for finessing sticky cloth apart. After a frustrating amount of time, she managed to hold down the backpack with one foot and scrape the top of the backpack open with the other.

But that was all she could do until Ace got tired of kneeling on metal and let go of her chin.

As the sun descended behind the Sierra Nevadas, the scattered developments that failed to connect Carson City and Refuge gave way to ragged hills rising above the eastern valley. Wind stirred dust across the landscape like a series of small campfires. Behind them, something bigger than a campfire spread like a smudge across the sky.

"Take the next right turn," Ace said.

Kimberli jumped, startled by the end to silence. "Does that mean it's okay to talk?"

"Sure," Ace said. "You're driving fine now."

Shaye warily stretched her neck. When his hand didn't reappear, she decided that he had been as uncomfortable as she had been. She scratched her lower leg, testing how much freedom Ace would give her.

He tossed his hat aside and rubbed his head like it itched.

"I'll be glad when the first hard frost comes and kills the mosquitoes," she said. "I got covered in bites out hiking."

Apparently he didn't care about the bugs one way or another.

They'd probably die if they drank his blood.

Pretending she was scratching, she slid her hand into the open backpack. She knew right where the emergency locater was. It was just a matter of getting it and turning it on without being killed.

She bit her lip against bubbling laughter, recognizing it as the first signpost on the way to hysteria.

Deep breath.

Yoga breath.

Her fingers reached the locater beacon. The SPOT 2 wasn't much bigger than a pack of cigarettes or an iPod. She just had to be sure she hit the right button. She really didn't want to activate the talk function and give away her best hope of getting out of this mess alive.

Her sweaty fingers slid over the face of the device. Her heart stuttered when she almost pressed the wrong button. Finally she found the recessed switch that activated the beacon's soundless pings.

Kimberli hit a hole in the deteriorating road.

The SPOT 2 squirted from Shaye's fingers. It seemed like forever before she found it again, but it had only been a few seconds since she first bent over. Adrenaline was screwing up her sense of time. Her finger slid off the switch, returned, and held it down long enough to activate the beacon.

"Are you all right?" Kimberli asked.

"Little nauseated," Shaye mumbled, stuffing the beacon deep under the front seat, wedging it out of sight. "Light-headed." She put her head farther between her legs as she felt for the bear spray. It was designed to convince six-hundred-pound bears that the human they were charging wasn't really worth it. The pepper-based liquid was powerful enough to shoot its spray more than fifteen feet. She'd practiced with a water version, but knew that moving targets were a lot trickier. Especially intelligent human targets.

There, in its loop on the side of the backpack. Smaller than a water bottle but not by much.

"Think I'm coming down with something," Shaye mumbled. She slid the spray canister free and hid it under her feet. "Haven't felt good all day."

"Sit up where I can see you," Ace said sharply. "Kimberli, watch the road. It gets worse in half a mile."

With a muffled sound, Shaye sat up. "Can I open the window?"

"A few inches, no more," he said.

She rolled it down and drew some slow, deep breaths. The air tasted of dust and sage beneath fading sunlight. She had thought she would feel relieved after she had activated the locater, but instead she felt tighter, like a spring being compressed and then compressed ever more until it quivered on the edge of flying apart.

Where are you, Tanner?

Why did I find you only to lose you?

There was no answer but her memory of Lorne's body and scavengers closing in.

She did some more deep breathing. The cylinder of bear spray felt comforting under her feet. The spray wouldn't kill Ace, but if she scored a direct hit, it sure would make him lose his focus.

"Now that you've had a chance to settle down and think," Kimberli said to Shaye, "you can see our point, can't you?"

Is she on crack?

"Kimberli's right," Ace said. "No need to let personal baggage get in the way of business."

Personal baggage? Does he mean Lorne?

Carefully Shaye shrugged. "I'm not sure just what the business is that we're talking about."

"Guess," Ace said.

"Since it all started with Lorne backing out of the Conservancy deal, I'll guess the business is his land." Mentally crossing her fingers, she said, "In the right hands, his ranch would make a beautiful—and beautifully profitable—resort."

"I knew you'd understand," Kimberli said, relieved and eager at the same time. "The whole thing is bigger than one old man and a run-down ranch nobody wants, including the one who supposedly inherits it. These small-town, small-time ranchers just don't get the big picture."

"Lorne sure didn't," Shaye said. That, at least, was the truth.

"He was just letting this incredible opportunity go to waste by being so stub—"

Abruptly Kimberli stopped talking long enough to make the right turn, miss second gear, and have to slow enough to start all over again in first. As if to make up for the mistake, she gunned the engine and jerked through the gears.

"Take it easy," Ace said. "This piece of crap is more than thirty years old. We've got a ways to go yet."

Not to mention getting back from wherever you're going, Shaye thought bitterly. *But I don't need to worry about that little thing, do I?*

"Anyway," Kimberli said with determined brightness, "we can put Lorne's land to work for everyone now. I just wish he'd had his heart attack after he initialed the contract and signed the letter of intent."

"Inconvenient of him," Shaye said neutrally.

"Exactly. See, Ace? I told you she'd understand. There's no need for all the rough talk. Shaye is our friend."

Kimberli half turned to glance at him in the backseat. The movement made the rhinestones on her silk shirt swirl like a mass of tiny suns shooting out her large, unlikely breasts.

"Lorne was at the end of the road," Ace said, his voice bored. "He just didn't know how close it was. Nobody ever does. There's no point in wailing over an old man's death. Emotion is a waste of energy anyway. The Conservancy traffics in nostalgia, but it's one thing to believe and another to use beliefs."

Kimberli blinked and turned her attention fully back to the road. "That sounds so . . . cold."

"Give me cold over stupid every time," he said. "Just up past those fences and over the cattle grate, turn left."

"I don't see a road," Kimberli complained. Her expression said she wasn't happy at the turn of the conversation.

"It's not much, but it's there. Follow my directions and you won't even have to use low range."

Kimberli gripped the wheel tighter. "It will be dark soon. You know I don't like night driving."

"You think I like banging my butt in the cargo space?"

She pouted.

How stupid are you, Kimberli? Shaye thought. *Do you really believe that Lorne died of a heart attack and that this is all just talky-talk business? A little seamy, a lot cold, but still, just business?*

"Stupid people live in the past," Ace said as if he had been reading

Shaye's mind. "Smart ones live in the present and plan for the future."

Kimberli nodded.

"Like a high-end resort on low-rent land," Shaye said.

"Among other things," he said. "The present always becomes the future. The intelligent choice is to understand that and not get tangled in emotions and the past."

"There's always a cost," she said, easing forward again as though to scratch her leg.

Her fingertips brushed the backpack. She flipped the top closed but didn't fasten it.

"Sure," he said with a smile. "Take notes, Kimberli. Your blue-jeaned protégée is about to name her price."

Shaye started to deny it, then realized how dumb that would be.

"Sure," she said, echoing his tone. "I want a job."

He laughed. "I was right all along. You were just stirring things up to see if there was a better payday in it for you. Self-interest is at the heart of every idealist."

"I've never met an idealist, so I wouldn't know," she said.

She doubted Ace had, either.

THIRTY-EIGHT

TANNER DROVE INTO the Mountain View Motel's parking lot the same way he had driven since the gas station—too fast. The first thing he saw was a champagne Lexus parked opposite number twenty-three. He pulled in next to it.

The Nevada license plate on the Lexus showed a rearing horse. The plate itself said SAVE IT. The plate holder said NEVADA RANCH CONSERVANCY.

A chill settled deeper into Tanner's gut. Despite everything, he still had hoped he was wrong, that Shaye was just asleep, safe, a cell phone with a dead battery on the night table beside her.

Now he knew that for the fool's dream it was. This was one too many in the string of coincidences clouding Lorne's death.

Okay, so Kimberli isn't just into conning rich men. She has a sideline in kidnapping. Or did she somehow talk Shaye into taking a drive? And where did Kimberli meet Rua? Did she pay him with sex? Can she even hold a handgun well enough to hit him at close range? Is she cold enough for murder one?

Tanner didn't particularly like Kimberli, and he knew that if pushed hard enough, anyone could kill, but he was having a hard time seeing her as having the brainpower or the sheer stones to pull off swindling Lorne, hiring out a murder, and then killing the murderer herself.

The important thing is to find Shaye and keep her safe. With me.

He reached under the front seat and hauled out his pistol in its belt holder. He kept the weapon in hand and clipped the holster to the back of his jeans. Nevada didn't require a license to carry a weapon in plain sight, so he wasn't worried about pulling his shirt out to cover the gun.

The air smelled vaguely of woodsmoke. Tanner didn't hear any sirens, so he ignored it. Keeping his pistol along his right leg, he climbed the stairs. The tag requesting maid service dangled in the fitful wind. Left-handed, he fished the key card out of his jeans pocket, unlocked and threw open the door to number twenty-three.

No sound.

No shots.

No body.

The room's stale air felt clammy after the dry, late-afternoon air outside. He breathed in cautiously but thoroughly. No scent of blood and human waste.

Thank God.

Tanner went through the two rooms with the speed and care of the cop he was.

Empty.

His pulse beat heavily as he put his pistol in its holster. Shaye wasn't dead or hurt inside the room, but that didn't make her being safe and alive anywhere else a certainty.

At least I don't have to worry about leaving prints, he thought as he began to search the room, *because I don't have any gloves on me.*

Just one more thing I didn't think I'd need in Refuge.

He didn't know what he expected to find in the room, but anything was better than what he had now. There wasn't enough sunlight left for a decent search, so he turned on every light in the place. The energy-efficient bulbs were slow, dim, and made everything a ghastly shade of greenish yellow.

The bedspread was a tangled mess, sheets whipped around it like sails that had come unmoored in wind. It could have looked like that for a perfectly innocent reason. He and Shaye had all but attacked each other in their rush to get skin to skin, need to need, heat to heat. The memory was both beautiful and bleak.

She should be here.

If only I hadn't left her . . .

Don't go there, he told himself. *Think like a cop, not a lover, because a lover won't do Shaye a damn bit of good right now.*

Since none of her clothes were tossed around the way they had been when he left, she must have gotten dressed before she disappeared. Even her jacket was gone. The furniture hadn't been moved. There were stains on the carpet, but none of them was fresh.

He opened drawers and found the courtesy pen and notepad undisturbed. He picked up the notepad, tilting and turning to catch the light, making sure that there wasn't an impression left by any note she might have tried to write.

The paper was unmarked. All the other drawers were empty. So was the closet. The bed was solid to the floor. Nothing was caught in the blackout curtains on any of the windows.

No water was drying on the shower glass or splashed on the floor. Two of the washrags and towels were rumpled. He had used one set for a fast cleanup. Presumably Shaye had used the other. A wad of toilet paper in the trash can—

Wait.

I didn't leave that. Did Shaye?

When he prodded the toilet paper, he felt something solid beneath. He grabbed a strip of tissue to protect his fingers and preserve any possible evidence. If this was the kind of crime scene he was afraid it was, technicians would be trying to lift latent prints from every surface, even the unlikely ones like toilet paper.

Gently he teased apart the wad of tissue until Shaye's cell phone lay in plain view. The phone was off. The SIM card was gone.

A combination of rage and fear flashed through Tanner, vaporizing the ice in his gut in the instant before he clamped down on his self-control. Shaye damn well deserved better than some hothead tearing around the landscape punching everything in sight.

He forced himself to breathe calmly, but his mind still clawed like a caged animal.

Nevada is a big, empty state. Lots of places to hide bodies.

Too many.

I could search for the rest of my life and—

Vaguely he realized his hand hurt. He glanced down, saw his left fist beating methodically on the cheap wood cabinet like it was a punching bag. Slowly he forced his fingers to unclench.

Use your head, he told himself savagely. *You can beat the hell out of something later.*

The sound of a maid's cart bumping along the cement walkway a story below focused Tanner. He strode out of the room, flipped the card to DO NOT DISTURB, and trotted down the stairs. He saw a young woman in jeans and a western shirt hauling trash from a room to the garbage section of her cart. She had the look of a pretty young mother with two jobs and not enough sleep. She probably had a gig as a cocktail waitress in the evening.

"Room twenty-three," he said, smiling and giving her plenty of physical space. Young maids were rightly nervous of being caught alone in a room by a strange man.

"Hi," she said, smiling. "I saw the service card out, and I'll be up as soon as I finish here. Should only be a minute."

"No problem," he said easily. "My woman was supposed to wait for me, but the room is empty. You notice anyone heading into or out of our room?"

"I was outside taking a smoke by the Dumpster a little while ago. Saw two blondes and a guy almost your size, wearing fishing gear and a floppy hat to cover up what looked like a bald head. One of the blondes looked like a rodeo queen, all big hair and makeup and glitter on her tight shirt. The other blonde was the real kind, but she could have used some of her friend's makeup. Real pale, you know?"

Kimberli and Ace.

Tanner's jaw tightened but he nodded amiably. "I know them. They're hard to say no to."

"Your girlfriend didn't look real eager."

"Any sign she was really unwilling? Last I heard, she was mad at them."

The maid shrugged. "She was on her own feet, not real happy but not fighting. Probably getting over her mad."

"You see which car they took?"

"Old orange Bronco. I didn't see where they went, because my break was over and I had to get back to work. Boss was driving into the parking lot."

He pulled out his wallet and gave her a ten. He knew what life working two jobs was like. "Thanks. And don't bother with room twenty-three. We're staying the night. She must have left the sign wrong-side out."

The ten disappeared into the woman's front pocket. "A lot of people do. Boss is too cheap to have separate signs. You sure about the room? I don't mind."

"I'm sure."

The woman stretched her back, stuffed an armload of sheets and towels in her cart, closed the door to the room she had just made up, and pushed the cart back the way it had come.

Tanner watched her without seeing her, caught by the memory of Rua dead on his back in his bedroom, lit by the unearthly glow of the aquarium.

Except it was Shaye's face, Shaye's body.

He grabbed his cell phone, found August's number in the memory, and called the deputy on his private phone.

"What's new?" the deputy asked. "Someone else drew second shift, so I'm off in thirty."

"Kimberli's car is in the motel parking lot. The maid saw two blondes—one flashy, one natural—and a probably bald-headed man get in an old orange Bronco. Shaye's cell phone was buried in the bathroom wastebasket. The SIM card is gone. Shaye promised she would be here when I got back from the wild-goose chase Ace sent me on to Reno. I'm assuming a hostage situation."

"Shit. Desmond, too? You're certain?"

"As much as I can be without having seen it myself. That enough to get the sheriff off his dead ass?"

"Doubt it. He can come up with more objections than you have answers or time. Desmond is a big supporter. Besides, the sheriff is on his way to El Dorado County."

The sound of computer keys clicking came over the phone as August talked.

"But," the deputy said, "I outrank Mercer. I just upgraded the BOLO to a potential felony in progress. Then I'll—damn, the other phone is ringing. Hang on. I'm not off the clock yet."

Tanner headed for Lorne's truck and waited. He was getting in behind the wheel when August came back on the line.

"SAR county coordinator got a call from a monitoring service. Seems that an emergency beacon used by one of our SAR people has been activated and is broadcasting."

"Search and rescue?"

"Yes. The ID matches the beacon we issued to Shaye when she volunteered for SAR duty. It's moving, so they can't get a real fix on it. Can't raise her cell phone, either, but after what you told me I won't try anymore. Her beacon's radio is on standby, so they can't get through to her. Besides, everybody but the three-legged dog is—"

"How close is the beacon?" Tanner cut in, starting the truck.

"South and east of Refuge. Our nearest four-wheel patrol car is at least an hour away, more if they keep going toward tribal lands. Some of the dirt tracks out there need high clearance."

"What about a helicopter?"

"Look to the west and what do you see?" the deputy asked.

"Mountains and some clouds."

"One of those clouds is a lot of smoke in east El Dorado County, burning over the line to Refuge County. People have been cut off and burned out. Everything that can fly is already gone. SAR is scrambling to check on hikers."

Tanner had seen too many brushfires in Los Angeles County not to know what an uncontrolled fire meant, especially with population in danger.

"Give me directions to the beacon's location," he said.

August did, then listened as Tanner repeated everything back to him verbatim.

"And do me a favor," Tanner added. "If any speed teams are still working, keep them off my ass."

"What are you driving?"

He described Lorne's truck right down to the license plate.

"Okay. You've just been deputized to pursue the BOLO. Leave your phone on. I'll tell you if the locater changes direction."

"I owe you," Tanner said, meaning it.

"Stuff it. Shaye is worth getting fired over. She's one of the good people. Find her. I'm taking a radio and following as soon as Mercer arrives and I can swap my patrol car for my own truck."

Tanner left the motel parking lot so fast he made marks on the old asphalt.

THIRTY-NINE

B ABY, I GOTTA pee," Kimberli said. "The bumps are really shaking things up."

"We'll be stopping just above the tree line. If you're feeling modest, you can use a tree for cover. Otherwise, go beside the car."

"You're kidding," she said.

"You see any toilets out here?" he asked. "Think about something else. You're not the only one with a dime bladder on a bumpy dollar ride."

Kimberli gave him a look, but didn't say anything. She kept on driving, but more slowly now, trying to avoid bumps.

Shaye looked beyond the Bronco. Far beyond. The desolation was complete. Way off in the Sierra Nevadas to the north and west, a fire was burning, making its own dirty cloud. The rest of the sky was clean except for contrails like fingernail scratches over the twilight, still too bright for a moon or stars. The fair-weather clouds were gone except to the south, where a wild storm cell was sweeping over the land.

But not here. Here there was a dry wind sucking moisture from everything, despite the almost-evening coolness outside. The land itself seemed unfinished, as if whoever created it had sketched only the outlines of what would come before giving up and abandoning the project. The remaining mountains were the bones of creation shoving through the land's thin, brittle skin.

In the high summer, being out here without water meant a day or two of survival if you found shade. In the sun, you could measure your life expectancy in hours. Even after the introduction of automobiles, the Emigrant Trail had claimed more than its share of travelers. The first person Shaye had ever gone on a SAR mission for had been out in the same kind of country she was seeing now.

Prospectors, mustangs, and wiry range cattle had left a spiderweb of scars on the thin-skinned land. Unlike the Sierra Nevadas, there were few springs in the rumpled, low mountains along the eastern edge of the valley and almost no running water during the summer. The only signs of humanity were the rutted dirt road ahead and a scant handful of windmills drawing water for range cattle lower down in the valley. More of the windmills were abandoned than still functioning. This was hardscrabble land, inhabited by little but jackrabbits, sagebrush, rattlesnakes, and wind.

It was also a dangerous land, with risks deeper than the obvious dryness and lack of cover. Old-time and modern prospectors alike had walked away from useless mines without covering the holes or fencing around them, leaving behind death traps for the unlucky or unwary.

Shaye understood the risks because she had been on three SAR missions in areas like this. At the bottom of an unmarked mine shaft, she had seen her first body. She knew others went undiscovered, unknown, lost.

She was terrified she would be one of them.

We'll be stopping just above the tree line.

Behind and below them, there was no dust lifted off the dirt road by speeding tires, no sign of a moving vehicle, nothing but the slowly, slowly fading light and the increasing coolness of a desert headed toward the cover of darkness.

Is the beacon transmitting? Shaye asked silently. *Is anybody listening? Does Tanner know I'm gone?*

They were coming up across the steep range of hills that would be called mountains if they were east of the Rockies. They had passed several dirt tracks leading to water or forgotten mines or even abandoned homesteads. They might have crossed into tribal holdings. Without a GPS reading it was impossible to tell. Out this far, few people bothered to fence the great dry lands of Nevada.

Even if Shaye managed to get away and hide, there was nowhere to go. Without the Bronco and its SAR beacon, she was as good as dead.

I wish I could talk to you, Tanner. Hold you. Feel the tightness of your skin over your chest. Smell the heat of you. Hear your heart against mine in passion and in peace.

The tree line was less than half an hour away, unless the road got worse. Then it would take as long as it took.

"Go north the next chance you get," Ace said.

"North?"

"Left," he said. "Don't you know where the sun sets?"

"Of course. It goes behind the big mountains beyond Refuge. What does that have to do with anything?"

"God," he muttered, "it's a wonder you don't get lost in the Conservancy's tiny parking lot."

Silently Shaye agreed.

The pout on Kimberli's face took on a wary, almost pinched look, but she smoothed it out and smiled at him. "We both know you're the smart one and I'm the one people like being around. No need to be mean about it."

Ace didn't answer.

Kimberli concentrated on driving so as to avoid the bumps that made her full bladder whine.

No one talked as they crept up toward the dark line where there was enough water for trees to survive the dry summer.

"Go left," Ace finally said.

"There isn't a—" Kimberli began.

"Just do it. There are old ruts. Follow them."

She turned on the high beams, ignoring his muttered protest.

Shaye didn't point out that it was easier to spot the track in the twilight without using the high beams. She was happy for Kimberli's inexperience in backcountry. Anything that slowed them down was fine with Shaye.

The Bronco was barely doing five miles per hour. Unless the driver shifted to low range, the engine would stall out soon.

Or they could run out of gas short of Ace's destination.

Shaye didn't mention that, either. If nobody had noticed that the gas gauge hadn't changed, she wouldn't point it out.

"Faster," Ace said. "It's not nearly as bad as you think."

Her face tight and her hands clenched on the wheel, Kimberli goosed the accelerator—and nearly high-centered the Bronco on a roadside rock.

"Not that fast! Jesus, don't you know how to drive?"

Saying nothing, hands clenched in grim determination, Kimberli returned to creeping along at barely a walking pace. This time Ace didn't object, even when she stalled out and had to start the engine again.

Too bad the ground isn't soft, Shaye thought grimly. *She would get us stuck in a second. Then we'd have to walk wherever Ace wants to go.*

She looked ahead and wondered where her grave would be.

On either side of the Bronco, the boulders increased in size, crouching like beasts. The light hung on with the stubbornness of life itself while shadows pooled in ravines that grew steeper the higher they went. Slowly the forest was increasing around them, dark trees sucking the radiance out of the sky.

Carefully, Shaye's hand crept toward the door handle. A little bit darker and she just might have a chance of getting to cover before Ace could stop her.

Something flashed at the corner of her vision. Metal.

A gun.

"This is my in-town gun," Ace said casually. "Just a .22, but it gets the job done. So relax and stop thinking about opening the door and making a run for it. Nothing out there anyway but a hard way to die. I'll make it easy for you, though. No fuss, no muss, no pain."

"Is that what you wanted, Kimberli?" Shaye asked. "Accessory to murder one?"

"You're being ridiculous," the other woman snapped. "What do you want everyone to do—crawl off and survive on welfare? No thanks twice. I was raised like that and I'd rather be dead than do it again."

"You'll get your wish."

"What are you talking about?" Kimberli said, looking at Shaye.

"Watch the road!" Ace ordered.

At the last instant, she jerked the wheel and just missed a boulder that had been lurking in the shadow of the headlights. The track pitched down into a forested ravine. Boulders gleamed everywhere like giant bones.

"Do you really think Ace is going to let—" Shaye began. Pain flashed behind her eyes, followed by a few moments of light-headedness.

"I told you not to snipe at Kimberli while she's driving," he said, his voice as emotionless as the gun that had rapped her head. "No more talking or you'll die now, here, the hard way. I'll smash your kneecaps and your elbows and leave you for the vultures."

Kimberli sighed and shook her head. Her attitude was that of an engineer at a séance—no real belief in the topic at all. Or else she was too terrified to believe, because that meant things were real and she really didn't want to know about it.

Shaye stopped talking. Unlike the other woman, she believed that Ace meant every ugly word of his threat.

Silently Kimberli concentrated on driving down the unraveling track, while Ace watched them both like the killer he was.

FORTY

TANNER SWERVED AROUND a moldy yellow Volkswagen covered with peeling stick-on daisies. He slowed only when he approached the faded sign indicating a crossroad. The road he turned onto was still paved, but it was as worn and patched as the motel's parking lot had been.

His phone rang. He hit the speaker button. "What?"

"Beacon is heading straight east now."

Tanner listened while August gave him more instructions.

"I checked with state patrol," the deputy added. "They're covering beats for cops in areas closer to the fire. Everyone from Reno to the state line is on standby for evacuation duty if the wind shifts and pushes the fire over. I can't leave."

"Got it." Tanner didn't like it, but he understood where August was. "Keep me in the loop as long as you can."

"Even on evac duty, I'll bridge for you with the SAR monitor. But the beacon will be out of the county soon. The next county's back-road vehicles were up north on a medical emergency at a ranch. One of them is rolling now toward the south to look for the Bronco."

"Hope he enjoys the ride. By the time he gets here, it will all be over one way or another."

"The good news," August said roughly, "is that Ace is going to run out of anything that even a four-wheel with low range can handle. Then they're on foot. How good are you at sign cutting in the dark?"

"Not since I was a boy. What am I heading into?"

"Contour map shows national forest and rangeland—scrub and granite at the lower elevations, pines and granite higher up. Rough country. No springs close to any road. Mines both abandoned and working. Rocks and dirt and a lot of thirst. Not a good place for hiking."

But a great place for stashing bodies.

Both men thought it.

Neither man said it aloud.

"You have GPS capability?" August asked.

"An app on my phone. That good enough?"

"Hell of a lot better than it used to be. When you get off the marked roads, call me. Don't want you to overshoot any turnoffs."

"Will do."

Tanner concentrated on the fading light and the county road that was crumbling at the edges and potholed in unlikely places. He went as fast as he dared, much faster than was safe or even sane.

So much country.

So damn little time.

He looked out at the empty tall hills folding up into small mountains. Rocky alluvial fans spilled out of ravines that were dry until it rained hard and often. Then they held flash floods that made boulders dance. The deputy's words echoed in Tanner's mind like a bell tolling.

Rough country.

Damned rough.

Tanner shoved away the fury and despair that were his own personal devils, but the truth was impossible to ignore. This place was uninhabited for a reason. Dust and stone and scrub rumpling up to sparse forest at higher elevation.

Rough country.

Damned rough.

No matter how hard he pushed the truck, Tanner felt like he was nailed to an endless present, motionless against the huge landscape. He would have killed or died to be a falcon, able to fly straight and high, predator's eyes zeroing in on any motion below. He would see Shaye, fall into a stoop, and tear out Ace's eyes for daring to threaten her.

A blind man wouldn't know how to hide.

But Tanner sure knew how to hunt.

Usually he enjoyed the wild desolation of Nevada's empty spaces. But not now. Now he dreaded the certainty that he was driving straight into a land that didn't care about human life or death. The country had been here for eons, it would be here for eons more. It ate the bones of the living with the same indifference that it absorbed heat or rain.

At least the Bronco is still moving.

No recent signs of off-roading along here.

No black signature of vultures gathering for a fast snack before the light disappears.

The only hope he had was the certainty that Ace was a canny man, not a greenhorn who would make mistakes out of fear or impatience. Ace was the kind who would make a woman dig her own grave to save him the trouble.

Don't think about graves.

Tanner drove into the deepening twilight, searching for lights ahead. He thought he saw several flashes near or in the tree line above. Enough to give him hope.

Enough to make him drive as long and as far as possible without lights. If the lights really belonged to Shaye's Bronco, Tanner didn't want to give himself away.

Or push Ace into rushing the job.

The phone announced an incoming call. Tanner hit the speaker button and said, "Where are they?"

"Up just past the tree line. Contour map places them in or near a deep ravine just north of the county road you'd be on if you were driving a race car. But in Lorne's old truck, you'll still be on the main highway. Can you give me your GPS coordinates?"

"Stand by." Tanner grabbed the phone and activated the GPS feature long enough to read off his coordinates.

"That far? Holy crap," August said. "Are you crazy?"

"It's a good old truck," Tanner said, eyeing the gauges warily. Engine was hot, but not dangerously so. Yet. "Tires are good. Mileage and suspension suck at speed but it goes like hell if you have the stones to push it."

"Jesus, man. You won't do Shaye any good if you roll over. Get ready to slow down. You'll be on gravel soon. Go for about three miles. Take the first ruts going north. It unravels into the countryside at an old mine just beyond the tree line. It's hard going. The locater is barely moving anymore."

"Coordinates," Tanner snapped.

As August gave the numbers, Tanner fed them into the GPS app on his phone. The display showed no roads worth mentioning, only dirt tracks that dead-ended for no reason in particular. "Where are the old mines?"

"Everywhere. You're not all that far from one of the biggest silver strikes ever made. Place is riddled by weekend prospectors. Or was. Metal fever comes and goes. How's the charge on your phone?"

"Good for at least an hour more. Two if I don't talk a lot."

"I've got a lock on your phone. I'm coming as fast as I can."

"What about evac duty?"

"Called off. Wind died down when the sun went behind the mountains."

"Small blessings," Tanner said.

"Amen. I'll catch up as soon as possible."

Neither man mentioned that August had a 99 percent chance of arriving too late for much more than identifying bodies.

FORTY-ONE

THE BRONCO FINALLY came to a lurching halt.

"Sorry, baby, but I gotta pee right now," Kimberli said, reaching for the door handle.

"You're not the only one," Ace said as Kimberli stalked off into the thickening dusk. He concentrated on Shaye. "Put your left arm back between the seats. Slowly."

Shaye hesitated.

"Do it."

The cold muzzle of the gun sank into her ear, telling her that she could die here, now, or she could obey.

Ace had been bad enough when Kimberli was around. Without her, he made Shaye's skin crawl in stark warning.

Slowly her left arm slid back between the front seats. As she partly turned, she saw a flash of hot pink. Disbelieving, she focused on the colorful open handcuffs trailing from blunt male fingers. Bright, fake fur padded the inside of the vaguely heart-shaped cuffs, providing a playful cushion for sex games.

But the cuff itself made a solid sound as it locked around her wrist. Even in bed, Ace played to win. The other cuff clicked closed around the metal brace underneath her seat.

"They look good on you," he said, his glance traveling over her body. "But then, they look good on any woman."

She forced back her hot words by thinking how different Ace was without Kimberli around. Blunter, colder, harder. Like a mask had been taken off to reveal the death's-head beneath.

He's helping Kimberli be as stupid as she needs to be, Shaye realized.

The knowledge was chilling and sparked a small flicker of hopeful fire. If the other woman could be brought to realize that she was going to die up here, maybe she would help both of them get out alive.

Once Ace was sure that Shaye couldn't escape, he pulled the keys out of the ignition and pocketed them. Then, loose shirt rippling in the wind, he walked quickly into the sparse cover of the forest.

She yanked on the cuffs hard enough to hurt. Twice, three times. Four.

Not enough time for this. I'll have to do what I can one-handed.

As she wriggled around enough to grab the canister of bear spray from under her feet, a surge of wind and grit peppered the Bronco like a handful of dirt at a graveside ceremony. She stashed the spray between her thighs.

The Maglite was next. It had four D-cell batteries inside and was heavy enough to break a person's nose. Or skull, if it caught someone just right. She shoved the flashlight between her butt and the back of the seat. Not comfortable, but comforting. Any chance, no matter how slender, was better than certain death.

Then she remembered the Leatherman. She had been thinking in terms of pure weapons. The knife on the Leatherman was more for cutting kindling than throats, but the handy little many-tools-in-one might be able to break open a link on the handcuffs.

It seemed like minutes, but really was only seconds before her fingers closed around the tool's leather carrying case inside the backpack. She opened the snap of the case with her teeth and shook out the Leatherman. Awkwardly using her cuffed hand, she expanded the jaws of the pliers, then positioned them around one of the links connecting the cuffs.

Her hand slipped, then slipped again. Vaguely she realized that she was sweating, clammy. Working by feel, she finally got the jaws around a link and squeezed. The cuffs might not have been law-enforcement grade, but they weren't aluminum foil, either. Nothing budged.

She twisted her wrist repeatedly, winding the chain until it was taut, humming. Then she clamped down on the pliers with all the strength of her desperation.

There was a grinding sound of metal on metal. Sweating, she sawed and gnawed on the metal with the tough little tool, trying to keep the link way back in the jaws, where there was a wire cutter. She thought she felt something move. Hope gave her a surge of strength.

Kimberli's shirt flashed in the headlights, a silent warning.

Biting her lip, wishing for Tanner's raw male strength, Shaye gave one last wrench.

Maybe it was hope, maybe it was the links, but she sensed that something gave. She yanked again.

And stayed attached to the seat.

She stuffed the pliers out of sight just as Kimberli got into the Bronco. The open door attracted bugs to the overhead light and ruined any chance of letting eyes adjust to the thickening dark.

Kimberli noticed the flash of bright pink connecting Shaye to the seat and snickered. "He's a playful one, isn't he?" she said, her voice teasing.

All that kept Shaye from trying to use the bear spray on the other woman was the certainty that the blowback inside the Bronco would put her out of commission as fast as it did Kimberli.

"Relax," Kimberli said soothingly. "Ace just talks mean. He's really a pussycat. All you have to do is rub him the right way. Didn't your mama teach you anything at all about handling men?"

The only way I'd touch Ace is with a cattle prod, Shaye thought bitterly. *Is Kimberli really stupid? Crazy?*

Dumb like a fox?

One of the other woman's most obvious and bewildering traits was that she could make herself sing cheerfully with any chorus she had to. Whether that made her crazy, stupid, or as coldly pragmatic as Ace didn't really matter. The result was the same.

Shaye was on her own.

But she didn't stop trying. Stupid could be educated. It just took more time than she was afraid she had.

"Do you know a man called Tonio or Tony Rua?" she asked carefully.

"Never heard of him," Kimberli said. "Sounds Italian, or maybe Mexican?"

"He was a mixed-martial-arts fighter, like your playful lover."

"Really," Kimberli said with a total lack of interest. She turned the rearview mirror to check her makeup.

"Rua had a specialty. It's called a heart shot. He used it to kill Lorne."

With a sigh that was somewhere between patience and irritation, Kimberli pulled lip gloss out of her tiny backpack purse. "Lorne died of a heart attack and everyone knows it. No wonder Ace is so moody, what with you and your hookup spreading rumors to anyone who will listen. Who benefits from that?"

"Rua died of bullets. Ace killed him after Rua killed Lorne."

Kimberli paused, gloss wand in her hand. Then she shook her head firmly, making her bleached hair stir. "Ace wouldn't really do something like that. It's just part of his tough-guy act." She went back to slicking her lips. "Honestly, sometimes I just don't understand you."

"Right now you aren't a murderer," Shaye said. "Ace is. You could walk out of here."

"Ace is a good businessman. He'll pay a generous price for Lorne's ranch and that money will be put toward buying three other huge ranches with a lot more acreage in mustang territory. Everyone will benefit, can't you see that?"

"All I see is Lorne's scavenged corpse."

"Oh, that's just nasty." Kimberli shivered. "Anyway, it's not like he was sixteen with all his life in front of him. He was an old man."

"He was alive," Shaye said doggedly. "Someone murdered him."

"Honestly, how a bright girl like you can be so stupidly blind about the simplest things . . ." Kimberli shook her head. "People younger than Lorne die all the time of perfectly natural causes. What is up with you? The Conservancy will sell the land to Ace for enough money to buy ranches on the mustang range. The people around Refuge will have work at the new resort. My bosses will be happy and the mustangs will be happy and I'll be promoted and Ace and I will get married and I'll never have to worry about money ever again. It's win-win-win."

"What if Ace decides to kill you and keep all the money?"

"Why would he do that? Nobody can blow him like I do. When you have control of a man's dick, you have control of the man."

Shaye tried another approach. "If Lorne wasn't murdered, why are you and Ace kidnapping me?"

Kimberli's face struggled to frown. Botox kept her from being successful.

"He wouldn't let me talk to you anywhere that he, personally, wasn't certain was safe," she explained. "He said it would be stupid because anyone could walk in or record stuff and make the Conservancy look bad. You know how the media is—bad news sells better than good. That's why he took away your phone."

Shaye felt the frayed threads of her temper slipping through her fingers.

"I didn't want to come all the way to the end of some no-name dirt road just to talk to you," Kimberli continued, "but he wouldn't listen. He doesn't trust you to know a good thing. Then you kept being bitchy and it just kept getting worse. As soon as Ace settles down and you guys have your talk, everything will be fine. When he's in a mood like this, a smart woman shuts up and doesn't push."

"And you're going to marry him?" Shaye asked before she could stop herself.

The older woman laughed. "I said he was rich and smarter than me, not that he was a purse-pet like Peter. Anyway, Ace is a lot better than my first husband."

"Tanner won't believe whatever setup Ace has planned. He will look for me until he knows the truth."

"The truth is, Tanner Davis will go back to L.A. a rich man." Kimberli capped the gloss with a gesture that said the conversation was over.

She's going to die, too, Shaye thought. *She's just too willfully blind to let herself see it.*

With a disgusted sound, Kimberli slapped her arm and squashed a mosquito. "What's taking Ace so long? Is his zipper stuck?"

Maybe he tripped and broke his neck, Shaye thought. What she said was, "Close the door. Light just attracts mosquitoes."

"What do they live on out here?" Kimberli complained.

"People who leave doors open."

The door slammed shut.

Shaye had been expecting the sudden darkness. If she hadn't been handcuffed, she would have been gone. As it was, she would have to wait until Ace returned. Unless . . .

"Do you have a key to these cuffs?" she asked calmly.

"Of course not. Ace keeps all the keys—it's the way he his, some sort of control issues."

"And you don't mind?"

"He's rich and smarter than I am. What's to mind?"

Shaye gave up. Reality had nothing to offer the other woman but getting old and dying.

Silently, Shaye thought about ways to escape and live. Only one seemed remotely possible.

First I have to get out of the cuffs.

Then the bear spray.

Even with both hands free, she would need a moment to pull the tab on the spray and turn the nozzle in the right direction. She doubted that Ace would give her that kind of time.

Whatever the state of his mind, cotton candy was no part of it.

Speak of the devil, she thought unhappily.

The door opened. In a flash of overhead light, Kimberli hopped out, letting Ace get inside. His bald head gleamed in the light.

"What took you so long?" Kimberli asked. "You didn't trip and hurt yourself, did you?"

"I tried to see if anyone was following us."

"Why would anyone do that?" she asked.

He handed the keys to Kimberli. "Just drive. I'll do the thinking. Keep to the left. There's a mine head up that way."

"Mine head? You mean, like a hole in the ground?"

"Do you know another kind of mine?"

"All I know about mines is that money comes out of them."

With that, Kimberli started the Bronco and crept up the unraveling track, keeping to the left.

Shaye wondered why some woman hadn't cut off parts of Ace while he slept.

"Don't worry about any gates, either," he added.

"I know, I know, you have the keys," Kimberli said.

"No, you do. It's called the accelerator."

Shaye understood, but even if Kimberli didn't, the other woman didn't ask any questions.

Tires crunching gravel and sage, the Bronco inched forward. Ace made grumbling sounds of impatience, but he didn't distract Kimberli by yelling at her.

Shaye didn't, either. She had an aching memory of the feel of a gun rapping against her skull.

I'm going to die here wearing these stupid sex-toy handcuffs. And Kimberli of the ridiculous tits and blond extensions is driving me all the way to hell.

Hysterical laughter rose like an acid bubble in Shaye.

Breathe.

Just breathe.

While you can.

FORTY-TWO

THE ROCKY RIDGES ahead of Tanner were dark, the copper glow of the setting sun only a memory. Everything was drowned in shadows darker than any bruise. The dirt road was a faint, pale thread leading to nowhere.

Tanner turned the wheel and shot off the battered asphalt to follow the dirt. Dust rose all around, nearly invisible, leaving grit on every surface. The dust around the truck gathered into a ragged banner, flickering with the least change in direction of the wind. He drove like screaming hell, sending dirt spewing everywhere when the road turned, barely holding the straight pieces, and still he felt like he was glued in place.

The knifepoint glitter of a few stars and a partial moon rising were the only illumination. In the rumpled land ahead of the old truck, night spilled out of ravines and spiked up the ridges.

No lights showed ahead of him, no flash or gleam to pierce the layers of darkness. The dirt road was a shade or two lighter than the surrounding brush. So were the boulders that stuck out without warning. One of them tried to eat the truck's right front tire.

I can't wait any longer, Tanner thought grimly.

He turned on the headlights, losing stealth but gaining visibility. Tire tracks leaped out on the dusty stretches of the road, the tread marks crisp enough to leave tiny shadows. His memory told him that was a good sign.

Someone was here recently. Wind makes short work of tread marks out here.

The bad news was that headlights announced his presence like a siren.

Can't see light ahead of me. They're probably in one of the folds in those small mountains. Can't see me.

I can't see them, either.

He pressed down on the accelerator and settled in for a rough ride. The road was made for maybe thirty miles an hour at best. He was doing twice that. The rutted dirt rose and fell, twisted and snaked, and generally behaved like something engineered by cowboys a century ago.

With one hand he brought his cell phone up and checked the battery and signal. Battery was good.

There wasn't enough signal to matter.

He hit the redial button just to be sure. The phone spun idly for three seconds, five, ten.

CALL FAILED.

Shit! August can't help me anymore.

Tanner wanted to throw the phone against the windshield, but he had better self-control, so he wedged it under his thigh. Depending on where the satellites were positioned in the sky, GPS could still be an option. But he suspected there were places out here that even GPS couldn't reach.

He hoped to hell he wasn't in one of them.

The image of Rua's dead face turned ghastly by the light of the fish tank kept eating into Tanner. That memory he could live with. It was the way the face kept morphing into Shaye's that was leaving a hole in his guts.

Don't think about it. Just drive.

And pray.

If Shaye doesn't come out of those mountains, I'll kill Ace.

It wasn't a prayer, but it gave Tanner patience when he wanted to explode right out of his skin. He'd seen people like himself before—parents of missing kids, families of miners waiting outside a mine explosion, waiting, waiting, waiting for news.

After enough time, even proof of death was a relief.

Stop thinking, he snarled at himself. *Do the only thing you can do. Drive.*

His hands gripped the wheel and he pushed everything else out of his mind. No distractions, no mistakes, nothing but the fact that Shaye needed him.

The phone chirped.

Tanner knew what had happened. There wasn't enough reliable signal to carry talk, but texts needed only an instant of connection to get through. He retrieved the phone and read quickly.

CELL SIGNAL GONE.
LOOK FOR TRACK ON LEFT.
MINES IN AREA. DANGEROUS.

That didn't surprise Tanner. People had been falling into abandoned mines when he was a boy. The mines hadn't been covered since then and human nature didn't change.

Easy to hide a body.

Forever.

FORTY-THREE

A GATE?" KIMBERLI asked in a rising voice. "You want me to drive through a closed gate?"

Ace grabbed a handful of her hair and twisted hard enough to get her attention. "Yes. Just aim and don't let up on the gas."

The gate loomed just at the edge of the headlights.

Shaye hoped they would crash or roll. Ace was more vulnerable in the backseat than they were in the front.

"But it's closed!" Kimberli squeaked.

"Do it."

From the corner of her eye, Shaye caught all the hard edges of Ace's determination. Kimberli took one look in the rearview mirror and gunned the engine.

The fence flew apart with a rending crunch. Chunks bounced over the windshield and side panels. Something caught in the grille, rattled, then fell off and spun out of sight. A plank caught in the undercarriage scraped along like a reluctant child. The sound made Shaye want to scream.

But then, she felt like screaming anyway. Her wrist was bruised and blood-slippery from pulling against the cuffs. The links didn't feel as solid as they had—and yet they kept on holding.

"There, that wasn't so bad, was it?" Ace said over the grinding noise of wood on rocky dirt. "Nothing to worry about. You've got to learn to trust me, baby."

Whether through fear or silent mutiny, Kimberli lost control of the wheel. Metal gnashed against a boulder with a chilling cry. Sparks exploded.

So did Ace. He cursed Kimberli in words that matched the shriek of metal on stone.

Grabbing the diversion, Shaye set her teeth and yanked. The noise of fender and rock covered the small sounds of her struggle—and of metal links giving way.

I'm free!

Okay, not really free, but not chained like a goat waiting for a tiger, either.

Though she ached to move her left arm, she didn't, not wanting anyone to notice that the cuffs had failed. With her right hand she eased the bear-spray nozzle until it was in position for a left-handed grab and a right-handed pull on the safety ring.

Slowly Ace ran out of curses.

Kimberli was as tight-lipped as only a poster for Botox could be.

"I think you got the oil pan," Shaye said, her tone matter-of-fact.

"Shut up," he snarled. But he leaned forward to watch the dashboard.

Shaye was watching the dials, too.

Nothing changed.

Damn.

"Almost there, baby," he said to Kimberli. "Just go up that rise and over the top. There's a shack on the right. And relax. You know I never can stay mad at you."

Shaye felt her opportunity to escape—to live—racing past her far faster than night had overtaken day.

"What would you have done if Lorne hadn't so conveniently died?" she asked Ace.

"We'd have gone the eminent-domain route," he said. "We'd have won, too, after spending a lot of time and money on attorneys."

"That would have raised a stink that'd make a skunk smell like roses," she said, watching Kimberli from the corner of her eye. "Nobody likes that kind of publicity, particularly Hill and Campbell. Conservancy would look like dirt, too."

Other than what might have been a flicker of discomfort trying to register on her unnaturally still face, Kimberli showed no response.

"Everyone would have survived it," Ace said. "At the end of the day, money makes everything sweet."

"Then why take Lorne out of the equation?" Shaye asked.

Kimberli opened her mouth. Nothing came out.

"Who says I did?" Ace asked with a complete lack of interest. "I was at the Carson casino when he died. Ask anyone."

"We tried to ask Rua," Shaye said, "but somebody had murdered him."

"Everyone dies. Fact of life. Some people die sooner than others. Boo fucking hoo."

Kimberli's eyes narrowed and she sort of hunched over the wheel. The farther down the road they went, the meaner and colder Ace became. Whether he realized it or not, his attitude was helping Shaye chip away at the other woman's certainty that Ace would never hurt her.

Shaye saw what Ace couldn't—Kimberli was looking more and

more scared. Maybe she finally understood what waited for her at the end of the road. She certainly had stopped whining about how much farther she'd have to drive, as if she no longer believed she'd be with Ace on the long trip home. She was also going so slow it would have been faster to walk, which was why the Bronco kept lurching and stalling.

Or maybe, just maybe, the gas tank was nearly empty, working only when it sloshed over the feed.

"We're far enough out here that nobody can overhear, no reporter is going to pop out from behind a boulder, nothing but nothing around us," Shaye said. "So why aren't you trying to talk me into coming over to the dark side and having a nice cup of Kool-Aid?"

"Impatient?" Ace asked, his tone baiting. "Don't worry, all the hassle and waiting soon will be over for you."

"I'm in no hurry to die."

"Like I said, fact of life."

The Bronco stalled out, bucked, stalled, and finally lurched over the ridgeline. Ace was too busy keeping his head from banging against the hardtop or the window to swear at Kimberli's driving.

With both hands, Shaye gripped the bear-spray canister. The next time Kimberli stalled out the Bronco—or if Ace noticed the handcuff was broken—Shaye was going to turn and give him a face shot and to hell with being in a closed car.

Kimberli made a whimpering sound that he couldn't hear, but Shaye could. The other woman was a ghost wearing rouge and mascara, a clown face driving a death car. Shaye didn't know whether to keep tearing away at the older woman's confidence or to get ready for the emotional train wreck that was coming.

Trees raked black fingers through the headlights. Off to the right, at the farthest edge of the high beams, the tilted hull of an old miner's shack loomed like news from a deadly future.

The Bronco coughed and died.

Kimberli ground on the starter. The battery did its part, but the engine didn't fire.

Shaye got ready to pitch herself out into the darkness.

Without warning, Kimberli broke. Suddenly she clawed at the driver's door and scrambled into the darkness.

"You stupid bitch!" Ace yelled, lunging forward and grabbing at her glittery shirt before it fled beyond his reach.

Kimberli jerked, then fell forward, ripping her shirt from his grasping fingers. While she scrambled to her feet, his gun flashed in the overhead light as he took aim through the open driver's door.

Shaye whipped the can of bear spray around, pointed the nozzle at his face, and pressed. The can hissed, gurgled, hiccuped, and stuttered.

The .22 went off with a sound like a very big whip cracking. Once, twice.

Kimberli ran faster.

Ace realized that the muted hiss and mutter he was hearing came from more than the engine. He glanced toward Shaye as she shouldered her door open while trying to get the bear spray to fire. He stared at her in disbelief and then pure rage, torn between aiming the gun at her and trying to protect himself by diving behind the front seat.

The bear spray finally kicked in with a huge hiss. An instant later came the whip-crack of the .22 firing and Ace's harsh curses. The smell of capsicum burned inside the Bronco, sticking to everything it touched like napalm.

Shooting wildly, Ace bellowed in shock and sudden pain, throwing himself behind the seat's protection.

Shaye hit the ground on her hands and knees, still holding her breath, eyes tightly closed against the blowback of the spray. She rolled and scrambled to her feet. The clank of metal on rock told her that she had instinctively held on to the flashlight. For an instant she considered making a grab for Ace's gun. Then common sense took over and she started running for the biggest patch of darkness she could see.

As she took her second stride she felt a numbing pain along the outside of her left calf that was so intense, she barely kept her balance.

Did I twist my knee? My ankle?

Doesn't matter.

Run!

She had to get to cover before Ace threw off the glancing encounter with the bear spray. From the corner of her eye, she could see the wink and flash of Kimberli's silver tennis shoes as she sprinted up the rough dirt track.

When his head clears, Ace will be on her like a wolf on a rabbit, Shaye thought.

Wind called hollowly through the sparse forest, making branches tremble and sway. Gently she tested her leg, which was feeling weird, almost numb, yet she knew pain was there. The leg wasn't out of commission, yet it wasn't quite reliable, like it was slow in receiving messages from her brain.

She could follow Kimberli but that would only make Ace's job easier. The best way to help the other woman was to take off in a different direction, forcing him to choose which target he followed first. No direction looked particularly welcoming, but if Shaye's orientation was correct, the arm of forest off the left bumper was between her and the twisty road back to civilization.

Making no effort at silence, much less stealth, she ran into the trees with a dogged, uneven gait. She had gone barely a hundred feet before she heard the Bronco's door slam open behind her.

Cursing, coughing, Ace started firing the .22. Bullets whined, ricocheting off rocks to the right of Shaye.

He had chosen his target and it wasn't Kimberli.

Shaye forced herself to run faster. Her leg was going from mostly numb to throbbing life. It hurt like hell burning, but it was more reliable despite the pain.

From a distance, back in the direction where Kimberli had run in a full-out panic, came a shrill scream. It was cut off sharply.

Did Kimberli fall?

No more screams came and there was nothing Shaye could do about it right now. Ace was closing in on her.

Get away from Ace. That's all that matters.

Run.

Shaye ran.

FORTY-FOUR

THE TRUCK BUCKED and jolted over the road, going too fast and not nearly fast enough. All that kept Tanner from a saner pace was the tantalizing come-on of the tire tracks ahead. As long as they continued, he would follow at breakneck speed. He bounced over another rocky rise, hoping to see the Bronco ahead.

Nothing but tracks slowly being sanded away by the increasing wind.

Can't lose them.

Faster.

He knew that he was covering ground quicker than the Bronco had, for its tracks showed none of the slipping and sliding that came from speeding over a bad surface.

Soon.

I'll overtake them soon.

Then he would be able to use the gun that was poking a hole in his back with every bounce.

And he knew just who he was going to shoot.

The engine made laboring noises. The stink of hot oil and metal filled the cab. He didn't bother to look down at the gauges. He knew the temperature needle was edging into the red zone. He'd break down soon—whether by blowing the radiator or breaking an axle. But right now he was going a whole lot faster than he could run, and that was all that mattered.

The only signs that the track had been used in years were the tread marks left by Shaye's Bronco.

Then his headlight picked out a bit of orange. In the instant that his heart leaped, he realized that he was seeing a ragged line of paint scraped off by a boulder that poked out into the road. The tree line was just beyond his headlights.

According to August's last text, he had less than a quarter of a mile before he caught up with Shaye's vehicle. Of course, that was a crow's-flight measurement. Out here, with the road twisting back on itself and snaking around obstacles as it climbed and dipped, it could be a lot more.

Briefly Tanner thought about going cross-country on foot, then decided against it. As long as the truck held together, it was the quickest way to Shaye.

The phone chirped as another text arrived. He glanced down, seeing the message in one quick sweep.

MINES AROUND U.
STAY ON ROAD.

Tanner gripped the wheel hard.
What is August, a mind reader?
The truck gnashed and hissed but kept going, spitting dirt, grit, and small stones every inch of the way. Tanner knew he owed the engine's

continued life to the coolness of the air. If the temperature had been ten degrees hotter, the engine would have seized.

It would anyway.

The only question was when.

Under the driver's relentless will, the truck bounced down the track, wallowed in the trough in the middle, and climbed up the rise like a swimmer gasping and plowing through heavy waves.

Suddenly he saw a light glowing between trees ahead and above him, off to the right. The light wasn't moving.

The Bronco had stopped.

Tanner didn't know if a trap waited ahead and didn't particularly care. The truck's temperature had gone into the red. Spectral wraiths of steam escaped from the hood and flattened across the dusty windshield, creating muddy tears. He kept the accelerator down on the floor, screaming toward the Bronco and Shaye.

Abruptly something cut into the path of the headlights.

A woman, running toward him on the road.

Shaye.

Or Kimberli.

Even on the uphill, he was going too fast to stop. He would hit her unless—

He wrenched the wheel hard to the left, away from the female shape and the miserable excuse for a road.

Between one second and the next, the going went from rough to deadly. The truck's wheels bounced over rocks as big as dogs. The steering wheel whipped back and forth, trying to break his grip. He fought it, but didn't win. The truck's center of gravity pitched up. What had started as a hard turn became a four-wheel skid. The world twisted around him like a freak show at a carnival. He braked and steered into the skid, fighting the heavy truck for control.

Headlights, tires, and metal frame did a slam-dance over the rocks and saplings at the edge of the road. He saw a boulder bigger than the truck on a collision course and knew the end of the ride was seconds away. He cramped the wheel to avoid a head-on and told himself to go loose and let the seat belt do its work.

He hoped his body listened.

The battle of metal and stone lasted only seconds that screamed like slow-motion minutes. Or maybe it was him. He was dimly aware of his head and right wrist whacking the steering wheel as the truck's front end tried to rear like a horse. His vision tunneled, then started to go black from the outside in.

At least I missed her.

Didn't I?

There was no way to answer the question right now. The truck slid sideways down the boulder and came to a wrenching stop. The diagonal ache that cut across Tanner's body from the seat belt told him that he was alive. He shook off the darkness and tried to release the belt with his right hand. It fumbled and sent back messages of pain, the kind that was in sync with his racing heart, telling him his right hand was pretty much useless right now.

Part of him noticed the steam shooting from beneath the truck's crumpled hood. The truck was finished, but he wasn't. Automatically he freed himself with his left hand and then opened the door with a well-placed shove of his shoulder. Before he got out, he made a grab for his pistol, automatically using his right hand.

With a searing curse, he switched to his left hand and awkwardly got the pistol free of its holster. The ache in his back told him he'd have a Glock-size bruise, but what really pissed him off was that as a left-handed shooter, he made a great dancer in a titty bar. But his right hand wasn't taking directions right now.

Tough shit, mook. Get going and find Shaye.

Holding the Glock in his left hand, he heaved out through the slanting cab door. He swept his glance around, saw nothing but the dim radiance of the Bronco's headlights through the tatters of steam that swirled around his own ruined truck.

If they're anywhere near, they already know someone has crashed the party.

"Shaye!" he yelled. "Are you all right?"

The *yap-yap* of a .22 firing came simultaneously with the whine of two small-caliber rounds hitting the truck. With steam blowing and hissing around him, Tanner couldn't even see a target to fire back at.

But somebody sure could see him.

No wonder Shaye didn't answer. She's hiding.

He refused to think about any other possibility for her silence.

Crouching, he kept under cover of the truck as long as he could. Whether it was Ace or Kimberli, the shooter would close in on the wreck, hoping to finish the job. At a distance, .22s were only a step up from throwing rocks.

Still bent over, he ran away with as much speed and stealth as he could manage. Keeping something between him and the shooter—trees, a boulder, a big cluster of scrub—slowed him down, but not enough to matter. Pain was there, keeping pace with his heart. That didn't matter, either.

A pure rage fueled him. It was the flip side of the fear that had iced his gut ever since he'd seen that the SIM had been removed from Shaye's cell phone.

Ahead, the pale shapes of boulders huddled together between dark trees.

Good cover.

He scrambled among the boulders. Then he crouched and forced himself to breathe slowly, carefully, while he listened for any sound from his back trail.

Several hundred feet away, the truck's engine hissed and gurgled in its death throes. Somewhere beyond the truck, someone coughed wrenchingly. He hadn't heard anything like it since he'd gone through pepper-spray training. He hoped it was Ace puking his guts out.

The coughs faded into a tense kind of silence. A waiting silence. All breaths held.

No sound of oncoming footsteps.

No sense of pursuit.

Nothing but the ringing in Tanner's ears from a head-butting encounter with the steering wheel.

Gradually the night brightened, a combination of his eyes adjusting and the partial moon shining through the ragged forest.

I can stay here and wonder about Shaye or I can get off my ass and go in the direction I saw the woman. If it was Shaye . . .

It can't have been Kimberli. No glitter anywhere.

And he was almost certain the figure had been wearing the kind of sensible trail shoes Shaye preferred.

Pushing aside any worries about wishful thinking, he began working his way back toward the place where he'd swerved to avoid hitting a woman.

Shaye.

It has to be her.

She has to be alive.

FORTY-FIVE

S HAYE SCRAMBLED BACK on her feet from the spot where she'd thrown herself when the vehicle came roaring up out of the night. She had heard the rending, endless battle of rock and metal, the echoing silence filled with hissing sounds, and then the quick snaps that could only have been Ace's .22.

The thought of him walking up to the wreckage and murdering the driver made her ache to be armed herself.

She was terrified that Tanner had been at the wheel.

She knew the driver had saved her life by wrecking the vehicle rather than hitting her. The square grille and placement of the headlights had been that of a truck, while the violent light and screaming engine had been the stuff of future nightmares.

Even as she had flung herself back, the truck had gone sideways, and the stark, spearing headlights had bounced and bounded until it all ended in a hideous crash that she hadn't seen because she was too busy trying to get to her feet.

Then Tanner's voice calling her name.

Followed by two shots.

He wrecked trying to miss me and now he's—

Viciously she slammed down on the thought.

The sound of Ace's gun wasn't that close, not really. He could have been shooting at me.

If so, he had missed by several hundred feet.

Tanner!

But she only screamed in her mind. If he was alive, he could be hurt, needing help.

And Ace was out there, somewhere.

Surely he has to be running out of bullets.

She could find out the hard way if he carried extra ammo, or she could be smart and try being invisible.

Remember, it's just business for Ace. He's got three people who know too much running around in the darkness. He'll go after the closest one first.

The truck.

He'll be coming in from the direction the shots came from. I have to get to the truck first. Tanner will be armed, and it won't be with a yappy little Chihuahua of a gun.

She headed down toward the truck as fast as she dared. Her leg had settled into a steady kind of burn that didn't get in her way. Most of the time.

The truck was in a small runoff channel. Moonlight gleamed on the pale rocks and dirt around it. She was tempted to shine her light through the windows, but knew it would only make her a target. Instead, she half skidded, half ran down the slope. If she moved quickly enough, she would be able to get the truck between herself and the source of the shots.

Maybe Tanner isn't alone. August could be with him.

The thought made her feel better, even as she doubted it. If the deputy had been present and conscious, he would have returned Ace's fire.

Her eyes readjusted to the dim moonlight again and she could make out a single headlight turning silver the ghostly seething of steam around the truck. Breath coming hard, she ran close enough to look inside.

Empty.

The .22 barked again. Glass broke as the single working headlight exploded.

Damn you, Ace!

Shaye abandoned the treacherous cover of the truck that was also a magnet for a killer. She followed the straightest line she could take and still keep under some cover, hoping that Tanner had done the same.

The gunshot had come from up the hill, almost a straight line from where Kimberli had fled the Bronco. Darting from one ragged shadow to another, Shaye waited to hear the next shot.

Nothing but her own breathing.

She saw another shadow ahead. Moving.

Tanner.

Shaye wanted to call out to him but was afraid she would only draw fire in their direction. Hoping Tanner heard her coming—she was hardly catlike in her scramble around trees and boulders—she sprinted toward him.

But the shadow was gone.

Was it my imagination?

Too late to change her mind. She knew Ace was coming and all she had was a flashlight she couldn't use and a prayer that she was afraid wouldn't come true.

FORTY-SIX

THE THIRD TIME Tanner tripped over a shadow and went to his knees he admitted that his head had whacked the wheel harder than he thought. Adrenaline was a great painkiller, but it didn't last long enough. The ringing in his ears was way too loud. And his eyes were having trouble with the faint, tricky light.

Need a few minutes to get my head clear.

He didn't have them.

Shaye. Get to Shaye. That's all that matters.

He levered himself up to his feet, waited for the double vision to pass, and kept going. The tricky light and shadows shifting in the wind weren't helping. His head throbbed, feeling like it was too big and then too small, like the brain and bone were trying to live in the same space at the same time. The gun in his left hand felt wrong, but holding it in his correct hand wasn't going to happen.

The moonlight barely revealed the next step in front of him. The distant lights of the Bronco were ahead and to the right, up the hill. So were the bigger trees and best cover. That was where Shaye had been.

But Ace held that ground.

Doggedly, Tanner picked his way through jagged blue-black shapes and the coy, flat light of the moon. Every few feet he paused to listen to the night. All he could hear was the heartbeat in his head and the ringing in his ears. His right wrist would have joined the chorus, but it didn't hurt enough to be heard.

Tanner glanced up the hill and couldn't see anything useful. If Ace was still up there, he wasn't allowing the Bronco's lights to silhouette him.

Wait. Something close. Just ahead.

Automatically, Tanner put his back to a small tree and brought the Glock up into firing position. Usually he didn't notice the weight of the weapon. Tonight it felt like holding a bowling ball at arm's length. He could do it for a while, but not for too long. He used his right forearm as a brace and held the pistol pointed at the place where he might have seen motion.

He waited, staring until his eyes hurt.

It was like looking at tar on black velvet at midnight. Nothing to see.

There it is.

Someone coming this way. Not making much noise either. Or the ringing in my ears is drowning out everything else.

He kept the gun up. If the person hadn't seen him yet, he couldn't move. Movement drew attention.

There. Again.

His finger tightened on the trigger.

Just a little closer. Be certain of the target.

Wait . . . wait . . .

FORTY-SEVEN

S HAYE HESITATED. SHE had seen someone in front of her, but now there was nothing. The figure hadn't been Kimberli—too big and no glitter. It hadn't been Ace—his khaki clothes were pale in the moonlight. That left Tanner in his dark T-shirt and jeans.

There was the faintest glimmer of moonlight off something. It could have been a gun.

Oh God. He can't tell it's me.

She could speak up and maybe get shot by Ace at a distance with a .22, or stay silent and get shot close up and for certain by a cop's gun.

Easy choice.

"Tanner," she said roughly. "It's Shaye. Don't shoot."

The shape dissolved and Tanner's voice said, "Jesus. I nearly shot you."

She felt tears stream down her face as she ran to him and buried her face in his chest. He flinched, made a rough sound of pain, and then gave her a one-armed hug.

"You're hurt," she whispered.

"Hit my head, right wrist is—"

Her fingers covered his mouth. "Too loud," she said.

He barely heard her past the ringing in his ears, but he lowered his voice. "This better?"

"Yes. We have to get to cover." She pointed toward the jumble of boulders just uphill.

"Been there," he said softly. "No good for two."

She pointed toward the bigger trees. "Ace."

Tanner made a circle-around motion.

She nodded and headed out, climbing up in a direction that would eventually lead to big trees.

Wanting to object, yet knowing she was right, he fell in behind her. Or tried to. He couldn't keep up.

"Wait," he said in a low voice.

At least he hoped it was low. The only thing that had real volume was the ringing in his ears.

She appeared by his side.

"Can you shoot this?" he rasped, holding out the Glock.

For the first time she realized that he was essentially one-handed.

"Yes. But I'm not very good."

"Extra magazines." He tapped his left jacket pocket.

She hesitated, then pulled out two magazines and put one each in the back pockets of her jeans. The instant she was finished, he placed something in her hands. It wasn't as heavy as other handguns its size, but it wasn't exactly a feather. The weapon was warm from his skin, but still it chilled her. She wanted to tell him she couldn't do this, then realized it wasn't true.

She just didn't like pistols. Too easy to screw up with them.

But Tanner didn't look real steady on his feet right now. She was lucky he'd had the training to wait and be certain of his target before firing.

He tapped the safety on the Glock, showing her the on/off control.

She nodded, worked the control until she could do it by touch alone, and turned back toward the slope. The pistol was an uneasy weight in her right hand. She considered asking him for the holster, but didn't. She would be slow enough getting the pistol into firing position as it was.

Wish I'd spent more time with handguns. But I didn't and it's way too late now. I know the basics.

It will have to be enough.

The night had tipped from cool to chilly. Wind sucked heat from anything warm, especially bare skin. The bigger trees that would give cover seemed to get farther and farther away.

Shaye listened, heard only the occasional stumble from Tanner. He was falling behind. She waited, listening carefully, and heard nothing beyond the two of them. Either Ace wasn't following them or he was used to stalking game.

A chill went over her at the thought.

As soon as Tanner caught up, she pushed on again, heading toward one side of the Bronco's gleaming headlights.

Is Ace doing the same?

Is he just waiting to get both Tanner and me at once?

Can I really shoot Ace?

FORTY-EIGHT

ACE WATCHED SHAYE and Tanner as he had once watched them from a ridge behind Tony Rua's house. The difference now was simple: tonight he would kill both of them. The only reason they were alive now was that he hadn't wanted to rush out and replace his .38 pistol so soon after he killed Rua. People might wonder why Ace needed a new handgun. It was a question he hadn't wanted to answer.

Some people would say he was too cautious, but some people were stupid. Ace wasn't.

No more long shots with a short pistol. I'll get up close and real personal before I put a bullet in them.

Besides, he hadn't decided whether it would be more satisfying to rape Shaye in front of her boyfriend, or kill Tanner in front of her and then rape her. And kill her, of course. He'd buried more than one body in an abandoned mine. Saved so many questions.

The top of his head still burned from the pepper spray, feeling like it was scraped raw, but his eyes had stopped watering uncontrollably. Now they just sort of dripped. He probably looked like he'd been bawling, when that was the furthest thing from his mind.

Shaye would pay and then pay again. He'd take a long time with her. A long, long time.

No. Something else might go wrong. Just finish it and move on. Especially with Davis here, even though he was moving like he hurt pretty bad.

Maybe he's already dead.

If not, he will be.

The thought of more work made Ace swear. It would be bad enough rounding up the stupid females and dumping them down a mine shaft, but Tanner Davis weighed as much as the two women together.

There's lots of room in the mine. It will all work out. I've got enough ammo.

Still, it irritated the hell out of Ace having his plans bumped off track at the last minute. But that was the way luck came—good and bad. He had his alibi. With a few nudges, Conrad would decide that the fool women had gone looking for mustangs or land or whatever, and when they hadn't returned, Davis had gone looking for them in a roaring hurry, wrecked, and ended up lost somewhere.

As for Ace, he'd have a mess of trout as proof of where he'd been—and there weren't any trout in these hills where he was right now.

He eased past the still-steaming truck. No one inside, but it never hurt to be sure. His vision wasn't really clear yet, because his eyes kept watering and he kept having to strangle coughs. His ears worked just fine, though. He could hear sounds ahead and upslope.

They aren't very far away at all. If I had my .38, I could kill or wound them from here.

But I can wait. The longer they head the way they're going, the closer they get to the mine shafts.

He didn't want to drag any bodies a foot farther than he had to.

For an instant he stopped, gun up, automatically tracking the motion he thought he'd seen. Then trees got in the way of any possible shot. But he was closer to them than he'd thought.

He picked up the pace, carefully closing the distance between himself and his prey.

It wouldn't be long now.

FORTY-NINE

TANNER LEANED HARD against a slender tree trunk. It shivered from his weight. These were not huge, sturdy pines like the ones on the west side of Refuge. Most of the trees here were barely twenty feet high. The soil was so rocky there just wasn't enough to nurture big trees. Where the land leveled out farther up, or in the creases of ravines, the trees were thicker and taller.

He couldn't see much, but occasional sounds from upslope told him Shaye was getting farther ahead.

Got to move faster. I'm slowing her down.

Doggedly he forced himself to pick up the pace, but the ringing in his ears and tunneling of his vision told him he wasn't going to be on his feet real long.

He nearly ran into her when she came back to see why he had slowed down. One look at his pale, sweating face and hearing his heavy breathing told her what Tanner refused to admit—he was too hurt to keep on.

He gave her a brief smile that turned into a grimace as pain stabbed behind his eyes. And he leaned on the tree way too hard.

Hurriedly she looked around, picking the deepest pool of darkness she could find.

There, where that thicket of pines is growing right beside the big boulder. Not enough cover for both of us, but plenty for Tanner.

She pointed and he heaved himself upright, stumbling behind her, forcing his way through pines until she stopped him and pushed him down into a sitting position. His skin was too cool, despite the exercise, which told her that he was balanced on the crumbling edge of shock.

"Stay here," she said very softly.

The night would provide cover, but that wouldn't last forever. He was going to need more help than she could give him right now, and he needed it fast. As battered as his face was, she didn't know how he'd come this far. He was physically strong, yes, but it was toughness of mind that got him out of the truck and up the slope.

I don't want to leave him.

But if either of them was going to survive, she had to stop Ace and activate the radio function on the locater. She couldn't do that from where she was. She'd need a decoy.

"Get to Bronco . . . get help," Tanner said, his voice barely a thread of sound. "Leave . . . me."

"Would you leave me?" she said, equally softly.

He breathed a curse. "You have to."

"If it's you or me, I choose us."

He didn't waste time or effort arguing. He just leaned and waited for the night to stop spinning.

Through wind-tossed branches, she could see the flickering of the Bronco's headlights. Night distances were too tricky to judge with any certainty, but she had a gut feeling Tanner couldn't go that far. She had to get to the Bronco and call for help.

"Rest here for a few minutes," Shaye said against Tanner's ear.

"What are you . . . going to do?" His voice was dry, rasping.

"Decoy."

He moved his head very slowly in a negative motion. "Don't like . . . sound of it."

But she wasn't waiting around to argue. Flashlight in her left hand, gun in her right, she worked her way through the thicket more quickly than Tanner could follow her.

Much more quickly.

I don't want to leave him.

So make damn sure you get back to him.

The wind rushed around her, covering the sounds she made, and any Ace might make as well. Branches clutched at her hair and raked her face. She ignored the scratches, her whole being fixed on getting far enough away from that thicket so that Ace wouldn't see Tanner and shoot him like an animal in a trap.

Shaye was breathing hard and sweating in the chill before she decided it was time to spring her own trap. She flicked on the powerful flashlight, sending a bright cone of radiance knifing through the dark. The beam didn't reach the Bronco, but it would be close enough to spook Ace into running back to cut off whoever was trying to get away.

Unless he knows that the Bronco could be out of gas.

Doesn't matter. It's the best chance I have.

FIFTY

W HEN THERE WAS a sudden flare of light against the trees up
ahead and to his right, Ace thought the pepper spray had truly
damaged his eyes. He blinked and blinked again. Then he realized he
was seeing the beam from a flashlight, bouncing around in an erratic
fashion, way too close to the Bronco.

Someone is injured. Or completely panicked.

About time I caught a break.

He knew Davis had been hurt in the crash, but not how serious his
injuries were. Even if the man was armed, if he was the one with the
flashlight, he was barely staying on his feet. It would be easy to sneak up
and kill him. Or her.

Both would be good.

Bang. Bang. They're dead.

*I'll take Davis out first. Then her. Even if she has a weapon, she doesn't
have the balls to kill a man.*

Ace was almost disappointed that the hunt was coming to an end so quickly. He had learned long ago that anticipation was the best part of any chase. The rest was just a bloody chore.

And I'll have one more to hunt after I take care of them. Not that Kimberli will be much of a challenge. She never has been.

Candy from a baby.

The light looked like it was moving toward the Bronco at a lurching pace. The beam was jerking around wildly, sweeping left, right, up, down, backward and forward, without any predictability. Once it even flicked over him, but he doubted he'd been seen. Whoever was holding the flashlight was a half step away from passing out due to pain or fear.

Goddamn Rua anyway. If he had just done what he was told, none of this would have happened. But no, he had to get greedy and steal from the old man even though I paid half up front.

Stupid amateur.

Serves him right.

The flashlight beam kept bouncing around up the slope. Ace followed, closing in as quickly as darkness and the landscape allowed. Several times he had to hit the ground when the light jerked toward him. The last time he ducked, he decided he was close enough to run the prey down without screwing around anymore.

FIFTY-ONE

SHAYE KEPT JIGGING the flashlight about like she was lost, hurt, panicked, or all three at once. She knew Ace was following her, because she had heard random sounds moving on a line that would intercept her light. The noises kept getting closer, then closer still.

This is far enough, she thought. *I want to trap him, not me.*

Panting, afraid, yet strangely exhilarated, she turned at an angle to the Bronco and kicked up her pace as if she had been terrified by something near the vehicle. All but running, she pushed through thickets of saplings and scrub brush, breaking off whatever she could, making as much noise as possible to lure Ace into being careless. Then she paused and flailed the light around, listening, trying not to pant.

There.

God, he's close!

Not where I expected him to be. And making enough noise for a bear.

The shot sounded like another branch snapping—right next to her ear. Reflexively she ducked, even though she knew that she couldn't dodge a bullet. Before she straightened, her mind told her that the shot hadn't come from the same direction as the crashing noises.

That's it. No more running. If Kimberli's thrashing around out there, that will be enough distraction.

Shaye tossed the light away and made a low sound, like the throttled groan of someone who had been hit. It didn't convince her, but she wasn't going for an acting award, just a diversion. She took cover behind three head-high saplings that were fighting for the same piece of ground. Then she forced herself to breathe slowly, deeply, quietly, instead of panting as she desperately wanted to.

The night and moon hadn't changed, but the thrashing sound wasn't as loud. Either whoever was making it had gone off course or wasn't running into as many things.

From a different direction came small crackles, like feet crunching weeds and stone, followed by the click of metal on metal.

Ace was reloading before he closed in.

She eased the Glock off safety, raised it, and waited for him to step into the flashlight beam.

And waited.

He was as wary as a wolf circling a wounded moose. He went completely around the flashlight before he made a disgusted sound. Stepping quickly toward the glare, he leaned down to pick up the flashlight. His gun and his bald head reflected the light, screaming silently of danger.

She pulled the trigger.

The weapon jumped in her hands as fire and sound exploded from the Glock's muzzle. She blinked and flinched against the noise and kick of the weapon. Without the ear protectors she wore at the shooting range, the noise was like a blow. Ears ringing, she steadied and fired again at the crouched form. The sound of the second shot joined the first, echoing from the rocky ridges.

That time she had kept her eyes open and braced herself to aim better. He spun fully around and stared at her with shock and surprise on his face. The .22 was at his feet and his right arm looked awkward.

She had wounded him.

Distantly she was aware of something moving again in the forest, back where she'd heard Kimberli a few minutes ago, but right now she was more worried about Ace. She hadn't hurt him enough to end the fight.

He made a throttled sound of rage and fell toward her.

Except he wasn't falling. He was charging her, head down, like a bull.

Shaking, she raised the Glock again to fire, but it was too late. He hit her like an avalanche. The Glock spun away into the darkness as she smashed to the ground, tried to roll, was knocked flat again, and finally scrambled wildly to get away from him. He rolled, too, but when he tried to spring up, he went full length in the dirt so close to her that she could smell his sweat and the metallic bite of blood flowing down his arm.

She clawed to her feet, tripped, and went flying. Her leg was scream-ing at her, refusing to take her weight, so she rolled over and over again, her only means of getting away from him. By the time she slammed against a tree and figured out which way was up, he was all but on top of her. He snarled in rage, lifted his foot to stomp her face, and brought the .22 into firing position with his left hand.

She jackknifed her knees and kicked out with both feet at his exposed crotch. He saved his balls, but just barely. Before she could coil for another kick, he shoved his .22 in her face.

"Game over, bitch."

FIFTY-TWO

THERE WAS A savage, animal growl in the instant before Ace went flying, literally kicked away from her by Tanner. Ace screamed—a high, thin sound of pain and fury. Then Tanner was on him.

In the glancing illumination of the flashlight, Shaye could see only a turmoil of arms and legs, the gleam of sweat and blood, eyes and teeth, a bald head thrashing. Jeans-clad legs kicked, scissored. There was a horrible *crack*—bone not bullet—and a silence broken by only one man's ragged breathing.

Tanner staggered from the darkness and fell to his knees by her. "Shaye? Honey?"

"Lost—your gun," she panted. "Ace—"

"Don't worry."

"But—"

"He's dead."

At Tanner's words, she felt like a balloon with all the air whooshing out. The night began spinning around her. She stretched out on the ground to steady herself.

With a groan, he crumpled alongside her, his body curled protectively around her.

"Tanner?"

"You okay?" he asked.

"Better than you. Just dizzy for a moment."

A groan was his only answer. She nuzzled against his sweaty neck. His good arm pulled her closer.

"Thought—I'd lost you," he managed.

"I'm not easy to lose."

"Stay with me. Promise."

"Always," she said.

He smiled and closed his eyes.

"We should get up," she said after a few minutes.

"Ladies first," he mumbled.

Then he groaned and got up, helping her to do the same. Her leg was unsteady, his head beat in time with his heart, and his right hand wasn't much good, but they were alive. Using each other as an uncertain brace, they hobbled toward the Bronco.

Neither of them glanced at the lump of darkness they left behind.

FIFTY-THREE

DAWN CAME SLOWLY, perfectly, to the old ranch house, filling the room with a golden blush of light. Still asleep, Shaye burrowed closer to Tanner. His arm tightened around her in silent reassurance. In the last eight days, they had held each other through nightmares and ecstasy, throttled screams and contented sighs. He watched her now, pleased by the shape and shadows of her in the soft light. With gentle fingertips he traced the curve of her eyebrows and lips and savored the warmth of her breath softly rushing over his skin.

He still needed physical touch to soothe him, to tell him that she was alive, safe, within reach. The cast on his wrist was a reminder of all he had almost lost.

She felt the same need for the reassurance of touch. Even asleep, she didn't move beyond the heat and textures of his body.

Easing ever closer to her, he mentally began making a list of calls he would have to make. Brothers to hear the latest cop gossip. The union rep to hear how the negotiations were going. The lawyer to—

"I can hear you thinking," she said in a voice husky with sleep.

"Just happy to be alive. With you."

She smiled and caught his fingertip between her lips in a gentle kiss. "Same here. How's your head?"

"Which one?"

Her laughter was another kind of sunlight, one that warmed him in places he hadn't known were cold before she came into his life.

"The one with brains," she said.

"That one is still asleep."

Her hand moved beneath the covers.

His breath wedged in his throat.

"This one is awake," she said.

"Really?" he asked.

Her fingers moved, measured, stroked.

He began to breathe again, more quickly.

"Really," she said. "Wide-awake." Her eyes opened, dark and mysterious, loving and teasing, radiant with the possibilities of dawn.

With a slow, easy movement he took her mouth, then all of her, giving himself to her at the same time. She gave and took with the generosity that was always new to him, better each time, deeper, hotter. They mingled breath and body, caressing, lifting, surging, until each was full . . . and then they overflowed into shimmering ecstasy.

Afterward they lay spent and at peace, listening to each other's breathing in the silence.

The next time they woke up it was full daylight and Dingo was giving his warning bark.

"Who needs an alarm clock when we have that mutt?" Tanner said.

Shaye stretched and watched while he pulled on his jeans, shoes, and belt holster. She loved the lithe ease of his body, the power barely held in check, skin sliding over muscle and tendon with each movement. She loved his intelligence and humor and . . .

She loved him.

And he, well, he hadn't said anything except that he was glad to be alive with her.

We're consenting adults. What did I expect?

Sometimes being an adult sucked.

"Better get dressed, honey," Tanner called from the living room. "It's the deputy. I'll plug in the coffee."

"August?"

"His truck. Assume he's driving."

She quickly pulled on some clothes and went to stand next to Tanner on the porch. Together they watched as August's truck raised dust on the road to Lorne's house.

Dingo shot out from behind a nearby water trough and barked sharply, once.

"Easy, boy," Tanner said. "I've got it."

The dog gave a last woof, waved his tail, and trotted over on dainty feet to stand next to the two humans he'd adopted. The vet had been amazed at Dingo's quick, complete recovery. When they brought him home, he had sniffed where Lorne had died, gone through the house like a tawny shadow, and never looked for Lorne again.

"I hope the deputy doesn't have any more questions," she said, flexing her sore leg. She had discovered that bullet burns were well named, but deep bruises took longer to heal.

"Cops always have more questions. Besides, he got your Bronco back for you."

"And towed Lorne's truck to the scrap yard," she said.

"Sure as hell neither one of us was up to it."

She inched closer to him, remembering.

He tightened his arm around her. He didn't like the memories of that night any better than she did. But almost dying clarified what was important in life and what just seemed important at the time.

"Too bad I could only break Ace's neck once," Tanner said.

"He broke it in a fall, remember? Trying to find Kimberli."

"Huh," was all Tanner said.

Kimberli had run flat out into an open mine. It had taken three days to recover her body.

August slowed down well before he came to the yard, a simple courtesy to keep the dust to a minimum. He parked beside the Bronco and walked up to the porch.

"Morning, Nate," Tanner said.

"Coffee's cooking," Shaye said.

"Morning," August said. "You two look better each time I see you."

"That wouldn't be hard," she said drily. "We were pretty scuffed up. Come on in."

"This visit official?" Tanner asked as he followed the others into the house.

"Somewhat. The El Dorado sheriff called and said he received an anonymous tip that some stolen gold might be hidden in Rua's fish tank."

"Huh," Tanner said.

"Yeah. I told him we had a report of missing gold coins in our county. It'll take some time and paperwork, but you'll get Lorne's gold back."

"I appreciate it."

"It was pure bad luck that Lorne was in such a hurry to get Dingo to the vet that he left the hidey-hole open," August said.

Tanner nodded. He and Shaye had pieced together Lorne's last hours.

"We figured that Lorne must have just come back from the lawyer's when Rua drove up," she said. "Lorne probably had been up all night, too mad to sleep. Never even changed his clothes. Then he found Dingo, grabbed a gold coin to pay the vet, and raced out."

August nodded. "Fits. He must have just come back from town when he heard Rua's motorcycle and ran outside to see who dared to trespass on his land. Didn't even take time to put on his hat."

"Did you ever find proof that Ace was Rua's fight sponsor?" she asked.

"Not court proof, but it doesn't have to be. Ace owned McCurdy's 8. That's enough of a connection for me."

Tanner waited, knowing that August hadn't driven out in the early morning to chew over the probable sequence of events the morning Lorne died.

"Any idea on the anonymous caller's identity?" August asked. "The one who jacked up the El Dorado sheriff so that he'd search Rua's home and find the coins and the throwaway cell phone with all the numbers on it?"

"Why would I?" Tanner asked, covering a yawn. "It's not my case."

"That's what I told the El Dorado sheriff."

Shaye looked at her shoes like she expected them to break into song.

"I talked to the judge this morning," August continued. "Sorry to tell you, Shaye, but Lorne's property goes to Tanner." He looked at him. "Your lawyer will be calling you later."

She glanced away from her shoes and said, "I've been expecting it. The Conservancy will be disappointed, but it was our mistake with the contract. We accept that."

"Congratulations on your promotion," August added. "I hear that you'll be running things for the Conservancy now that Kimberli is dead. The ranchers are real happy about that. They like you."

"It's just temporary, until they can hire a fund-raiser."

"Not what I heard," August said. He looked at Tanner. "You going back to L.A.?"

"I left a lot of loose ends there," Tanner said. "Some of them have to be handled in person."

"And you're the type who likes to tie everything up right and tight," the deputy said. "You'll be getting an official pat on the back from the Refuge County sheriff added into your files."

Shaye hoped nothing showed in her expression. She'd always known Tanner was going back. She just hadn't wanted to think about it.

"Coffee inside," she said hoarsely, turning away.

By the time the men came into the kitchen, she had worked the knot out of her throat. The one in her stomach would have to wait. The one in her heart . . . well, she'd just have to learn to live with it.

At least she was alive.

When Tanner started for the coffeepot, she beat him to it.

"You still have coffee stains on your cast from the last time you tried to pour left-handed."

"I'm a lot better shot left-handed than I was."

She didn't argue. Both of them had spent a lot of time firing at targets he'd made. Neither one of them ever wanted to take a chance on missing again.

Tanner waited until she sat down before turning to August. "What's up?"

"Can't a man just have coffee with friends?" the deputy asked, deadpan.

"Long way to drive for coffee."

The deputy smiled. "The judge and I decided that part of what we know shouldn't be put in writing."

"How does your sheriff feel about that?"

"Didn't you hear?" August said blandly. "His doctor discovered a problem with his heart. The sheriff will be resigning, effective today."

"He deserves worse," Tanner said, his voice as flat as his cop's eyes.

"We can't prove it. Same with the others. No law against doing business together on cheap cell phones."

"What about Rua?" she asked.

"So he bought a throwaway cell phone and had the number of his old boss and his new one on it. And Ace's, who was probably his sponsor at McCurdy's 8. So what?"

"What about Hill?" Tanner asked, to save her the trouble.

"He's a politician. He talks to hundreds of people all the time. Just like Campbell and Hill and Kimberli and Ace did. Real shame about their deaths, too. Loss to the community, and—"

"Blah blah blah," Shaye cut in.

"Easier for everyone that way, most especially your lover," August pointed out mildly. "Hard to keep a woman satisfied when you're behind bars."

"But Campbell—" she began.

"Leave it be," August said. "Campbell knows if he so much as farts in public, I'll be all over him like greed on a miser."

"I doubt if he really knew what was going on anyway," Tanner said, shrugging. "Ace wouldn't have told him anything. Hill, either. You ever know a politician who could keep a secret? As for the sheriff, he's not the first official to back the people who support his campaign."

August nodded. "It's a shame that Kimberli got so excited about seeing real, live mustangs that she followed them and lost track of time and geography. And it was real brave of Shaye and Ace to try to find her in the dark with abandoned mines everywhere. Lucky you didn't get lost or break your neck, too, like Ace did. As for Tanner, he wrecked trying to avoid you when you waved him down to help."

Shaye opened her mouth, then shut it again. Some things you simply agreed with. Less complicated that way.

"Yes, we were lucky," she said, her mouth dry.

"Keep it in mind," the deputy said. "Sometimes the easy explanation actually is the just one."

"Sleeping dogs and all that," she said.

"Not to mention that the Conservancy comes out looking good," Tanner said. "As you told me, you have to live here. And the Conservancy checks out as one hundred percent honest."

"Kimberli was the bad apple," August agreed.

"I'm glad," Shaye said simply.

"If Shaye and I don't have any kids," Tanner said, "the Conservancy will get the land."

August looked from one to the other. "Kids, huh? Congratulations."

She felt like saying the same thing: *Huh?*

Tanner gave her a slow smile. "A man can hope."

Her smile was slow and wondering. "So can a woman. But . . . I thought you were going back to L.A.?"

"Only as long as it takes me to sign papers, pay bills, and pack." He gave the deputy a hard look. "Isn't it time for you to get back to the office or on patrol or—"

August ignored him. "I also hear that Tanner's retiring early, and your captain said that you were an outstanding cop and he was sorry to lose you, but with all your hard work and being hurt and all, he agreed with the union that you should get ninety-three-point-four percent of your retirement pay, plus the rest of your vacation time."

"The captain is a prince," Tanner said.

It was Shaye's turn to snicker.

"Yeah, I'll just bet he is," August said. "We're taking applications for an opening in the department. With your years of experience as a cop in L.A., you would be hired before the ink was dry on the form."

"Have you been talking to a man called Brothers?" Tanner asked.

"He said to tell you to invite him to the wedding."

"I told him I had to catch her first."

"From here, doesn't look like she's running too hard."

Shaye cleared her throat. "She hears quite well."

"Go away, August," Tanner said. "I need to close the deal."

"I was going to give you some pointers on that."

"Trust me," she said, "he, um, points just fine."

The deputy laughed, finished his coffee, and left them in peace.

"So you like the way I point," Tanner said.

"You have outstanding form. Function, too."

"You willing to marry a retired cop who can guarantee long hours and short wages as a deputy and rancher?"

"Are you the cop?"

"Yes."

"Then I'm willing," she said.

"Even if it means living on a rural ranch?"

She traced the edges of his mouth with her fingertips. "Especially then."

Tanner's smile made Shaye's breath stop.

"Let's go back to bed," he said. "I've got a pointer for you."

"Just one?"

"If it's good, it only takes one."